A MARISKA STEVENSON THRILLER

CHARLES LEMOINE

PRESERVATION

TO UNLOCK THE PAST
SHE MUST RISK HER FUTURE

Preservation
A Mariska Stevenson Thriller

ISBN: 9781731493941

Cover art and formatting by Incredibook Design

PRESERVATION

A Mariska Stevenson Thriller

CHARLES LEMOINE

CONTENTS

PROLOGUE

Southern California ~12,000 BC during the Pleistocene Epoch

The spear struck the tree, mere inches from her head. Bark splintered on impact, sending bits of wood flying into her eyes, blurring her vision. She rolled away from the weapon and ran for her life. Tears flowed but didn't slow her progress. Deeper into the dark and dangerous wooded region she went, her tiny canine companion following close. She'd entered the forest, thinking it would offer more cover and places to hide than the vast expanses of land that met the morning sun, but the tracker found her anyway.

She stole a glance back, but with all the shadows and dense vegetation, she couldn't see him. Now, crashing through the trees and underbrush, she was sure to leave plenty of clues for a decent tracker to find, and he was the best one from the clan. Her only chance was to put as much distance between them so she could have enough time to hide or set up a trap of her own.

Exhaustion was taking over; her legs felt heavy, and her lungs burned. Had she put enough distance between them? She'd been running for what seemed like forever, but had it been long enough? Her pace slowed, and she looked down for her little friend. His tongue hung thick and heavy from his mouth and drops of saliva fell to the forest floor with each rapid pant. He too was tired. Without warning, the toe of her bearskin shoe caught on a fallen limb, and she slammed to the ground with a thud. She scrambled on all fours, desperate to stand, desperate to keep running, but fatigue won out. She collapsed in a heap. Her little brown dog stopped too. Next to her head, he lay facing her. His hot breath came in rapid puffs, making her cough. His tongue gave her a loving kiss on the nose, and she sat up to better take in the surrounding area.

She was now deep in the forest, further than she'd ever been. The thick canopy of trees filtered out much of the sunlight. Now a kaleidoscope of light and shadow swirled around her as the wind blew high above her head. The trees whined and sang a mournful song only they knew as they swayed and danced with the force of the gale. The clan often told stories about this place. It was rumored to harbor the Howler. The hairy-man who screamed at the moon and stole from their hunts. She reached into her shirt and pulled out the band that was around her neck. The tooth and square beads had been strung together by her mother's people generations ago. It was a necklace of protection, from man, from the hairy-man whose teeth separated the beads of the stars. Her mother slipped it around her neck the night she escaped. Had her mother not risked her own life for her daughter, she'd have been sacrificed to the gods. An offering for the return of the mammoth, their main source of food.

She shivered. Sweating from exertion, she was beginning to cool, and the ever-disappearing forest floor indicated it would soon be night. The creatures of the dark would then awaken to hunt, and she'd have more to fear than the murderous man who pursued her. With effort, she stood and surveyed the large tree next to her. It would be difficult, but if she could secure little Kada in the buffalo skin coat, she might be able to climb high enough to wait out the long period of darkness in safety.

She bent low to pick up Kada when a cacophony of sound erupted from everywhere. A huge cloud of birds took to flight and screamed a sound of alarm. Had the tracker found them? On shaky legs, she ran for her life. Deeper into the woods she went, branches hitting her face, but not slowing her. A wall of rock lay in the quickly approaching distance. She looked at both sides for a way around. There wasn't. She was going to have to climb. The first large boulder was no match for her. At a full sprint, she threw herself up and scrambled up the wall. Kada was right on her heels as he scampered around the side and up another way. Almost to the top, she stopped when a hand grabbed her by the leg.

In a panic, she kicked and tried to pull herself free, her hands still clinging to the rocks above her. She stole a glance down; she couldn't help it. The pounding in her chest continued, but when she saw it wasn't the hunter, but her beloved from the village, a calmness settled over her. He had followed her. He was there to save her. She wasn't alone, anymore.

She grabbed him by the wrist and helped pull him up next to her. Hugging him tight, she pressed her forehead to his and breathed a sigh of relief. But it was short-lived. Kada growled behind them from the top of the rock outcropping. They both turned, and she saw the danger. The hunter was coming, his spear up and ready to be thrown. Without a word, she stood and yanked her love by the animal skins, pulling him with her as she fled. To the top of the high mountain of boulders they rushed, headlong and without caution for potential of falling. Rocks skittered down the mound below them as they went.

It was barely but a moment and they were safely over the crest and starting down the other side. As they set foot on the ground, a sickening smell overcame her. She coughed, then gagged, before sucking in air between her teeth. The earth wasn't hard here; it was mushy, sticky. Her feet felt stuck in place. With great effort, she pulled up one foot and then the other and moved further away. Tucking her nose and mouth under her animal skins, she looked back to her love for help. Only none came.

The man she loved and trusted, looked at her with sadness in his eyes. Why wasn't he running? The hunter cleared the top of the outcropping, and she grabbed for her lover's hand to run with her, but he yanked it away. Tears in her eyes and out of breath, voice thick with emotion, she pleaded, "Hurry, my love. Come with me." But he didn't move. Looking back at the hunter, he signaled for him to throw and then turned away.

He had chosen the clan over her.

Without another moment of hesitation, she turned and ran for the dense forest on the other side of the clearing. Fear clouded her mind as the sense of betrayal tore her heart to pieces. Sobs wracked her body as her lungs began to burn for more air.

Each passing step became harder than the last. She looked down at her feet, now submerged in a thick black liquid. She pulled up hard, but couldn't budge her feet. Kada, near her, barked, his stressed vocals kicked her in the belly. A sickening omen. Kada jumped into her arms, knocking her backward. She sank into the soft, liquid ground, first her hips and then her arm as she tried to push up to stand. Through tears and ragged coughs, she struggled to breathe, struggled to stand, struggled to live. A rustle from the bushes drew her attention to the side. It was her lover. Standing near the edge of this terrible place she now found herself, a large rock poised over his head.

She shook her head but didn't beg for help. Didn't beg for her life. Without warning, he threw the rock. An explosion of pain on the side of her head as she registered the breaking of her bones. A ringing in her ears didn't completely drown out the snarls and then whimpers of her four-legged companion. She couldn't save him or herself. Another crushing pain as a second rock smashed into her face. No longer able to raise her head, she craned her head to look at the man who betrayed her. The hair pulled from her scalp, and she cried out from the searing hot pain.

They locked eyes in time for her to see the third large rock that he hurled. It connected with a thud, sending her into the vast darkness of her ancestors. No longer in pain. No longer running in terror. She was now a memory.

CHAPTER ONE

Mariska studied the bones. Skull and pelvis. Ribs and limbs. Ancient. Thousands of years old, the partial skeleton of a woman, meticulously preserved by the very thing that killed her. She noticed something inside the skull that didn't belong—a foreign object, woven cloth. Her heart raced, but she swallowed her uncertainty. *Where the hell had that come from?* No, there'd be time—for all of it.

Her gaze drifted over the swirls of brown and black that had seeped into the skeleton's pores like smoke, staining them dark with time and tar. The acrid scent of petroleum seeped deep into her nose as she took a calming breath meant to soothe her building excitement. Answers to the questions that plagued Mariska for as long as she could remember danced within reach. Who was this woman? Where did she come from? How did she get here?

They were all there and, finally, she was going to learn the truth.

The announcement was to be made today—her grant proposal might finally be approved. Rumor had it she'd get her funding, and almost immediately, the whispers began. Her colleagues speculating on their own *whys* and *hows*.

She's Mariska Stevenson. *What else did you expect?*

You know who her father is, right? He probably funded the grant himself, just to make her happy.

I wish my daddy would buy me a museum to play with.

Mariska pushed it aside. None of it mattered, not right now.

If true, she was going to be given full, official access to the La Brea Woman and her findings would be published. Not even the petty jealousy of her colleagues could ruin it for her.

She put her ruby-red Swarovski crystal purse down on the table and leaned in close, so close her breath fogged the glass case that separated her from the bones. She saw her reflection in the glass, her shiny black hair a stark contrast to her light skin and bright blue eyes. Many said she looked like a movie star, but she didn't care for that description—she was a scientist. But she did smile when she saw her dangling earrings as they sparkled in the light. Mariska always enjoyed pretty things. The remains inside the case looked back at her. "I'm going to identify you," she said quietly, the diamond drop earrings she wore swinging softly against her neck. "And I'm going to take you home."

"She can't hear you, you know."

The voice, familiar and warm, brought a playful smile.

"How can you be so sure?" Mariska straightened to find David Beaumont, her best friend and colleague, watching her from the doorway. "And how'd you know I'd be here?"

"You're kidding, right?" David rolled his eyes. "Where else would you be?"

He was right, of course. Several times a day, she snuck down here to see the set of preserved bones. Nothing more than a partial skeleton, the La Brea Woman had been in the museum's basement archives for over a decade now. Rows of multi-tiered metal shelving filled the vast underground lair. Deep underground, the repository of ancient and irreplaceable treasures was kept protected from sunlight, great temperature swings, and the killer of all antiquity—moisture. The skeletal remains had been taken off display in an attempt to stave off controversy; left unexamined to avoid having to give her back to her rightful people—whoever they turned out to be. Multiple groups of people, who wanted her returned to them, had made their desires known.

Mariska planned to change all of that. Not only was she going to identify this ancient woman positively, but she was going to bring her home.

"I must've lost track of time." She smoothed her hands over her gown. White silk couture. Like the earrings, the dress was a gift from her mother for the occasion. The woman would use any excuse to go shopping.

David leaned against the open doorway, smirking. He looked good in a tux—standard attire for museum gala fundraisers—but his tousled dirty blond curls and horn-rimmed glasses kept him from full-fledged James Bond status. Kept him *David,* just the way she liked him.

"Snyder is looking for you," he told her, souring her mood.

"I'm sure he is," she muttered. Dr. Snyder was the head curator of the Page Museum and their immediate supervisor. "Probably wants to make sure I'm sufficiently silenced for the evening."

David patted his hands over his suit. "And look at me—I forgot my duct tape," he joked in an obvious attempt to lift her fallen mood. "He really chewed your ass, huh?"

"*Dr. Stevenson, I don't care who your father is—*" she said, imitating their boss's snooty tone perfectly. "*If you breathe one word about your* little project *within earshot of any of the Independent Review Board members tonight, your hope and dream of* officially *studying the La Brea Woman will come to an abrupt and permanent end. Understood?*"

David whistled low. "Harsh."

"As if being granted the funds to do something no scientist has been given permission to do for more than a *century* qualifies as nothing more than a *little project.*" Mariska fumed, still stinging from Snyder's threat. She could read between the lines—mention her grant to anyone at the gala tonight, and her hopes were up in smoke.

"He's retiring in less than a month and can feel the loss of power nipping at his heels." David shrugged, crooking his elbow away from his impeccably cut suit. "Don't let him get to you."

She looked him over. "You clean up nice."

"Armani." David looked down at himself before grinning in her direction. "And rented. And don't change the subject."

"Well, you still look nice." She circled the wide expanse of glass and steel that held the bones and made her way toward him. "How bad is it upstairs? Has Kathy started sucking up to Dr. Snyder yet?" Mariska's assistant had been a pain in her ass since the day she started, but she'd been powerless to fire her. No doubt the woman had friends in high places.

"I'm sure she's got her nose up some rich guy's ass. And I'm sure once you get past the protestors outside, it's your average annual Page Museum dog-and-pony show." He handed her a flute of champagne.

She winced as she slipped her arm through David's, pulling the door to the archive room closed before letting him lead her to the bank of elevators and back upstairs. "That bad?" She watched him remove his keycard and swipe it through the reader, summoning the car.

"We roll over and beg for table scraps from millionaires, celebrities, and politicians." He tucked his keycard back into the breast pocket of his rented tux. "*Bad* isn't the word I would use."

She knew what word he'd use. *Humiliating.* Since her parents happened to be among the millionaire patrons they were supposed to be schmoozing upstairs, she kept quiet as they stepped onto the elevator together. She took a sip of the champagne. *Damn, that's good stuff.* It wasn't her first glass tonight, and wouldn't be her last.

"So do you," David said to her, punching his finger against the call button, staring at his shoes.

"So do I what?" She felt her stomach drop slightly as the car shot upward.

He looked down at her for a moment. "Clean up nice," he said, saving them both from an awkward moment with another lopsided smile. "Come on, Dr. Stevenson—I'll buy you another drink to *quietly* celebrate your smashing success."

She flushed at the mention of her grant approval. "The drinks are *free*, Dr. Beaumont." She raised her half-empty glass with a laugh as the elevator doors slid open and he walked out. "But I'll take what I can…" She stopped and looked down at her empty left hand. She'd forgotten it.

Her beaded clutch. She'd left it downstairs.

She handed her drink to David. "I have to go back. I left my—" The doors slid closed between them. She pushed the button marked B, for the basement and waited.

Mariska couldn't forget her purse. Another gift from her mother, it probably cost more than a good used car, it matched her shoes, and if she wasn't carrying it, her mother would take note and start asking questions. The last thing she wanted to do was hurt her mom's feelings.

"No one has to know about this," she muttered to herself as the car came to a halt, its doors sliding open. Her mom had warned her not to let the purse out of her sight. *She knows me better than I know myself*, Mariska thought.

Stepping off the elevator, she noticed it right away. The door to the archive room was open. Not much, slightly ajar—but she was sure she pulled it closed behind her before she left. Glancing down the hall, she saw what she expected to see: a long stretch of darkened hallway, doors pulled securely shut.

Advancing as quietly as her strappy red Louboutin heels would allow, Mariska crept toward the open crack. Stopping in front of it, she reached out a hand, pushing the door open slowly, widening the breach so she could see inside. The archive room came into view, her gaze locking onto the scarlet crystals of her beaded clutch almost instantly. It was where she'd left it, perched on a crate of plant fossils awaiting carbon dating. She grabbed the purse and turned to leave. A scrape of a shoe against the tiled floor sent goosebumps building over her body.

Something was wrong. The case with the remains…was empty. On the floor in front of her, she saw the same fabric she'd seen inside the La Brea Woman's skull. Reaching down, she plucked the small pouch from the floor.

Another scraping from behind her sounded. Without thinking, she shoved the pouch into her purse and rushed toward the exit.

Heart pounding in her ears, her eyes went wide as she looked over her shoulder. *I'm not alone.* The realization overwhelmed her senses, a second before a blow to the back of the head plunged her into darkness.

CHAPTER TWO

Mariska picked at the bandage on the back of her head. The pain was bearable if she could get herself to lie still. But all she wanted to do was go home.

Detective Eric Wulf stood at the foot of her hospital bed, small flip-pad in hand. No less than six-foot-two-inches tall with broad shoulders, and a square jaw, he had warm blue eyes and a full head of dark hair that Mariska would have found quite attractive, had it been under different circumstances. "Dr. Stevenson—" he said, adjusting his black tie before putting his hand in the front pocket of his black slacks. His gray suit jacket hung on his muscular frame like a well-tailored drape.

"Please, call me Mariska." She wasn't feeling well enough to make this formal.

Leah Stevenson stood at her daughter's bedside. "Really, does this have to be done right now? Robert…tell him to come back after she's had a chance to recover."

Mariska's father looked every bit as weary as she felt. His tux was rumpled and bowtie undone, hanging from his neck. "Detective? Is there any way you can come back later? The doctor recommended rest."

"Yeah," David said, stepping into Mariska's limited view from the hospital bed. "She needs to rest."

The detective studied their faces for a moment, but his expression remained neutral, cold. "I'll try and make this quick. The doctor said she's going to be released tonight…Mr. and Mrs. …?"

Robert Stevenson cleared his throat. "Stevenson. This is our daughter."

The detective remained quiet, but it was clear he was processing the scene before him. Mariska was Caucasian while her parents were both African-American. They'd found and adopted Mariska as an infant and spent the rest of their lives together ignoring ignorant people's look of surprise or in some unfortunate cases, disbelief.

Leah turned to Mariska and reached for her hand, her dark brown skin a beautiful contrast to Mariska's light pigmentation. To be someone's child didn't always mean you shared DNA, and Mariska couldn't have been more fortunate to have been chosen and raised by Leah and Robert Stevenson.

"It's okay, Mom. I can answer a few questions." Mariska offered an encouraging smile. "It's getting late. Maybe, you and Dad should go home and get some sleep."

Her mother began to protest, but her father wrapped his arm around his wife and pulled her close. "How will you get home?"

Before anyone else could say a word, Mariska said, "David will take me." She looked at him with urgency. "Right, David?"

"Of course, Dr. and Mrs. Stevenson. I'd already planned on it."

Detective Wulf cleared his throat, drawing the room's attention. "If you all don't mind, I'd like a moment alone with your daughter."

Mumbled protests, and worried glances filed out of the room, into the hallway. She knew David was soothing her parents' fears, despite his own.

The room fell silent. The pain in the back of her head throbbed into her ears.

"I'll try and make this quick." He took a step closer to the side of her bed.

"I appreciate that," Mariska said, rubbing the pain from her temples. "Can you grab a chair? You're making me nervous?"

He strode over to the small, metal folding chair in the corner of the room and slid it over to the side of the bed. The scrape of the chair legs on the linoleum floor echoed through her skull like a jackhammer. She clenched her eyes shut, but she heard him shove the chair toward the head of the bed, closer than she was comfortable with. He sat with a huff, and she opened her eyes. He didn't say anything. Didn't make eye contact. He flipped through the small green notepad while his jaw worked hard on a piece of gum. Finally, he said, "How are you feeling?"

Mariska started to say she was *fine*, but when she looked up into his eyes, she felt he wasn't asking it as part of polite conversation. He was studying her. Why did she feel like she was in trouble for something? Wasn't she the one lying in a hospital bed?

"My head hurts." She touched the swollen egg-sized lump at the back of her skull.

He grabbed her nurses' call-button and moved it out of her reach. "I'll be sure to summon the nurse for you as soon as we're done."

"Fine." *What an asshole,* she thought. Mariska returned to rubbing her temples for relief. "I don't think the headache will go away for a while no matter what anyone does for me."

"You're probably right." He flipped the page of his notebook and clicked the pen in preparation of his questioning.

"Just so you know, my memory seems to be a bit foggy." Mariska winced as she tried to straighten up in the bed.

"I'll make it easy for you," he said. "Is there anyone at the museum that would want to hurt you? Or steal from the institution?"

He thinks it's an inside job? She wracked her brain trying to make sense of it all. "I can't think of anyone. I…" she paused for a moment. "My boss and I share an assistant. Her name's Kathy Wellington."

"And you think she might be a part of this?" He stopped writing for a second and looked up.

"I don't know…maybe? I didn't see who did it."

"Okay, why don't you tell me something about Kathy Wellington? It might help shed some light on why you think she had motive to hurt you." He sat quietly, waiting for her to continue.

"Kathy has a background in science…paleontology in particular. Unfortunately, there was a bit of a scandal at the university where she was accused of stealing research conducted by a fellow student.

I don't know all the specifics, but it basically ended her career before it started—blacklisted, at least in the academic arena."

Wulf said, "How did she end up coming to work at the Page Museum? You know, if she'd been blacklisted."

"Her dad has a ton of money. He's a Hollywood guy. Lots of friends in high places. Not only did he give a substantial donation to the museum, but a good amount of his friends did too. I'm not saying you can buy favors from the museum, but institutions such as the Page have struggled recently to make ends meet."

"How does this lead you to the conclusion where she wants to hurt you?"

"She doesn't like me. I think she views me as a threat or competition. From what I've been told, the museum wanted to use me as the public face—you know, put my image on the billboards and brochures."

"And you think she wanted that to be all about her?"

Mariska nodded. "Absolutely. I know that for a fact."

"Okay," Wulf said as he continued to jot information down into his notepad. "Anything else?"

"Yeah, I overheard Dr. Snyder telling Kathy last week there'd been some threats made against the museum."

"What kind of threats?" Wulf arched his eyebrows with interest.

"There was an anonymous letter sent by someone demanding the remains of La Brea Woman returned to her rightful descendants."

"Did Dr. Snyder make any suggestions as to who he thought sent the letter?"

Mariska rolled her eyes. "The local indigenous peoples." She slapped the side of her bed. "But I think that's ridiculous. They have peacefully requested her return for decades…never once have they made any threats."

He shrugged. "Maybe they got tired of waiting?"

Mariska didn't respond but looked away, annoyed.

"How about you? I know you work for the museum, but what is your exact role and background?"

She nodded. "I am the lead Paleontologist. I have multiple doctorates. One in Paleontology and the other in Anthropology with an emphasis on Archeology and Field Research."

"Impressive." He took notes and then asked, "How was someone so young able to get such an accomplished set of credentials?"

"It wasn't easy. I double majored and then had to petition the school to allow me to present two separate theses during the same year. They agreed, and here I am—look at me now." She opened up her arms in a sarcastic gesture of success.

"You primarily conduct research at the Page? Like, you dig stuff up?"

She snorted. "Yeah, I dig stuff up. But I also conduct tours for visitors. That's one of the best parts of my job. I get to take people who are interested in the cool, big, sets of skeletons and explain what they were and how they were discovered. There's nothing more satisfying than seeing the children's eyes light up when they are standing under the gigantic Columbian Mammoth, looking up and the immensity of it all." She smiled. "It's fantastic."

He smiled but continued to take notes.

"What else do you want to know?" she asked, her energy a bit more renewed.

He looked up from his pad. "Tell me what happened."

That's kind of a broad question, don't you think? "The last thing I remember?"

"Sure. Let's start there." He took a fresh piece of gum from his pocket and popped it into his mouth. The muscles of his jaw rippled as he chomped down. The smell of his peppermint-laced breath filled her nose and made her mouth water. She glanced in his direction and couldn't help but notice a few flecks of gray in his otherwise dark brown hair. How old was this man? She'd have guessed thirty…maybe thirty-five by the hint of wrinkles around his eyes when he was concentrating on his little notebook.

She closed her eyes and thought about the events that landed her in the hospital. *The purse.* "I'd forgotten my purse in the basement and when I went back down to get it…I don't remember exactly what happened."

"Had you been drinking?"

'Sure. A glass or two of champagne. I didn't black out and hit my head if that's what you're getting at."

"You don't remember falling? Hitting your head?"

The memory wanted to come out…it was in there, somewhere. A memory-flash of the Tomb…the door hadn't been closed, it—

"Guess it must've been a pretty nice purse," Detective Wulf noted.

"Excuse me?" Mariska blinked a few times as the memory vanished.

"You went back for a purse, but you were in the middle of a very important gala, weren't you?"

She hesitated for a moment. The purse *was* pretty and expensive, but those hadn't been the reasons. She hadn't wanted to disappoint her mom…but there seemed to be more to the story. She struggled through the fog in her mind. Then, all at once, the memory came flooding back. Her heart began to race, and she took a deep breath to regain control. She'd put the artifact in her purse. She hadn't intended to, but someone was in there with her that shouldn't be. She'd needed to escape—protect the pouch. An internal voice told her she'd better keep the real answer to herself, for now. What she did was still technically stealing even though it'd been unintentional. "My mother gave me the purse."

He jotted something down in the flip-pad and then refocused his attention on her. He tapped the pen on the end of his chin. "What were you doing down there in the first place?"

"Dr. Snyder was to announce who'd been awarded the grant proposal to research the La Brea Woman." It had come down to her or David. Either way, they'd both be participating, but she'd heard rumors she had the grant all locked up. "The anticipation was killing me, so I stepped out for a while and went to see her. I…I couldn't wait to see her." Mariska shifted her weight on the mattress so she could sit up a little straighter. *Would he hurry up? I need to find my purse.*

"And, did you see her?" The detective's intense stare put her immediately on edge.

"Yes, of course. I was examining her until Dr. Beaumont came down to get me."

He paused in his questioning as he flipped to a new page. Scribbling down a few more notes, he looked up. "When you saw her, did you happen to notice anything unusual? Maybe something out of place or that didn't belong?"

"No, why?" Her memory started getting foggy at this point in the timeline. The La Brea Woman was there, her bones visible through the glass front of the storage crate. That's when she'd first noticed the unusual cloth bag. A secret she still hadn't shared with anyone. But the detective couldn't possibly have known about that. She'd been alone. And why would he care? "Is there something you're trying to say, detective?" Her anger over the presumed accusation was tempered by the guilt she felt from her wrongdoing.

"Just gathering information for the investigation. You mentioned Dr. Beaumont came down to the basement. Is he working on the research with you?"

"No, not last night. And shouldn't you be more concerned with who attacked me?"

The detective paused, "How much did you have to drink last night?"

"It was a celebration. I had a drink." She crossed her arms. "Last time I checked, it wasn't a crime."

A memory flash of her waking up on the floor of the elevator—alone. How had she gotten in there? Mariska closed her eyes and put a hand on her stomach.

Detective Wulf put his pen down for a moment. "Are you feeling okay?"

She didn't answer but grabbed for the emesis basin on the bedside tray.

"Here," he said, handing her the small kidney-shaped bucket. "I'll get you a towel."

Detective Wulf went into the bathroom and reemerged a few seconds later with a washcloth. He handed it to her. The cloth was scratchy but cool and moist. She dabbed it on her forehead, cheeks, and down the sides of her neck. The urge to vomit subsided.

"I'm sorry," Mariska said. "I felt like I was going to be sick. I think I have a concussion."

He sat back down in the chair next to the bed. "I won't be much longer." His voice carried a soft, caring tone.

Mariska sighed. "Best finish your questions before the nausea comes back."

Detective Wulf sat quietly looking through his notebook while she composed herself. She took a few sips of water and closed her eyes, resting her head against the pillow. She started to feel the familiar tug of sleep, a weightless, painless bliss. Without warning, she was brought right back to reality with a few firm words.

"Mariska." Detective Wulf tapped her hand. "Don't sleep."

Her eyes fluttered open. His eyes met hers with a kindness she hadn't expected. His command was clearly more to keep her safe and conscious than to simply wake up and answer his damn questions. Maybe he wasn't such a bad guy after all.

"Do you have any more questions for me?"

"Who were you working with?"

Mariska narrowed her gaze. "Are you accusing me of something, Detective?"

"Just one more question. What did you do with the La Brea Woman?"

"Excuse me?" She struggled to maintain eye contact as she tried to straighten up in bed. A memory-flash came through, and her head once again began to pound. There she was, in the Tombs. She'd gone back for the purse, but something wasn't right. "Her storage case was gone."

The detective leaned in closer to her. His face not far from hers. Mariska's heart began to pound in her chest. Her breaths were tight and fast. Who'd been down there that night—watching her and waiting to attack?

"The La Brea Woman's been stolen."

Mariska rolled to the side of the bed and vomited in the basin. And it had little to do with her headache. La Brea Woman was gone—stolen. Mariska's life's work…had all the hours of research, countless pages written, and hundreds of hands shaken been for nothing?

The detective tossed her a towel he'd retrieved from the bathroom. "Here," he said and pointed to her chin. "You've got some…right there."

Mariska swiped the scratchy towel across her mouth and tossed it to the floor. She rolled onto her back and took a sip of water, swishing it around in her mouth before spitting it out into the emesis basin."

"Dr. Stevenson, what did you and your accomplice do with the remains? It's clear you had help." Detective Wulf stood and loomed over the bed. Gone were all attempts at civility. The man who stood before her now oozed contempt and the disgust of a career dealing with liars.

She didn't know whether to laugh, cry, or scream at this asshole cop in front of her. She shook her head. "I didn't take her…I would *never* take her."

"And why is that?"

Mariska hit the bed with a fist and looked the cop dead in the eyes. "I have spent my entire life wondering who the hell I was. Where did I come from? Who were *my* real parents? Why did they throw me away like a piece of trash?"

Detective Wulf shrugged his shoulders like he didn't care, but his jawline softened enough to betray he still had a heart. "What does that have to do with the remains?"

"Don't you get it?" Mariska spit the words out in disgust. "Of course, you wouldn't. You don't see it at all. No one knows who the La Brea Woman was or where she came from…who she belongs to. I had the chance to find out those answers. Me, a woman who's been unable to piece together her own beginning was going to help solve the mysteries of another woman's life. Bring her, closure." Mariska's eyes narrowed into angry slits. "Without her body…I can't do that."

"Rumor has it you didn't get the grant." He shrugged. "Just like you said. Without her body, you couldn't study her."

But she had been granted the rights to study the La Brea Woman…hadn't she? From what she could remember it was nearly final—nearly. Frustration and anger welled up in her and poured down her cheeks.

The detective offered her nothing. No reassurance. No sympathy or understanding. She looked up at him after a few moments. "I'm the one lying in a hospital bed as a victim of assault, and you're accusing me of a crime? Short of a cavity search, you can clearly see I don't have the remains."

The detective's hard stare softened a touch. He turned and stepped toward the door.

"I guess this means I'm a suspect?"

Hand on the door, he stopped and turned back. His jaw was set, but his eyes betrayed the compassion he must have been feeling. "Please don't leave town."

CHAPTER THREE

Detective Eric Wulf stepped out of the hospital room and was immediately confronted by the suspect's friend.

"So, what did Mariska say?" David said. "Does she remember anything?"

Wulf put his hands up in front of him to give him a foot of personal space. "Please back up a step."

David looked down for a second. He must have realized he was a bit too close as he took a couple steps back and said, "Oh I'm sorry. It's been a terrible night."

"Understandable." Wulf scanned the hallway for Dr. Stevenson's parents. "Did her family leave?"

David turned and flicked his head at the alcove of empty seats. "Yeah, they took off. Her mom was pretty upset. I think Mr. Stevenson took her home to get some rest."

That's fine. They aren't a flight risk.

Wulf motioned over to the seats and said, "Let's have a seat for a moment, shall we?"

David looked at the closed hospital room door and then back to Wulf. A moment of hesitation. Wulf pushed on, "It'll just take a minute or two."

"Yeah, sure, okay." David hurried over to the nearest seat and sat. "I can't believe this happened. And to her of all people."

"Why do you say that?" Wulf asked, taking out a notepad and pen. "What about this is so unexpected?"

"What?" David wiped his hand across his face. Everything about his body language said he was tired. Tired and worried. Dark circles under his bloodshot eyes. Mussed hair.

"Where were you when Dr. Stevenson was attacked?" Wulf asked.

"I thought I'd gone over all this before." David sat back into the chair. "I was in the Tombs with her, and we decided to rejoin the fundraiser Gala upstairs. We got into the elevator and then…"

Wulf looked up from his notepad. With arched eyebrows, he urged him to continue. "Go on."

"I don't know, she just handed me back the champagne glass and stepped out of the elevator." David looked off in the distance, lost in his memories. "It's like she forgot something."

Wulf nodded. "Yes, she mentioned a purse."

David rolled his eyes. "A stupid purse. No doubt one bought for her by her mom."

"Why do you say that?"

"Her mom is always buying her expensive things. It's like she feels guilty about something…I have no idea." David huffed. "This all could have been avoided if it wasn't for that damn purse."

Wulf continued to take notes. David stood and said, "Unless there's something else, I think I should to be with her."

This guy has it bad for the girl.

"Absolutely," Wulf said. "I'll be in touch if I need anything else."

David looked at him for a second and then nodded. "If you'll excuse me?"

Wulf stood and stepped to the side so David could pass by more easily. David stopped at the hospital room door and glanced at Wulf before stepping into the room and closing the door behind him.

What would be the motive behind this crime? Greed? Sabotage? Hate?

Making his way out of the hospital and into the parking garage, Wulf's mind ran through one scenario after the next, trying to make sense of it all. Cases like this were time-sensitive; they grew stagnant very quickly. If Wulf made a wrong turn this early on in pursuit of answers in this case, there might not be time to right the ship before it went cold.

Things he already knew were the La Brea Woman's remains had been stolen. The Paleontologist potentially assigned to researching her was attacked the night she thought she was to be given the official go-ahead to start her project. And the usual: no one saw anything. No one heard anything.

He unlocked his car and got inside. Turning on the airconditioner and headlights, he began to ease out of the parking space and go back to the police station but stopped. He pulled out his phone and started searching the internet for general public information regarding the La Brea Woman and the Page Museum. As he scrolled down the links that popped up first, he soon came across the controversy surrounding the remains.

The woman was found in 1914 by the owners of the land and subsequent founders of the Page Museum, Mr. Ashton. He clicked on the highlighted link and found that Mr. Ashton had a son and granddaughter associated with the museum as well. Ingrid Ashton, the founder's granddaughter was the last remaining living relative of this wealthy and influential Los Angeles family. Under her name, the word *Controversy* was highlighted in blue.

Wulf clicked it and was immediately sent to another page containing a petition. The local Chumash tribe had been gathering signatures for decades trying to pressure the museum into releasing the La Brea Woman's remains. As he continued to scroll, Wulf found what he was looking for. The subheading read: *Threats Shut Down the Museum*. It was dated back to January 3, 1971.

After clicking the link, an image of a local newspaper clipping filled his screen. It showed a picket line surrounding the museum. The signs read: *GIVE HER BACK. SHE DOESN'T BELONG TO YOU. LET HER COME HOME.* And, *WE WON'T REST UNTIL SHE CAN.*

The article went on:

The local Chumash people continue to picket the Page Museum, demanding the return of who they say belong to them. Museum officials have repeatedly denied their request stating, "She will be returned to them when proof becomes available indicating her true lineage." Local officials have been wary of wading in on such a tinderbox subject. According to Douglas Whitman, a local expert on such matters, "The Chumash people believe that specific ceremonial adornments and rituals are required for a member of their people to pass through to the afterlife." Recent threats of violence and even a bomb threat has caused the museum to close its doors to the public for an indefinite time period. Clearly, this is a high-stakes he-said/she-said, and the people of Los Angeles, as well as the rest of the world, wait to see what happens next.

Wulf turned off his phone. He'd lived here his entire life, and it was as if none of this ever happened. Sure, there were picket-lines whenever the museum had an annual Gala, but there had never been threats of violence in recent memory. If the Chumash had never received the La Brea Woman's remains, why did they stop trying? Surely, by now they would have taken the matter to court and yet there wasn't a record of that happening.

Why now? Why Dr. Stevenson? Very good questions that he intended on getting to the bottom of, and soon.

CHAPTER FOUR

Mariska sat in silence while David drove her home. He'd been concerned when he walked into her hospital room and saw she'd gotten out of bed. Somehow, she'd managed to get dressed, find her purse, and stash the mysterious objects she'd found that night into her bra for safekeeping before he walked into the room. She ignored his protests and pushed the doctors for a quick discharge. Afterward, she used her best puppy-dog-eyes to make sure David would still be willing to give her a ride home. It worked, although she started to feel guilty for manipulating him. No wonder he was upset with her. Had the roles been reversed, she would have felt the same way.

"I know you're irritated with me," Mariska said, looking out the window as they passed by the many closed businesses at that early morning hour.

He turned to face her. She could see his reflection in the window, and his eyes were weary, almost sad.

"I'm not mad," he said. "I'm worried about you."

"I'm fine. The doctors said—"

"I don't care what the damn doctor said." David smacked the steering wheel. "You were just in the hospital with a head injury, and you're pushing yourself too hard."

She turned and glared at him. "I wanted to go home, so I'm going home. You didn't have to take me."

"I didn't have a choice. Your parents were already gone."

"You always have a choice. We all have choices, David. I'm choosing to go home, and you're choosing to take me there. I could have taken a cab, Uber, or maybe even called my assistant."

"Kathy?" David said with a sarcastic tone. "She doesn't even like you."

Hearing the statement out loud, hit her in the stomach, but it wasn't a surprise. "Who gives a shit? She doesn't have to like me. Kathy's my assistant, and she does her job without bitching about it."

David rolled his eyes, letting out an exacerbated sigh through his nose. "Well, maybe not to your face, but…"

Mariska turned back to look out of the window. David was so overprotective at times it could be smothering. But how could she tell him he was smothering her when he was her friend, her only real friend?

"I'm sorry," David whispered.

"It's fine." Mariska kept looking out the window.

He reached for her hand and gave it a squeeze. "I really am. I just worry about you sometimes. I think you are so…so…"

She turned and gave him a look that said he better pick the right words and yanked her hand free.

He kept his attention on the road. "I worry your stubbornness might come between you and…well, your life."

Her clenched jaw and pursed lips turned into a smirk. "You're so dramatic."

"Me? Dramatic?" He clutched for his imaginary pearls.

Laughter broke the tension in the air, and they both settled into a comfortable silence. David turned the car into the alleyway behind her apartment. When they came to a stop, Mariska felt a sudden and overwhelming fatigue she hadn't felt before, not even at the hospital.

"Are you, okay?" David asked. "You look like a wet noodle."

She yawned and stretched her arms out above her head, slowly bending her neck from side to side. The stiffness had set in on the car ride, and she suspected the drugs she'd been given in the hospital were wearing off.

"I'm just tired...and sore." She took off her seatbelt and opened the door with a groan. "I think I'll be better once I get a nice, long hot shower."

"That does sound nice." David's face flushed red, and even in the poor lighting of the overhead car light, Mariska noticed it.

Was she ready to turn their friendship into something more? Yesterday, despite their mutual decision to not pursue a romantic relationship, she might have let it happen. But now was not the right time. Despite the butterflies of attraction, she said, "You're more than welcome to take one too, but I'm first."

"Great," he said, getting out of the car and hurrying around the side to help her. "Here, grab my hands."

She let him assist her to her feet. Her body swayed ever so slightly, but she fought hard not to let it show. Last thing she needed was David to throw her back into the car and rush her to the hospital.

Mariska threaded her arm easily between David's elbow and torso. Their bodies linked together like they belonged that way. She leaned against him while they walked. His body helped to warm her on the cool, damp evening. The streetlight at the entrance to the apartment parking lot did little to illuminate their path, but it was nice not to squint past the headache. When they reached the long, steep, metal staircase that lead to the upstairs apartment, she looked up at the daunting challenge. When she'd found her apartment, she'd loved the fact it was located above a Korean market. A screech of tires behind them made her tighten her hold on David's arm. Now she wished she'd chosen the posh high rise her mother tried to foist on her. It had an elevator.

Just the thought of stepping into another elevator tightened the breath in her chest. She had a sudden flash of memory, bright and blurry. She'd been in a hurry to retrieve her purse. After a dash down the hall, her hand settled on the knob to push the door to the Tombs open. She could still feel the cold metal in her grip. Her heart began to race. The La Brea woman was gone. A sound—movement behind her. Pain—

Someone had hit her from behind.

"Are you sure you're okay?" David's face swam into focus, inches from hers, concern etched deeply into his brow. "That's it. We're going back to—"

"No we're not," she told him with as much edge to her voice as she could muster.

He hesitated at the bottom of the stairs. "Are you sure you can make it?" David asked, giving in with sigh. "We can always go back to my place."

"Nope, I can do this." She let go of his arm and grabbed both railings.

She counted each step in her head, feeling accomplished with each one she left behind. The first two or three steps weren't that bad, but they became more and more difficult as she climbed. With less than five steps remaining, her quads started to shake, and her knees threatened to buckle. She paused for a moment and took a deep breath.

"Are you okay?" David anchored his hand below her elbow.

"Just a bit tired. I'll be all right."

Determined to make it to her apartment so she could take a shower, slip into something comfortable and relax in her own bed. She gritted her teeth and continued up the stairs. The last two were downright painful, but she made it to the landing.

"Here, let me get the door," David said as he wiggled the key into the lock. "Are you sure this is the right key? It won't unlock."

"Oh yeah. The lock sticks." She changed positions with him and pulled out the key. "You just have to use a bit of finesse." She slid the key all the way into the lock then backed it out just a touch. "And then you…" She banged her fist against the door, above the knob, and turned the key. "Easy, enough." Mariska grinned, despite the fact that all the banging and jiggling made her a bit nauseated.

David wasn't nearly as impressed with her door opening skills as she was. "Right," he said, giving her another furrowed-brow look. "You should get that fixed."

David ushered her inside, and Mariska was sure to lock the doorknob and both deadbolts. It wasn't the best part of town, although it could have been much worse. The apartment itself was great. The only one in the building, it was expansive and the owner, Miss Yi, allowed her to decorate it however she wanted. Of course, her mom hired one of Los Angeles' premiere interior designers, and the apartment went from a storage attic to a posh, postmodern living space that Mariska loved. And despite her mom's protests, she'd been faithfully paying her parents back without fail for the renovations.

"Is there anything I can help you with?" David reached for her purse. "Here, why don't you give me that and you can go in and start getting ready for that shower you've been talking about."

Mariska hesitated, but after placing a hand to her chest, handed the purse over to David and smiled. "If you wouldn't mind, could you put it in the second bedroom's walk-in closet? There's a section for my accessories."

David's mouth flattened into a straight line, "For sure…the accessories section."

They walked together down the hallway. She knew David hadn't grown up in a life of luxury, and she might have felt bad about it, but between her headache, fatigue, and desire for a shower, she let it go. If he seemed weird about it later, she'd say something. He turned to walk into the second bedroom, and she stopped him. "Thank you for all your help."

He smiled and gave her a nod, reaching for her hand. She let him. His strong, warm hand felt good around hers—comforting.

"You know I'd do anything for you, right?" David said.

"I do." She squeezed his hand back. "And I hope you know how much you mean to me."

His fingers relaxed just a bit. "I do."

She released her grip, letting her arm fall to her side. "I shouldn't be too long. Maybe twenty minutes."

"Okay, I'll put this away, and if you don't mind, I'll meet you in the living room. There's got to be something fun on television to watch."

"There was a marathon of an alien conspiracy show on yesterday, so there's probably ten or more episodes on the DVR."

"Great. See you when you get out." David turned, and she watched him head for the walk-in closet to put the purse away.

She walked into her own bedroom and closed the door behind her. Leaning heavily against the door, she again put her hand to her chest for a moment. Maybe she *had* left the hospital too soon. She took a deep breath and let it out slowly. *No,* she'd be fine. Mariska cracked the door open and snuck a peek into the hallway. David was a stand-up guy, so why was she being so secretive about what she'd done? About what she had found?

As she was about to close the door, David emerged from the second bedroom. His effortless gait. The bounce in his step, despite the late hour of night. The way his rumpled tux clung in all the right places. He caught her staring.

"Everything all right?" he asked, stopping in mid-stride. His brow once again furrowed.

"Oh, yeah. I thought I heard you call my name." She looked down and smiled—biting her bottom lip ever so slightly, before closing the door in front of her.

Mariska heard his footfalls, slow at first, pause at her door before continuing down the hallway toward the living room. She started to turn away but stopped. Looking down at the doorknob, she reached into the top of her dress and pulled out the pouch she'd stashed away in her bra. She'd managed to sneak them from her purse before they'd left the hospital. Had this discovery she'd made in the tombs this evening been related to her attack and the theft?

La Brea Woman's remains were missing, but she still had this—a pouch filled with pieces of the puzzle. Contemplating their significance for a moment, she closed her fist around them and locked the door.

CHAPTER FIVE

The reflection in the mirror made her glance away. Eyes sunken deep into their sockets, dark circles punctuating her fatigue. Mariska looked like she'd aged years in the past few hours. The mirror showed the bruises were forming on her arms, legs, and back. There were scratches on her back and legs that were now red and inflamed. *Had she been dragged into the elevator? But by whom?*

The hot shower behind her was filling the small bathroom with steam. The mirror fogged over, releasing her from the trance she'd fallen into. She put the white evening dress on a hanger attached to a hook over the bathroom door. The steam would help relax the wrinkles that had multiplied on the delicate silk fabric. She turned the dress over and saw no less than five tears. She brushed her hand against the dark stains. It was ruined. She hung her head and massaged her temples.

Damn.

She sat on the toilet and took off one shoe at a time, massaging her toes and instep. The shiny red heels were beautiful, but hurt her feet more than she'd like to admit. She set the shoes down on the floor next to her and closed her eyes. An image of the gem-encrusted purse she'd gone back into the tombs to recover flashed into her mind. Had she left the purse behind, she wouldn't have been attacked, but she might not have found the mysterious pouch that'd been left behind. The find had been unexpected, and there'd been no time to examine it. Mariska palmed the woven material, rolling it around in her hand. Soft and worn, the find had enough weight to make her wonder what it contained. She'd wanted to pull it from the skull, but knew better than to do it before having the official permission. But when she'd found it on the floor of the tombs, there hadn't been time to think…or act with a scientific mind. The pouch was old and hand woven with a cinch at the top. Cloth material like this was not found in America ten thousand years ago, so it hadn't belonged to the La Brea Woman. While old, possibly turn of the century, she suspected the pouch itself was not of any real scientific significance. But how did it get inside her skull? And why?

With extreme care, she opened the cinched top and emptied the contents into her palm. The unexpected surprise made her gasp. A large tooth along with nine crudely carved beads. Each bead was cubic in shape and of a different color and had a hole bored through. Part of a necklace? And a tooth? Shaped like a human eyetooth, it was far too big. At least three times too large. These artifacts had to have been related to the theft, why else would it have been there? Her mind swirled with more questions than answers, and she started feeling weak. She returned the mysterious items back into the pouch and hid it inside the vanity. Better take a shower.

Water hot enough to sting helped wash away the day's devils. That and the cherry blossom bath soap her mom and dad brought back from their recent travels to Japan. Her skin was red and hot but had now adjusted to the temperature. It felt so good, the water massaging away the aches and pains. Soon her headache was gone—mostly. After turning off the shower, she stood for a moment, listening to the water circle the tub drain.

The slow drip of the showerhead kept her focused the problem. *Where was the La Brea Woman? Who else wanted her? And who the hell had access?*

A shiver brought her back to the here and now. The water had completely emptied from the tub, leaving her cold and wet. Goosebumps covered her body and the shivering intensified. She threw back the shower curtain and grabbed for the towel. Once she was dry, the fluffy terrycloth bathrobe slipped around her shoulders in a warm, comforting embrace. She snugged it tight and breathed in its freshly laundered scent. It was a wonderful, yet temporary reprieve from the terrible day.

She jumped at the unexpected knock on the bathroom door. She'd completely forgotten David was still there. Such a good man, agreeing to stay the night—on concussion watch. Even though it would've been nice to take a shower in peace.

"Are you doing all right in there?" David asked. Mariska could hear the concern in his voice.

"I'm good, thank you. Just about finished." *Hadn't she locked her bedroom door?*

"Good, just making sure. The doctor did say the steam from the shower could make you woozy."

"Nope, I think it made me feel better." Mariska began towel drying her hair. "Thank you for checking, though."

"I'll meet you in the living room. *Ancient Aliens* is on, and they're talking about the Annunaki. I swear the commentators are nuts, but I do agree the Sumerians knew more than we give them credit for."

She couldn't help but smile at his enthusiasm. "Sounds good. I'll be out in five minutes."

She smiled. David was such an open soul. Believed in everything from aliens and Bigfoot to the Loch Ness Monster. Maybe even mermaids. She loved that about him. While she was someone who believed there were still many mysterious things that haven't been proven, seen, or explained, she still had trouble admitting it to anyone other than David.

Guilt nagged her belly as she dug the pouch out from the bottom drawer of the vanity. Why didn't she tell David about it? It was for his own protection. No sense in risking implicating him in what she'd done. But if there was anyone in this world that could and would truly appreciate the potential find, it was him. Yes, she'd tell him about them—eventually. But not until she had a better idea of what it all meant. After all, if she was still somehow awarded the grant, he would be her right-hand-man. But for now, it would stay her secret.

She walked out of the bathroom and straight over to the bedroom door and locked it. On the long dresser under the window, there was a small decorative box. It was covered in multicolored glass mosaic tiles. It had a trick lid that popped opened when the bottom was pulled down. Opening the pouch, she took out the beads and palmed them. She placed the beads into the box and closed the lid. There hadn't been room for the pouch and tooth, so she needed a second hiding place.

She took a moment to examine the fossil. It didn't fit any animal she'd ever seen before. Too long to be from a dire wolf, too short to be from a saber-toothed cat. Possibly a bear, but at three inches from tip to base, it didn't fit any of the usual suspects in that area of California. *What was that?* Mariska held the tooth up to the light. A tiny hole on each side of the base. Part of a necklace? Had the La Brea Woman been wearing the beads and this tooth when she died?

There wasn't the time or equipment in her apartment to give the tooth a proper scientific examination. That's when she spotted the perfect hiding place. On the bookshelf, there was a geode she'd picked up at a local flea market. The felt bottom could be pulled back to reveal a hide-a-key opening. She padded across the room and opened the secret compartment. After putting the tooth back into the pouch, she placed it inside the geode and replaced the felt bottom.

A jiggle of the doorknob made her jump. The knock that followed pissed her off.

"I'm getting dressed," she said.

"Sorry, just checking on you." David's voice was soft, kind.

She took a deep breath and let it out slowly. With nothing to be upset about, she put the bookend back on the shelf and got dressed into her matching green and white Zed the Mammoth pajamas. The long sleeves and pants were made of a thin, soft, cotton-blend and they always relaxed her nerves when she wore them.

Hurrying out to the living room, she sat next to David on the leather couch, pulling the throw off the back and onto her legs. Despite the summer heat, her apartment was always cool inside. She snuggled into his side a bit further.

The two of them sat comfortably together on the couch, watching television, and it felt amazing. Good enough for her mind to wander to the long term. Could she and David be…*a thing? No.* David was a great guy, and there might've been a time where they could've been something more, but they both decided that their friendship meant too much.

"You feeling any better?" David asked.

She slid over and rested her head on his shoulder, "Yeah. I am now."

He wrapped an arm around her shoulders. "Good. I'm sorry the gala turned into a nightmare for you."

"Me too." She sighed. "Dr. Snyder was going to give one of us the go-ahead to start our research on the La Brea Woman. He was supposed to make it official with an announcement tonight. Not that it matters now."

David tightened his arm into a hug. "It still matters…and he pulled me aside just before the gala started and told me it was you who was getting the green light."

"Me? He told you that?" Her heart raced at the idea, but a pit formed in her stomach. *I'll probably never get the chance to do it now.*

She tilted her head and arched her eyebrows. "David?"

"Yeah?"

"I didn't tell you everything that happened when the detective questioned me."

He looked at her, his forehead crinkled, deep furrows forming between his brows.

"He tried to say that—"

Mariska's cell phone rang. She grabbed for it. "It's Dr. Snyder."

"Better answer it. Maybe he'll still give you the grant?"

She took a deep breath and let it out, slow and controlled. "Hello, this is Dr. Stevenson."

"Dr. Stevenson, how could you?"

The unexpected volume of his voice caused Mariska to pull the phone away from her ear for a moment. "Excuse me?"

"You've stolen museum property." Each and every word was a dagger straight into her gut.

"I…I didn't." There was no way he knew about the beads. "I don't know what you're talking about."

"You know damn well. The La Brea Woman is gone. You've stolen her. Even the police think you're involved."

"No, I—"

"You did." Dr. Snyder's voice came through as scratchy bursts of anger. She could envision the spittle as it left his violently shaking jowls. "The detective told me he interrogated you at the hospital. Clearly, you have to admit they think you're involved somehow."

"The police told you I did it?" Mariska felt sick and struggled to keep her voice steady.

"The detective didn't say you were guilty, but it's obvious to me you're a suspect."

"If I'm a suspect, then we both are. You were at the Museum Gala, just as I was…sir."

"Excuse, me?" Dr. Snyder's voice cracked, betraying his surprise at her defense. There was a moment of silence where she assumed he was gathering his composure. "The museum has suffered a great loss—an assault really. I do not have proof that you're directly involved, but you've been so obsessed with the La Brea Woman, I can't just dismiss the possibility. Maybe you acted with an accomplice, but I believe you're involved. Somehow you found out you might have been passed over for the grant money and you just couldn't bare the idea of giving up your research."

Mariska's stomach sank, and she swallowed back tears. "I didn't get the grant? I thought it was set in stone. I had no way of knowing it wasn't. You've got to believe me. I'm sorry this has happened. I want you to know I have had nothing to do with this…I swear to it. I'll take a polygraph—whatever it takes."

"I think in the public eye, it's too late for that," Dr. Snyder said before clearing his throat and putting on his boss' tone of voice. "I want you to resign from your position. I want the negative spotlight off the museum. Every day that goes by without a resolution…coupled with your continued employement, puts the museum—and the funds that keep her afloat—at risk."

"Please, Dr. Snyder." She clenched her fist to keep her emotions in check. "I was attacked…I'm a victim here."

"No, the museum's the victim. And as much as this pains me to say, if the police prove your part in this, expect that you will be pursued with every resource we have at our disposal."

"I'm going to be cleared of any wrongdoing. I would hope you'd use the museum's resources to find the culprit who committed this horrible crime. This witch-hunt is a waste of their money, your time, and is beneath the reputation of the museum."

"I am so incredibly disappointed in you, Doctor Stevenson."

She swallowed the lump in her throat. *What could she say to that?*

Dr. Snyder huffed. She could image him sweating, shaking with pent up hostility and unsaid comments he was forcing to remain that way. He'd never liked her. He'd railed against her initial hire and then again, her promotion to lead paleontologist. He would soon be retiring as head curator, and it must have hurt him to hear her name floating around as a possible replacement.

"If there is the slightest bit of evidence you're involved in this, Dr. Stevenson, your career is over. And until this investigation has been completed, you are not to touch, access, or research anything at the museum that is related to the La Brea Woman. I don't want your name associated with anything that is linked to the remains. Period. You mess up at all, you're done. Are we clear?"

"Crystal." She hung up the phone and sank further into the sofa, her head resting against David for comfort. "He—"

"No need to say anything. I heard that smug asshole, loud and clear." David wrapped his arm around Mariska and held her tight. "I'm so sorry you're going through this. Do you think he's making it up about the grant? It's like he's trying to pin in on you."

She would have cried if she wasn't so pissed.

CHAPTER SIX

Mariska hunched over a backlit table sifting through bits of dirt, bone, and tar-covered debris from Pit 23. The pit adjacent to the one La Brea Woman was found in over a century ago. The strain in her lower back was spreading up her spine and into the back of her head. David's warnings about returning to work too soon after the attack had fallen on deaf ears. If she didn't take a break soon, she'd end up with a migraine. She sat up, arched her back, and stretched her neck from side to side. The throbbing in the back of her head made her eyes and teeth hurt.

"Are you okay?" her college intern, Theresa Krieger said. She was a graduate student from USC and had proven a solid scientist. She stood and reached up overhead and stretched her back. The young woman wasn't extremely tall but was as lanky as they come. Long spindly legs, shoved into skinny-jeans, and long blonde hair made her appear even skinnier than she really was.

Walking around the room, Mariska shook out her arms and legs, getting the blood to flow back into them.

"I'll be fine. Just a bit bruised and sore from last night. Still can't believe what happened."

The pain ebbed a bit once she was standing and moving around the dark laboratory. But her mind wouldn't shut down, or even slow, for that matter. Who took her, the La Brea Woman? And, why? There had to be something incredibly valuable about her…and it couldn't have been her historical or educational value.

There was a coffee pot outside the lab. No food or beverages were allowed inside to avoid contamination. She thought about how she'd already done so much to hurt her career. Shaking her head, she sighed. What made her think it had been okay to take the woven pouch in the first place? To touch it without gloved hands was iffy, but to take it from the museum was something else entirely.

Mariska turned to Theresa, who was still hunched over a back-lit table, sifting through bits of material. "I'm going to step out for a second—clear my head and take a walk around." She opened the door and walked out into the dark storage area of the Tombs.

She took a sip of coffee and looked back through the glass wall into the lab and saw the clock inside read ten o'clock. It was way past closing time. She and Theresa were the only souls in the building. Thankful for the company, it helped keep the creepiness of the Tombs at bay. Long, dark aisles of shelving with storage boxes filled with the remains of long-since extinct animals and plant life. Each box holding a new discovery, yet to be analyzed and recorded. But whenever Mariska closed her eyes and was alone among the remains, she felt the collective energy of this makeshift mausoleum. Not someone who identified as a religious person, or had a belief in souls or the afterlife, Mariska couldn't deny there was an energy that flowed through this place.

Maybe it was the fact she'd been attacked there less than twenty-four hours ago, but she felt like there were eyes on her. She looked up and spotted a security camera. That was new…wasn't it? The dust from a freshly drilled wallboard dirtied the floor below it. Definitely, new. Had it already been hooked up? She took a step to the right and a couple to the left. The camera didn't move, the glowing red light the only indication it was even turned operational.

Mariska drew a line in the air, following the direction of the camera angle. It hadn't been put in to view the tombs, but the coming and going of the employees who worked in the underground laboratory. Dr. Snyder had been pushing for security cameras for years, but it hadn't been in the budget. This latest incident clearly pushed his agenda through the budget committee.

Theresa popped her head out the door. "Anything fun going on out here? The sample I'm sifting is sucking the life out of me." She took a full step out of the lab and let the door close behind her.

Mariska thought back to the previous evening, recalling how David had mentioned the Gala was protested by the Native American community. "Do you recall the protests from last night?"

Theresa nodded. "Yeah, what about them?"

It wasn't unusual as the local tribes had petitioned the museum to return the remains of the La Brea Woman for the past three decades. The museum's position had always been they were conducting research on the remains. If and when evidence came to light indicating the Chumash tribe were her rightful heirs, she'd be turned over to them.

"Dr. Beaumont mentioned they were protesting and I couldn't help but wonder if they were behind her disappearance."

"From what I've always heard, the museum was going to return her when the research was complete," Theresa said.

The problem was Mariska knew no one had ever performed any research on her, as the museum never wanted to risk giving up ownership. That was one of the reasons she'd been so anxious to get her hands on her. There was an unknown amount of treasured information Mariska could glean from the remains. Unfortunately, the museum had gone as far as taking body off display and had stashed the remains into storage. Out of sight out of mind? The museum hoped so, anyway. Recently, there'd been a huge shakeup in the board of directors, and the great Ingrid Ashton had taken a more prominent role. Mariska smiled when she thought about all the amazing things this woman had accomplished, even when it wasn't widely accepted for a female to do—like scientific research.

"Dr. Stevenson?" Theresa's voice was sheepish.

Mariska looked up. "Yeah?"

"I know the glass case she'd been held in was left behind, but do you wonder how the intruder could have managed to remove the entire body so quickly? Without anyone seeing it? I mean, she was a full-sized human."

The speed at which the body had been removed hadn't yet piqued her interest, but it sure did now. "I hadn't thought about that. I was unconscious…so, I guess I just assumed they had time."

"Seems like Dr. Beaumont emerged from the elevator only a few minutes before you did."

"What exactly did you see?"

"Dr. Beaumont exited the elevator, and I remember he had a smile on his face like he'd just thought about something funny. He went and got two flutes of champagne and went straight back to the elevator."

"I had left him for a second to run back into the lab to retrieve my purse. He probably thought I was scatterbrained…or tipsy." Mariska chuckled. "I can assure you; I was neither of those things."

Theresa smiled. "He was definitely bringing you another glass of bubbly to celebrate your success. He's such a good guy."

"Then what happened?"

"He pushed the button for the elevator return, and when the doors popped open, you were lying on the floor. People started screaming…at least your mom did, anyway. The other stuffy bastards mostly looked annoyed." Theresa rolled her eyes. "I can't understand why they think you're involved."

"I feel like they suspect I had an accomplice and staged my assault and injury." Mariska shook her head in annoyance.

That entire ordeal couldn't have taken much time. Maybe five minutes for whoever had attacked her to remove the body and get out without setting off any alarms. Mariska looked into the coffee cup, swirled it around a few times and took a couple more sips of the lukewarm swill.

"We might as well get back to work. The dirt and tar won't sift themselves." Mariska opened the door for Theresa. Her stomach felt tight, and a nagging nausea wouldn't leave her, she had no idea if the IRB would still give her the grant, or take that money and use it for something else—like continued security upgrades. In the meantime, she would need to stay focused on her other duties as the lead paleontologist.

Today, those duties included a bucket full of debris that needed to be painstakingly sorted. Her tools consisted of tweezers, a tiny brush, and a fistful of aspirin. Each bit of debris could hold the key to a new discovery. Every piece was important. The tar preserved all kinds of things, bone, bugs, and even some plant life. The sticky substance bubbled up to the surface entrapping thousands of creatures over time, ultimately killing them, but also preserving them. The process was slow but efficient and successful.

Another hour of work, she'd catalogued four pill bug insects and eight Giant Sequoia seeds. "Having much success?" Mariska asked her student.

"Just a few seeds is all." Theresa sounded as disappointed as Mariska felt.

When Mariska first started working at the museum, the tiniest of discoveries didn't impact the way they did now. She'd wanted to find a new species of mammal or bird. Something on a large scale that put her name in lights or at least on the cover of a science magazine. But the longer she worked there, the more she came to realize the importance of the small discoveries. The Giant Sequoia seeds, for example, represented trees that thrived in southern California during the Pleistocene Epoch. These same trees were now confined to more northern areas, indicating a significant climate change. The sheer pleasure she garnered from discovery and increased knowledge that could be shared with the future generation way outweighed any magazine cover or perceived notoriety she'd sought in the past.

"Devil is in the details," Mariska said.

During her tenure at the museum, they'd discovered a type of algae that had very specific requirements to survive, including temperature and humidity. The moisture levels of both the atmosphere and soil had to be very specific. These required levels were no longer possible in Southern California. Again, indicating a shift in climate that changed the entire ecosystem of North America. These other, physically smaller discoveries, painted the true picture of what life was like during that time.

Every visitor to the museum asked: *What happened to the Mammoth? Why did the giant ground sloth disappear? Whatever happened to the Saber-*

Toothed Cat? Mariska hoped one of these discoveries would one day reveal the answers.

Mariska's cell phone buzzed with an incoming call. She picked it up and saw that Dr. Snyder was calling.

"Hello?" Mariska said, with as much pleasantness as she could manage. The man was nearing retirement and could barely contain his disdain for the younger and up-and-coming generation.

"Dr. Stevenson, I've met with the IRB. We have our final decision." His voice was clipped, hurried. "I'm on my way to the museum—can you meet me there tonight?"

"Yes, I'm here already. Theresa and I have been sorting and cataloguing a portion of Pit 23." Mariska looked at Theresa and shrugged. Why would Dr. Snyder be coming to the museum at this hour?

He cleared his throat. "I haven't authorized any overtime."

"HR changed my status to salary when my promotion to lead paleontologist became official." What the hell was his problem?

"Right…the promotion. Meet me in my office in twenty minutes." The phone went dead as he didn't bother waiting for a response. Mariska shrugged. He didn't have to wait, he was the boss, and it wasn't like she would have told him no.

Theresa drew Mariska's attention away from the phone. "Dr. Stevenson, I was thinking about something…and I think it's important."

Mariska barely registered her words. She had a strange feeling about her conversation with Dr. Snyder. Something was wrong. Was there more to this meeting than a discussion about the status of the grant? Was her job in jeopardy?

"…the dog is still here, right?" Theresa said, but Mariska hadn't heard the beginning of her statement. "Might be some clues in there."

"Clues?" Mariska said. "I'm sorry. I wasn't listening. Dr. Snyder is coming here tonight, and he demanded to see me in his office in twenty minutes. He sounded pissed off."

"That sounds, serious." Theresa furrowed her brow and bit her bottom lip. "You don't think you're in trouble, do you? They can't fire you…right?"

"I think I'll be fine. They can't fire me unless it's proven I had something to do with the theft. I mean, innocent until proven guilty and all that…right? Personally, I think he's the only one who thinks I had anything to do with it and it's because he doesn't like me for some reason."

"That's a relief." Theresa made an exaggerated sweep across her forehead. "I've been thinking about something important, and I don't think you've thought of yet."

Mariska looked at her intern's face. Her expression was one of excitement and concern. She looked at the clock, eighteen minutes to go. "Okay, lay it on, me."

"The La Brea Woman was found with a small canine in her arms."

Mariska wasn't following her train of thought. "And?"

"Last month, when you were submitting your proposal to the IRB, we separated the remains. We stored the canine in a separate storage container because he wasn't part of the proposal."

Mariska's heart started to pound, and her face felt flushed. However small, there might be a chance that some of the La Brea Woman's DNA could be found with the canine's remains. After all, they had died together, spending the last ten thousand or so years with their bones interwoven together. Mariska bolted for the exit. She pulled the door open, hard. The calendar mounted on the wall behind it, fell to the floor as she ran past, deeper into the Tombs.

Knowing right where the canine was stored, Mariska hurried past three rows and turned right. On the second shelf, two boxes from the end, she spotted her prize. Without hesitation, she pulled the box from the shelf and onto the floor. Pulling out her cell phone, she turned on the light as she lifted off the lid. The noxious smell of asphalt penetrated Mariska's nose but didn't slow her down. Inside, the small canine, no larger than a Corgi, lay at the bottom of the wooden box. There were a few stones and a layer of dirt and tar at the bottom of the box. No materials were discarded until they could be sorted and sifted through under magnification.

The bright, flat, white LED light made shadows grow and deepen behind the illuminated skeletal structures.

"Thank god no one took you," Mariska said. That's when she noticed something she hadn't before. The bright light seemed to make the bones glow against the flat dingy surfaces of tar and dirt. Between the second and third costal bones on the underside of the skeleton, something was there that didn't belong. Or, at least didn't belong to the canine.

Mariska pulled a pair of latex gloves from her back pocket and reached inside and tried to wiggle the object free. It didn't immediately come loose. It was cemented in place by thousands of years of tar and sediment buildup. Mariska reached under the canine and lifted it up off the bottom, no more than an inch. She used her other hand to grasp the boney object and tapped it with her finger. It didn't budge. Unwilling to damage it, no matter how important she thought it might be to finding the La Brea Woman, she used the edge of her gloved fingernail to scrape away some of the sediment. Flecks of dirt and hardened asphalt crumbled away and fell to the bottom of the box. She then grasped the bone between two fingers and slid it along the costal bones of the canine until it reached a wider opening. Pulling back with a gentle nudge, she felt the bone come easily free.

Slowly, she brought the bone into the light, her heart racing away. Turning it over and over in her hand, she couldn't believe her eyes. It was a human phalange—a finger bone. Somehow, years ago, when the bodies had been separated, this bone had been left behind. No, doubt a result of it being partially encased in debris not to mention the majority of skeletons were incomplete when discovered in the first place. It wasn't uncommon to find ancillary bones months, if not years later that could be reunited with the rest of the body once matched.

A scraping noise sounded behind her, followed by a sharp huff of exacerbation.

"What the hell are you doing?" Dr. Snyder said. He was early.

From the way he was breathing, he'd speed-walked in from the parking lot and came straight to the Tombs to find her.

Mariska's body went stiff. She was holding in her hand the only remaining vestige of the woman she'd obsessed about for the last decade. She'd been forbidden from coming into contact with anything La Brea Woman related, and here she was, caught red-handed. *How the hell am I going to get out of this one?*

"Stand up, and step away from the box." Dr. Snyder's voice grew into a menacing growl.

She hesitated. This couldn't be happening. Not now dammit. *I need answers.*

"I said, step away from the box." He used the flashlight to emphasize the direction he wanted her to go.

Resignation and regret was all she felt. Mariska took a deep breath and stood.

"Show me what's in your hand."

She held up her palm with the La Brea Woman's finger bone in it and let out a sigh. "I'm sorry."

He aimed the flashlight onto the box and then on the content of her hand.

"I told you," Kathy said, stepping out from behind Dr. Snyder. "She can't be trusted." She glared hard enough for Mariska to feel it physically.

"Why is she here?" Mariska asked.

"It's none of your concern." Dr. Snyder flicked the light up into Mariska's eyes, and she flinched away from it.

"Tsk tsk, Dr. Stevenson." Kathy sauntered on high heels toward her. Each heel click against cement, a stab into her heart. "First, the remains…now, this?" She pointed to Mariska's hand. With pouty lips and feigned sadness, she whispered out of Dr. Snyder's earshot, "Looks like I'm going to take your place."

Mariska narrowed her eyes and swallowed down the venom welling up inside her. "You don't even have a degree."

"Don't, I?" Kathy shrugged her shoulders. She raised her voice, "I graduated last week."

"And she'll be handling some things in your absence," Dr. Snyder snapped.

"But..."

He put up a hand silencing her. "Too bad, Dr. Stevenson." He shook his head. "I knew you were impulsive...or maybe it's just youth. But I never took you for being this stupid."

What could she say? His face was a mask of disappointment and anger, and she knew he wouldn't listen to what she had to say. She'd messed up, and she'd done it to herself. "I'm..." She looked away.

"I know you're sorry, but that doesn't negate the fact you went against a direct order. You were clear on the rules. You broke them. And, now you're done here." He pulled a decorative handkerchief from his jacket front pocket and said, "Hand it over."

She did as she was told before turning away. Unable to speak, there wasn't anything else to say.

"You are not to set foot on museum property again until this investigation is over. If I have my way with the board of directors, your position here will be terminated." They made eye contact, and she felt a lump rise into her throat. "You deserve this, Dr. Stevenson. I can't afford to retire and leave this revered institution in the hands of a reckless showboat. The museum has been here for decades, and it contains artifacts from thousands of years ago that have withstood millennia of environmental changes, social and political turmoil, advancements in industry and knowledge only to be put at risk of being destroyed by the careless actions of an amateur. I won't have it. Leave, and do not return, or I'll have you arrested for trespassing."

Mariska flinched at the harshness of his words. Over his shoulder, Mariska spotted Theresa as she slunk away, back to the lab. Suddenly, the walls began to close in on her, making it difficult to breathe. Fighting back tears, she pushed passed him on her way to the exit.

"No one can help you now, Doctor," he said to her retreating form. "Paleontology is a small world, and you're done...finished."

She ran for the exit, barely able to hold back the sobs of frustration and sadness. What could she possibly do now?

CHAPTER SEVEN

Mariska hadn't called ahead. There was still a chance to run away, but she needed to fix this. Her parents lived on a sprawling Cliffside Drive estate, having recently moved there from Holmby Heights. It'd taken her a while to get used to visiting them at their new place. Sure, it was a beautiful home with lots of land for her mom to enjoy puttering around in a garden and grove of fruit trees. Not to mention the view—the Pacific Ocean as far as the eye could see. But it still wasn't the home she'd grown up in. The thought of her old bedroom and the attached playroom where she'd set up fake archeological digs played out the struggles of times past, and so often lay on the floor imagining the giant creatures that she read about in textbooks and choose-your-own-adventure novels, made her belly ache. She missed it. Adulthood had proved not to be all that she'd thought it would be.

She pushed the doorbell; the chime played a tune from *The Sound of Music*. Her resolve to ask her parents for help, faded by the second verse. Mariska turned to leave when the front door opened behind her.

"Mariska?" Jane the housekeeper said. The tone in her voice revealed how much more excited she was to see her than Mariska was to be there. The woman's upswept gray hair normally hung at shoulder length and remained thick despite her age. Her short, strong body had physically worked hard most of her life. She'd no doubt outlive Mariska herself. The idea brought a smile to her face. Had it not been for Mariska's mom, Jane would have been happy to wear the same clothes over and over as she wasn't one to splurge on herself.

Mariska turned and with outstretched arms, rushed over and gave the woman a huge hug. "It's been way too long. I've missed you."

"Honey, I've missed you too. I know it's none of my business, but I heard about your accident." The middle-aged woman reached out a hand and smoothed Mariska's hair. "Are you, okay?"

Jane had been a part of the family since before Mariska was even born. She lived in a casita on the property although Mariska's parents had asked her to come and live with them in the main house. Jane wanted her independence.

"I'll be fine." She gave Jane another big hug. "How are they doing?"

"They miss you." Jane leaned in a little closer and lowered her voice. "Your mom mentioned at breakfast that she's distraught over what happened to you last night. She even asked your father if he could make you move back in."

"Make me?" Mariska laughed.

"I know, honey. You know how worried your mom gets." Jane grabbed Mariska's hand. "I'll keep her busy. The less time on her hands to worry about you, the better."

"Thank you." Mariska gave her a hug. "You know my parents can't survive without you."

"Well they better figure it out, I'm not getting any younger, you know." Jane had been saying this for the past ten years or so. Her parents had a maid service come in to clean, and a landscaper took care of the expansive property. Mariska's parents continued to pay Jane, provided her with housing, food, and companionship. It was a win-win situation for everyone. And as long as it was never spoken aloud, it would continue that way until the very end.

Mariska said, "I need help, and as much as I hate to do it, I have to ask my parents for it."

Jane's expression grew thoughtful. "I can't imagine they'd ever say no to you."

"That's part of the problem. I know they'll help me. I'm scared to get them involved. What if my dad tries to use his influence and they somehow suffer the consequences of my actions? That'd make two tragedies in one day."

"Oh, believe me, I know. You were such a stubborn, headstrong child."

Mariska feigned shock. "Sweet, little old me?"

"With all seriousness, Mariska. They want to help you. They need to help you. You're their only child." She put a hand to her chest. "Trust me, they want to provide for everyone they love, but especially you."

"I know." Mariska looked around the front of the home for a moment. "Something looks different."

"Remember that hideous monstrosity of a fountain?"

Mariska turned around to find the gigantic black stone water feature gone, replaced by a beautiful Japanese pine tree.

"How did you ever convince my father to get rid of that thing?"

"It wasn't easy." Jane took a quick glance over her shoulder to ensure they were still alone. "Your mom had a brilliant idea. She had me back the car out of the garage."

"But you hate to drive my parent's car."

"Precisely the point. I backed your father's Land Rover right into it. Cracked that son of a bitch clean through." She let out the most glorious cackle but stifled it before it got out of control.

"I love you," Mariska said, still giggling to herself.

"Where are my manners?" Jane looped her arm through hers, and they hurried inside. "Let's go out back. Your mom is going to be so excited to see you."

They walked arm-in-arm through the mansion. They passed pieces of priceless art and artifacts from ancient Egypt, Greece, Rome, and Mariska's favorite, the Pleistocene Era. Prehistory was often more interesting then ancient history. There were so many mysteries still to be solved. They passed through the kitchen, into the formal dining room, and made it to the side exit that opened up to the pool. Her childhood home in Holmby Heights hadn't had a pool. Well, it did, until her mom had it filled in. She always said it was too big of a risk to have small children around water.

"She's right over there," Jane said, pointing to the far side of the property. Right at the edge of the manicured lawn was a small grove of lemon, lime, and pomegranate trees. The trees were confined to one side, blocking the view of their only neighbor to the north of the property. The unobstructed view of the Pacific Ocean never ceased to be amaze. High up enough on the cliff to keep the smell of seaweed away, the clean, cool breeze was always refreshing.

Mariska turned and gave Jane a hug. "Thank you."

She hurried across the huge property, careful not to step on any of the randomly placed sprinkler heads. Her heels sank into the soft sodded lawn, and a sprinkler head would spell certain disaster. Mariska stopped at the tree line. The scent of rosebushes drew her attention to the left. Her mom had been hard at work in the garden. Perfectly manicured, the roses were in full bloom and caught the light just right. Red, white, yellow, and pink. All beautiful. All well-loved.

Mariska turned back to find her mom sitting on a folding chair under the canopy of fruit trees, crying. She rushed to her side.

"Mom, are you hurt? What's wrong?" She threw her arms around her mom and squeezed. "Please don't cry."

Leah tried to stand, but Mariska kept her planted firmly in the chair, arms wrapped around her mom's waist and head resting on her bosom.

"Oh baby. You're here. I've been so worried about you."

Mariska sat back on her heels and looked up at her mom. "Please don't worry about me, Mom. I'm okay. Really."

Leah wiped the tears from her cheeks. "It's just that you were hurt—in the hospital. And…there was nothing I could do. I couldn't protect you."

"But I'm okay. Please don't cry." Mariska gave her mom another hug, and they remained in the embrace until she could hear her mom's breathing relax and tears no longer flowed. "I love you."

"I love you more." Leah kissed the top of Mariska's head as she lightly rocked her back and forth. "I've been thinking."

Mariska sat back on her heels and faced her mom. "About what?"

"Your father and I would love it if you'd come back to live with us…you know, just for a little while." Her mother's eyes were bloodshot but hopeful. "Just until you recover…and they catch whoever did this to you."

"I can't come running home every time life gets hard."

Leah took Mariska's hands in hers. "I want to know you're safe."

"Bad things can happen no matter where I live. I know it's not the answer you wanted, but you and Dad raised me to be independent. Even though it doesn't seem like it sometimes."

"We raised you to be kind and make good decisions." Leah looked out over the ocean. "I thought I was going to lose you last night. My only child."

"Mom, please don't think that way." She leaned in and kissed her mother's cheek. "It was just a bump on the back of the head. I promise you it won't happen again."

Leah's eyes locked with hers. They both knew it wasn't a promise anyone could keep, but it needed to be said. "Did I ever tell you the story about when your father and I took you home for the very first time?"

Many times, Mariska thought. "Tell me again."

"You'd been found outside the Page Museum, hours after you'd been born and abandoned."

Found in the dumpster. Thrown away like garbage. "You found me," Mariska said.

Her mom continued, "I heard a soft mewing sound when your father and I were leaving the annual Page Museum Fundraising Gala. I turned to him, and we couldn't for the life of us figure out what it was. Well, I decided even if it was an abandoned kitten, my dress wasn't worth more than a life, and I hopped up into the dumpster."

Thank, God for you, Mom. I love you. Mariska sat in silence listening to her mom recount that day.

"Anyway, I was knee deep in boxes and discarded food from the party when you let out a cry that could wake the dead. I always told Robert that you must have thought it was your last chance."

"I think I knew you were the one. You and Dad were meant to be my parents."

Leah's eyes welled up with tears. "It was meant to be. Your father and I lost two children during the second trimester. We'd given up hope that we'd ever have children…and then we found you."

Mariska swallowed hard.

Leah continued, "I've never asked you this before, but do you ever wish things were different?"

Different? Mariska's searched her mom's features for an explanation. *What did she mean by that?*

"What do you mean?"

Leah dabbed away tears with the sleeve of her shirt. "Do you feel like you've missed out on anything? Was it strange for you to be raised by parents who didn't look like you?"

"I've got questions no one can answer, but I can't imagine anything better than I already have." Mariska spoke the truth. She'd often wondered who she was and where she came from. There'd always been a part of her that felt a bit empty or lost. Curiosity about who she really was and who her real parents were would never go away. And in some ways, she felt that drove her with her work and research. The need to find answers to questions that were theoretically impossible to solve. Like who was the La Brea Woman?

"Do you mean that?" Leah asked.

"Absolutely. You and Dad are my parents, and I love you both with all my heart. I couldn't have asked for a more loving and happy childhood." Mariska hugged her mom and stood. "Let's go inside. I need to talk to you and Dad about something important."

A snap of a twig made the women turn and see Robert Stevenson standing there under one of the larger Lime Trees.

"How long were you standing there?" Mariska asked.

Her dad cleared his throat, his face betraying the emotions he'd been feeling just moments ago. "Long enough."

Mariska went over and hugged her father, the cologne he always wore soothing her nerves almost instantly as his arms squeezed her back. She led him the last few feet to where her mom now stood, the Pacific Ocean, bright blue and beautiful stretched out behind them as far as she could see.

"So, to what do we owe your visit?" He looked tired, the little lines around his eyes seemed deeper and more plentiful than she remembered.

"I came to ask you for some help."

The pair both feigned being blown over by a gust of wind. "You rarely ask us for help."

She deserved that. They were always trying to help her, offer her their influence and connections to powerful people, but she'd always declined. Somehow it seemed like cheating. David, her best friend, had also managed to graduate from a top-notch school with straight A's and landed the same job she did at the museum. He did it all on a shoestring budget and absolutely no friends in high places. So, while she accepted her family's financial support to get through college and find a decent place to live, she enjoyed it when she could do more for herself, and never asked her parents to get her a job or influence her acceptance into school or graduate programs. If David was able to do it, there wasn't any reason she should be different.

"Please don't make this hard for her, Robert." Leah smacked her husband's arm. They turned to face, Mariska. "Whatever you need. We would be happy to help. Right, Robert?" Another smack to the arm.

"Absolutely, honey."

"Okay," Mariska said. "I got a phone call last night from Dr. Snyder. He wanted to meet me at the museum to tell me something important."

"Please tell me he was calling to offer you a vacation. After all, you've been through so much already." Leah's expression was so hopeful, Mariska felt a pain deep inside to have to break the truth.

"Not exactly," Mariska said. "I was fired."

"Fired?" her parents said in unison.

"He is under the impression that I have something to do with the disappearance of the La Brea Woman."

Leah looked from Mariska to Robert. "That's absurd. You adore that woman. Why would you have done something to her remains? It's been your life goal to research her. I mean, hadn't you been given the grant?"

"It hadn't been officially announced yet, but I knew I was going to get it." Mariska ran her fingers through her hair and looked away from her parents. "And, there's more."

"More?" Leah said.

"He demanded that I remove myself from the La Brea Woman research to ensure that the museum was always kept in the best of light. And, well…I messed up."

Her father threw his hands up in the air. "You did what?"

"I swear to you, Dad. I planned on staying away from her, but then something came to mind, and I knew it would help us identify who she might belong to and in turn help us to find her. I know it was a huge longshot, but I felt like I had to try." Mariska looked from her dad to her mom. "Dr. Snyder caught me and fired me. I'm sorry."

"We know you are honey," Leah grabbed Mariska's hand and gave it a squeeze. "Did you say that to Dr. Snyder?"

"Absolutely…but, he doesn't care."

Robert stepped forward and put an arm around Mariska's shoulders. "What can I do?"

She wrapped her arms around him and gave him a big bear hug, looked up into his face with the large, tearful eyes and said, "Snyder is going to go to the board of directors and petition them to fire me—despite the outcome of the investigation. I was hoping you could talk to him…or them…on my behalf? Maybe just ask them to hold off judgment until after the conclusion of the investigation? I mean, you know I'm innocent. That has to count for something."

"Is there anything else?" her dad asked.

"My laptop is at the Page still, and I'm not allowed to go on the premises to get it. So, if you could ask him for it when you speak with him, I'd appreciate it."

Robert took Mariska by her arms and gave her the most fatherly look she'd seen as an adult. His eyes were full of doubt. Her heart sank. Was it he couldn't pull the right strings, or was he unwilling to help? After all, it was her own fault. "I'll make a call and see what I can do."

The three of them hugged. It was time to leave. She needed to go home and make a game plan on how to proceed, with or without help from her parents. Her father assured her that as soon as he heard anything, he would give her a call. She gave them both a kiss on the cheek and hurried back across the lawn, only looking back once. Her heart sank as she saw them watching her go. No matter what happened, she had to keep them out of harm's way. If she could at all help it, this would be the last time she asked them to get involved in one of her messups. What would she do without them?

"Please don't wait so long before coming back for a visit," Jane told her as she walked Mariska to the door.

"I won't. I miss you all too much to stay away."

"Good girl." Jane hugged Mariska and gave her a kiss on the cheek. "If you need anything let me know. I have some pull with your parents, you know."

Mariska smiled. "Thank you, and yes, you'll be the first to know." She turned and started walking to her car. Turning back at the sound of Jane's voice.

"Be very careful out there. I have a sinking feeling about all this." Jane clutched at the collars of her shirt, despite the warm weather.

Mariska jumped in her car and waved goodbye as she circled around the tree in the driveway. The middle-aged woman's image grew smaller in the rearview mirror as she hurried home to wait for her father's call.

CHAPTER EIGHT

It had taken an hour and thirty-nine minutes to drive from her parents' home to her apartment. Another two minutes and five seconds to climb her stairway and successfully fidget with the lock that should have been fixed months ago and enter her apartment. And yet, still no call from her father. *How long did it take for him to pull some of his strings? Call in a favor? Ask a colleague for help?* There was nothing she hated more than asking her family for their help, except waiting for the help to arrive.

There was no better way for her to lose track of time, than getting immersed in work. She didn't have the La Brea Woman's remains to examine, but she did have the beads and the tooth. Rather than taking them out of safekeeping, she started with the internet. It'd been a long time since she'd completed research without having her hands on something to touch, feel, examine and smell.

If she had her laptop or the backup files at work, she'd have access to the research she'd already conducted, but her home-desktop computer would have to do. She poured herself a glass of wine and plopped down at the desk in her living room. Where was she going to start researching? The beads. The tooth was organic material, and she would need more equipment to get anything done. She tried multiple searches through Google. *Traditional Indigenous beadwork. Ancient Californian beads. Styles and types of beadwork from Indigenous Americans.*

Nothing. Or at least nothing helpful. Everything she found looked alien compared to what she'd found on the La Brea Woman's body. *Maybe they don't belong to her. Or, maybe she wasn't an ancestor of a local tribe. Maybe her people were just moving through the area, following the herds of Mammoths?* So many questions and so few answers. She felt like Bones, the doctor on Star Trek. She needed to perform a task she wasn't qualified to do. She wanted to scream: *Dammit Jim, I'm a paleontologist, not an anthropologist.*

Frustrated, she tilted back in the office chair and let out a huff. Two more large swigs of wine and the glass was empty. Her mind began to wander. Who would want to steal the La Brea Woman's remains? And, who would want them bad enough to assault her?

Her phone rang, and she dashed across the room and into the kitchen where she'd left the cell phone on the counter. She reached it by the third ring. *Dad*—his phone number lit up the screen.

"Hey, Dad." Mariska's heart pounded from more than the sprint across the apartment.

"Honey, I did the best I could." He sounded defeated. "Unfortunately, I wasn't able to completely strong-arm Dr. Snyder into letting you come back to work."

She kicked the bottom cabinet drawer and held the phone away from her hear while she took in a couple deep breaths, letting them out slow and smooth through pursed lips. Swallowing hard, she said, "Thank you for trying."

"On your behalf, I requested that all personal belongings…including the laptop computer, be returned to you."

"And?"

"Dr. Snyder was not too happy about it. But after I reminded him there was no proof of your involvement, and he was under legal obligation to return your personal belongings, he agreed."

Mariska pumped her fist in a silent celebration. "Great. I'll head over there now and pick it up."

"Not so fast." Her dad's tone suggested there was more to be worried about.

"Yeah?"

"While I didn't get your job back, I did manage to get your official status changed from *terminated* to *suspended.* It'll depend on the outcome of the investigation."

"That's awesome. Pretty much the best outcome I could have hoped for. Thank you so much, Dad. I can't believe you were able to get him to agree to that."

"There are conditions to be followed. This isn't just a get out of jail free card."

"Go on."

"You aren't able to set foot on museum grounds until the investigation is completed. You're suspended. Dr. Snyder can easily switch your status back to terminated if you break his rules. Understood?" His tone was more serious than she'd ever heard it. He wasn't asking or requesting her to comply, he was demanding it.

"Understood…but, how am I going to get my stuff back?"

"He said he'd have it delivered to you."

"When? I mean, I can't just sit around and do nothing. I've—"

"You can and you will." His voice was angry, and he went silent for a moment. His voice returned to the loving father she'd always known when he continued, "Baby, I want you to have everything you've ever wanted. I'm going to do everything I can to protect you and keep you healthy and safe. But I need you to be careful. Follow my suggestions. They're for your benefit."

"I know." Mariska knew he was right, but it all didn't sit well with her. "I love you too."

"Keep me in the loop?"

"Of course." Mariska hoped she'd be able to keep all her promises. She'd do what she could to follow his lead, but there was more at stake than her career, and she needed to get to the bottom of it. "Thank you, again. Please give Mom another hug for me."

"I will, and you're welcome." His voice softened back into her loving father's usual tone. "Oh, one last thing. I'll be sending Jane over this week. Your mom ordered you some new bedding. You know how she gets when she's worried."

Mariska laughed. "Understood. Should I leave out a hide-a-key?"

"No, I had a copy of your key made, and gave it to her after you moved in."

Mariska wasn't surprised they'd do something like that without asking, but Jane was family anyway. "Will she need help bringing it all inside? Last time Mom bought me stuff because she was worried about something I nearly filled the spare bedroom with it." Mariska shook her head. Her mom used any excuse to buy her new things, whether she needed them or not.

"I doubt it. This time it's just some things for your bedroom. She said she wanted to spruce it up a bit. Said you were letting the room go stale."

"Nice," Mariska said. "I look forward to seeing it."

"Love you."

"Love you more. Thanks again, Dad." Mariska made a kiss noise before hanging up.

Mariska wondered how long it'd take to get her things back from her horrible boss. He could theoretically hold them hostage for weeks, and she wasn't sure she could wait that long.

There was a knock at the door. No way was Jane there already. She would have thought it would be later in the week. Maybe even on the weekend when there was less traffic. Mariska rushed to the front door, unlocked both deadbolts and pulled off the chain. When she opened it, she took a step back.

"Hey, Mariska. It's good to see you." Theresa stood on the top landing holding a large cardboard box.

"Oh, hey. What are you doing here?" Mariska said.

"Dr. Snyder sent me." Theresa sagged a bit under the weight of the box. "Can I come in?"

Mariska pushed the door all the way open. "Oh my, God. Yes, I'm so sorry. What is all this?" She reached out and grabbed the box out of Theresa's arms and immediately regretted it.

The box was heavier than it looked and fell from her grip, hitting the floor with a thud and the sound of rattling glass.

"Shit," Mariska said. The box hadn't opened up when it fell, and she reached down and tried to pick it up. Using her legs to save her back as she learned in school. Some of the fossils she'd dug out of the ground had been quite heavy, and body mechanics was essential.

"Here let me help you." Theresa stepped around to the opposite side of the box, and together they heaved it off the ground. "Dr. Snyder said I had to bring this to you. I think it's your personal stuff from the museum."

"Really?" Mariska had just gotten the phone call from her dad. "I just found out that he was allowing me to have my things like five minutes ago."

"He had all this packed yesterday. The only thing he added was your laptop before he *commanded* me to bring it to you." Theresa never was one to talk badly about anyone, but there weren't very many people who liked, or even tolerated, Dr. Snyder. "Where do you want to put all this stuff?"

"Might as well leave it on the kitchen table." Mariska led the way in the doorway and the few feet to the table. "Right, here will be fine."

They gently set the box down on top of the heavy wooden table, when Mariska had a sudden revelation. There was no way she was going to have access to all the research equipment she would need to conduct the in-depth analysis of the beads and tooth without some help.

Theresa gave her an awkward smile and said, "Well, I guess that's it then. I'll see you…around—"

"Wait." Mariska stepped over to the door and closed it. "Do you need to rush back to the museum or do you have a few minutes to talk?"

"I guess I can stick around for a bit." She looked around the entryway to the apartment, before nervously crossing her arms, avoiding eye contact. "There's something I wanted to talk to you about too."

"Okay, you first." Mariska smiled and offered her a chair.

Theresa sat and began wringing her hands.

"What's wrong? You look nervous."

"I…I can't believe this all happened to you," Theresa blurted out. "I mean…you're the most dedicated and hardworking person at the museum."

"Thank you," Mariska said, patting her on the knee. "That means a lot coming from you. You've been a wonderful student and assistant. Someone I've grown to rely on…trust."

Theresa's eyes lit up, wide and eager. "Do you mean that?"

"I really do. You've proven to be smart, resilient, and resourceful. I wish there was some way we could still work together." Mariska tapped her finger on the tip of her chin and then said, "Maybe there's a way we could help each other."

"I wish there was, but I heard you were fired."

"Actually, I've just been suspended. Pending the investigation. And, considering you and I both know I didn't do what they're claiming…I fully expect to be reinstated. I should have my job back before summer's end."

Theresa stood and clapped her hands together once, grinning from ear to ear. "That would be fantastic. If that were to happen, you could still be my clinical instructor. And, you could still be a coauthor on my research paper."

"Yep, which would also mean you wouldn't have to start completely over with another mentor from the museum." Mariska smiled. "It'd be awesome. A win-win."

"So…now what?" Theresa asked. "How do we make this happen?"

Mariska stood and grabbed a box cutter from the top drawer of the cabinet near the table. She slid the blade out two clicks and slashed the tape open on the top of the box. "I'll need your help."

"Anything."

"I'm glad you said that, because it won't be easy. But I think we can work together on both clearing my name and finding the La Brea Woman. The quicker we do that, the better…for both of us."

Theresa thought about it for a moment and then nodded.

Mariska continued, "You have access to equipment and computer systems at the Museum, and I don't right now. While I'm not technically fired, I have been forbidden from setting foot on the premises."

"That asshole has it out for you, huh?" Theresa shook her head in disgust.

"Yes, he does. But the good thing is that we can get around him. We don't need him if we keep this quiet. Just between us. Agreed?"

"Absolutely." Theresa motioned as if to zipper her mouth shut and threw away the key.

"Perfect." Mariska smiled and pulled the laptop out of the box. She turned it on and entered her password. "What the hell?"

"What's wrong?" Theresa stepped closer to look at the computer screen.

"Most of my files have been deleted. How'd he do that? He didn't have my password." She frantically searched through the computers trash file and looked for the backup folders.

Nothing. It'd been wiped almost completely clean.

"I saw Kathy in his office earlier today. They had your computer, and they were looking at something on there. But I didn't know they were deleting stuff."

"Kathy," Mariska said. "She knew where I kept my passwords in case of emergency. I guess having a stone cold, power-hungry bitch as an office assistant has its downfalls."

"What's left of your files?"

"Just my personal stuff. Nothing work related. None of my files on the La Brea Woman are here. Not even the preliminary research I'd completed while still in school." Mariska slammed the lid closed. "Dammit. All my backup files are on the server in my office." She paused for a second before continuing. "Do you think you could go back to my office and bring me the storage drive?"

Theresa shook her head. "There's nothing there. I was in your office helping to gather up the last of your personal stuff, and the only piece of equipment was the computer. Are you sure you didn't use the off-site internet storage?"

"I wonder if Dr. Snyder took it?"

"Why would he do that?"

"That's a very good question. But being the boss has its privileges."

"I bet he considered it museum property." Theresa put a comforting hand on her shoulder. "Now, what do we do?"

Mariska turned to her and affixed her with a determined stare. "This is where we work together, in secret. If we can find the La Brea Woman…or at least who took her, we can clear my name, and I can have my job back."

"And I can finish my internship and graduate," Theresa added.

"Exactly. I think the best place to start is going to be researching who was at the Fundraising Gala that night. Maybe someone there had motive?"

"I am not familiar with the guest list. I wasn't even invited to the party."

"But I could have sworn I saw you there that night?" Mariska said. "Sometime early on in the evening."

Theresa gave Mariska a coy, innocent look. "I said, I wasn't invited. I ended up sneaking in the employee back entrance. I wasn't there long; just wanted to see what all the fuss was about."

"I knew I liked you for a reason." Mariska fist-bumped her intern. "Maybe you can find a list of vendors or delivery people who came to the museum that day."

"Great idea. I know where Kathy keeps the invoices. I'll start there." Theresa started for the door but turned back. "I feel like Nancy Drew."

Mariska couldn't help, but giggle at the thought of them creeping through the museum at night, flashlights in hand, and searching out clues.

"Do you think that the protestors outside the museum the night of the Gala are suspects?" Theresa asked.

"I hate to think so, but considering I'm a suspect, I guess they are too."

Theresa drew silent for a moment and then said, "I bet there's a way to recover the files from the computer. You know, like through forensic means."

Mariska hadn't thought about that. "I wouldn't have any idea how to do that, or even who to ask."

"Hmm, I'd say there's a few places to check first—like a computer repair shop." Theresa crossed her arms. "Or, as a last resort, I had a friend recover a forever-lost term paper from an ad online. There's a ton of people offering services, and some of them are freaking geniuses. Here." Theresa took out her phone and scrolled through her contacts. "Do you have a pen?"

Mariska retrieved one from the kitchen drawer and handed it to her.

After jotting down a web address, she handed it back to Mariska. "That's the guy my friend used…in case you don't find someone else."

"Really?" She thought about it for a moment after taking the paper and put it into her pocket. Weighing the pros and cons. "I guess as long as I don't try to hire a serial killer, I'll be fine."

Theresa shrugged. "It's up to you. So, when should we meet again?"

Mariska thought about it for a few seconds. If they were being watched or followed, meeting regularly would be a red flag. "I think it'd be safest to keep in contact via phone. No text messages, unless you disguise what you're talking about. Vaguer the better. If we need to meet, we should try and change the location each time."

"Okay, sounds good. I'll start with the vendor list. What will you be doing?" Theresa asked.

"There aren't that many people who even know about the La Brea Woman. She'd been taken off display years ago. Step one will be to figure out which guests did know about her. My research would have brought attention to her, maybe making her more valuable to them."

Theresa pulled her keys from her pocket and stepped toward the door. "So, you think someone did this out of greed?"

"I think someone might have had a lot to lose and it either pissed them off or scared them. Self-preservation can be a great motivator."

"Kind of like us," Theresa said. "We're trying to preserve our jobs, careers, and future."

"I've got it. If we need to meet in person and we can't text why, because it could give something important away, we will use a code word. And every time we use this code word, we meet at the same place each time. Are you familiar with the *Marie Calendar's* across the street from the Museum?"

"Of course. I love their cornbread. How very *Nancy Drew* of you. Okay, what's the code word?"

Mariska took a step toward her and with dead seriousness said, "Preservation."

CHAPTER NINE

Mariska's instructions had been to park a block away from the meet-up location. At midnight, she was to enter the building at the address provided. The man she spoke with seemed like he was disguising his voice as it sounded almost metallic—electronic. His instructions had been conveyed without emotion and either rehearsed or at least read to her. All she knew was she was supposed to ask for *Badger* when she got there. What kind of name was Badger? The conversation had ended abruptly, leaving her with many more questions than answers. After she realized all her computer files pertaining to the La Brea Woman were gone, her on-site storage at the museum had been taken, and she'd been left with nothing, she knew she had to take matters into her own hands. If she didn't act fast, it might result in her reaching the end of the road with her research, and that was unacceptable.

But then an advertisement had come on the television offering hope through computer file recovery at one of the large box stores in the neighborhood. They touted having an entire group dedicated to solving electronics and computer related issues. After contacting them, it became clear they wouldn't be able to help her. Not only was the computer so out of date it was considered obsolete, but when she'd asked the guy about hacking into a mainframe computer system, she thought she heard his voice crack. She was going to need professional help—maybe the kind that didn't work at the neighborhood chain-store.

After hours of scouring the internet for other options, Mariska decided to take Theresa's suggestion and check out some of the online ads and social network sites. There were hundreds of advertisements with pretty outrageous claims, but she had no idea who she could trust. She took the paper Theresa had given her and typed in the web address. The screen changed to black with an email symbol in the center of the page. She'd clicked it and left her cell number and computer problem. Less than ten minutes later her cell phone rang. The unknown number belonged to the man she was here to meet. Their brief but bizarre conversation resulted in uneasy feelings mixed with hope. If this is what it took to get her files back, to get La Brea Woman back, then she was willing to do it.

Mariska checked the time on her watch. Five more minutes to go. Plenty of time to walk down the block, turn right, and cross the street. The address was in Santa Monica. After Google mapping the exact location, she discovered it was in an older section of town. The street view on the computer made it look like it was in a commercial district, although the address itself was for a long-since closed fire station. Did the man have his office in there? Or was it where he lured his unsuspecting victims?

Mariska shivered in the cool night air. The dull streetlights did little to push away the sketchiness of the situation. After a deep breath, she set off down the street. All the businesses were closed for the night, dim light shone through the display windows, but did little to illuminate her path. Mariska managed half the block before her imagination started running wild. Behind her, the sound of a shoe scuffing on the concrete set the little hairs on the back of her neck on end. She glanced over her shoulder.

No one was there, but her gut quivered anyway. She was being watched. Steeling herself against the unknown, she pulled her jacket a little tighter and kept moving—only this time a bit faster and with her hands balled into fists, her car keys sticking out like daggers between the fingers of her right hand.

As she closed in on the final destination, an incessant thudding grew louder. The familiar sounds of a party or rave reminded her of her college years. The constant, never-ending beat, thumping through the night air made her relax a bit. At least there were other people close by, just in case she needed them. Although, no one would hear her screams.

Standing in front of the two-story run-down property, Mariska checked her watch. Midnight, on the dot. *Now what? Do I knock? The door looks thick, solid.* Would anyone hear the knock over the pounding music? Above the door was a security camera, the red light was on so she waved. The door didn't open. She put her car keys into her pocket and pulled her sleeves up to the elbow. Then, just as she drew her fist up to pound on the door, she heard a click.

The heavy door slid apart in the center. The six-inch gap was dark, nothing visible inside. She leaned in a bit closer, her heart beating faster with each inch she moved. The closer she got, the more she could see, although she couldn't make out anything specific, but it was clear there were people inside. Light and shadow danced about with the incessant thud that punched itself through the opening.

"Stop right there," a man said. His voice boomed through the gap in the door.

Mariska jumped back at the unexpected voice. A moment later the doors opened wide; the man inside stepped into the dull lights of the street lamp above them. He was huge. Six foot five and at least two hundred eight pounds of muscle. His dark skin and bald head didn't intimidate her. But his posture and cold stare made her rethink what she'd gotten herself into.

"I'm here to see Badger." The quiver in her voice betrayed her internal fear.

"No one sees Badger unless they can answer three simple questions. No mistakes." The man put a finger to an earpiece and nodded. He refocused on her. "Do you understand?"

"Actually, I don't. I'm supposed to meet someone that answered my online ad. Why would I need to answer your—"

The man took a giant step toward her, and she nearly dropped her computer bag. She stumbled backward toward the curb when the man's huge hand grabbed her wrist and steadied her. Stabilized, she readjusted the bag and straightened her jacket. "Thank you."

"You must answer three questions. One wrong answer and you're done, no second chances."

Mariska nodded her understanding.

"Question number one. What was the full name of your first pet?"

Full name? Who were these people and how would they have this information? She thought for a moment, just to make sure she wasn't forgetting anything. "Sir Augustus Poncherello Stevenson the Third."

He put his finger to the earpiece and nodded. "Second question. What is your father's favorite color?"

That depends, she thought. He told everyone it was blue, but Mariska knew it was yellow. But her father made her promise not to tell anyone that as he thought it made him seem less manly. Would Badger know the real answer? "Yellow."

The man once again put his finger to his earpiece and a few moments later nodded. "The third and final question. You must answer this correctly to enter and meet with Badger. What is the one thing you are most obsessed with?"

The La Brea Woman…or was that too easy? She was also obsessed with learning her own past. What was the right answer? What was he looking for? Then it dawned on her. "The truth."

The man stepped aside and said, "Come with me."

As she moved through the doorway and into the dark, he held her by the wrist and led the way deeper into the darkness. Flashes of light danced around the room with a strobing effect, like an indoor lightning storm. The deeper she went, the louder the music became. The man who led her came to stop in front of wall of glass. She couldn't see inside, but it was clear by the door and the men standing on each side, it was a protected area.

"Is Badger in there?"

He didn't answer but knocked on the door in a series of fast and slow raps. The code could have been anything, but she suspected Morse Code…or maybe some kind of binary. The door opened, and they stepped inside.

The room was a huge glass box. The walls, ceiling, and floor were one-way glass, and all around them was a huge rave. People bounced up and down to the incessant thump of the beat. Multi-colored rays of light spun from globe-shaped light fixtures that hung from the ceiling. Strobe lights flashed with the beat, and the crowd remained spellbound, not wise to the inside of the room she found herself.

She looked around the glass-walled room. It was lined on all sides with glass booths. Each room glowed green and red. Empty rooms were green, and the ones that had an occupant glowed red. The people in the booths were hunched over laptop computers, and they wore headphones. Whatever they were working on, it appeared important. They weren't distracted by the music, lights, or anything going on outside of the computer screen. At the front of the room was a gigantic display screen that flashed from one news story to the next. She recognized CNN, Fox News, and Headline News, but many of the stations were from overseas. Under the images, a series of zeros and ones scrolled down to the bottom in a never-ending sequence.

What the hell was going on in here?

The man who led her there pulled her toward an empty booth and punched in a code, and the door slid open with a swoosh. "Please, go inside and open the computer. Badger will be with you shortly."

"But..." She stepped inside and turned back around. "I'm scared."

He blinked and put his hand to the earpiece. "Don't be scared. You're safe here." He nodded again at the voice only he heard. "My name is The Guardian. I will be waiting outside. When Badger says you can leave, I'll be here to walk you out."

The door slid closed with a hiss. The booth filled with absolute silence and the red light turned green. She pushed on the door, tried to pull it open, and kicked it. Mariska was locked inside. She turned and rushed over to the computer, opened the lid, and put on the headphones that were plugged into the side.

The computer screen flashed, pixels scattered over the screen like little bugs. The swarm of dots swirled into the hurricane and then went black. A blinking cursor at the bottom right was the only sign the computer was even running. Mariska used the finger pad to click on the blinking light. The image of a forest and trail showed on the screen.

Mariska cocked her head to the side. The picture was familiar. It looked like Griffith Park, just to the north of the observatory. She regularly went there to think, solve the problems of the week. How did Badger know so much about her?

Instructions appeared: USE THE FINGER PAD TO MOVE DOWN THE TRAIL

She followed the instructions and quickly made her way down one of the many trails she'd hiked on her regular visits to the Observatory. It was a place she went to think, clear her head, solve problems, or just relax. A place where she felt connected to the universe even when she didn't feel connected to anyone or anything in the world.

The trail came to an abrupt end. What was she supposed to do now? She hit the escape key, and the screen flashed, exploding into a snowstorm of white pixels. Within seconds they condensed into an image. A badger.

"Now we're getting somewhere," Mariska said.

The badger spoke to her from the screen. "It's good to meet you finally."

She remained silent.

"Oh, you can speak freely here," he said. "I can hear you."

"So, what is all this?"

"You asked for my help."

"I know that, but why are we going through all this…" Mariska looked around the booth. "Why did you bring me here?"

"I'm assuming you want the short answer."

She nodded.

"I don't trust anyone. This place… The Hive is where people come to learn the truth about all kinds of things. Answers to questions that governments, religious organizations, and even private corporations have been trying to keep secret for as long as anyone can remember."

"But if you know everything…why would you want to help me? What could I possibly do or offer you?" Mariska's heart pounded. Was she officially in over her head? Screw it; she needed answers.

"No one knows everything, but we can learn just about anything…if we try hard enough. You'd be shocked to know my clientele."

No doubt he was right. She was sure that many inspiring and equally as frightening things were revealed in this place. She looked out through the glass door for a moment. The rave was continuing at full steam. No one the wiser to the fact they were being used as cover. A distraction to espionage…or whatever the hell this was.

Badger drew her attention back to the computer screen. "You mentioned briefly over the phone that you needed some deleted files restored."

"Yes, my boss deleted everything related to the museum off my computer before he would return it to me. These files are a culmination of years of research. *My* research."

"Depending on what software he used to clear your computer, I cannot guarantee an outcome or timeframe. Are you okay with that?" The badger turned and faced her on the screen. Its large eyes, blinked as he waited for her response.

"I would appreciate anything you could do to help me."

"Answer the question: Would you be okay with a bad outcome?"

What kind of a question was that? Of course, she wouldn't be okay. Countless hours of research, gone. No way to clear her name. No way to continue her research. No way to find answers. "No. I need answers."

"Good," Badger said. "I needed to know you are in this one hundred percent."

"In that case, I have a question of my own."

The badger said nothing. It waiting for her to continue. Its large, blinking eyes, piercing her gut.

"Why me? Why help *me*?"

"I'm always looking for my next challenge. Something interesting to keep me motivated. When I saw your request for assistance, I almost kept scrolling, but there was something in the words you used. I sensed your desperation."

"So, you get off on desperate women? Great…that's encouraging. No red flags there." She rolled her eyes and slumped back against the booth.

"I find you intriguing."

"Intriguing? Well, I guess that's better than desperate." Mariska sat back up straight. "So, how do I pay you? I'm sure you don't do any of this for free."

"You're right. I don't work for free. However, my payment is based on how much I have to do to bring you the answers you're looking for."

"What happens if the files have been permanently erased from the laptop? Is that it? We're done?"

"We're not done until I say we're done."

The computer screen flashed white and then went black. The light in the booth changed from green to red and the door lock disengaged with a click. She turned toward the door, and it slid open. The Guardian was waiting for her.

"Leave the laptop on the booth," he said.

"But…"

"Badger will ensure its safe return to you." He took her firmly by the arm and pulled her from the booth. She looked back at the laptop as the booth door slid closed. The red light went out as the booth went completely dark. The once see-through glass, now opaque.

A light breeze tickled the hairs on her neck as she stepped through the door that opened out onto the street. She shivered as the heavy metal door slammed closed behind her. Suddenly, the dimly lit streets of Santa Monica didn't feel safe anymore. The distant sound of a dog's bark grew louder and more intense. She stepped off the curb when she heard tires squeal from somewhere in the night, sending her into a frantic adrenaline-fueled sprint for her car.

What have I gotten myself into?

CHAPTER TEN

Detective Wulf sat in his car like any good stalker, only he was on official police business. He'd followed Mariska to what had previously been known as an abandoned building in Santa Monica. He'd have to make a report to the authorities at the city the site was anything but abandoned.

Loud, thumping music pounded its way down a full city block. Amazing no one had called to report a noise disturbance in the area. She'd been inside the building for quite some time, but there hadn't been any indication that anything was wrong. No need to break his cover. Not yet, anyway.

He opened his laptop and synced it to his phone, so he could use it as a Wi-Fi hotspot. He searched the internet for information about the old fire station. The results were from official sites addressing the issues behind the station closure. In an ironic twist of fate, the fire station hadn't been up to new fire codes implemented in all city, state, and federal buildings in the state of California. The building had been shut down a few years back, and there had been talk about turning it into a local firefighting museum, but the repairs and modifications to the building had been mired in bad luck, greedy politicians, and a general lack of funding.

A dark SUV drove by slowly, pausing at the front of the building for a half second and then continued on its way. Wulf craned his neck to see the license plate, but it was too far away, and the little lights next to the plate were not working. He continued to watch as the vehicle slowly pulled away and out of sight. Without warning a fluttering deep in his belly formed goosebumps over his body. He rubbed his arms to get rid of them, but suddenly felt he wasn't the only one watching Mariska this evening.

Torn between following the SUV and sticking with his original plan, he stayed put. Focusing back on his internet search, he came across a couple social media sites. They touted the abandoned building as the hottest new club. Low admission prices, great drinks, the latest music, and in a great location. He up and thought to himself, if he'd been younger and looking for a good place to party he could see how this place would fit the bill. According the website, admission into the club was exclusive and don't bother simply dropping by, you won't be admitted.

Had Mariska somehow been invited to this place? From what he could tell, she was let right inside as if she'd belonged there. But much like himself, she didn't seem to fit the standard age or type to be a regular here. Not to mention the fact she was wearing jeans and sweatshirt tonight, definitely not standard attire for a night out dancing at the hottest new club in Los Angeles.

Movement in front of the building drew Wulf's attention outside the vehicle. The front door opened and Mariska stepped out onto the sidewalk in front of the building. She looked confused. Standing there in the dim light of the street lamp above her, she reminded him of a scared, lost, young woman. Someone on the run, in a strange, unfamiliar city. What had happened inside the former fire station?

Wulf rolled down his window and listened. A dog barked in the distance, but other than that, surprisingly silent. Then without warning, a squeal of tires tore through the still night. He turned in the direction of the noise, but when he looked back, Mariska was on the run. She was spooked. He would have felt the same if he'd been in her shoes.

She was headed right for him. To avoid being seen, he reclined his seat and turned away from the window. A few seconds passed when he heard pass by. With breaths almost as rapid as her steps, she didn't slow as she went by. Wulf waited a few more seconds, until he no longer heard her footfalls through the open window.

Then he sat up and readjusted his seat.

Mariska had since rounded the corner of the block and was out of sight. He put the car in drive and made a U-turn, following her, making sure she would make it back safely to her car. His cell phone buzzed. The screen lit up with an incoming message. Stopping the car at the corner, he watched as she got into her car and peeled away from the curb.

The message read: *Thank you for making sure she made it back to her car.*

Wulf looked behind him. The street was dark but empty. He looked back at the message. There was no indication as to who sent it or a return number.

"What the hell?" he said. He tried to reply to the message, asking who had sent it. But, the message wouldn't go through. An error message flashing *Undeliverable* in red further fueled his annoyance.

He threw the phone down on the seat next to him. All of his investigating had turned up little to no evidence. Everyone associated with the museum came back with clean background checks. Not that a clean background check proved anything other than the person hadn't yet caught yet doing something illegal. Or that the other names and aliases hadn't appeared in the background checks yet.

Wulf *had* uncovered a few unexpected details uncovered. While Mariska was clearly adopted, the details to her birth were anything but clear. She didn't have a birth certificate, or at least not one issued from a hospital. Digging through the young woman's past, he discovered she had been abandoned at birth in a dumpster outside the Page Museum. He shook his head as he thought about the irony. She'd been born at the museum—and almost died there.

He'd been unable to determine who her birth family had been. Most likely, no one knew…maybe they didn't even care. For some reason, it nagged at Wulf; even though it seemed like an important detail to this case. Call it a hunch or intuition; he couldn't shake the feeling it was going to be these small details about her past that would help solve this mystery.

Wulf started to pull away from the curb, but a large vehicle roared past, nearly taking off his side mirror. "Damn it, asshole!"

The dark SUV swerved to the side, braking hard, and sliding to a stop at the far end of the street. Was that the same SUV that stopped at the front door a few minutes ago? Wulf stomped on the gas. The squeal of tires filled the car with noise.

Wulf managed a few meters down the road when the front door to the SUV opened, and a huge, shadowy figure got out and faced the oncoming car. Without a sound, a flash of light lit up in the distance.

"Shit," he said as he slammed on the brakes and ducked away. The right front tire exploded, roking his car. He looked up to see a second and third flash, followed by the shattering of his windshield.

That jackass is shooting at me, and he's got a silencer. Definitely not a random gang-style attack.

He threw the car in park and pulled out his gun. Aiming straight out through the missing front windshield, Wulf fired his weapon. Without a silencer of his own, his return fire was loud. But he missed. Ears ringing in he started reloading, but watched in frustration as his attacker got back into his SUB, shut the door, and sped away.

Wulf was pissed. Not only had he failed to stop the murderous man, but now he had a mountain of paperwork to do tonight. Any chance he had at getting some rest evaporated after he fired his weapon. He sat back into the car seat and let out a huff.

"Well, fuck." Wulf reached down into the center console and retrieved his police radio. "This is Detective Wulf. I'm out at the old abandoned fire station in Santa Monica. Shots fired. No known injuries, but I'll need a full team here." He answered all of the dispatcher's questions and then rested his head back into the seat.

He took out his cell phone and placed a call to his chief. While he waited to be connected, he got out of the car and took in the damage to the car. Two flat tires and a shattered windshield. He was going to need a tow…and some coffee.

CHAPTER ELEVEN

Despite being exhausted from the day before, Mariska barely slept. The adrenaline that flowed through her veins after meeting Badger just now began to ebb. She took a sip of coffee and yawned. What was she going to do now? She didn't have a way to contact him. Last night she hadn't even thought to ask him for a phone number. Craigslist. That's how they'd made contact in the first place.

Mariska logged into her account using her cell phone. Nothing. It was too soon, and she knew it. She sent a quick message to the Craigslist account Badger had used to contact her last night. A few seconds later a message appeared in her inbox.

"That was quick," Mariska said.

She clicked to open the message. After the first line, it became clear it was a generic message from the website. It informed her that the person or entity she was trying to contact was no longer using that email. The account had been closed.

"Be patient," she said, putting the phone back down on the kitchen table.

In the meantime, she was going to need a plan of action. She grabbed an unopened cable bill and turned it over. Mariska began to make a list.

1. *Find out who would want to take the La Brea Woman and why.*
2. *Do any of the people at the Fundraising Gala, guests or workers, have motive?*
3. …

She began tapping her pen on the table. Within a few seconds, she slammed the pen down and stood. *What is the next move?* There was not much to go on. She was about to give up and take a shower when her phone rang.

She snatched the phone up and didn't recognize the number. Maybe it was Badger? "Hello?"

"Hey, there. How're you feeling?"

Mariska paused for a second. "David?"

"Yeah. Expecting someone else?"

She looked at the phone again. "Where are you calling me from? Your name didn't pop up?"

"Work. I'm using a backline. Why?"

Mariska started an internal debate. Be honest and have to listen to him tell her how dangerous it was for her to meet a stranger she met on Craigslist in the middle of the night. Or she could save herself the headache and lecture and lie to him.

"Oh, just curious." She took a deep breath and let it out slowly. "I didn't sleep well last night. I think I'm still in shock from everything that's been going on." Not a complete lie, anyway.

"I'll tell you what. As soon as I'm done here, I'll come over and make you dinner." His voice was so hopeful her stomach tightened.

"Um…"

"Please, say yes. I…I, really want to make you my grandmother's chicken fettuccine alfredo. It's delicious."

Mariska smiled. "I thought you said your grandmother specialized in French cuisine?"

"Okay, fine. I downloaded the recipe on Pinterest a few minutes ago. It looks super good though."

There was so much she wanted to try and get done today, but dinner with David sounded nice as well. "I would love that. What time should I expect you?"

"Does six work for you?"

She looked over at the clock. If she could get her act in gear, there would still be plenty of time for her to do some digging. If there was one thing that watching investigative television shows had taught her, if the trail goes cold, it's harder to find what you're looking for.

"Six o'clock sounds great," Mariska said. "Hey David, before you get back to work can I ask you something?"

"Of course. I've always got time for you."

"Has Dr. Snyder said anything about me? Have you heard anything at all about the La Brea Woman, my job, or the grant?"

"I think you should focus on *you* right now," David said. "I mean, you were just in the hospital. You need to take care of yourself, first and foremost."

Mariska's blood started to heat up. "I don't need advice, David. I need answers."

"I'm just saying that—"

"You're just being overly protective. I don't need another father. I need a friend. One willing to help me." She pictured him sitting behind his desk, running his fingers through his unruly hair. Contemplating his options. Piss her off and eat alone, or do what she asked. Oh, she hated being that person, but truth be told, she needed answers if she was ever going to move on.

"Dr. Snyder got a call from Ingrid today."

"Ingrid…*The* Ingrid Ashton?"

"The one and only. She called this morning. Insisted on talking with Dr. Snyder."

"What about?"

"No idea. He took the call in his office with the door closed."

Ingrid was the head of the Institutional Review Board. There were four people on the board, plus Dr. Snyder, who voted in the event of a tie. They decided which research projects were awarded grant funding from the Museum. Ingrid controlled the board with a sweet smile, nerves of steel, and a lineage dating back to the beginning of the Page Museum itself. Her grandfather was one of the original researchers there. Rumor had it that the Page Museum was supposed to be named The Page Ashton Institute, but that there'd been a falling out between Mr. Page and his chief scientist, Dr. Ashton. Although Mariska suspected it truly was a rumor since the Ashton family has continued to be an integral part of the institution since its founding.

Mariska had a thought. "Was his assistant lurking around? Maybe she heard something."

"Kathy? Even if she did, she wouldn't say anything to me."

"She's such a bitch. I'm sure you could bribe her into talking." Mariska said as she walked into her bathroom and turned on the shower. "I heard that she might even have the hots for you. Maybe you can flash her a boob or something."

David snorted. "Flash a *boob* or something?"

"Okay, remember when we were all sitting in the Sexual Harassment Seminar last month? When the guy mentioned boobs to the innocent, young female coworker, Kathy turned around and looked at you."

"No, she didn't. She was looking at you because you started laughing," David said.

"The entire scenario was so ridiculous. Anyway, she looked at you."

"Even if she did, I don't like her…at all, really." David sounded defensive. "Not to mention the way she eats her salad at lunch. Total turn-off."

"Oh, you don't like it when people eat plain chopped lettuce out of a zip-lock bag, using their hands? Each piece of lettuce plopped into their mouth like it was movie popcorn?"

"Exactly. She's creepy."

"No, she's desperate for attention. Kathy's a product of a family who's famous for making their money on shady business deals. And from what my mom told me, she has major daddy issues—always trying to live up to some ideal that her father never accepts." She shrugged. "I mean, it's kind of sad, but she's never been nice to me so there's not much I can do about it."

"To be fair, she's not the only person I know with issues," David said before going quiet. No doubt kicking himself for what he said.

"We aren't talking about me. Anyway, I need to get going. I've got things to do."

"Okay," David said. "I'll do it."

"Do what?" Mariska was ready for this conversation to be over.

"I can ask around, but I wouldn't hold your breath. I can't imagine Kathy will tell me much of anything…that's even if she knows anything."

"There isn't much that happens at the museum that she doesn't know. She's in everyone's business."

"Not to change the subject." David cleared his throat. "But are you taking a shower?"

"Just about to jump in when you called."

David paused for a moment. "I can't wait to see you tonight."

Her stomach growled. "Fettucine Alfredo, you said?"

"The best."

Mariska threw back the shower curtain, "Okay, I'll see you at six. Have a great rest of your day."

"You too," David said.

"And if you hear or see anything, please let me know. You know how important all of this is to me."

"Absolutely, you have my word." David turned to leave. "See you later."

Mariska made quick work out of her usual morning routine. She was feeling much more like her usual self, except for an underlying fatigue. She suspected a good solid night's sleep would help fix the problem. And closure would, no doubt, help her get that much, needed sleep.

If Ingrid needed to talk to Dr. Snyder, then she needed to talk to Ingrid. Mariska looked up Ingrid's address, mapped it on her phone, and grabbed her car keys on the way out of the apartment. Ingrid wouldn't mind an unexpected visitor, would she?

Mariska rushed out the door and got behind the wheel of her dark-blue BMW coup. She closed her eyes for a moment and thought about what she was about to do, what lead her to this point, and the potential consequences. The La Brea Woman's remains came into focus. This was more about her than it was Mariska. Although, she was mixed up in this mess every bit as deep as the ancient woman. She put her foot on the brake and turned the ignition. The sporty car roared to life and sent an excitement through her she hadn't felt in the past few days. She was on the right track, and she knew it.

CHAPTER TWELVE

Mariska turned onto Mulholland Drive and checked her phone for directions. According to the app, she'd be pulling up to Ingrid's estate in less than twenty minutes. The extra time was due to the slow speed limit on the winding road filled with hairpin turns. It wasn't the hairpin turns, as much as the steep drop-offs that worried Mariska whenever she drove on this road. There were far too many news stories this year about bicyclists and motorists meeting an untimely end on this stretch of road. Usually, speed or intoxication were to blame. She hadn't been drinking, and she planned on keeping it at or below the speed limit, even if the anticipation of making it to Ingrid's killed her.

Her cell phone rang. Checking the mirrors for signs of cops, she picked up the phone. It was Theresa. "Hey there."

"I wanted to check and see if you were able to make any progress with the computer?"

Mariska hesitated. Could she trust her? All this paranoia was going to make her legitimately crazy. Should she go ahead and reserve a room at the local Mental Health hospital?

"Well, let's just say I found someone to help."

"A computer expert?" Theresa asked.

"That is exactly right. He said he would be happy to help. So, tell me, what do you have for me?"

"I'm sorry, Dr. Stevenson. I haven't been able to find anything helpful yet."

"I thought we went over this already. Please don't call me Dr.

Stevenson. Right now, I'm not your boss. We are…partners in this endeavor. Call me, Mariska. Please."

"Okay, I'll try and keep that in mind." Theresa sounded like she was smiling while she spoke. "So, in that case. What do you have for me?"

"That's the spirit. I'm going to see Ingrid Ashton. Speaking of Ingrid, I heard she called the Museum today and demanded to speak with Dr. Snyder."

"I heard that too. I'm the one who answered the phone."

"Oh, yeah? What exactly did she say?" Mariska could feel her excitement growing. She was getting somewhere.

Theresa didn't answer right away, and Mariska could hear her moving around. No doubt, she was still at work and was looking for somewhere more private to have this conversation.

"Sorry about that, I needed to change offices. You know, too many rat ears in this place."

Mariska laughed. "Oh, trust me, I know what you're saying."

"Ms. Ashton called this morning. She asked to speak to Dr. Snyder. I told her that he was in a meeting. I didn't tell her this part, but Dr. Snyder and Kathy had been huddled up in his office for the past couple of hours. Seemed strange to me, but what do I know?"

"No, I can tell you something strange was going on there too. We can get to that next. So, what happened then?" Mariska said as she slammed on the brakes. "Shit."

"What's wrong? Are you, okay?"

Maybe this was why the state of California had banned the use of cell phones while driving? Damn, she almost drove straight off the cliff. The turn had come up out of nowhere, and she must have missed the warning sign because she was talking on the phone.

"I'm fine. Just lost track of where I was driving."

"Be careful out there. So many crazy drivers," Theresa said.

"Oh, yeah. Lots of crazy drivers out here. What happened next?"

"Ingrid mentioned she wouldn't take no for an answer. She started telling me how much money and time she puts into the Museum every year. How she has been a founding member and her family helped make the museum what it is today. I mean, I knew all that shit, but I was shocked she was being such a bitch about it. It's not like any of this was my fault."

Mariska said, "Wow, I've never seen her act like that either. Something must be upsetting her...more than just the fact she couldn't talk to that asshole boss of ours."

"But what?"

"I'm not sure, but I intend on finding out," Mariska said.

"Oh, yeah? How are you going to do that?"

"Simple, I'm on my way to her house now."

Just as she spoke something slammed into the back of her car, hard.

"What the fuck?" Mariska looked in the rearview mirror.

"What happened? Are you, okay?" Theresa asked, her voice elevated with concern.

A dark SUV pulled dangerously close to the back of her. She couldn't see the license plate, but the grill was clear. The Cadillac emblem grew closer, and she stepped on the gas.

"Mariska? Are you, okay? Hello? Are you there?"

"Someone just rear-ended me. Oh, shit, here they go again." Mariska braced for impact.

This time, the SUV rammed her and kept pushing. It didn't relent. She dropped the phone and grabbed on to the steering wheel with both hands. She slammed on the brakes, but only slowed for a moment, then continued on up the road. They were pushing her. Smoke billowed up from her back tires. She tried turning the wheel toward the oncoming lane, desperate to keep herself from going over the cliff. The car started moving to the left, but the SUV countered. An oncoming car blared its horn, and she adjusted to the right to avoid a collision.

The road ahead was clear. Mariska pulled the wheel to the left once again. This time the SUV sped up, pushing her straight toward the rocky cliff-side. She pulled hard to the right, but it was too late. The car went straight into the mountainside. Her seatbelt instantly engaged and she felt arms and head fly forward, pulling up short of hitting the dashboard by the seatbelt. The sudden stop came with a crunch of metal and the smell of burning rubber.

Wiping the hair out of her face, she opened her eyes. The windshield was splintered into a spider-web of cracks. The engine was still running, but there was a lot of smoke coming from the hood of her car. Fire? She looked in the rearview mirror. The SUV was backing away. Her car rocked side to side as the Cadillac pulled itself free. Who the fuck was trying to kill her? And, why?

Mariska thought she better get out of there while she still could. Hopefully, the car would still drive. She slid the car into reverse and edged the car backward toward the road. She looked back to the front. How was she going to see through the front windshield to drive? She rolled down the driver-side window and looked out. That would have to do. She inched the car back some more, across one lane until she got the car facing the direction she needed to go to finish her journey to Ingrid's house.

She stopped the car and put it into drive. Sticking her head out the window to see where she was going, she pushed on the gas. The wind in her hair felt good, drying her face and hair from the sweat that soaked her. Her phone. She needed her phone. As she drove slowly up the winding road, she searched around the inside of the front of the car. There it was, in the footwell of the front passenger seat. If she could just reach it. Lunging to the right, she took her chances. Her fingers closed around the cell phone, and she pulled it up with her as she straightened up in the chair.

A squeal of tires caught her attention, and she looked out the window. She passed the SUV. It had been waiting for her. She pushed the gas pedal down to the floor and her car gained speed. Normally, the car was a high-performance vehicle, great at taking corners at high speeds, but there was something wrong. The car's steering was off, not responding the way it usually did. The faster she went, the less control she seemed to have. She let off the gas, for a split second. And when she did, the SUV made impact with her once again.

The BMW whined as she slammed on her brakes. The SUV was

once again pushing her forward. Only, this time, she couldn't steer the car away from the cliff's edge. With a sickening sensation that accompanied free-fall, the car went over the edge. Broken shards of glass and her cell phone that she'd dropped again began to float up from the floor. But only for a second, as the car hit the side of the cliff wall, bouncing away from it, before slamming into the ground at the bottom of the cliff. Her seatbelt engaged, tightening around her like a boa constrictor. Air pushed from her lungs, with the feeling of a cracked rib, and then the snap her head forward.

She tried to breathe, but couldn't. Her vision blurred and then began to tunnel. Her world was going black, and there wasn't a damn thing she could do about it. A ringing in her ears and a stream of blood running from her mouth were the last sensations she felt before her world went dark.

CHAPTER THIRTEEN

Dust swirled through the air in a suffocating cloud. Mariska coughed, gagged on the tiny particles that now coated her tongue and restricted her airway. *Where was she?* It was hard to breathe, and the struggle made it hard to think. She started pulling at the strap that pressed against her chest and waist. *What was going on?*

Mariska tried to yell for help but instantly regretted it. A series of coughs once again wracked her body. Her lungs burned. Her throat ached. She tried to swallow, but couldn't. A sudden clarity awakened her logical thought process. The steering wheel in front of her, the seatbelt suspending her in midair, and the shattered windshield told the story.

She'd been run off the road and was now nose down in a deep ravine.

Reaching down between the seat and the driver side door, she blindly felt for the seat belt release button. *Where the hell was it?* Her fingers closed around what she'd been searching for.

Click.

Mariska used her feet to brace for impact. The airbag had deployed but was now a dusty half inflated bag, useless for cushioning her fall onto the steering wheel. Lying flat against the steering wheel, she used her left hand to search the car door for the handle. A few frantic seconds passed before she pulled it, the door swung open. A breath of cool air engulfed her body, chilling the sweat the covered her skin. It felt like Heaven but was short-lived as she pushed herself up and over to exit the vehicle.

The fall to the ground outside the car didn't hurt so much as it woke her up. Woke her up to the situation she was now a part of—someone had tried to kill her. Again.

A few seconds passed while she cleared her head. It hurt when she breathed. Pushing her fingers along her ribs, she pinpointed the fourth rib and intercostal. Pushing a little harder, she winced. There wasn't any grinding or crunching when she applied significant pressure, probably bruised rather than broken. Wiggling her fingers, toes, and all four limbs, Mariska determined she would live. Nothing broken, but she hurt like hell. Although, her mouth tasted of blood. Sitting next to her on the ground was a piece of her side mirror. She picked it up and looked at her reflection. Hair in all directions, matted against her face and partially slick with sweat, her makeup gave her raccoon eyes, and blood drying on her lips and down her chin.

She swallowed. More blood. Opening her mouth, she looked in the mirror again. Her tongue was lacerated and seeping blood. She'd bitten her tongue. It didn't hurt too badly, but she knew it would later. Visions of her many friends in college who'd went and gotten tongue rings. *Oh, it doesn't hurt. You should get one.* They'd been drunk, and silly. But the next morning couldn't eat, barely drink. Coffee in the morning would have to be iced.

Surveying her surrounding, Mariska replayed the events that led her to this spot. She'd been a few minutes' drive from Ingrid's home. Closing her eyes, she mentally put herself on the map. A mile, maybe two. She could walk that far. Forcing herself up to stand, she stretched. *Snap, crackle, pop.* Everything began to fall back into place. Looking up the side of the ravine that she needed to climb she started to laugh. How the hell was she going to do this? It might as well have been a sheer cliff or Mount Everest—she was in heels.

"A journey of a thousand miles starts with the first step…or something like that," Mariska said as she took off her heels.

After retrieving her purse and cell phone from the car, she tucked the heels into the back of her pants, slung the purse over her neck, and tiptoed to the wall of dirt and rock. Taking her time, she looked ahead and plotted out a few hand-holds so she wouldn't get stuck in no-mans-land. The rocks hurt her feet and hands, and she was going to need an emergency pedicure when she could find the time, but she was going to make it. What seemed like forever, was over in ten minutes—according to the time on the cell phone. She sat at the top of the ravine, alongside the roadway. Breathing heavily and sweating profusely, she was safe.

Mariska tried to call David, but couldn't get a signal. She stood, put on her heels, brushed the dirt from her clothes and tried to straighten her hair. A revving car engine drew her attention up the road to one of the many switchbacks. There, maybe a quarter of a mile ahead was a dark SUV. A breath caught in her chest. That was the son of a bitch who ran her off the road. Who were they? She squinted, trying to get a better look at the man who stood outside the vehicle. She didn't recognize him. He was too far away to see any distinguishing features, but he was a tall man. Thick, broad shoulders, wore a suit, and sunglasses. They'd been watching her. Probably waiting to see if she survived the crash.

She pulled out her cell phone again, pretending to make a call. That did the trick. He hopped back into the passenger side of his vehicle and started pulling away. *Take a picture, you idiot.* Fumbling with her phone, she managed to open the camera and take a picture before the SUV had completely disappeared from sight. Mariska zoomed in on the picture, trying to make out the license plate. No use. Too far away. She'd keep the picture anyway, just in case. *Maybe Detective Wulf would want to see it.*

Mariska spent a few minutes wandering around trying to get a signal with her phone. Her phone suddenly beeped. A text message managed to sneak through the spotty coverage. Opening the message, she saw it was from an anonymous number. The message read: *You're in Danger! Badger.*

"Now you tell me." She tried to reply to the message by asking how he knew and asking if he knew who was trying to hurt her, but the message had essentially come from no number at all. The cell phone prompted her to put in a number before the message could be sent.

Mariska put the phone in her back pocket and started up the road. A couple miles walk in heels shouldn't be that bad. She'd done it before with minor blistering. The hour passed about as fast as it does in the dentist chair, but she made it to Ingrid's mansion. The sprawling estate was at least ten acres, hidden away in the hills outside L.A. city limits. It was quiet up here in the hills, very little traffic and even fewer neighbors. The acreage was stamped in the middle with a gorgeous white and stone mansion. From where she stood on the roadside, she could only make out a small portion of the front of the main house. She'd been told there were a couple separate buildings that housed the help. Rumor had it that Ingrid even had a collection of antiquities, artifacts, and fossils that would leave a fully established museum, green with envy. The gate in front of her was at the base of the driveway. Locked up tight. Mariska pushed the intercom button and waited.

"Can I help you?" a man's voice said over the intercom.

"Yes. My name is Dr. Mariska Stevenson, and I would like to speak with Ingrid, please."

"Where is your car?"

Mariska saw that the intercom also had a camera. "I was in an accident. I left the car about two miles back."

There was a long pause. Long enough for Mariska to question if she was going to get a response at all.

"Ingrid will see you."

There was a buzzing noise, and the gate immediately started to open. Mariska didn't wait for it to finish opening and slipped in through the ever-widening space as soon as she could fit. Speed walking up the long, bricked driveway, she managed it in less than a minute. She rang the doorbell and used her selfie setting on the phone to straighten her hair and makeup. She was still a mess when the door opened.

"Dr. Stevenson, welcome. Miss Ingrid will be with you momentarily. Your *unexpected* arrival has found her in the middle of some pressing matters." The butler ushered her inside and closed the door. Mariska followed him to a sitting room a few feet from the entrance.

"Can I offer you something to drink?" the butler asked.

"Some water would be wonderful, thank you." Mariska remained standing and waited in the middle of the sitting room.

The butler returned moments later with a tall, cold glass of water. She took a sip; it was refreshing and felt good on her sore, dry throat.

"Thank you," Mariska said. "This is wonderful."

The butler nodded and walked over to one of the ornate chairs in the room and placed a white cloth down on the seat. He led her over to the chair and said, "Please, have a seat. Miss Ingrid shouldn't be much longer."

She took a seat in the uncomfortable yet elegant chair. The clawed feet and arms of the chair gave it a medieval appearance. In fact, the entire room reeked of old, expensive decor. Oil paintings of aristocrats, Chinese vases, and Egyptian art with cartouche carvings hung from the walls. Covered the tables and filled the built-in display cases that lined the walls of the room. Beautiful art. Expensive and historical things. Someone with a more discerning eye for such pieces might call them relics or artifacts.

She fought the urge to get up and look around. Pick up and hold each piece. Try to feel the historical significance of each item. Much like she did when examining the bones and fossils of animals…and of the La Brea Woman. Mariska prided herself in the ability to feel the energy, the significance of fossils. It was like the wooly mammoth was alive when she touched its bones. Her colleagues would joke from time to time about her attachment to the specimens she examined. *They aren't alive anymore*, they'd say. *They can't hear you, Mariska.*

The only person at the museum who seemed to get her was David. He would look at her, watch her while she worked. How many times she'd look up to find him smiling. His attention on her, rather than his own work. He made her feel like a genuine, authentic person. Not a title. Not a paleontologist or scientist. Not a daughter. An individual, with feelings, desires, and passion.

Mariska smiled and pulled out her phone. She'd send him a text. They were going to have dinner later tonight. Maybe he could pick her up at Ingrid's and drive her home. An image of him, freaking out, coddling her like a child. *Nope, not in the mood for that shit.*

She got up from the chair and started surveying the room a little more closely. There were some photographs on the long wooden table in the back of the room. Mariska bent down to get a closer look. Black and white pictures of people standing over a large pit. She recognized the pond in the background. It was taken at the Page Museum. Actually, before the museum ever existed, but from the grounds where the building was eventually built. Next to the pit there were two men dressed in dirty work clothes, the pants held on by suspenders. The picture looked like it dated back to the early 1900s. The men were skinny, dirty, but happy. The man with the pickaxe and shovel stood next to a large mammoth bone—a femur, the back leg. The next picture caught her attention. Two adult men and a young boy, maybe ten to twelve years old. They stood next to large, deep pit. Mariska leaned in closer to the photograph. The angle of the picture didn't allow her to see all the way to the bottom of the pit, but there was something sticking out, barely visible.

A human arm.

The La Brea Woman was the only human ever unearthed at the La Brea Tar Pits, so it had to be her. Which dated the picture to 1914, the year she was discovered. Mariska picked up the picture to get a better look at the people. She didn't recognize them from any of her history books or displays at the Page Museum. Although, it was possible that one of them was Mr. Page, the founder of the Museum. She hadn't seen pictures of him as a young man, plus the picture quality wasn't the best.

Mariska put the framed picture back on the table. The third and last photo was harder to make out. The image looked smeared like the camera was moved while the film was exposed during the shot. She looked behind her, Ingrid still hadn't arrived. Turning over the picture frame, she started to undo the clasps in the back. She wanted to see if anything was written on the back of the picture.

"What are you doing?" The voice from behind her startled Mariska. The picture she held seemed to jump from her hands on its own. In desperation, she fumbled with it, trying to regain her grip. The beautiful, wooden frame, and priceless, one of a kind photograph hit the floor with a crash.

CHAPTER FOURTEEN

Ingrid rushed over to where the picture had fallen. Her tall, thin frame was aged, but sinewy, and strong. With an ease of someone thirty years younger, she bent down to the floor and scooped a piece of her family history up into her arms. Clutching the frame to her chest, she slowly took a look at the picture.

Mariska held her breath as she craned her neck to inspect the damage. The glass covering the photograph was shattered, a few shards had come loose and speckled the wooden floor near where Ingrid kneeled. With a sure hand, Ingrid ran her finger along the cracks in the glass, inspecting the photograph below.

"Oh my God," Mariska said. "Ingrid, I'm so sorry. I wanted to look at the back of the photograph…and I guess I was startled. I feel terrible. Is there something I can do to fix it?" Mariska reached down and placed a gentle hand on Ingrid's shoulder.

Ingrid pulled away from her touch and stood. A few short strides and she reached a nearby desk. She slid the top drawer open and placed the broken frame inside. Without a word, she took a deep breath before closing the drawer and turning to face Mariska.

Mariska took a step back. The look on Ingrid's face was not the kind, experienced scientist she'd met once before. Ingrid looked her up and down before clearing her throat.

"You look a frightful mess, my dear," Ingrid said as she walked around her, leaving a wide berth between them. "I see my butler, Thomas, has provided you with a towel to sit."

Ingrid took a seat in the chair facing the one with a protective towel. She motioned for Mariska to sit as well. Without a word, Mariska rushed over to the chair.

"I'm sorry about the picture." Mariska fidgeted with her shirt. She looked up and saw Ingrid smile. Before she could muster up the courage to speak again, Ingrid waved a dismissive hand.

"Mistakes happen. Thankfully, the photograph itself was undamaged, although the frame was an antique I picked up on my travels through Europe. Irreplaceable, expensive, but not priceless."

Mariska felt two inches tall. This woman had been a mountain in the scientific community. A woman who wasn't afraid to get her hands dirty. In a male-dominated field of study from the start, archeology and paleontology have had extremely thick glass ceilings. Somehow this woman had managed to achieve more than any man Mariska had met. The daughter and granddaughter of two men who originally found the La Brea Woman on Mr. Page's land during an excavation of one of the tar pits. In short, she was Mariska's hero, idol, life-goals personified.

"I will pay to have it fixed."

"That won't be necessary, dear." Ingrid took a glass of water that had just been brought in by Thomas. "Thank you." She took a sip and smiled. "Refreshing. Would you like some water?"

Mariska looked around for the glass she'd been drinking from a few minutes ago, but somehow in the midst of the chaos, Thomas had taken it away, before she could break that too.

She looked at her hands and then with palms out said, "I better not. I seem to have a case of the dropsies."

"Indeed," Ingrid said with a genuine smile. "Thomas, if you'd be so kind as to give us a moment alone."

They waited while he left the room.

Before Ingrid could continue, Mariska said, "I'm really sorry to show up unannounced. I needed to talk with you about something important."

"What is it? Is everything all right?"

Mariska caught herself smoothing out her hair and clothes. A nervous habit, but one that fit in this case. She was still quite a mess after the accident.

"Dear, why do you look like that? What happened?" Ingrid's concern was evident in her voice. She put the glass of water down and leaned forward to get a better look at Mariska.

How do you tell someone you were attacked, run off the road and left for dead? "I was in an accident. On my way here, an SUV crashed into me, and I went off the side of Mulholland Drive."

"Have you called the police? Do you need an ambulance? Are you okay?" Ingrid's questions came with concern etched across her face.

"I haven't called anyone, yet. At the site of the accident, I didn't have cell coverage and couldn't call anyone. I walked the last two miles to your house. I figured I could call them from here." Mariska wanted to tell her everything, but didn't know who she could trust. She closed her eyes as she tried to push the ever-growing fear away.

"Of course. If your phone doesn't work here, you can always use the house phone." Ingrid stood and went into the hall outside the room. She must have been speaking with Thomas, but Mariska couldn't make out what they were saying. When she came back into the sitting room, she said, "Thomas will fetch the police or a doctor. Would you like him to make a call on your behalf?"

If anyone showed up now, she wouldn't have a chance to really converse with Ingrid. This entire trip would have been for nothing. "I don't think that's necessary. Before I go, I'll call my friend David. He can pick me up. We're supposed to have dinner together anyway."

"What about the police? They'll need to know about the accident." Ingrid stood a few feet away, arms crossed over her chest. She reminded her of her mother. The woman definitely had more to say but was keeping her opinions to herself—for now.

"Before any of that, I would like to ask you something. The whole reason I came up here in the first place was to discuss the La Brea Woman."

Ingrid uncrossed her arms and placed her hand on her hips. Pursing her lips together, she offered nothing, but a few rapid eye blinks. "What about her?"

"I'm sure by now you've heard. She's been stolen?"

Ingrid's face fell at the mention of it. "Of course, dear. The board of directors was immediately called, and we convened the following day. Do you know what kind of damage bad press can do to a museum like the Page?" Mariska didn't speak but nodded. "I'm sure you have an inkling, but the full ramifications can be devastating. Bad press can mean the difference between getting funding to continue with the digs or close the doors forever."

"What did the board discuss? The appearance of my involvement?"

Ingrid pursed her lips and arched an eyebrow as her red-hot stare took in Mariska and her current state of messy clothes and hair. "We discussed how we were going to keep the details out of the press for as long as we could. One way we were able to do that was by not mentioning you by name."

Mariska was relieved she wouldn't be having to answer questions to the press as well as the authorities…or at least not yet. Despite her innocence in regards to the disappearance of the remains, she couldn't help but feeling sad when she looked at the older woman. La Brea Woman was such an integral part of her life. Ingrid had often been quoted as saying the ancient woman's remains was both inspirational and pivotal in her desire to become a scientist. The mysterious skeleton had provided her with motivation to keep pushing through a testosterone saturated field of study, staying one step ahead of her male colleagues. Another reason Ingrid was such an inspiration to Mariska.

"I appreciate you keeping my name out of the media," Mariska said. "It would only have added to the stress of this whole thing."

"We didn't do it for you. My hope is to find the La Brea Woman's remains before she's lost forever. God forbid she ends up on the black market or halfway across the world in some rich asshole's living room on display." Ingrid stepped over to Mariska and plucked a tiny leaf from her hair. "You were attacked…and now run off the road."

"Some luck, huh?"

"Do you think the two incidents are connected?" Ingrid asked, still holding her hand.

Mariska wanted to laugh at the absurdity of it all. "I would like to think they aren't, but who knows? I haven't heard of any leads regarding my attack…or about the La Brea Woman."

"Surely, the police have investigated? Haven't you heard anything about it at the museum?"

"That's the thing, Ingrid. I've been fired…well, suspended thanks to the influence of my father actually. Pending the outcome of the investigation, Dr. Snyder said he would decide then. If there is a shred of evidence I was involved, I'll be fired and then prosecuted."

"I can't imagine that'll happen. I mean, you're not the cause of this mess. You were the one attacked, for God's sake."

"You have no idea how much it means to me to hear you say that. I was so worried you might believe the rumors." Mariska squeezed the older woman's hand.

"If I believed rumors or even listened to the gossip or innuendos I've been subjected to over the years, I would have gotten nowhere with my life." Ingrid gave a sweeping motion with her arms indicating the enormous amount of success she'd accomplished.

"I'm glad you feel that way. I have something I need to ask you."

"Ask me anything you'd like, dear."

"All of my research has been deleted from my computer, and I no longer have access to anything at the Museum. To make matters worse, since the La Brea Woman is missing, I can't redo any of the research that's already been done on her. I have nothing." Mariska's voice grew high with her emotions.

"Calm yourself, Mariska." Ingrid put a reassuring hand on Mariska's shoulder. "Do you think if every time I was upset about something in my career, I flew off the handle or cried, that I would have been taken seriously by the establishment? Not on your life. Now, continue. Tell me what you need. Tell me how I can help."

Mariska took a moment to collect her thoughts and pushed down her emotions. "As the head of the IRB for the Page Museum, you were aware I had been granted money for research, or that's what I'd been lead to believe. I thought I was going to be allowed to complete an in-depth research study on La Brea Woman's remains. For the first time, we might have been given an insight into who she was, where she came from, how she ended up in the pit, and who she belongs to. Really, belongs to."

Ingrid's eyes were searching hers. Mariska could feel the electricity in the air. The energy of a woman who's been at the forefront of innovation and international research, for decades. *Say something...anything*, Mariska thought.

"You're absolutely right. I was overjoyed to be at the helm of the board responsible for allowing the research. But with the remains missing, what would be the point on even considering it? I'm not one to give up on a cause or a course of action simply because the road is hard." Ingrid's jaw visibly clenched. "Without a body, the research would never justify the grant of precious funding."

"I agree, but that's why I'm here."

"Go on." Ingrid raised an eyebrow in interest.

"Your father and grandfather were the ones who unearthed La Brea Woman back in 1914. If I know anything about you and your family, it's that you keep meticulous documentation. The research your father did on the first giant sloth unearth was nothing short of inspiring. I can't even imagine what it must have been like to pull bone after bone out of the earth with absolutely no idea what it was. The species of animal was no longer in existence, so there was no reference by which to piece it back together. It was through his copious notations, photographs, and measurements that made it all possible."

"He was truly an impressive man."

"That's why I have a feeling you may have the key," Mariska said.

"Key to what?"

"Finding the La Brea Woman. Think about it...your family members were the first to take notes, photographs, and document details regarding the La Brea Woman. So, while we no longer have the actual remains, we have the next best thing: their first-hand evidence. There may even be something that points to a clue that could help us find her."

"How? I don't understand where you're going with this." Ingrid shook her head, obviously unconvinced.

"There may be clues in their writings as to who she belonged to or how she ended up in the pit, to begin with. I've been wracking my brain for days now trying to figure out why anyone would want to steal her remains. The only thing I could think of was the fact that there were protestors outside the Gala. Maybe one of them snuck in to take her."

"There's always protestors at the big events. The local tribes feel she belongs to them, but they can't even agree as to which tribe has the rightful claim on her. Why now? Why would they attack you and take her now? She's been housed in the museum for decades."

Mariska gave it some thought. "I don't know. I need more information. That's what I'm hoping your father and grandfather's notes would provide. Not to mention in the event she's lost forever, I'd like to use their documentation to put together research with what we do have."

Ingrid didn't say anything for a few agonizing moments. She reached out and took Mariska's hand in hers. She led Mariska across the room to the bookcase on the far wall. "Take a look at these books here. Many of them are old and first edition."

Of course they are, Mariska thought. She wouldn't have suspected anything less from Ingrid. The woman was all class and knew the value of history and artifacts.

"If you were to pick one book from this collection as being most important to you. One that seemed to have the most impact on your life or career, which one would it be?" Ingrid asked. Her face was bright and alive. Her energy was contagious. Mariska felt a tingle run up her spine, and she shivered.

Mariska looked over the selection. The books ranged from *20,000 Leagues Under the Sea*, to *Moby Dick*. There didn't seem to be much of an order or theme to them, other than they were old and probably signed first editions. Then one book, in particular, caught her eye. *Fifty Shades of Grey*, by EL James. No, way.

"This one," Mariska said, pointing to the book.

"Ah." Ingrid crossed her arms and turned to Mariska. "How'd I know you would say that?"

Mariska smiled and cocked her head to the side as if to say *you've got to be kidding me.*

"Now, reach up there and tilt the book down," Ingrid said. But as Mariska reached up to touch the edge of the book, Ingrid stopped her. "Carefully."

The women shared a soft laugh, although Mariska cringed internally. With all the care in the world, Mariska tipped the book toward her. When the book reached a forty-five-degree angle, there was an audible click. Mariska turned to Ingrid with a questioning look.

"It's a secret room." Ingrid reached up and pulled on the bookcase. A hiss of air and a scraping sound as the bookcase slid across the wooden floor. "I keep most of my family's research in here for safekeeping. A fireproof room, hidden from prying eyes."

Mariska took a step forward, entering the room. The temperature was at least ten degrees cooler, dry, and pitch black. She turned to ask if Ingrid could turn on the lights when the older woman flipped the wall switch. Mariska gasped, the bright light making her wince and shield her eyes for a moment. Blinking rapidly as her eyes adjusted to the bright illumination, things began to come into focus. The room was a vault. A time capsule.

Ingrid came up behind Mariska and whispered in her ear, "Now, that you've seen this place, I can't let you leave."

CHAPTER FIFTEEN

Mariska turned just as Ingrid took a step toward her. Heart pounding, her eyes darted around the room but found nowhere for her to hide. Nowhere to run. *This can't really be happening?*

"What do you mean?" Mariska said, taking a step back. *Had her luck just run out?*

Ingrid let out a hearty laugh. "I've always wanted to say that." She reached for Mariska's hand, but Mariska pulled it away. "Oh dear. I wasn't thinking straight. I didn't mean to scare you."

"Well, you did."

"I see that now. Considering what you've just been through, it was definitely in poor taste." Ingrid reached for Mariska's hand once again. This time, Mariska allowed the older woman to hold her. "I've been called many things in my life, but never a comedian. I am sorry I scared you."

Mariska took a moment to respond. "Of course, I'm just a bit jumpy. With everything that's been going on lately, I just overreacted."

"I, for one, am glad you didn't hit me. When I get scared, I tend to lash out. Or, I did when I was younger." Ingrid released Mariska's hand and walked across the room to a large built-in cabinet and drawers. "My father always said I was his fiery redhead."

The cabinets were, of course, museum-quality and reminded Mariska of the storage areas of the Tombs. They were made of dark wood: large single panels made up the upper cabinets, and the lower drawers had industrial style pulls and were faced with ornately carved designs. Ingrid went over to the top drawer and pulled it open. Mariska crossed half the distance to get a better look. From her new vantage point, she saw that Ingrid was fingering through files. What they were marked, Mariska couldn't see from this distance. A few moments later, Ingrid located what she'd been looking for.

"Here it is," she declared as she pulled out a thick, white folder that had begun to yellow with age. Ingrid turned and smiled. "You must see this. I think this is what you've been looking for."

Ingrid brought the contents over to a large table in the center of the room and laid the folder open on it. Mariska was there in a flash, willing her hands to keep to themselves. Ingrid slowly, but with a measured hand, turned page after page over until she reached the first photograph in the pile.

"Ah, this is my grandfather and father standing with Mr. Page. They'd just discovered the La Brea Woman. Look at their faces. They were so happy—proud."

Mariska couldn't agree more. The men looked practically giddy, with huge open mouth smiles, the youngest man slightly doubled over with an explosive laugh. This was something that Mariska had found to be a rarity for the time period. Photographs of people back then were almost always posed, and the people were almost always deadly serious.

The next picture was just the younger man, but this time he wasn't laughing, wasn't smiling. The closer Mariska looked, the more interesting the photograph appeared. In the background was the pit where the La Brea Woman was discovered. Next to it was a tarp covering what Mariska assumed were her remains.

"Is this your father?" Mariska asked.

"Yes, John Matthew Ashton. Wasn't he a good-looking young man?"

Looks were in the eye of the beholder, but it wasn't the man's appearance that drew her attention. "What's in his hand?"

Ingrid smiled, "I've often wondered the same thing."

Mariska said, "Do you have a magnifying glass?"

Ingrid opened the second drawer of the archival table and handed it to Mariska. She used it to look closer at the young man's hand. His hand fit almost entirely around the object, just a tiny bit showed between the thumb and index finger. Since the photograph had been taken over a hundred years ago and was in black and white, there were limited clues to tell Mariska what was in his hand.

"Did your father ever record anywhere what he was holding?"

"Like I said, I've wondered my entire life what was in his hand. As a child, I looked at these pictures over and over again. I asked my father about it many times."

"And what did he say?" Mariska put the magnifier down and turned to Ingrid, anticipation eating a hole in her belly.

"He always said that in time, the truth would be revealed. Believe me, when I tell you this. It was one of the things that kept me motivated to accomplish what I managed to do with my life. I've been searching for answers my entire life. My father didn't live a full life. His being cut short by disease he'd picked up on one of his many international travels. I didn't have a lot of time as an adult to ask the right questions before he passed."

"I'm sorry. How insensitive of me. When I see a mystery, I want to solve it. I don't always think about what stands between me and the answers I want to find."

"It's okay, dear. Why do you think I've never been married? There wasn't time…I had too many mysteries to solve." Ingrid's expression told a truth Mariska hadn't expected. Ingrid, the headstrong, powerful, intelligent woman had regrets. "A husband would have only slowed me down."

Mariska could have sworn she'd read somewhere this woman had a family of her own. *Why would she lie?* Now, wasn't the time or place to ask a question like that.

As Mariska went to pass the photograph back to Ingrid, she noticed something unusual. She quickly pulled the photo back to take a closer look. "Who's that?"

"Excuse, me? I just—"

"Oh yes. I know that's your father. I'm talking about that person…there," Mariska pointed to the far top corner of the image.

"He doesn't look happy. Not happy at all." Mariska kept looking at the image but noticed in her periphery when Ingrid turned away.

Facing the exit, Ingrid said, "No one to concern yourself with."

Silence grew uncomfortable and thick between them. Mariska looked from the photograph to Ingrid, and back. The man wore similar clothes to her family but appeared darker skinned. His black hair was straight and longer than what was traditional for the time.

"Was he a local Native American?"

Ingrid turned back around. Her expression, hard. Eyes, angry. "That man made everything difficult for my father."

"How, so?"

"He's a tribe member of the local Chumash people," Ingrid said, her voice scratchy and dry.

"Chumash? Is that the same tribe that's been protesting the Page Museum…for as long as I can remember?"

"Longer. They've demanded the La Brea Woman's remains be brought back to them. As if they own her." If words could burn, Ingrid's could have set the entire room on fire. "The thing is, it didn't have to be this way. It hadn't always been this way…" Her voice trailed away.

"But maybe they—" Mariska began to offer another way to look at things, but Ingrid's eyes told her to remain quiet. It wasn't the time or place for this discussion.

Change the subject and stay focused, Mariska, she told herself. "Was there another photograph taken right after this one? Where we might be able to see what he's holding?"

"I'm afraid not. When my father passed away, he donated a lot of his research papers and photographs to the Los Angeles Public Library for their archives section. All I have are the leftovers." Ingrid offered a dramatic sweep of her arms and a smirk.

"Pretty decent leftovers, if you ask me."

"I agree. I've been blessed in my life." Ingrid began to pack up her things. "Would you like copies of the photographs?"

"That'd be fantastic."

"I'll have Thomas make you some, and we'll have them delivered by courier to your home."

They walked together toward the exit when Mariska noticed a large tarp draped over something in the corner of the room. "What's that? Under the tarp?"

Ingrid didn't even look in its direction. She simply hooked her arm in Mariska's and held her tight. "That's for another time."

Mysteries everywhere. What Mariska wouldn't do to have full access to Ingrid's home. No one around to make sure she kept her hands to herself. She could spend days in the secret vault alone. So much history. So many unanswered questions.

Ingrid pushed the sliding bookcase back into place and said, "Have you decided whether you want to call and report your accident now, or when you get home?"

Back to reality. "I'll call when I get home. I don't want to take up any more of your time. I appreciate all your help."

"Would you like Thomas to give you a ride home? Or, I think you also mentioned a friend? A gentleman…I assume."

Mariska's face flushed hot. "Yes, but we're just friends."

"I see," Ingrid said. "By his choice? Or, yours?"

"We've talked about it in the past. Our friendship is so important to us that we didn't want to risk it."

"Well, it's none of my business, but that sounds like something you decided. In my experience, men don't mind risking the friendship." Ingrid turned and walked into the hallway entrance of the mansion.

Mariska shook her head. This woman was more than a scientist who specialized in ancient civilizations and extinct creatures; she knew the human condition. Maybe it was age. Maybe it was a discerning eye that noticed subtle changes in body language. Either way, Ingrid was smart and knew what she was doing.

She followed the older woman into the entryway. "Thank you for your time, Ingrid. I really appreciate it."

"Any time." Ingrid smiled. "But next time, try not to break anything."

Mariska cringed. The blow was in jest, but well deserved. "I promise."

"I've summoned Thomas to bring the car around. He'll take you home or wherever you want to go."

"Thank you, so much."

Ingrid gave her a hug. "I have some other business to attend to, so if you don't mind, I must leave you now."

"Absolutely," Mariska said. "I will wait for Thomas right here."

Ingrid turned and started walking away into the bowels of the expansive home when Mariska thought of something she'd forgotten to say. "Ingrid." The older woman must not have heard her as she turned the corner and disappeared from view.

An internal debate began. Tell her later or go after her now? All she wanted to ask her was for the library location where her father's belongings were stored. There were multiple locations in L.A., and there was no telling which one had his documents on file. The archival files wouldn't be available online to search, and she'd need to visit them in person. Getting the information now would possibly save her two or three days of searching.

Charging up the long hallway in the direction Ingrid went, Mariska slowed to a silent crawl when she reached the end of the hallway. Something told her to peek around the corner rather than entering like a proverbial bull in a china shop. Pressed up against the wall, she stole a glance around the corner.

Nothing. No one was there. *Better try one more time*, she thought. This time, when she looked around the corner, she took a bit more time. Peering around the corner, the room came into view. An expansive ornate room filled with luxurious furnishings. A set of large mammoth tusks caught her attention. They were mounted over the fireplace at the far side of the room. Mumbled voices could be heard, but were too soft for Mariska to make out with any kind of understanding. She held her breath and listened, again. Ingrid was talking to someone, but it was only her voice Mariska heard. She had to be on the phone with someone. Straining to hear, she took a small step into the opening of the doorway. *Where was Ingrid?* To the right of the room was another hallway. She must be in there. Mariska slipped off her heels and tiptoed across the hardwood floors in silence. The closer she got, the more she could hear. Ingrid said, "That's not needed… No, I'm telling you, it'll be fine… Yes, less than you, trust me."

Who was she talking to? Was it about, me? Mariska's heart pounded. If she were caught eavesdropping, there'd be no plausible explanation as to why she was there.

Ingrid continued, "Yes. I understand. As you wish. Oh, and do me a favor…run the sample, stat."

Mariska heard the woman hang up the phone. *I need to get out of here.* She took a couple steps backward when she bumped into something. She turned just as vase sitting atop the table she'd collided with began to topple. *Shit.* She grabbed for the ceramic masterpiece that was probably worth more than Mariska's life. With both hands, she scooped it up into the air, but something inside the bowl rattled loud enough to be heard in the next room.

"Thomas? Is that you?" Ingrid said from the other room.

Mariska placed the vase back onto the desk and snatched her shoes from the floor and ran. Headlong, she raced through the expanse and into the hallway. Just a few more meters to the front door. With one last painful lunge, she reached for the door and swung it open. Her bruised ribs screaming out at the stretch she'd put them under.

"Dr. Stevenson?" Thomas stood in the doorway.

"Thomas," Mariska said, out of breath. "Are you ready for me?"

A confused expression crossed his wrinkled, old, face. "Is everything okay?"

"Yes, thank you." Mariska looked behind her. Ingrid stepped into the hallway and cocked her head to the side. Mariska waved, "Thank you again."

Ingrid waved. Mariska pulled the door closed behind her and rushed over to the limousine.

"Dr. Stevenson, your purse is in the backseat. Is there anything else you'll be needing before we leave?"

"No, thank you." Mariska swung her legs inside the vehicle as

Thomas shut the door.

Mariska couldn't wait to get home. She had some digging to do.

CHAPTER SIXTEEN

Thomas pulled open the door just after he parked the car in the small lot behind Mariska's apartment. She grabbed her purse and took his hand as he helped her out of the backseat. The adrenaline had long since left her body since the accident earlier in the day. Her back and all four limbs were stiff and sore. The bruise had begun to form on her left arm and knee. She'd have to do a more in-depth examination in the privacy of her own home.

Accepting the offer of help out of the car, she pulled on the older man as she came up to stand. Her ankles were a little more, shaky than she'd expected them to be.

"Thank you, Thomas." She shook his hand. "Will you please thank Ingrid again for her time?"

"Of course, ma'am." He offered a nod and returned to the front seat. Seconds later, he was pulling out of her lot, and she was left all alone.

Motivation at an all-time low, made the metal staircase leading to her second-floor apartment appear insurmountable. It might as well have been Mount Everest. And here she was without any Sherpas to help her to the summit.

That's when it hit her. The importance of what she'd learned and seen at Ingrid's house. The old woman might hold the key or at least be a conduit to the key to finding La Brea Woman…or at the very least finishing her research. Energized, she took the first six stairs without a second thought. It was the final six that sent pain up the back of her legs and into her hips and low back.

A few seconds of struggling with the tricky lock and sticky front door, she muscled the door open with her shoulder. She looked at the clock above the sink in the kitchen. She still had a few hours she could do some research before David showed up with dinner. Not to mention she was going to need to contact the police regarding the car accident. Accident? No, it was no accident.

First things first, send Theresa a message. Mariska took out her phone and sent a text to Theresa asking if there was anything new on her end. Next, she placed a call to Detective Wulf.

She got his voicemail and left a message. "Detective Wulf, this is Mariska Stevenson calling. I wanted to report to you…an accident. I was driving on Mulholland Drive, right around mile marker fifteen. There's a steep drop off at the second switchback. A dark SUV ran me off the road. So, I guess maybe it wasn't an accident? Anyway, call me back. You have my number."

Mariska hung up the phone and went into her bedroom. She hurried to the dresser and bookcase and retrieved her hidden, stolen treasures. The beads and mysterious tooth. Taking them over to the bed, she opened the box and took out the pouch of beads, pouring them out onto the bedspread. Ten, in all, crudely made and of a cubic structure. At first glance, they were small, about the size of Mariska's thumbnail and rough in texture. The beads were not made of a familiar stone, or at least, Mariska didn't immediately recognize them. They didn't appear to be made of similar stones found in the tar pits. They weren't from the local area. She held them up to the lamp she turned on next to the bed. Without magnification, she saw that the beads weren't just rough, they were carved. Or, at least that was her best guess right now. Her expertize was animals, not humans, and she had yet to find a mammoth that wore jewelry or carved their initials into their tusks before ending up in the tar pits. She would need more magnification at the very least, to further study them.

The tooth was a different story. Definitely, not human. The tiny holes on the sides made it clear it was part of the necklace, along with the ten beads. Was there a significance to the necklace? Would it help to identify who La Brea Woman was…or at least who she belonged too? The weight of the tooth wasn't what she'd expected it to be. Usually, fossils were heavier, unless they were preserved in the tar itself. She put the tooth in her palm and compared it to a small Tyrannosaurus Rex tooth she'd found on a dig in Montana when she was in graduate school. They were of similar size, but not the same. The T-Rex tooth had turned to stone over millions of years, the minerals being slowly replaced by the surrounding soils and ultimately being turned into stone. This mystery-tooth was not like that. It was similar to the weight of a preserved tooth, not a petrified or fossilized one.

For Mariska, it told her that the tooth was of a living, or recently deceased creature dating back to the Pleistocene Epoch, and wasn't already a fossil dug up by the La Brea Woman before being fashioned into a necklace. The unknown creature was something that must have existed as recently as ten to fifteen thousand years ago. Just like the La Brea Woman. Finding a new Dinosaur species was cool, but still happened quite often in the paleontology world, but finding a new Megafauna species dating to the Pleistocene Era, and in America…that was rare, exciting. Something that could not only make an already good career, spectacular but also bring an added piece to the puzzle she and her predecessors slaved away at the bottom of hot, smelly pits to bring to the scientific community at large.

Her phone chimed with an incoming text from Theresa. *I haven't come up with too much yet. I'm trying to warm up to Kathy to see if I can get any information. She's an ice queen.*

Mariska sent a text back, *Keep trying. I think she might know more than we give her credit for. We'll also need to make a visit to the Los Angeles Library, but I'll need a ride. What day would work for you?*

Another chime, *I can pick you up tomorrow. What time?*

Perfect. How about after you get off of work? Five o'clock?

Theresa responded almost immediately. *I'll see you at your place at five.*

Mariska put the phone down and picked up the tooth and beads, rolled them around in her hands, and closed her eyes. She normally spent time thinking and imagining times past at the Griffith Park Observatory. But she didn't have a car to take up there. So, she laid back on the bed and tried to imagine she was in the wilds of California, fifteen thousand years ago. The smell of the huge pine and conifer trees. In the distance, an unknown animal bellowed. Probably a *Bison Antiquus*, a huge animal weighing over three thousand pounds, the bones told of a heavily muscled animal that had a thick skull and sharp horns. A stiff breeze blew, cooler than modern-day California, but not bitterly cold; she got a whiff of something…musky. Animal, for sure, but what kind.

Unconsciously, Mariska rubbed the tooth between her fingers, its smooth surface ending in a point. Scrolling through a memory bank of potential creatures that would meet the needed size and classification for such a tooth, she smelled another strong odor. The sensation sent a tingle through her body that woke her from her meditation. Sitting up, she brought the tooth and beads closer to her face. Like a child, trying to feel, taste, and smell everything to gain as much information as she could from the world around her, she took a sniff. Nothing, but a faint smell of tar. The noxious, sticky substance, would continue to ooze out from the porous material, over the course of decades.

A knock at the front door took her out of the moment. She put the tooth and beads back into their perspective hiding places and went to see who came over uninvited. Although, maybe David came early. He'd been known to do that in the past. But she thought she'd broken him of that by not answering the door until the scheduled time.

She snuck a peek through the peephole. Definitely not David. Mariska unlocked the two deadbolts and removed the chain. Swinging the door open, she tried to affix a pleasant expression to her face.

"Detective Wulf. I wasn't expecting you."

He cocked his head to one side, "Really? You called me."

The car accident. "I did. You're absolutely right." She took a step back and said, "Would you like to come in?"

Wulf gave a nod and stepped past her into the entryway.

"Honestly, I thought you would have just called me back. I didn't know you would come to my home." Mariska closed the door behind them and walked through the kitchen toward the living room, with Wulf following.

"We had a couple calls come in regarding an accident on Mulholland. One, call said they saw a black Cadillac Escalade push a small BMW off the side of the cliff," Wulf said, before taking a seat where Mariska had shown to him. He lowered himself onto the sofa, and she sat across from him in a high back leather chair. "When you left me a voicemail, the police were digging through your glove box and reported back your name and address. Clearly, this wasn't an accident."

"So, you came to take my report? Or…?"

"That's how it's done," Wulf said. "Before we go any further, I'm telling this for your own good. Never leave the scene of an accident again. It's against the law and I have every right to arrest you for this." He gave her side-eye. "I'm not going to this time, but don't let it happen again. And while I'm lecturing you, have you called your insurance company?"

She shook her head. "I will as soon as you leave."

He cleared his throat. "Now, we've taken paint samples from your car. They also took swabs of the blood, when we thought we were going to need to identify the victim. Although we will be sure to match them to you…since we've collected them, might as well test them."

"Of course." Mariska looked down for a moment and then said, "Would you care for something to drink?"

"No, thank you. I'm on duty."

Mariska chuckled, "I was thinking water. Bottled, but non-alcoholic."

"Oh." He fidgeted a bit with his tie. "Still, I'm fine, but thank you."

So, he's uncomfortable now, she thought. *Good to know*. "Do you have any leads?"

"It's far too early to have any leads, but it's good to see you're doing okay. Have you been to the hospital to get checked out?"

"Nah, I didn't hit my head. Nothing's broken. I'm good." Mariska looked down and saw her skirt was torn on the side and stained with blood. "I mean, I've looked better, but I'm physically doing, okay."

"It would be better to be checked out by a doctor…to make sure."

"You don't know me very well, Detective. I'm not one to run to the hospital or the police for help when I need it." She gave a short laugh. "I've been told I'm stubborn."

"Oh, yes. I remember."

"You, remember?" Mariska's smile disappeared. "You're acting like you know me, or something."

He cleared his throat and looked away for a split second. "I…I'm referring to our encounter at the hospital. You were being pretty darn stubborn. If, I remember correctly."

Mariska narrowed her stare. Who was Detective Wulf? The tingle in her gut told her there was more to him that he let on.

She broke eye contact as he said, "What can you tell me about the person who ran you off the road?"

"Not, much. Once, I climbed up the rocky embankment to the street; I saw a man watching me from the SUV. He wasn't the driver, so there were at least two of them. He was too far away to see anything really, but…"

"But?" Wulf scooted to the end of his seat.

"I took a picture. Wait here." She ran into her bedroom and retrieved her phone. Scrolling through her apps, she continued, "I don't think it's a detailed picture by any stretch of the imagination, but it might be of help."

She turned the phone, so Wulf could take a look at the picture.

"May I?" Wulf said, asking to touch the phone so he could get a closer look.

Mariska handed him the phone and sat back into the chair.

Wulf squinted and put the phone up close to his face. He zoomed in on the photograph to get a better look. "You're right. It's not a good picture."

Mariska rolled her eyes but smiled.

"It's better than nothing. I'd like you to text me that picture please." Wulf handed her back the phone.

"Sure," she said, sending him the picture while he waited.

His phone beeped with the incoming text message.

"Anything else?" he asked.

"Nope, that's about it. It looks like someone tried to kill me twice now."

He shook his head. "I would say your luck has been anything, but good. At this point, there's no way to tell if these two incidents are related…you know, other than they both happened to you."

"I'm not sure if that makes me feel better, or worse."

"What were you doing on Mulholland?"

"Excuse me?" Mariska blinked back her irritation and tried to tame down her tone. "Not that it matters, but I was going to visit a colleague…of sorts."

"Of sorts?"

"We don't exactly work together, but she is a member of the review board for the museum."

"Who's that?" Wulf pulled out a small notepad and pen.

"Ingrid Ashton."

"Did anyone else know you were going up there?"

She thought about it for a moment. "Not that I know of…I don't remember telling anyone about it."

"Was she expecting you?" He looked up from his pad, eyebrows arched.

Mariska shook her head, "Actually, no. I went unannounced and unplanned. Kind of a spur of the moment decision." Suddenly, a memory flashed. Badger had texted her a word of warning. That she'd been in danger. How did he know?

"You, okay?" Wulf asked.

She pushed away her thoughts. No sense in bringing up the man she contacted on Craigslist, that she never met, never saw, and has no idea how to contact. No, it would be too messy, and she didn't feel like explaining herself. Not right now and not to him.

"Yeah, I'm fine. I just have plans for this evening, and it's getting to be around that time." She looked at her watch, but she hadn't been wearing one. *Damn, it.*

They both stood when she heard someone knock at the front door followed by the sound of it opening. She hadn't locked it. *Damn it.*

"Mariska?" David hollered into the apartment as he closed the door. He stopped short, mid-stride, wine in one hand, flowers in the other.

Mariska and Detective Wulf, stood at the entrance to the kitchen in silence as she saw what looked like confusion turned into annoyance cross his face. David's gaze settled on Wulf. He said, "What's going on, Mariska?"

Damn it.

CHAPTER SEVENTEEN

David slammed the front door closed and locked it. "Care to explain?"

"Explain, what?" Mariska crossed her arms and refused to look away. "So, you're mad, now? That doesn't make any sense."

"I'm not mad," David said. He walked past her and started putting water in a vase for the flowers he'd brought. "I don't know what you're talking about."

"The way you slammed the door shut, I'd say you're mad."

David turned away from the sink and walked over to the kitchen table. He placed the vase filled with beautifully arranged, pink and white tiger lilies in the middle of the table. The flowers were spaced with greenery, and a ribbon was tied around the base of the container. Under different circumstances, Mariska would have been impressed. Tiger lilies had always been her favorite. So, while the flowers were gorgeous, Mariska would have preferred the wine.

"I'm not upset. What you do in your apartment is none of my business."

"Damn, straight. It's absolutely none of your business. But since I'm not sleeping with the man, I'm open to answer whatever questions you may have." Mariska poured herself a glass of chilled white wine. "Want a glass?"

He didn't answer at first. David looked back at the door for a moment. He must have made the decision to stay, because he said, "Sure, pour generously."

At least they had that in common. The small bottle emptied

between the two large wine glasses, Mariska handed him his and walked into the other room. "Come in here, and I'll explain everything." Knowing full well after seeing his little jealousy-induced fit, her description of the day's events wouldn't be with full-disclosure. Not yet.

David sat on the sofa and Mariska settled into the large recliner perpendicular to him. Close, but far enough away that it wouldn't be awkward. In silence, they sipped wine and looked off in opposite corners of the room. *Might as well tear off the bandage*, Mariska thought. No sense in prolonging the inevitable. Chugging the last three gulps of wine, she reached forward and put the glass down on the coffee table.

Before she could utter a word, David said, "Your hair is a total mess, and your makeup is smeared. The top button of your blouse is missing, and it's not tucked in."

Mariska absently smoothed her hair on the side while looking down at the mess she'd become.

"I assumed I'd walked in on something I wasn't meant to see," David said. He too took the last of his wine in short order and put the glass down on the coffee table.

Mariska looked away for a moment. She owed him an explanation. He was her best friend. "I can see why you have questions. Although, since we are just friends, I don't like the accusation."

"Just friends," David's words came out with a bitterness she hadn't expected. "You know how I feel about you."

"We discussed this a long time ago," Mariska said. "I mean, you're the one who said our friendship was too important to risk on a relationship."

The fire in David's expression went from red hot to extinguished, in seconds. His puppy dog eyes tugged at her heart, and she wanted to take back everything she'd just said…and how she'd said it. "David…"

"No, you're right. I did say that. And, at the time, it was the right thing to do." He looked at the empty glass on the coffee table.

"Geez, the wine got to me pretty quick."

The poor attempt at deflecting his feelings was obvious to them both. Desperate to cut the tension in the room, Mariska grabbed his hand. David, at first, flinched under her touch but didn't pull his hand away.

"Thank you." Mariska locked eyes with him. "Thank you for caring about me."

He smiled, but he still looked sad. "I will always care about you."

"Then this might be hard for you to hear." Mariska pulled her hand away. "You're absolutely, right. I look like a mess, and there's a really good reason why."

David didn't respond, only looked at her with his expectant eyes. His brow furrowed and his mouth drawn into a thin line.

"Maybe I should open another bottle of wine," Mariska said.

"Maybe you should tell me what's going on. Are you okay?"

"I was in a car accident."

"What?" David stood and then quickly knelt in front of her. "Are you, okay? What happened?" His eyes searching her entire body for signs of injury.

"I'm fine. Nothing, broken."

"Why didn't you call me? Where did this happen? I was wondering why you were home and your car wasn't parked out back." David sat back into the couch but kept ahold of her hands.

"I didn't want you to worry. Plus, I was fine, so it wasn't like I was in any real danger…well not anymore, anyway."

"What does that mean?" David squeezed her hand. "And why was Detective Wulf here? He's a detective, not a regular cop."

"I called him. See…my accident, might not have been an accident in the true sense of the word." Her face scrunched up as she watched the words sink in. Before he could say anything, she cut him off, "I think I was run off the road…on purpose."

"Run off the road? What the…?" His eyes searched hers for more answers. "Where did this happen?

"I was on Mulholland Drive…"

"Mulholland? Why the hell were you driving up there?" He

paused for a moment. "Does this have to do with what happened at the museum?"

"Yes. I mean, I think so. I don't know. I was going up to Ingrid Ashton's home to ask her a few questions."

"Ingrid Ashton? Why?" David looked almost angry. Why the hell would he be angry?

Enough, with full disclosure. David was clearly too upset to hear all of this, so she was going to stop the escalation of emotions. "I wanted to ask her about my grant."

"But…" he paused for a moment. "Oh. The grant."

"Yeah, nothing that unusual. I wanted to ask her if I were to be reinstated at the museum if she'd be willing to still award me the grant."

He let out a sigh. "Well, that's a relief."

"A relief? I almost died."

"You just said it wasn't a big deal. Now you almost died?" David laughed. "Which is it?"

"First of all, asshole, I was run off the road, and my car is totaled."

"I'm sure your dad will replace it." David stood and started walking into the kitchen. "Should I start making us some dinner?"

Mariska hopped off the recliner with such explosive energy that she toppled the wine glass sitting on the coffee table. "That's uncalled for. You know I don't like taking handouts from my family."

"And yet you do. How'd you get the car in the first place? This apartment?"

"They were graduation gifts." Mariska pinched David's arm hard enough to hurt him, but he didn't give her the satisfaction of reacting to it.

"Guess what I got for a graduation present?"

Mariska didn't answer.

"I'll tell you. I got a twenty-five-dollar gift card to Red Lobster. So, tell me again how much you hate taking handouts from Mommy and Daddy?" The coldness in his eyes matched his tone of voice.

And they both hurt her more deeply than she'd expected.

"You're right." She shrugged. "I do accept financial help from them. Who cares? As long as I work hard and accomplish my professional achievements on my own, I don't think it's wrong to accept help from my family." Pausing only to take a quick breath she continued, "I think you're missing the point. I was in an accident and could have been seriously injured. And, I wouldn't be surprised if this had something to do with the attack at the museum."

"Even if it was related, why would someone run you off the road?" David started back into the kitchen, pulling out pots and pans he would need to make his 'famous David's pasta'...if she'd let him stay that long. She was still undecided at this point.

"Detective Wulf believes me. And quite frankly, he has shown more concern for me than you have." She looked away. "I don't think I'm all that hungry."

"Mariska." David grabbed her by the shoulders and looked squarely into her eyes. "I'm sorry. I really am. I think the shock of finding you and the detective together, then hearing about the accident, and then the immediate relief I felt that you were okay...it skewed my feelings. So, of course, I'm concerned about you. You know this."

"I guess." She wanted to be alone.

"Do you want to tell me about the accident?" David said. "Is there anything I can do to help you?"

She thought about it for a minute. *Yeah, you could leave and give me some space*, she thought. "Nah, no sense in talking about it. I gave my report to the detective. I'm sure if there's any more developments, we will find out together."

"Great. It's a deal. Now, would you like the marinara sauce or the alfredo?"

Mariska grabbed his hand and squeezed it. "I don't feel much like eating. It's been kind of a rough day, and I think I just need to get some rest."

"You're not going to eat?"

"No, I'm not really all that hungry." Her stomach growled, but

David didn't seem to notice. "Can I take a raincheck?"

David looked around the kitchen and shrugged his shoulders. What else was there for him to say? "Sure…I guess."

Mariska walked with him to the front door, unlocked the deadbolt and opened it for him. "Thanks for the wine. Prosecco—you always know my favorites."

"Just to be clear. You believe me, right?" David looked away.

She sighed. "Yes, I promise you I'm not mad. I just need to get some rest."

"I'll call you tomorrow?"

How about in a couple of days? "Sure, that sounds great." She smiled. "I hope you have a good day at work tomorrow. Wish I could be there too."

"You will. It shouldn't be long. I mean, you didn't have anything to do with the missing remains. I'm sure once the investigation is complete, Dr. Snyder will retire, and you will be back. It'll be like old times." David looked out the door. "Well, I guess I better get going."

"Thanks again." Mariska gave him a gentle hug and closed the door behind him.

Why did that man have to be such a dick, sometimes? She went into the living room and retrieved her cell phone. After placing a call for some Chinese takeout, she called Theresa.

"Hey Mariska," Theresa said as soon as she answered the call.

"There's been some developments."

"Go on."

"I was in an accident. Only, I don't think it was accidental…if you know what I mean?"

Theresa paused for a moment. "Are you hurt? Do you need me to call anyone?"

"No, I wasn't injured. And, I've reported it to the police already."

"How can I help?"

"I was reminded of Dr. Snyder's upcoming retirement. Can you ask around…and investigate if there have been any offers made to purchase the La Brea Woman's remains?"

"Sure, I can do some digging. Do you suspect Dr. Snyder of

selling her?"

"I really don't know what to think at this point. But I visited a friend this afternoon, and…" Mariska heard a strange series of clicks coming from the phone. She pulled it away from her ear and saw the display flickered on and off. "What the hell?"

"What's going on, Mariska? Everything okay?"

"I'm not sure. I think we should discuss this in person, rather than over the phone."

"Okay, tell me when I pick you up tomorrow," Theresa said.

"Thank you. I'll see you then." Mariska disconnected the call.

After calling and reporting the accident to the insurance, she needed to make another call. One, she was dreading, but one that needed to happen. Sooner, rather than later.

"Hello?" Mariska's mom said.

"Hey, Mom." Mariska cleared her throat. "I need to ask you for a huge favor."

"Really? I love helping you. What can I do?"

Not only was it a bit embarrassing to ask her family for a new car, but she was going to have to explain what happened—she hated worrying her mom. "Let me start off by saying, I'm sorry, and I promise to you pay you back…I have some money in a CD, but I can't touch it for another four months."

"What is it, dear? We're here to help."

"I going to need a new car."

CHAPTER EIGHTEEN

Wulf sat in a booth at a local greasy-spoon diner. He thought about the exchange between himself and Dr. David Beaumont. He couldn't blame David for being less than polite toward him. Mariska was a beautiful woman, and they had a long-standing friendship. He suspected David wanted more than that and had some jealousy issues. Wulf made a mental note to ask Mariska the next time he saw her if she knew her friend was harboring some unresolved feelings for her. He knew it wasn't professional, but it might bring up some interesting information about their past…and who knew, maybe it would help the investigation.

Wulf opened up his laptop and read through his account of the night he was nearly killed by the man in the SUV. Not that he could shake the images from his mind, but it always helped to read the details. He hadn't told Mariska that according to her description of the SUV that ran her off the road and from the color of paint transfer found at the scene, it was plausible the man who drove her off the road was the same one that had followed her to the club. Forensics was still working on a definitive link between to the two incidents.

"Can I take your order?" the waitress asked.

Wulf looked up from his computer. "I'll stick with the coffee."

"Are you sure I can't tempt you with a few hot biscuits?" The waitress snapped her gum and gave him a wicked smile.

He smiled back. "Nah, the coffee's good, thank you."

"Suit yourself." She blew a bubble, popping it between her teeth, before turning away to go harass one of the other men sitting alone in the restaurant.

Shaking his head, Wulf couldn't help but laugh. He had what his friends called the seven-seventy-rule. All the females loved him as long as they were seven and younger or seventy and older. In other words, he was hopelessly single.

Getting back to the business at hand, he scrolled through his police reports regarding the incident at the club. He then brought up the picture that Mariska had taken at the crash scene. She hadn't taken a good one, but with some software enhancement back at the station, he might be able to make it usable. He could only tell that the truck looked like the one he encountered the other night outside the club.

He sent an email with the photo attached to the computer expert in the police lab. If anyone in the department could enhance this photo and give him a suspect to hunt down, it'd be that guy. After sending the message, he checked his inbox. A message marked: *Urgent,* caught his eyes. Wulf opened the message.

It read:

Det. Wulf,

We have a mutual acquaintance in need of help. Dr. Mariska Stevenson is innocent and in danger. We will need to join forces to save her life. Through unofficial channels and methods, I was able to intercept a communication between the man who has been following Mariska and who I believe to be his employer. I can tell you the hitman goes by the name Gambo. His employer goes by the initials, C.H. As of right now, they have managed to cover their tracks very well. I have no further information. I'm sending you this email from a dummy account so don't reply to this message. My name is Badger and I'll be in contact as I find out more.

That makes two times this Badger person has contacted him. It was time to investigate whoever this was as well. And with things escalating quickly in the case, he'd better find out answers…and soon. Mariska's life was at risk. Thankfully she'd managed to survive the couple attempts to kill her up to this point. She was a tough woman. He sent an email to one of his buddies in the cyber-crimes division at the Bureau, asking if he'd ever heard of someone who went by Badger. It was clear to Wulf that whoever this Badger was, this wasn't the first time he'd been involved in some serious technology crimes or at the very least was being monitored by the Bureau. He closed the laptop and ran his fingers through his hair. A heaviness weighed on him, one he hadn't felt in a very long time. It was a worry about someone he cared about who was in trouble.

Something had changed. He hadn't spent much time with her, but one thing Wulf prided himself in was his ability to read people. Mariska was good. She was kind. She was genuine. For these reasons, he found himself thinking about her, more and more. Was she okay? Was she putting herself in danger? Should he stop her from risking her life? Risking it over what? A woman's remains from thousands of years ago?

It didn't make sense to him what her obsession was with the remains…although he did understand being consumed by his job. Obsessing over details. Dreaming about the cases he was working on as if his brain was solving them in his sleep. Some people said it was admirable how dedicated he was to the job, while others worried about him losing himself in it.

It hadn't always been this way. There was a time when he loved more than his career and taking bad people off the streets and making them pay for their crimes. He closed his eyes and tried to push his memories away before they got the better of him.

Too late.

A memory flash of his wife, Julia. The heaviness he was feeling a moment ago grew ten-fold. He opened his phone and scrolled through the photo albums until he found the one labeled, *Julia.* Picture after picture of them together tore his heart in half. He stopped at an image of their prom picture. He was holding her in that goofy way everyone seemed to pose back then, his arms wrapped around her from behind. High school sweethearts, inseparable.

He kept scrolling through the photos, the memories of their high school and then college graduations—purposely going to the same college, although different fields of study, so they could remain together. His heart sank even further when he stopped on the picture of her standing out front of Cedar Sinai Hospital. She was all smiles in her Nurse Practitioner's white lab coat. They had a storybook relationship…but, unlike in the stories, nothing lasted forever.

Julia's smile flashed through his mind and tore into his heart. Oh, how he'd missed her over the years.

The ever-tightening knot in his stomach pulled him out of his internal thoughts and pain. Mariska was in danger. He knew it, but couldn't yet prove it. But to save her, meant he had to solve this case before it was too late.

Wulf gulped down the last of the bitter, black coffee, and threw some money on the table. It was time to get back to work.

CHAPTER NINETEEN

Theresa and Mariska pulled into the underground parking garage for the library. Theresa's black GMC Yukon SUV barely fit into the parking space marked for full-sized vehicles. Their ride from Korea Town to downtown hadn't taken long, but it was long enough to have filled the vehicle with awkward silence.

"So, tell me," Theresa said to her.

"Tell you what?"

"You said last night you were in an accident, but then said you had to tell me the rest in person. I've been fighting the urge to ask you about it the entire ride over here."

Mariska fully intended on telling Theresa everything as soon as she saw her, but became gun shy. Who could she trust? There were just a couple people in her life she was willing to open up to, let alone put at risk by full disclosure. Surely, she couldn't talk to her parents. David and Theresa were all she had at this point.

"Long story short, I went up to see Ingrid about my grant funding as well as to garner information about the La Brea Woman. I figured she would have the most detailed accounts that I could use to study her considering the fact that the remains are missing."

"So, Ingrid smashed your car? Please tell me that's not what you're trying to say," Theresa said with an eye roll.

"I wish it was that easy. Actually, I was run off the road on Mulholland Drive."

"Oh my god," Theresa gasped. "Are you okay? Who did it and why?"

"I'm not sure who or why, but I think it was deliberate. When I finally crawled out of the car and back up the ravine to the road, I looked ahead and saw them watching. They must have been looking to see if I was alive. I took out my phone and tried to get a picture of them, but they took off before I got a good shot."

"Damn. I was worried about you. I had a gut feeling something was going on," Theresa said.

What an odd thing to say, Mariska thought. "Why would you say that?"

Theresa's expression took a shyness that Mariska hadn't seen before. "I had a pit in my stomach ever since we last talked. I sometimes get that when bad things are about to happen. Or, at least I like to think that. Anyway, it's nothing scientific…women's intuition, I suppose."

"Remember how I was going to meet up with that guy, Badger, regarding my computer?" Mariska asked.

"Yeah, what about it? Did you hear back from him?"

"I got a text on my phone at the time of the crash. It was warning me of danger." Mariska looked through her phone to show her the message. She tapped the screen and held it up for her to read.

"Wow, that's strange. I wonder how he would have known…unless…"

"Unless?" Mariska asked.

"Do you think Badger is associated with the bad guys? Whoever they are?"

Mariska thought about it for a moment. "That's a good question. I can't imagine he would have warned me if he wanted me dead. Plus he could have had me killed the night I met up with him at the rave. My god that place was crazy. No one would have heard me scream, I can tell you that."

"Maybe you should get a gun? No harm in protecting yourself." Theresa tried to offer a smile, but Mariska wasn't buying it.

"I'm not the type to use a gun. First of all, I don't know the first thing about them. I wouldn't feel safe having one until I've been trained in using it." Mariska put the phone back in her purse. "I do have *this*." She pulled out a canister of pepper spray and pointed it at Theresa.

"Hey, put that away." Theresa backed away, pushing herself up against the door. "I think you're right; you shouldn't own a gun. But think about at least getting a Taser."

"I'll think about it." Mariska put the pepper spray back into her purse. "Now, let's get going before the library closes. I'm not sure how late they stay open."

They got out of the vehicle and headed straight for the stairwell. Theresa locked the SUV remotely, with a confirming beep. Theresa reached the door to the stairwell first and pushed it up. The bang from the door echoed around them. The poorly maintained heavy metal door swung open with a screech of metal. They started up the stairs, as the door slowly closed behind them. Up to the first landing and around to the next set of stairs they continued to climb. Mariska heard the door come to close with a scraping sound, but then immediately the sound of screeching once again as it was reopened. As Mariska picked up the pace, taking two steps at a time, she stole a glance over the handrail down the flights of stairs. A black-gloved hand held onto the railing two floors below. It was moving quickly along the length of the bar moving up toward them.

"What floor do we need?" Mariska said softly.

"Fourth…right here."

They took the last two steps in one leap and opened the door leading out to ground level. The rush of fresh air hit her face and instantly dried the perspiration that'd covered her face.

Mariska looked around for the entrance to the library. It'd been years since she'd been there. In fact, the last time she visited this library location she'd been in graduate school. This library had the *Special Collections* room. Only students and faculty of universities and local institutions of higher learning and research had access to the collections. Mariska hoped her museum ID was still valid so she could get inside. There it was, just ahead. Marked *Library Entrance*, the sign was partially hidden by a tree that'd been allowed to grow freely without being pruned into a compact column.

Hurrying across the lawn toward the entrance, Mariska heard the door open from the underground parking garage. Without turning around, she pulled Theresa along by the elbow. "We should hurry."

"What's going on? Are we in danger?" Theresa's eyes went wide. She turned her head and looked behind and to both sides. "Mariska?"

"I'm just feeling a bit jumpy—I might revisit the idea of a gun. Okay, we should get inside while the library is still open."

Five more hurried steps and the two women entered the building that housed the library. Its multiple floors contained a vast array of books, offices, archival research repositories, and learning centers for people of all ages. A series of escalators brought visitors up or down to the various areas depending upon their needs. Her surroundings suddenly became familiar as a flood of memories came back from the many hours she'd spent in this building.

"Do you know where we're going?" Theresa asked.

"If they haven't rearranged things since I was here last, we need to go down two floors to the *Special Collections* area." Mariska stepped onto the first escalator and began walking downward as it moved. Theresa followed close behind. "Ingrid said that her father's things had been donated to the library. There would be no way something so old and important would be held in regular circulation. Plus, it has a direct tie to research being done in both university research, the L.A. historical society, and the Page Museum…maybe even the Los Angeles Natural History Museum."

Mariska and Theresa stepped off the final down escalator and turned left toward the entrance to the library research section. A quick glance behind them, Mariska didn't see anyone following them. The escalators were all clear. In fact, the entire library was eerily quiet this evening. She hadn't noticed before, but they were the only ones there, as far as she could tell. With a quick sigh that did little to calm her, she pushed the enter button to the library's special collections section. The door automatically swung open, and they walked inside.

The ambiance of the room instantly teleported her back in time.

The awe and wonder of this place brought her back to the college years. So many hours were spent here doing research, looking up obscure information for research papers and presentations. The heavy silence of the room calmed Mariska's nerves. Like a heavy blanket calms a child with sensory integration issues, this place immediately settled her, smoothed out the chaotic jumble of unanswered questions and problems banging around inside her mind. There were answers here, and it was time to do some real research.

Mariska and Theresa approached the information counter where the woman wearing horn-rimmed glasses with a chain that looped around her neck. Her hair was tightly permed and dyed an unnatural bright blonde. The name tag read *Peggy*. Peggy looked like a by-the-book type of gal. Mariska screwed on a stewardess smile and said, "Hello, Peggy. We're here from the Page Museum and would like to access the Special Collections archive to conduct some research. Would that be acceptable?"

"Of course," Peggy said. "I'll just need to see your library card, museum identification cards, and driver's license."

"Would a retinal scan be required today as well?" Mariska said. Security was tighter than she remembered.

Peggy turned to her and with all seriousness said, "I have been wanting to implement such a policy for the past two years. I'm glad someone else finally agrees with me."

Theresa said, "You can never be too careful these days."

They produced all the required identifications and laid them out on the counter. Peggy took each ID and ran it through a scanner that entered it into the computer. Similar to checking out a book, a person accessing the Special Collections needed to check themselves *into* the room. The computer beeped. Peggy pulled out Mariska's museum ID and reentered it into the scanner. Another series of beeps.

Peggy took the ID and placed it on the counter in front of Mariska. "Seems that the ID is registering as being invalid."

"Invalid? How could that be?"

"I'm not sure," Peggy said. "There have been a few glitches in the system these days. I mean, just the other day a woman came in here and wanted access, and her ID was rejected. Come to think of it, *she* had a Page Museum badge."

Mariska and Theresa exchanged a look. Who could it have been? Mariska couldn't think of anyone who had recently left the museum. Why else would the ID register as invalid?

"Do you remember who she was? Maybe we know her?" Mariska asked.

"Do I remember? No. But I wouldn't be Peggy Peterson-Paulson, if I didn't keep a record of it."

She rushed over to the other side of the counter and rummaged through a drawer and file folders until she found what she was looking for. "Here it is," she said pulling out a yellow folder marked *Rejects*.

Peggy flopped a photocopy of the ID in front of Theresa and Mariska. The badge photograph was Kathy, Dr. Snyder and Mariska's assistant and resident Page Museum bitch.

"Wait a second," Theresa said. "Look." She pointed to the name under the photograph.

Bethany Jacobson. Why the hell was there a fake ID with Kathy's picture and a fake name?

"Did the woman who tried to use this look like the photo?" Mariska asked.

Peggy took a closer look at the picture. "Yep, that was her. A real sarcastic little thing. I explained that her ID wasn't coming up as valid under the Museum database. The museum and library have a direct link between them. She threw a real fit. Told me that she would have my job terminated if I didn't let her in the room."

"I assume you stuck to your guns and didn't let her inside?" Mariska said.

Peggy's face revealed a woman riddled with guilt. "I've been working for the library for twenty-nine years. If I can get through one more year, I'm eligible to retire. I really need that pension to survive." Peggy clutched her blouse. "Please don't tell anyone."

Mariska turned to Theresa. "I wonder what she wanted from in there? Could she be looking for the same thing we are?"

Theresa shrugged.

"When was she here?" Mariska pointed to the photocopy.

Peggy flipped the page over and said, "It was two days ago. See," she pointed to some writing on the back. "I wrote it on here myself."

"Do you know if she checked anything out of the archives?" Mariska asked.

"Oh, no. We don't allow people to remove anything from here anymore. Too much liability. The research in there is irreplaceable." Peggy slipped the photocopy back into the reject file and put it back in the drawer. "Again, please don't tell anyone."

"Your secret is safe with us," Theresa said. "One more question…do you happen to know what she was researching inside the archives?"

"Yes," Peggy said. "That I do know. She left it a mess, and I had to put it all away. I can't believe some people. Think they own the place…"

"What was it?" Mariska asked.

"Some very old handwritten research that had been donated from a private collection, years ago."

Mariska's heart began to pound. She and Theresa exchanged worried looks. "Go on," Mariska said.

"It dated back to the early 1900s," Peggy said.

"Who donated it?" Mariska asked, holding her breath.

"The Ashton estate."

Mariska wanted to vomit. Was this going to be another dead end? What the hell was going on?

"We need to see what she was researching for ourselves," Mariska said.

"I'm sorry, you can't go in there." Peggy shook her head. "Your ID doesn't work."

"Is there any way you can make an exception for me…just this once?" Mariska smiled and put her hands together like she was praying to the older woman. She looked behind the woman and noticed a donation sign with a sad-looking dog on the front of it. *Save Homeless Pets*—a great cause for sure. "I'll tell you what. I see you're doing a fundraiser for that charity back there." Peggy turned her head for a moment and then nodded. "I'm assuming you get credit for anyone you get to donate to the cause?" Again, Peggy nodded. "Great. I'll make a thousand-dollar donation right now if that'll make my ID work?"

Peggy stepped back, eyes widening. "That'd push me into the lead for sure."

"Well, that settles it then. Can I use my credit card?"

"There'll be a three percent fee incurred." Peggy pulled out the credit card machine and placed it on the counter. "I don't like rich people coming in here thinking they can get special treatment, but," she glanced back at the donation can for a moment. "This'll be the first time I've won it since I started working here."

"I'd say you're way overdue for a win, Peggy." She pulled out her Visa and put in the chip. "Make it twelve hundred."

Peggy punched in the numbers, and the receipt started printing. "I'll buzz you in," Peggy said, a hint of guilt passing over her face. She picked up Mariska's ID again and studied it. "Please don't stay long."

"Thank you," Mariska said. She and Theresa walked over to the entrance to the archival room and waited for the buzzing noise and then pulled the door open.

"I wouldn't have taken Peggy for someone who could be bought like that," Theresa said.

"The important thing is, we're in. So let's get a move on before she kicks us out."

They looked for the year 1914 and found the drawer marked 1900-1950. Mariska pulled the open the drawer. Inside, a series of large hanging folders that contained research from various scientists of the area. It didn't take long to find the folder marked: Ashton. Mariska carefully removed the hanging folder and brought it over to the large examination table located at the center of the room. Flipping on the overhead lamp, she opened the file. There was a pile of notebooks, loose photographs, hand-drawn schematics, and various images of the tar pits.

"So, what are we looking for here?" Theresa asked.

"Honestly, I'm not one hundred percent sure. We need to find anything that's related to La Brea Woman, specifically. Maybe something that hasn't been published on the woman or any controversial issues surrounding her at the time the documents were written."

Theresa and Mariska combed through the stack of papers. When they heard, the door click open behind them. Mariska turned and saw Peggy standing in the doorway.

"Can I help you?" Mariska asked.

"I…hate to tell you, but we will be closing soon," Peggy said, backing slowly out of the doorway.

Mariska turned to Theresa. "We should hurry. Anything that looks interesting or useful, take a picture with your phone. We can compile the photographs later."

"Good idea. I can even print them out at the museum so we can easily examine them. Enlarge or enhance them as needed." Theresa pulled out her cell phone and started to snap photographs.

Every page Mariska turned, there appeared to be information that could prove important. There wasn't time to really read everything to determine if it was something previously unrecorded or not. She found herself taking pictures of everything. She suspected Theresa was doing the same thing as she too took an unknown number of images. That's when Mariska turned the page of a handwritten notebook that Ingrid's father had recorded in 1914. An image that looked almost identical to the picture she'd seen at Ingrid's home. The picture showed Ingrid's father, grandfather, and Mr. Page standing together, they were all grinning from ear to ear.

She turned the page. It was a drawing of the second photograph she'd seen at Ingrid's. It was of the pit where La Brea Woman had been found. This drawing showed Ingrid's father standing next to the pit with the remains at the bottom of the pit. The young Native American man stood in the background with an angry expression.

She turned the page again. Could this have been what the smeared photograph was depicting? Ingrid's father stood next to the remains of La Brea Woman. Next to his foot was her skull. But there was something doodled next to it. Squares and a triangle? With a question mark next to them? She took a photograph of all three pages with her phone.

"Time's up, ladies," Peggy said as she barged into the room. "Pack this up. If you need anything else, you'll have to come back at a later date. And please have a valid ID with you next time." She gave Mariska a wink and whispered, "Thanks again for your donation."

"And thank you for all your help," Theresa said to Peggy. "We were able to get what we needed."

Peggy stood in the doorway as they put all the repository materials back into their proper storage area and left the room. They walked straight for the exit but stopped short of leaving as Peggy had one last statement to make.

"I don't know what you ladies are up to, exactly, but if I were you, I'd pick better friends."

"Excuse me?" Mariska said. "What are you talking about?"

"There was a man in here looking for the two of you. I mean, he didn't ask for you by name, but it was clear you were who he was looking for."

"Did he say who he was and why he was looking for us?" Mariska asked as she turned to Theresa. A worried expression began to form on Theresa's face, and Mariska felt a pit growing in her stomach.

"Nope. But then again, I didn't ask him. One thing I've learned in my twenty-nine years working in the heart of a big, scary city like Los Angeles, is the fewer specifics you know and the fewer questions you ask…the better."

Mariska felt sick. Worried for herself and for Theresa. Was the man now stalking her? How else would he know to find her at the library?

They said their goodbyes to Peggy and ran back to Theresa's SUV. Out of breath, scared, and with her imagination racing out of control, they reached the vehicle. Jumping into the front seats, Theresa started it and quickly pulled out of the parking space. Driving a bit too fast for the cramped spaces of the parking garage, Theresa suddenly slammed on her brakes. They lurched to a stop, seatbelts tightening around Mariska in a painful constriction she'd felt the day before.

"What's wrong?" Mariska asked.

"Look," Theresa said, pointing to the back. "I just noticed. Someone broke out the window."

Mariska's belly tightened, and her heart raced. "Get us out of here, now."

Theresa squealed the tires as they reemerged at street level, not slowing to merge into traffic.

CHAPTER TWENTY

Mariska waved goodbye to Theresa and watched her leave from the safety of the metal staircase while she pulled away. She turned away and climbed the remaining steps to the top landing. That's where she froze. The brand new, heavily reinforced metal door, was dented inward around the handle. She looked behind her, hoping Theresa was still within sight, but no luck.

She reached for the doorknob and squeezed, but didn't try to turn it. Her heart began to race, and her belly felt queasy. Should she check to see if it was still locked or call someone for help? Indecision plagued her. She looked back toward the street, again. It was dark and quiet, deserted by Los Angels' standards. There was no one around that would be offering to help her. With every ounce of care in her body, she turned the doorknob. It moved freely. Bending down to look at the lock, she saw that the wall around the door had been damaged. Splintered wood and scrape marks told the tale. Someone had used a crowbar to break the lock and pry the door open.

Mariska opened her purse and felt around for her cell phone. She could call David, her parents, or even Theresa to come back and go inside with her. No, she couldn't put the people she cared about in danger, simply because she didn't want to keep involving the cops. She placed the call to the police.

"9-1-1, state the nature of your emergency."

"I think my apartment's been broken into," Mariska said, her voice barely above a whisper.

"You're inside your apartment, and you heard someone break in? Is that right, ma'am?"

"No, I'm standing outside. When I got to the door, it was pried open."

"What is your name and address, ma'am?"

"Mariska Stevenson. 5116 and a half Wilshire Boulevard. My apartment's above the grocery store, Seoul Foods. Please hurry, and let the officers know that they have to access it through the alley behind the store."

"The police have been dispatched. They should be there shortly. You should leave immediately. Do you have a safe place to wait for them?" The woman's voice was trained. This wasn't her first rodeo.

Mariska looked around the alley. *Not really*, she thought. "I can wait behind the dumpster in the alley."

No response.

"Hello?" Mariska said. "Hello?"

Nothing.

She looked at the phone. The screen was black. The phone was dead.

"Fuck." Mariska threw the phone back into her purse.

She started down the stairs to wait in the alley when she suddenly stopped. Her artifacts. Could someone have broken into her apartment to steal the last remaining bit of the La Brea Woman and the only possible lead she had to find her remains? Mariska looked back up the staircase. What other choice did she have? Pushing down her natural desire for self-preservation, she took the steps back up, two-by-two.

Crouching low, she turned the knob and pushed the door open. A few inches at first, and then a few more. The apartment was dark inside. Even popping her head inside, to peer around the corner, she couldn't see any further than a few feet. The ambient light from the street lamps did little to help since she kept her blinds closed most of the time.

The idea of losing the last remaining vestiges of her life's obsession, steeled her resolve as well as her shaky legs.

Acknowledging the fact that she was nuts for even thinking about going inside, she knew she had to protect the artifacts. She entered the apartment that suddenly felt foreign to her. She could have walked from room to room with her eyes, closed, but the idea of someone possibly lurking inside made her feel unsure of herself. Unsure of her decision. But she persevered. One foot in front of the other, ever mindful to make herself small, keep to the shadows, and remain silent.

Mariska crept past the oven when she stopped. Three more feet and she would step onto squeaky floorboards. Behind her on the kitchen counter was a heavy meat tenderizer. She grabbed it and tested how it felt in her hand. She'd smacked a few steaks and chicken breasts with it, but would it be heavy enough to tenderize someone's skull? It would have to do, for now. She crept forward. Her toe touched the spot on the floor she knew would squeak. Not a loud noise, but in this situation, it might as well have been a jet plane landing in her kitchen.

Squeak.

Tightening her grip on the weapon, she held it up above her and ran headlong into the apartment. Turning the corner from the kitchen, past the apartment's bisecting hallway, and into the living room, she ran. Her mother had often encouraged her to stash weapons around the home—just in case. Thank God her mom grew up in Harlem and was as street-wise as they come. Two more feet and…

Someone collided with her from the side, sending her sprawling across the living room floor. The left half of her body bouncing off the sofa, she rolled with the fall, the weapon flying from her hand. Whoever hit her was like a truck. She hadn't had a chance. The living room was nearly pitch black, and she couldn't see where the meat-tenderizer landed. The only visible light came from the digital time display on her cable-box. Looming above her was the intruder. A seemingly inhuman-sized man, bathed in darkness. His immense form slowly moved closer.

Crab-crawling backward, she dove like an Olympic backstroke

swimmer. Her hand sliding under the far side of the sofa where she'd stashed a telescoping metal baton. With no time to think, she extended the length with a quick jerk and swung it at the attacker. He must have seen the glint of LED light on the black metal because he stopped his advance. She swung it again and again, screaming, "Get the fuck away from me."

Blinking back sweat and shadows, she saw the shadowy hulk of a man begin to move away from her. His footsteps, heavy and solid against the hardwood floor. A few seconds passed, and she heard the kitchen floor squeak and then the front door. He'd gone. She collapsed back against the floor and breathed hard, and fought back tears.

After a few moments, the realization kicked in: she was alive, but the artifacts might still have been stolen. A new wave of adrenaline entered her bloodstream, and she found the strength and motivation to get up from the floor. Flipping on the living room lights, the room was bathed in the soft white light of energy efficient bulbs. The sofa cushions were scattered across the floor, the stuffing pulled from them and lay in a myriad of small white piles. The leather recliner was flipped onto its side, table lamps toppled and in various levels of destruction. The Tiffany lamp her mom had given to her for her birthday sat on its side next to the end table. The multicolored glass shade was in pieces, and the cord had been pulled from its base.

Mariska turned in a quick circle. There was almost nothing in the room that hadn't been either destroyed or at the very least moved from its original position. Despite the loss of security and things, what she needed was to know about the artifacts. Baton in hand, she stepped over the debris and hurried into her bedroom. Nothing in there had been spared destruction. Her mattress now sat against the far wall, the underside slit open like a gutted animal. The mattress material protruded from the gash like the entrails that had yet to be cut away.

Her bookcases had been pulled from the walls and now overlapped each other in the middle of the room. Books, knickknacks, and framed pictures had been strewn about the room in a violent attempt to find something in a hurry. Where were her treasures? Sifting through piles of items on the floor, she located the decorative box that held the beads. Mariska reached down and picked it up. The top was missing. She took a closer look and saw that it looked like it'd been torn from the bottom as if the person who removed it didn't know the trick to opening it. The edges had damage, and the side was dented.

Mariska looked inside the box; it was empty. She pulled out the small red cloth that lined the bottom and gasped. The small blue bead had been missed. The intruder had either been in too big of a hurry or had been interrupted in his thieving; he missed it. Without a second thought, she shoved the small, blue, cube-shaped bead into her front pocket and started looking for the geode that hid the unidentified tooth. Up against the large front window of the room, the hide-a-key geode sat atop the long short bookcase, untouched. The intruder had definitely been interrupted. The entire room was in shambles, but this one spot. High-stepping over the mess in the room, Mariska reached the geode in two steps.

Placing the baton on the top of the bookcase, she peeled back the false bottom of the stone hiding place. The woven pouch that held the tooth fell into the palm of her hand with the satisfying heaviness she'd remembered and let out a deep sigh of relief. She removed the tooth from the pouch and brought it up close, to get a better look. She rubbed her fingers along the undamaged length of it. She hadn't lost it all, but she'd lost so much. What was next? What was left to lose? Tears welled up in her eyes and threatened to roll, but she held her breath and swallowed hard. Fighting the involuntary wracks of her body as the sobs of pain, fear, and frustration threatened to undo her. From childhood, she'd hated to cry. Often preferring to be alone where no one could see her lose that control of emotion, control of herself. She released the breath and kissed the tooth.

An unexpected thud from the front of her apartment jolted her back into control. This wasn't yet over, and she would fight to the end. She shoved the pouch and tooth into her pocket and grabbed for the weapon. Securing a tight grip on the handle, she swung it around to charge out of the bedroom.

"Police. Drop it," a female voice commanded from the doorway. A bright flashlight shown into her eyes, obscuring her sight. Was this a trick? The memory of calling the police before entering the apartment made a sudden return.

Mariska's first instinct was to raise both arms straight over her head. She blinked and squinted as she turned her head away from the incessant bright light.

"Drop it," the officer commanded once again.

Arms stretched high above her head, she released the weapon as she'd been told. It struck the floor next to her foot with a solid thud. The officer holding the flashlight stepped toward her, and as she did, Mariska could see it wasn't just a flashlight pointed at her.

The officer held a gun in one hand, the flashlight in the other. The two objects coming together in a show of force in front of the officer.

"Put your hands behind your head and take a step back," the officer said. "Now, get on your knees. Keep your hands behind your head."

Mariska did as she was told.

A second officer, one she hadn't seen, approached from the right. He picked up the baton with a latex-gloved hand and handed it back to whoever was standing in the doorway. The lights in her face continued to obscure her vision.

Mariska felt a strong hand close around her right wrist, and then the left. Her hands were quickly forced down behind the small of her back. Without a word, the officer clapped a set of cold, metallic handcuffs on her and shoved her face down onto the floor.

"Wait," Mariska said. "I'm…I'm the victim, here. I called you." She started struggling against the restraints. A familiar sensation began to surge through her body as the claustrophobia set in. It started with a tingling in her face and chest, followed by rapid breaths, and profuse sweating.

Panic.

"Be quiet," the officer said to her and then addressed one of the others, "She's secured."

"I called you for help." Mariska felt a knee in her back, and a hand pressed firmly against her head. She closed her eyes and retreated within herself. *I need my mom*, she thought.

CHAPTER TWENTY-ONE

Detective Wulf sat across the desk from Mariska. His cool, blue eyes, studied her like he was going to have to draw her from memory. She would have thought the police station would have been a little more subdued at this hour, but it was clear law and order was a twenty-four-hour a day operation. A woman screamed as she entered the room. Mariska was the only one who turned to look as the woman wearing a scant green dress with hooker-heels and fishnet stockings was shown to a seat against the far wall. The officer who led her there removed the handcuffs as she sat. Mariska couldn't help but notice the woman's makeup was smeared across her face, lipstick smudged half way up her cheek, and the eyeliner was definitely not water resistant. Her bloodshot raccoon eyes, torn stockings, and mussed hair told a story.

"Mariska?" Detective Wulf said. "Are you okay?"

She looked back at him and then to the woman again. Mariska started feeling sorry for the woman. She'd clearly been through hell tonight. No one deserved to be mistreated, but…the woman kicked at the officer standing guard over her. He took a step back, but not in time to avoid the loogie she spat on him. Mariska looked away before she puked.

"Sorry, I was distracted," Mariska said, motioning to the scene quickly deteriorating at the far end of the room. The detective's expression remained one of concern. "I'm fine, really."

He smiled and leaned back in his chair, stretching his back, and then sat forward again. "It's been a long day."

"Yeah, tell me about it."

"First of all, I wanted to thank you for coming down to the police station," he said. "I know you didn't have to. I mean, you weren't under arrest."

"Wasn't I? I seem to remember being slammed to the ground and put in handcuffs."

He cleared his throat and addressed her in a tone adults used when explaining things to a child. "You reported a break-in and then hung up. How were the officers to know you weren't the one breaking into the residence? Why the hell did you go inside in the first place?"

She couldn't have agreed more but hated his tone. Glaring, she said, "Whatever you say. Now, the *non-arresting* officer said you requested I come down to the station. You know, while he was dragging me to my feet."

"He was helping you to your feet." This time his tone was markedly different—kind, caring. His eyes were soft around the edges and his brow furrowed with worry.

"I guess they were doing their jobs." She shrugged and let out a deep sigh. "I'm tired."

He nodded and reached across the desk and put a calming hand on hers. "You've had a rough night."

She nodded. "Please tell me you have something important to share with me? Or did you just want to see me again?" Their eyes locked for an intense moment sending butterflies fluttering in her belly when he didn't look away. She slid her hand out from under his and ran it through her mussed hair.

She made a grand gesture of looking around the room, pausing to watch the woman being subdued on the floor against the far wall, screaming and kicking. The woman had the officer's pant leg in her mouth, and she didn't appear to want to let go of it. Turning back to Detective Wulf, Mariska arched her eyebrows and tilted her head slightly to the side. "A coffee shop would have been better atmosphere for a first date…if you were going for that sort of thing." She smiled behind her hand and looked away.

"You're sassy this time of night," Wulf said. "We need to take your report. Not to mention, I have been researching the SUV that ran you off Mulholland Drive."

"Oh?" Mariska sat up a little straighter in the chair. "Do you have a lead?"

"Sort of. We had a couple leads, but they haven't panned out yet. I took the image of the vehicle you took with your cell phone. I copied it to a digital enhancement program and sent it over to the CSI team. Even after being tweaked, enlarged, and ran through a predictive program that fills in the grainy portions of the image, it still isn't NASA quality by any means."

"But…" Mariska started to say.

"But we were able to determine the make and model of the SUV."

"That's great." She waited for him to say something more, but he didn't. "Isn't it good?"

"It's not a smoking gun if that's what you're asking." He sat back in the chair and rubbed his brow. "There are virtually thousands of vehicles registered locally that meet that description, let alone in the surrounding area. At this point, there wasn't much to narrow down the search."

"So, what you're saying is, we have absolutely nothing." Mariska crossed her arms and looked away. "Great."

"I do have these." Wulf flopped a large book onto the desk in front of her.

"What the hell is that?"

"Mug shots." He sat back in the chair, resting his hands behind his head. "I compiled them based on some scumbag assholes that have committed similar crimes and are currently at large."

Mariska sat up straight and leaned in to take a better look. She opened the book of photos. She was immediately struck by the gravity of the situation. Here she was, the daughter of a rich and powerful family, and yet sat in the police station in the middle of the night flipping through a book of mug shots. God, how grateful she was her parents weren't there to witness this.

"Take a good look at these guys," Wulf said. "I'm curious if anyone's familiar to you."

"Why would they? I didn't get a good look at the people that ran me off the road—and like I told the officers at my apartment, it was too dark to make out a face. All I know was the guy was big. Really big." Mariska flipped the page to the next set of photographs. It seemed like each subsequent page, the men got scarier and meaner looking.

"I know that. But it's possible one of these guys will jump out at you. Maybe, you crossed paths at the grocery store, coffee shop, or on a tour at the museum?"

She shot him a skeptical look.

"Hey, anything is possible." He put his hands up in defense. "I've seen a case solved when the victim identified the bad guy from one of these books. He just so happened to be the man that jogged past her house every day when she left for work."

"Really?" Mariska said.

"Really."

She continued to flip through each page, scrutinizing each image. She even occasionally closed her eyes to try and picture where she might have seen some of these goons. Nothing stood out to her. Mariska turned the last page and sat back in the chair. "I'm really sorry."

"Don't be sorry. I figured it was worth a try. No harm, no foul, right?"

"I guess." She ran her fingers through her disheveled hair, smoothing it out. "I wish I could be of more help. Things seem to be getting worse. Theresa and I were followed."

"Theresa?"

"My student intern at the museum."

Wulf nodded. "I haven't had time to read the full report. Please, go on."

"I asked Theresa to take me to the library this evening to do a little research on the La Brea Woman. When we were getting ready to leave, the librarian said a man came in looking for two women that met our description."

"Did you see this man?"

"No, Peggy told him we weren't there. She must have thought it strange that he was looking for us."

"Peggy?" Wulf sat up and started looking something up in the computer.

"Oh, yeah. She's the librarian. Sorry, I get ahead of myself sometimes when I'm telling a story."

"No, it's not that." He continued to type and sporadically use the mouse to navigate whatever he was operating on the computer. "Peggy Peterson-Paulson?"

"That sounds right."

"*Was*...what her last name *was*." Wulf cleared his throat and sat back in the chair. "Peggy Peterson-Paulson, fifty-nine-year-old Caucasian female, brown hair, and brown eyes?"

"Yes?" Mariska's heart began to race. "What's going on?"

"She was found dead tonight in the parking garage at the L.A. City Library."

"Dead?"

"Murdered would be my guess. Even though it can't be ruled as anything other than suspicious until the coroner determines cause of death. But by the look of that ligature mark around her neck, I'd say she was murdered."

Mariska reached for the computer monitor to angle it toward her so she could see the image he was referring to. Wulf was just quick enough to prevent it. "You don't want to see that. Trust me."

She stood, wanted to yell. Wanted to run away. The room seemed to close in, but at the same time spin out of control. Mariska clutched at her chest. Why couldn't she breathe? She took a step but started to stumble forward.

"Oh shit," Wulf said, jumping up from the desk. "Here, have a seat. I'll get you some water." He held her by both arms and assisted her back into the chair. A few seconds later he returned with a paper cup filled with cold water.

She took a sip and handed back the cup. Leaning forward, she brought her head down into her hands. Breathe in, breath out, and repeat. When she opened her eyes, she was relieved to see it had stopped spinning.

Wulf, squatted low beside her chair. She turned to face him. His expression was full of compassion and kindness. His brow was furrowed and his eyes, soft with concern. All she really wanted was a hug. Mariska closed her eyes for a moment. A sudden familiarity struck her. Did she know this man from somewhere? When she reopened her eyes, the feeling vanished.

"Mariska…Mariska," her mother, rushed to her side and immediately wrapped her in an embrace. "Are you, all right, baby? Look at me, honey."

Leah had Mariska's face in her hands, and she kissed her daughter on the forehead.

"Mom, what are you doing here? Where's Dad?"

"I'm here," Robert said.

Mariska turned and saw her father. He stood with his arms crossed. His face pinched with emotion.

"I called them," Wulf said.

She glared at him, "Why would you do that?"

"I asked him to," Robert said as he stepped up alongside his wife.

Mariska stood and gave her dad a hug. His strong arms wrapped around her in a protective shield that she sometimes wished would last forever.

"Your dad asked me to contact him if I ever hear of an incident…you know, involving you." Wulf stepped around the desk and offered a handshake to both of her parents. By the way her mom took his hand into both of hers, Mariska could tell how much it meant to them. Knowing they had someone on the *inside*, keeping an eye on their daughter.

Robert took her by the elbow and led her away from where her mother was talking with the detective. He squared up with her, looked into her eyes, and said, "What are you doing?"

"What do you mean?" Mariska said.

"Are you pursuing this…this, insane notion that you have to

solve this crime? That you have to find the La Brea Woman?"

"Insane?" Mariska took a step back. "How dare—"

"No," Robert said, his voice harsh and breathy. He stepped closer. "How dare you? How dare you put your mother, and me for that matter, through this?"

"I'm not doing any of this to you on purpose." Where the hell was this coming from? She was the one attacked and nearly killed…more than once. She took a deep breath. "I understand you're upset."

"You're damn right I'm upset. My only daughter, the little girl who we cherished from the moment we set eyes on her, is putting herself in danger. And, for what? For some stupid bones that no one really cares about? No one even knows anything about her. Not really." He shook his head and looked away.

His words struck her as hard as a punch to the face. Tears welled up in her eyes, but she refused to let them fall. She cleared her throat. The emotion threatened to take control of her words, and she fought hard to reign it in. "Kind of like me."

"Excuse me?" His hard expression softened and then turned to concern as his own words sank in.

"No one cared about me, either. Thrown away like a piece of trash in the parking lot." She pulled her hand away when he tried to reach for her. "I wonder if my mom felt a sense of relief. Squatting behind the dumpster like a dog, pushing me out of her onto the cold concrete floor. I'm surprised she even bothered to throw me away. Why not just leave me there? Didn't want to litter?"

"Mariska," Robert said and grabbed her up into an embrace. "She wasn't your mom. Your mom is the one standing over there worried sick about you. She cries herself to sleep at night, thinking that you're in danger…that you might not be…" His words trailed off for a moment. He pulled her way to look her in the eyes. "I don't know how much more she can take of this. I'm sorry for what I said before, but truth be told, there is some truth to it. You mean more to us than the La Brea Woman."

"I know," Mariska said. "And, please believe me when I say that

I am so sorry that I have upset you both. I don't want to hurt either of you."

There was a moment of silence between them. "Your mother and I will support you in any way we can. But we won't help you get killed."

"What exactly are you saying?"

"I'm saying, that your mother and I love you very much. But I have to look out for your mom's best interests as well. I won't allow you to hurt her. I won't allow you to put yourself in more danger."

Mariska's anger began to grow. "Allow? I'm not one of your gardeners."

"Indeed." He turned to walk back to his wife and the detective. "Just be careful, Mariska."

She followed him. Leah turned to them, searching their faces for any indication of what transpired in their private conversation. Mariska saw her father's face take on the CEO façade. "Everything is good here," he said, taking Leah's hand in his.

Leah looked at Mariska for confirmation. Mariska nodded with a smile. They hugged, and soon her father joined the family embrace.

"The nice detective filled me in on what happened to your apartment," Leah said.

Mariska nodded, "Yeah, it's a total mess. But it's nothing that can't be fixed."

"Nonsense," Leah said. "We'll hire a cleaning company. I'll have them remove all the broken things, and you and I will go shopping for new. All, new."

"I don't need all that. Maybe a nice cleanup and then we can go shopping for some new things for you and Dad?"

"Honey, didn't you already get Mariska some new bedroom things?" Robert said.

"I did." She smiled. "I'm going to have Jane bring some of them over in a couple days. Let's get that mess cleaned up first."

Robert offered the detective another handshake. "I want to thank you again for all your help."

"Any time." Wulf nodded.

"If there isn't anything else, I think we'll take our daughter home," Robert said.

Wulf shook his head. "Nothing more tonight."

"If it's all right with you guys, Detective Wulf offered to take me home," Mariska said, giving him a knowing look.

Wulf looked from her to Robert and Leah, and then back to Mariska.

"Plus, he says he wanted to check out the apartment one last time when he drops me off. You know, make sure there aren't any bad guys or monsters hiding under the bed." Mariska gave Wulf a friendly slug to the arm.

"Is that right, detective?" Leah asked.

"You bet. I'll make sure the apartment is secure before I leave."

Despite the flippant way she'd made the suggestion, it would put her more at ease to have him make a sweep of the apartment before leaving. She gave her parents a hug goodbye and followed the detective to his vehicle. It too was a large dark colored SUV. Did everyone in this city drive a gas guzzling vehicle similar to the guy trying to kill her?

CHAPTER TWENTY-TWO

After an off-handed comment about on the ride home about pancakes, Mariska found herself sitting in an all-night diner. The *Greasy Spoon*, or something…maybe *Greasy Floor* would have been more accurate, although far less appetizing. The torn vinyl seats, graffiti-covered tables, and less-than-clean silverware accentuated the absurdity of the establishment.

"This is the best place you could come up with?" Mariska asked.

Wulf feigned hurt feelings and tucked the paper napkin into his shirt. "What? This place is awesome."

"Awesome?"

"Oh, you're too snobby to appreciate a place like this," Wulf said. "I see things never change." He smiled but looked away.

Snobby? What the hell was he talking about? Again, a sense of familiarity struck her. His gaze settled on her and she felt her tummy flip-flop. The little butterflies inside her were getting excited, despite the fact she didn't want them to. "And for the record, I'm not snobby. I just prefer to eat at places I'm not going to catch an intestinal parasite."

He laughed. "We've already ordered coffee."

"Okay, we can stay, but I'm not sure I want to order anything to eat."

"I'll tell you what. I'll order some pancakes. We can split them. If you don't like them…I can finish the entire plate." He patted his stomach. She heard the rock-hard thump of tight abdominal muscle. Didn't see the slightest bit of jiggle. And found herself wondering what was underneath his shirt.

She felt his eyes upon her once again. Face flushed and hot, she tore her attention away from his midsection. "So, tell me, what got you into law enforcement?"

"Long story, short…my dad was a cop, his dad was a cop. I kind of always felt like I was destined to become one too."

"That's great. I bet your family is very proud of you."

He didn't say anything for a while. He took a sip of coffee and put the mug down on the table. "My mom hates me being a cop. My dad, he's dead. Killed on the job."

"Oh my god. I'm so sorry. I had no idea." Mariska reached for his hand but pulled back almost immediately. Tucking her hands into her lap, she fidgeted with her shirt. "I didn't mean to bring up painful family memories. I really am sorry."

"Don't be," he said.

The waitress came by and refilled his coffee. Enough of a distraction to allow her to change the subject. Hopefully, to something more pleasant. When the woman walked away, Mariska was about to say something, but Wulf started to slide out from behind the booth.

"Gonna hit the head." He stood went toward the back of the diner.

Mariska leaned forward, resting her head on her arms, and closed her eyes. No sooner did she do this when she felt the table rock gently as he sat back down opposite her.

"That was quick," she said as she lifted her head.

Sitting across from her was not Wulf. It was a very large man, white, dark hair, brown eyes, and a five-o'clock shadow. His shoulders were wide and well-muscled, and his jaw was set, angry…no, determined.

Her initial surprise turned to fear as she realized, this man could have been the intruder in her apartment. While she hadn't seen his face, this guy's build was similar. Huge. She tried to slide out of the booth, but the man's hand clamped down on her wrist and squeezed. Hard. Mariska pulled but didn't even budge him. He squeezed harder, and her hand started to pulse with the pressure of the trapped blood, his fingers a virtual tourniquet.

She tried to stand, as she continued to struggle. Looking around the diner, she realized the place was deserted. Where the hell was Wulf? She took in a large breath, prepared to scream when he said, "Shut your fucking mouth." He squeezed even harder. How was that even possible? The pain in her wrist grew exponentially. Fingers going numb, but wrist bones moving under the pressure of his grasp sent shooting pains up her arm.

Her breathing grew rapid under the pain. "What do you want from me?"

"I've come to collect." His voice was deep and menacing. The man's eyes narrowed and bored holes through her. The intensity scared her. This man wasn't angry. He wasn't emotionally invested in what he was doing to her. What truly scared her was she could see in his eyes her life didn't matter. What happened to her, meant absolutely nothing to him.

"I don't know what you're talking about." He twisted her wrist down and to the right. A whole new level of pain. Mariska knew bones, and she could see them breaking inside her. He could snap her in two. He was going to snap her in two.

He leaned in closer, and she could smell the tobacco on his breath. The sweetness of a cigar, but the stale stench of old coffee and decay. Is that what a dead soul smelled like? He breathed out his words with a hint of a growl. "You have something that doesn't belong to you. Give it to me, or I'll start taking. And you won't like what I take."

"I swear to you. I don't know what you're talking about." Mariska wanted to plead with the man. Beg him just to leave her alone. How could he even know about the tooth and bead, if that's what he came for? She'd found it. She'd been alone. "Please…"

He glanced over her shoulder and back. "Close your eyes and put your head down, now."

She did as she was told. How was this man so brazen to do this while there's a cop in the building? He's either really stupid, or he doesn't care if he got caught…but why? The smell of his breath seeped into her nose once again, but it was his words that made her feel sick. "You had your chance, bitch." And then with a sick, childlike voice, he whispered, "It's going to hurt. I promise you. It's going to hurt."

The table jiggled as he slid out from behind the booth. Her stomach threatened to purge, but there hadn't been anything in it.

"Are you tired? We can get going if you want." The table jiggled again as Wulf sat across from her.

She looked up but didn't speak. Mariska sat up tall and craned her neck as she searched the diner. Her breathing continued to be quick, and the sweat that had formed over her body began to trickle down her back and along her hairline.

"Are you okay?" Wulf asked. "What happened?" He looked down at her hands. "Oh my god. Your wrist…"

Her wrist was discolored. The distinguishing marks of fingers were growing darker by the second, and the swelling in her hand made her fingers feel like stuffed sausages. Mariska pulled her hand in close to her body, cradling it like a delicate puppy.

Wulf stood next to the booth, scanning the diner. "Mariska, tell me what happened. Who hurt you?" He didn't look at her but continued to look around the restaurant.

"I…I think it was the guy that broke into my apartment," she said, her voice thick and raw.

"Quick, tell me what he looked like." He paused. "Mariska. Hurry. What was he wearing?"

"Umm, I'm not sure. He was so big. Dark hair. White guy. Umm. Black leather jacket…maybe?" She shook her head. "I'm not sure."

"Stay here. I'll call for backup." He thumbed a number into his phone and hurried outside into the parking lot.

Mariska looked around the diner, feeling very alone and scared. No one saw the guy come in or leave and here she was sitting alone, again. Searching the table and surrounding booths for some means of protection, the butter knife on the table drew her attention. She picked it up and palmed it. Holding it like a dagger, she slid out from behind the booth and went to the far back corner of the main dining area. Sitting on the floor with her back against the wall, she tried to make herself invisible. A fake potted tree and chair stood between her and whatever dangers were hiding there.

"Mariska?" Wulf said as he entered the diner. She watched him as he hurried back to where they'd been sitting. She didn't make a sound. He rounded the corner, his expression focused, but concerned. "Mariska?"

He spotted her. A few hurried steps, and he was there, bent down on one knee. He slid the tree and chair out of the way and said, "You're safe now."

"I didn't hear any gunshots. So, I'm guessing you didn't get him. How again am I safe?" She started to push herself up from the floor, but Wulf helped her stand.

"He got away, this time."

Mariska brushed herself clean and swallowed hard. It was time to pull herself together. "I gathered that. Please take me home; I need to get some rest."

"Let me make a call." Wulf pulled out his phone. "I can bring you to your parents' house. You'll be safer there."

She put a hand on his arm and pushed it down, pulling the phone away from his ear. "No, take me home. And don't you dare call my parents."

The look on her face must have told him how serious she was because he put the phone away and took her arm in his. Wulf lead her out of the restaurant and to his SUV. Opening the door, he waited for her to get inside and closed the door. She heard him get in the driver's side but didn't look over at him, preferring to stare out the window.

In silence, they made their way through the ever-busy streets of Los Angeles. But at that hour it didn't take long to reach her apartment. She'd waited on the landing for him to make the initial sweep of the inside and then followed him inside. He led her through the kitchen, living room, and back into her bedroom, flipping on all the lights along the way. Despite the disaster of overturned furniture and broken things, she preferred to be home, rather than anywhere else.

"Do you have a piece of paper?" Wulf asked. "And a pencil?"

Now, what? She thought. "Sure, in the kitchen."

He went and sat at the kitchen table while Mariska retrieved the items he'd requested.

When she reentered the room, Wulf was hanging up his cellphone. "Here." She placed them in front of him and sat in the chair across the table. "What do you need them for?"

"I was hoping you could give me a description of the guy who attacked you."

"I don't know what else to tell you."

"Okay, I'll ask you about each one of his facial features. I find it helps if you close your eyes and think hard. Place yourself back at the diner and really try and see it in your mind," he said.

It was worth a try. "Are you planning on drawing it?"

"Yes, I'm going to try, anyway." He put the pencil to the paper. "I called the station, but there weren't any artists available. Technically, I've passed all the training needed to do it myself, but I prefer the allure of detective work to sitting at a desk with paper and pencil. Anyway, whatever I draw is considered official so why not give it a go?"

"I never really thought of cops being artists. Where did you learn to draw?"

"School. High school, mostly." He smiled. "I had a good teacher."

"I guess we do have something in common. I loved my high school art teacher."

"Small world," he said. "Okay, if you're ready, let's get started."

Mariska closed her eyes and answered all of his questions. As she thought about the man, she started to see details of his face. The three pockmarks on his left cheek. The cleft chin, uni-brow, and the lopsided jawline. It had to have been broken and poorly set. She recalled his smoker's teeth and blood-starved greyish gums. His breath.

"Unfortunately, the sketch isn't a scratch and sniff," Wulf said. "You can open your eyes."

Mariska looked at the picture and sat back for a moment. "That's him. That's the asshole." She gently massaged her bruised wrist and flexed her swollen fingers. "Damn, you're good."

He smiled, "So I've been told."

His eyes twinkled, and she looked away. A moment later she yawned and looked at the clock above the stove.

"It's getting late," he said. "I should let you get some sleep."

They stood from the table and faced each other. She looked around the brightly lit apartment and felt a chill.

"I've never been afraid in my own home before." She took a tentative step toward him.

"You've been through a lot." He moved in her direction and rested a hand on her shoulder. "I'd be more worried about your mental state if none of this bothered you."

She reached up and took his hand in hers. "Would you spend the night here…tonight?"

His expression didn't change, but he didn't answer right away. She was about to laugh away her invitation when he said, "Sure…if you want me too." His voice was a bit more strained than what it had been a few moments ago. He moved ever closer to her as she could feel the heat emanating from him. Looking up into his kind eyes made her belly flutter. His lips parted as if inviting her in for a kiss and his large hand tightened around her with a sense of protection she couldn't remember feeling before.

She nodded. "Yes, I want you…to."

He brushed a stray hair from her forehead with such care; she melted under his warm, affectionate touch. Then suddenly, as if the moment grew too uncomfortable for him, he cleared his throat and stepped back, but didn't let go of her hand.

She was unable to contain her smile. "Thank you for staying." She led him into the living room which was still a disaster area. "If you wouldn't mind helping me to flip the couch back over and put the cushions back on, I'll get some sheets."

He let out a soft snort through his nose, "No problem. I'd be happy too."

Relief. Security. She'd sleep much better tonight knowing Wulf was nearby.

CHAPTER TWENTY-THREE

The night sky began to swirl above her as constellations took form before her eyes. Ursa Major, more commonly known as the Big Dipper, was known down through history as the Great Bear. To Mariska, the pictorial imagery looked like a hybrid animal or one that no longer existed. A bear-like body with some feline features and a wolf-like tail. Considering this constellation has been part of the written and oral histories dating back more than thirteen thousand years, it seemed possible an unknown animal from the Pleistocene Epoch could have been the inspiration.

The North Star or Polaris remained in its spot while the rest of the heavens seemed to spin around it as an axis point. Science, nature, and history…they always brought her focus and calm in a modern world of chaos and danger.

Mariska's imagination had been taking her to far-flung parts of the world and in times past when suddenly light from the horizon began to emerge. She sat up straighter in the recliner and listened to the end of the astronomer's presentation at the Griffith Park Observatory.

The astronomer's voice was tailor-made for this kind of work. Equal parts soothing and inspiring, she brought the entire auditorium to places many could only imagine. Holding a glowing sphere up over her head as the lights in the planetarium slowly brightened, she said, "Our ancestors, tens of thousands of years ago, looked up into the night sky with wonder. They made up stories to make sense of the movement and positioning of the celestial bodies.

Even without telescopes, computers, or cameras…man was able to observe, remember, and predict the movements of the stars, planets, and moon. They used this information to predict the seasons. Seasons for hunting, planting, and migration. We know more about the heavens today than we did in times past. However, the more we see…the more we know, the more we wonder. We are a curious bunch, we human beings, it seems the more we question the universe around us, the more we desire and seek out answers. Until then, keeping looking up into the night sky. Maybe, you'll be the one who makes that next discovery, or solves that next mystery."

The glowing orb she held high above her head, slowly darkened. Without a word, she lowered it and walked to the back of the planetarium, out of sight. The mesmerized crowd sat for a moment in silence. At first, one by one and then as a large group, the audience filed out of the auditorium. Mariska found herself alone, the room dimly lit with soft blue, twilight colored light around the base of the domed screen. She felt at peace, filled with wonder and awe for the mysteries of the universe that were still there, waiting to be solved.

She always came here to the observatory when she wanted to think—clear her head to allow for problem-solving. It'd helped her get through college, and she hoped it'd help her figure out her current situation. Not wanting to be disturbed, Mariska only told Theresa she was coming here in case she needed to get ahold of her. She closed her eyes, seeing the night sky once again, replaying in her mind how the constellations moved across the sky signaling the change in seasons. Then it struck her. The La Brea Woman. Had she been a night sky watcher? Were her people attuned to the sky as many others down through history had been, like the Mayans, Greeks, Romans, and the Iroquois people?

Mariska patted her jeans and felt the lone blue bead and mystery tooth she'd planned to keep on her person until she knew what she was dealing with. She got up and walked out of the darkroom and into the bright light outside on the lookout deck of the Observatory. In the distance, the city of Los Angeles laid spread out in all its glory. A general haze of smog, or marine-layer, as her socialite friends often referred to it. From her vantage point, she could see all of downtown, Century City, and with a turn of the head, the iconic Hollywood sign. At night, the city would be lit up with awesome, glitzy lights, but even at midday, it was beautiful. The best part of being up in the hills was the silence. She couldn't hear the traffic, sirens, or horns. The ever-present background noise of life in a big city was absent. It was the perfect place to think. Many of her big life decision had been made in the hiking trails of the surrounding park and in the hallowed halls of this time-honored institution of learning, exploration, and imagination.

Mariska walked around the side of the building to the entrance to the telescope. The door was locked at this time of day, but that was fine with her. She was more concerned with finding a less trafficked area to take another look at the bead. Sitting down onto the top step of the entrance, she fished the small hand-carved blue cube from her front pocket. In the bright light of day, she held it up and let the sun gleam off its surface.

She didn't know what the bead was made of, but it was definitely stone of some kind. Rubbing the pad of her index finger over the surfaces, she felt the tiny imperfections, worn by time and tar. On the underside of the bead, she felt a rough patch of solidified tar. Using her fingernail, she picked at it. Careful not to scrape away any surface structure, Mariska managed to remove the adhesive substance.

Taking a closer look at the newly cleaned surface, a series of tiny indentations became visible. The tiny carved holes made up a pattern of some kind. It wasn't something that readily came to mind, but could it be a constellation or part of one? She'd better ask. Back inside she went, but this time, down into the basement. Two flights of stairs and a few minutes of hunting, Mariska spotted an elderly-gentlemen in a red sweater-vest. His, white, frizzy hair reminded her of the crazy scientist on the classic 80's movie, *Back to the Future*.

Mariska hurried over to him and waited patiently while he explained to a couple of German tourists how much they would weigh if they were standing on the surface of the moon. The woman smiled from ear to ear, clearly wanting to make the trip where she'd be a whopping thirty-three pounds. The old scientist was thrilled he'd made her day, patting her on the shoulder before turning away. Mariska stepped into his path and smiled.

"Excuse me." Mariska extended her hand, and he shook it. "Can I ask you a question?"

"Absolutely," he said. "Would you like to know how many moons orbit Jupiter?"

Mariska shook her head, "I know that at last count there were sixty-seven named moons orbiting Jupiter."

The man's eyes widened with surprise. "That's correct. Very well done. I can see you've been studying your astronomy…" He paused and waited her for her to introduce herself.

"My name is Dr. Mariska Stevenson. I'm a Paleontologist down at the Page Museum."

"Ah, impressive. My name is Dr. Conrad Billings. My friends call me, Doc."

Of course they do, Mariska thought with an inner smile. "I need your help with something."

"You name it."

Mariska took him by the hand and led him to the back of the hands-on-learning center where people of all ages could weigh themselves on the planets of the solar system, study the methods used to garner scientific information regarding planets we've never set foot on, and how to track the path of comets, among other things. A second of doubt filled her belly as she wondered if he'd somehow know she'd taken the bead without permission. But how could he? She shook off the self-doubt, and once they were alone, she pulled out the bead and showed it to him.

"What's this?" he asked.

"It's a bead."

He looked at her with a questioning expression. "I don't see how I could possibly be of any help. I've spent my entire adult life studying objects in the sky, not down here on Earth."

"I kind of figured you'd say that." She turned the bead over and showed him the tiny carvings.

He gave a chuckle. "I'm going to need a magnifier for this. My eyes aren't what they used to be."

Doc turned and began walking into the back room, through a door she hadn't even noticed. She followed close. There was no way she was going to let the bead out of her sight. The doorway opened into a short hallway with offices on both sides. The second office door on the left was marked with Doc's name, and he entered without the use of a key.

"Have a seat." He walked around to the other side of the desk and sat.

He took out a magnifying glass from the top desk drawer and began studying the bead. He turned it over and over, making little sounds of interest.

"So? What do you make of the carved pattern?"

He put the magnifier down on the desk and handed the bead back to her. "Again, this is not my area of expertise, but I think this relates to my field of study. The pattern is far from perfect, but resembles the Long Sash Constellation of the Tewa people."

"The, what? Who?" Mariska shoved the bead back into her pocket. "Tell me more…please."

"The legendary Long Sash told the story of a people moving westward. They were seeking a new land a refuge from their enemies that had been attacking villages. But once settled into the new land, the people began to fight among themselves. Long Sash was then said to make an ultimatum. The people of the village could either choose to stay or make a new trail. But if they stayed, they would have to give up all violence."

"Who are the Tewa? Are they local here in California?" Mariska asked.

"They are a group of Native Americans who settled near the Rio Grande in New Mexico or Santa Fe."

"That's so strange, considering the bead was found in California." Mariska sat back in the chair.

"Not completely surprising," Doc said.

"Why's that?"

"Constellations are observed all over the world." Doc reached behind him and pulled out a book, plopping it on the desk. "Greek." He turned around and grabbed a couple more books. One by one, he dropped them onto the desk. "Roman. Norse. Iroquois. Pawnee. Inuit." He stopped and looked at her for a moment. "Each of these books contains a list, description, and the mythological stories provided by each of these civilizations. Many of them overlap. They are looking at and using the same groupings of stars, but often telling completely different stories."

Her head was spinning. How would she ever narrow this down?

"Even within the same region. Take the desert southwest for example. There could be multiple Native American tribes that carved or told stories about the same constellations as the neighboring tribe. I think I remember a totally different story about the same set of stars as what's on the bead, from the Navajo." Doc leaned against the desk. "What I'm trying to say is, it would be hard to identify the bead's origin without other associating factors."

"Like, what else? DNA?" She sat up straight and leaned in.

He looked shocked and sat back against his chair. "You're the expert, Dr. Stevenson. To determine the origin of this bead, you would need the exact location of discovery. Not to mention looking for other artifacts at the same location and depth. For example, pottery, other beads or jewelry, maybe even human remains…bones."

Other beads. Bones. *The La Brea Woman's bones*. But everything was gone.

"Where did you find this artifact?" Doc asked.

She cleared her throat. "You'll never believe it. I was at an estate sale in West Hollywood, and I found it in a jewelry box I'd purchased." Mariska fidgeted a bit in the chair. There was no telling who she could trust, even within the scientific community.

"You're absolutely, right," Doc said. "I don't believe you."

Suddenly, the calm and centeredness Mariska had felt moments ago, had been stripped away. The confines of Doc's basement office began to close in around her. The tightness in her chest threatened to stop her from breathing.

"Thank you, Doc." Mariska stood to leave. "I have to go."

She was about to pull his office door closed behind her when he said, "I'd love to get my hands on that bead again."

Without a word, Mariska closed the door and ran down the hallway. She was going to need a new place to meditate and solve her problems.

CHAPTER TWENTY-FOUR

Mariska burst through the front doors of the Observatory, down the steps and onto the lawn where she slowed to a walk. Three school buses in the parking lot opened their doors and a flood of screaming children spilled out of them. It was a good thing she'd already done her meditation. She made her way to the far Eastern end of the property which led to the parking area as well as the hiking trails when her cell phone rang.

It was her mother.

"Hey, Mom."

"Hi, honey." Her voice was so chipper and brought a smile to her face. "I wanted to see how you liked the car we had sent over to you this morning."

"Oh Mom. I tried calling this morning but got your voicemail. Practically squealed when I saw what you'd picked out for me."

"Your father and I were out to brunch with a few city officials, and I wasn't able to pick up the phone. It was so boring." Her mom chuckled.

"I can imagine it would be." Mariska shared her amusement. "You and Dad are so generous. Thank you very much for all the help. I promise you that I'll do everything I can to pay you guys back as soon as I can."

"I'm happy you're happy. Your father is friends with the owner of the dealership and he handled the entire transaction, but I picked out the color." Mariska could almost hear her mother beaming with pride.

"And it's perfect, Mom. I love you."

"I love you more." Her mom paused for a moment and Mariska took that second to turn and find a place to sit and continue their conversation. Spotting a cement bench not too far away, she made a beeline. Under a large pine tree, it would at least offer some shielding from the sun.

"Your father wants to know if you're remembering to eat." Mariska knew where the question originated. Her mom had always been worried about her eating habits during times of stress—she'd lost too much weight one semester in college and her mom threatened to force-feed her pizza and milkshakes.

"I sure am. Let Dad know I had an egg and cheese sandwich for breakfast."

"Of course." Leah sighed, no doubt with relief.

"I hate to bring up the car again, but I'm a little surprised you got me such an expensive one. I feel guilty you guys fronted so much."

"Oh nonsense. You deserve it."

Mariska laughed. "I wouldn't go that far, but I appreciate it. And, I love the color. Black with tinted windows. I hope when David sees it he won't give me crap about it being a Mercedes."

"Your father was going to get you a red car. I told him that wasn't your thing. You prefer stylish and low-key. David's a good boy. I can tell he really likes you."

Mariska didn't say anything for a moment. Her mom must have sensed the awkward silence. "I'm sorry. I know, I know, it's none of my business."

"It's not that. I honestly don't know where we stand these days. And, until I know, I'd prefer not to talk about it." Mariska pulled the phone away as she heard a beep from an incoming text message.

"Hey, I have to go. Can I call you later?"

"Yes, dear. Your father and I will be going to a fundraising banquet later, but feel free to call me anytime. Lord, knows I'd rather talk to you than those stuffy socialites."

They shared a quick chuckle. "Love you, Mom."

"Love you, more."

Mariska disconnected the call and went to her text messages. It was from an unknown sender, which could mean only one thing. Badger. She clicked on the message, and it read*: Follow my instructions.*

Mariska typed a reply, but the phone wouldn't send the message since it was from an unknown number. So, she sat and waited for further instructions.

Beep

Last week when you came here you spent some time on the trails. Go to the large tree that you rested under and wait for further instructions.

How long has Badger been watching? There was no way it was a coincidence that he answered her online ad for tech support. Too many coincidences. He knew too much. She thought back to last week, and the time she'd spent up here in the hills. So much had happened between now and then. There was a favorite place on the trail she rested though. That must be where Badger was referring. She got up from the bench and jogged to it. It didn't take, but five minutes to reach the spot. She stopped and looked around. Mariska hadn't noticed before just how deserted this part of the park was. Even a week ago being alone didn't seem as unnerving as it did now.

Beep

Follow the path behind you. Four hundred feet. Stop. Turn right.

Mariska followed the instructions precisely as she was told. Using the average stride length of an adult female being close to two feet as a guide, she paced off two hundred paces. But when she turned right, there was a steep ravine that looked treacherous.

Beep

Jump.

"Not on your life, Badger." Mariska looked around with her arms crossed. There was no one in sight. From this height, she could see loose graveled trails snaking around the park. Through the trees and over and around the many hills. In the distance, the people jogging, hiking and walking their dogs; all looked small. Far enough away, they wouldn't hear her scream for help.

Beep

Just kidding. I left the package at the edge of the ravine. It's what you've been waiting for.

Maybe he left me my laptop? "Why couldn't you drop it off at my house?" Mariska said. She looked at the phone. Nope, he didn't respond. *Where the heck is it?*

The earth had crumbled at the edge of the ravine, and she stepped up to it. Hugging a pine tree and peering over the edge, she saw a brown cardboard box about twenty feet down. The damn package had fallen over the edge—dammit. Thankfully, she was dressed in jeans and sneakers. Had she been in heels, there would be no way for her to climb down the steep wall. Moving to the edge, she sat on her butt, letting her legs go over the side. She inched forward and lowered herself down to the first little ledge. This was where it got interesting. Surveying the path she planned to take, it seemed pretty straightforward. Work herself down the hill slowly, always have one limb braced against something solid at all times, and don't fall. It wasn't so steep that she'd die from the fall but she'd definitely be in a wheelchair for the next eight months.

Mariska turned to face the wall of loose rock and began working her way down the side. Every few feet, the small pebbles and crumbling rock skittered over the ledge and down the side of the cliff. *Don't look down*, Mariska kept telling herself. *Look at the wall in front of you.* She was almost there. A few more feet down and she could rest. Her heart raced, and she was covered in sweat. Partially from the exertion, but mostly from fear. Facing the wall, she sidestepped over to the next ledge where the prize was waiting for her. Setting foot on the five-foot-wide landing, she was able to take a sigh of relief. From there, she could rest before going back up.

Beep. Another text message came through.

Good job. Once you open the present, follow the instructions.

"Yeah, yeah," Mariska said. Although, she wasted no time tearing into the cardboard box. There it sat, her laptop. "Yes."

She opened the lid and pushed power. A few seconds later the screen came to life, and a word repeatedly flashed on the screen. *Click, me.*

Mariska clicked, and the image of a cartoon Badger came on the screen. She pushed the volume up button a few times to make sure she could hear what was happening. The Badger began to talk.

"Some of the files contained on this laptop have been corrupted beyond repair. Many of them have been erased completely," Badger said.

"Damn."

"There are a few files pertaining to the La Brea Woman that have been retrieved. You will find them saved to the desktop under LBW. That's not all. I have reason to believe you are in serious danger."

"No shit," Mariska said. "I've almost died a few times now."

Badger continued, "I have determined that your computer was used on the night of the Fundraising Gala to access financial records for members of the Independent Review Board, Dr. Snyder, and some of those who were in attendance at the Gala. Many of the people are rich and powerful. Some of them you know."

Mariska's heart sank. Could they be talking about her own father?

"There is also a list of vendors that were there the night of the Gala. Some of these vendors have ties to Gala attendees as well as local groups staking claim to the La Brea Woman's remains." The Badger bowed and disappeared. The blank screen was replaced by the desktop containing two folders. One marked: LBW, the other marked: Top Secret.

Mariska turned off the computer and closed the lid. Looking back up to the top of the cliff, she shook her head. How was she going to get back up there while carrying this laptop? She tugged on the waistband of her jeans. There was a little play, so she sucked in her belly as far as she could and shoved the laptop down the front of her pants. She did a quick twist and bend and managed not to break the laptop. No other options, she took a deep breath and started climbing.

Three-quarters of the way up, she did the one thing she always told herself not to do, looked down. Her hands instantly began to sweat, the dust that covered them became slick and messy. Mariska wiped them on her jeans and chastised her stupidity. Facing the cliff, her body pressed up against the crumbly rock wall, she side-stepped up the narrow pathway to the top. A few more feet and she'd be safe where she'd started this insane journey. Pausing for a moment, she took a deep breath. She was almost there but exhausted. Looking up, she saw that the ledge was within reach, but unlike when she started her way down, she was going to have to pull herself up and over the edge. The computer was going to get damaged if she didn't take it out of her pants.

With shaky hands, she let go of the jutting rocks in front of her and slid the computer out of her waistband. She grabbed a hold of the rocks with her left hand and used her right to hoist the computer up and over the edge. On tiptoes, she managed to get it safely up there. Now, to get herself up there too. Bringing the left foot up onto a rock that stuck out from the wall, she stepped up and used both arms to steady herself on the flat ground above her.

Where was her computer? With her upper body resting on at the top landing and the bottom half dangling precariously over the edge, she saw a man a few feet away. He looked back at her over his shoulder. It wasn't the same monster that assaulted her last night, and he wasn't all that big. This asshole was stealing it. With a move, straight out of a ninja movie, she flung her leg over the top and rolled sideways onto her back. Scrambling onto all fours she yelled, "Hey, that's mine."

The young man, dressed in a dark grey hoodie and blue jeans stopped for a second.

"Please give me back my laptop." Mariska started walking toward him. He wasn't more than fifteen feet away from her. Maybe he'd mistakenly thought the computer didn't belong to anyone? Or, had she been followed?

Nope, he started running. "Asshole." Mariska jumped into pursuit. The guy's baggy pants and unlaced high-tops sneakers were slowing him down, and she was gaining ground. They were running downhill toward the Observatory parking area. He tried to turn down a path on the right, but the loose gravel made him lose his footing. Rocks skittered out from under him, and he grabbed for a tree branch to keep him from falling. It slowed him down just enough for her to close the gap separating them.

Without a thought for her own safety, she threw herself at the young man. Her shoulder connected with his midsection. Wrapping her arms around his waist, she didn't let go as they tumbled down the steep rocky path. Mariska barely registered the stones scraping off pieces of flesh as he rolled over the top of her. The laptop slid from his grasp, and he struggled to stand as he kept trying to run, but his legs weren't fully under him. He bent low to reach for the computer, but Mariska kicked at his legs, causing him to fall forward once again. Flat on his face he slid a few feet down the path, giving her time to right herself. On her feet, she rushed the man and kicked him in the ribs with every ounce of her strength. She felt her ankle pop, but there wasn't any pain.

Taking a step back, she wound up again and kicked him. This time, she heard him cry out in pain. He turned over on to his back, and she saw a kid. He couldn't have been older than eighteen years old.

"Who sent you?" Mariska said, coming to kneel on his chest. The point of her knee pressing into his sternum, the pain etched across his face as he struggled to take in a deep breath. "Who the fuck sent you?"

The boy tried to wiggle free. He shifted his weight to the side, but it was no use. She had all the advantage. Mariska pushed down harder onto his chest, but then brought her hand to his neck. She clamped her hand around his throat and applied enough pressure to scare him, but not crush his trachea. His face grew red, and the little blood vessels on his forehead, temples, and neck began to bulge. The kid started to cough.

Mariska loosened her grip enough for him to talk. "I'm going to ask this one more time. Who sent you?"

His eyes grew wide, "I can't tell you." He turned his head enough to look down the trail they'd been running on. The kid craned his neck so he could see past the tree line. Mariska followed his gaze and saw a man in the distance, watching their struggle. He was too far away to make out, but she could tell he was an adult male. The man was of indistinct race, his hoodie obscuring his face. His size was smaller than the hulk that'd broken into her home. How many people wanted to kill her? How many people wanted the La Brea Woman and the information about her whereabouts?

Mariska turned back to the kid and said, "I'm going to let you up, now. Don't try anything stupid. I'm going to retrieve my laptop, and you're not going to do shit about it. Understood?"

The boy nodded.

She didn't have any choice, but to believe him, and take the chance. Mariska took her hand off his neck and then stood. The kid rolled away and ran for the observatory. She hurried over to the computer, scooped it up and ran for her new car. Hopefully, it was still in one piece and whoever was after her, didn't break out all the windows or set it ablaze.

Mariska rounded the corner and crossed the parking lot without slowing down. Fishing the keys out of her pants in a dead run wasn't that easy, but it was necessary. Clicking the unlock button, she threw open the door and got inside, slamming the door closed behind her. She locked the doors and started the engine. A week ago, the idea that she worried her car could blow up when starting it would have been absurd. Today it was a relief. Pulling out of the parking space, Mariska called David.

"Hey Mariska," he said as he answered the phone.

"I am headed back to my apartment. What time are we doing dinner tonight?"

"You know, you're not supposed to be driving while talking on the phone." His voice was lighthearted and fun. "I'll come by your place around seven o'clock. Will that work?"

"Perfect, see you then." Mariska hung up the phone.

Great, there would be enough time for her to get home, shower, and address the bloody scrapes on her back and sides. David would kill her if he knew what she'd been up to, and how she almost died, again. Thankfully Theresa made a great partner in crime; she didn't seem as worried about Mariska's wellbeing. Mariska needed to meet with her but wasn't sure how to contact her. There was no telling who was monitoring her phone calls and text messages.

The secret code word.

Mariska sent Theresa a text message: *Preservation. Tomorrow at noon.*

CHAPTER TWENTY-FIVE

Mariska squinted against the bright lights that shown into her eyes. The midnight-blue truck had turned its headlights on, right as they'd pulled into the parking space in front of it.

"I'm really surprised you decided to go out for dinner. I kind of expected us to eat at my place. I even chilled some wine," Mariska said.

David turned to her. "What? A guy can't take a beautiful woman, who also happens to be his best friend, to dinner? It's been a while since we've gone for a swanky, night out."

They got out of the car and started toward the restaurant. Preston's was a steakhouse with flare. It showcased water features, illuminated art pieces along the walls, and even a professional violinist that brought beautiful music to each and every table. When David had asked if she'd been there, she told him no. It was very expensive, and she knew he couldn't really afford to go in the past. She wondered what'd changed. Her family, of course, had been invited to its opening night and she'd gone a few more times since then.

"It's got great reviews online," Mariska said. "But it's marked as the highest average price according to the ratings."

"Money is just money. Right?" David took her by the hand and led her to the entrance.

The line was long, and Mariska's stomach growled. This was going to be a long wait. Maybe a waitress would drop a piece of bread on the floor as they passed by. She wasn't above diving to the floor and eating right there in front of everyone. They approached the haughty-looking hostess.

She gave David a look of disdain and said, "Without a reservation, you'll be waiting three hours."

"Dr. Beaumont, party of two. We've made reservations for seven o'clock." He turned to Mariska and smiled. "Look at me, all grown up and planning ahead."

Mariska was dressed in an elegant light blue dress with a white satin shawl that helped hide the bruising she'd received the past couple days. She wrapped her arms around him and leaned against his shoulder. He'd dressed in a nice black suit. It wasn't expensive, but it fit him well. He really was a good guy. Going out of his comfort zone to show her a good time. The hostess brought them to their table and handed them menus without prices on them. Mariska asked for a bottle of wine to start things off, and the hostess offered a nod and walked away. It was going to be sticker-shock when the bill came, but she brought a credit card, just in case.

"So, what made you decide to take us here, to Preston's? It couldn't have been on the spur of the moment since you made reservations."

He took a sip of the wine that'd been brought to the table. "I had something important I wanted to share with you."

David looked nervous. He wasn't making eye contact, and that made Mariska's tummy tighten. She picked up her glass of wine and gulped it down. Not the entire glass, she was a lady after all.

"Do tell." Mariska tried to seem nonchalant.

He reached into his jacket pocket and pulled out a small box. Mariska's heart began to race. Had he gone and lost his mind? David couldn't possibly be proposing. Fighting the need to dive for the nearest fire alarm, pull it, and run into traffic, she swallowed hard.

"What's that?" Mariska pointed to the box.

"Open, it." He pushed it across the table to her.

She looked down at it for a moment, wishing this moment had never happened. Taking a deep breath, she pulled the top off and looked inside. It wasn't a ring. With a sigh of relief, she didn't know whether to laugh or cry at her near panic attack. Clearly, there were some issues she would need to discuss with her therapist…once she got one.

"Can I touch it?" Mariska asked.

He tossed her a pair of purple, latex gloves. "Sure." He was smiling from ear to ear, and his mood became contagious.

Mariska picked up the delicate toe bone of a dire wolf. She'd seen thousands of these, but this one was bigger than the rest. Significantly bigger, when comparing the averages from the six thousand partial to full Dire Wolf skeletons, that had already been found at the Tar Pits.

"When did you find this?" She slipped on the gloves and picked up the bone to examine.

"A month ago," David said, his tone sheepish.

The bone wouldn't look all the impressive to the layperson, but to Mariska it was marvelous. Many of the toe-bones she'd excavated, cataloged, and studied were about four inches in length, marginally smaller for females. She turned her hand over and placed the bone along her middle finger. The tip of the bone stuck out past the end of her finger, making it roughly four and a quarter to four and half inches. Relatively huge in comparison. Her tummy tightened with excitement. She rolled the bone around in the palm of her hand, looking at it from every angle. This was a magnificent find. Then, it struck her, the timing of this find.

"I was still active at the museum when you found this." She handed the bone back to him. "Why didn't you tell me before? I shared everything with you."

He looked away for a moment, putting the bone back into the protective box and slipped it back into his jacket pocket. "I didn't want to share it with you until…" Again, he broke eye contact.

"Until, what?"

He cleared his throat. "I don't want to do this here. Not, now."

She leaned forward and forced eye contact. When she had his full attention, she said, "Until, what?"

"Until…I found out the IRB awarded me the research grant to

study the remains." David looked away, but Mariska's glare could still burn holes into him.

"How could you?" Mariska's voice broke as emotion welled up inside. "The Page only award one grant per year. Sometimes, only one grant every two or three years, depending on the size of it."

"I know, but—"

"But what? You decided that my research subject was missing, so why the hell not? You knew I was going to get her back…and when I do the money for my grant won't be there anymore."

"What? It's not like I'm stealing your grant money? I thought you would have been happy for me. I'm finally getting the chance to head a research team and make a name for myself." David's face quivered as he talked and fought to keep his composure.

Mariska slid her chair back and stood. "You're right. I'm just upset right now. This is another nail in my research coffin."

He looked up at her. His eyes begged her to sit back down. "Please, Mariska. I swear…I never meant to hurt you. They came to me. The museum came to me."

She knew she was being overly emotional, but it didn't seem to matter at the moment. Right or wrong, she felt betrayed by her best friend. Marching out of the restaurant, she ordered a ride from an app on her phone and left David sitting at the table alone. When she saw him next time, she'd offer to pay for half the bill, but for now she just wanted to tell him to shove the wine up his ass. The driver pulled up moments later and she got into the backseat. The ride home started off with her pissed and ended with her feeling like a complete bitch. With each passing mile, the realization sunk in a bit further. His words kept echoing in her mind, "They came to me."

Of course they did. The IRB had multiple proposals for the grant money. She'd been the original winner and lost it when the body went missing. David must have been the runner-up. He probably didn't even say anything before because he didn't want to seem like he was competing against her. Mariska tipped the driver, got out of the car, and climbed the stairs to her apartment. By the time she fished the keys from her purse and worked them into the lock, she felt sick with guilt. How could she have treated her best friend so terribly?

The doorknob turned without the key. It hadn't been locked? She pushed the door open and entered the apartment. On the kitchen table by the entrance, sat three huge designer department store bags. Jane must have dropped them off. Leah had mentioned she was going to have her drop them off for Mariska. Her mom always wanted the best for her, and she always wanted it to be exclusive…or at least expensive.

Mariska decided to call and apologize to David later. It'd give them both time to calm down, and she wanted to make sure she said all the right things. In the meantime, she could spend some much-needed one-on-one time with the person who's always made her feel good about herself. Jane was like a second mom to her, and she could use a hug right now.

"Jane?" Mariska called out as she put her keys on the table.

No response. Was she still here?

"Jane? Where are you?" She slipped the white shawl off from around her shoulders and hung it on the back of the kitchen chair. "Jane?"

Mariska went through the kitchen and into the living room. With each passing step, the rock in the pit of her stomach grew heavier and more unsettling. An unfamiliar smell hung in the air, and it too seemed to grow stronger and thicker in the air as she advanced through the apartment.

"Jane?" Mariska stopped in the doorway between the living room and the hallway that lead to the bedrooms. "Are you here, Jane?"

The master bedroom was fifteen feet away, but the journey seemed insurmountable. One foot in front of the other, she crept toward the door at the end of the hallway. The door was ajar. All she had to do was push it open. With a shaky hand, Mariska opened the door.

On the far side of the room, Jane lay on the floor, partially propped up against the wall. Blood was everywhere. Red splatters covered the wall behind her. From floor to ceiling, sprays of death ran in trails. Mariska unleashed a guttural scream that tore through her throat and soul like a blowtorch of pain. She threw herself forward, stumbling over an overturned lamp and landed face down a few feet from Jane.

She pushed herself up and crawled across the saturated carpet. Mariska's fingers sank into the fibers, hands submerged in the beloved woman's ichor. The woman lay supine, her legs spread wide with arms flopped out to the side. Jane's dress was torn and slashed but covered the deep wounds Mariska knew were there. She reached for Jane's neck to check for a pulse, hoping and pleading with the universe to give her a miracle, but jerked her hand away. Her throat had been slashed.

Mariska began to sob. Over and over again, she cried out to the woman, "Jane."

She tried to stand but felt too weak, incapable. So, she kneeled next to her precious friend. Jane hadn't deserved any of this. Had Mariska heeded her father's advice to stop pursuing the La Brea Woman, she would still be alive. And Mariska wouldn't be covered in her gore.

"Jane, I'm so sorry." Mariska wanted to look away. Never see the horror splayed out in front of her, again. But she couldn't stop. Sobs came once again, wracking her body before she collapsed next to the slaughtered woman who once read her bedtime stories.

A few moments passed, and she knew she needed to call for help. It was too late for Jane, but maybe the detective could find her killer. She forced herself to stand. Mariska took one last long look at Jane when a squeak of the floor made her freeze in place.

On the floor, next to Jane was a phone. She must have tried to call for help before she was killed. Mariska started to go for it, but thick, muscular arms wrapped around her waist and neck. He squeezed and her airway closed. Frantic kicking and clawing at the killer's limbs did nothing to loosen his grip. She tried to pull free, lifted her legs off the ground for leverage, but nothing worked. The man was stronger than her, bigger than her, and she couldn't even turn her head to look him in the eye.

The seconds passed with agonizing slowness. Mariska tried to blink away her fading vision, needing to remain conscious. She had to continue to fight, but her arms and legs grew heavy, and the tingling in her face began to intensify. Unable to take in a breath, her vision started to tunnel, and she felt her eyes grow wide with desperation to see. That's when the message became clear. Written above Jane in her own blood, scrawled across the wall in the killer's own hand, were the words of warning she'd been given the night before at the diner.

I TOLD YOU IT WOULD HURT.

CHAPTER TWENTY-SIX

Mariska woke up, face down, in a congealing pool of her own blood. The pain on the top of her head, no doubt from a scalp wound that bled profusely. Judging by the lack of fresh blood, the bleeding had stopped, and she'd live. Or, at least not die from exsanguination. She tried to push herself up from the floor, but her hands had been tied together, and she was lying on them.

A quick check of her legs, she was able to bend them at the knees, but they too were tied at the ankles. A sound from the other room made her stop her struggle. She held her breath and tried to listen. The man who grabbed her must have still been in the house. From what she could tell he was in the living room, pacing back and forth. Her mom's words rang in her ears: *It's better to die at the scene fighting than to be taken alive.*

Rolling to her side, hurt, but she used all her might to push up from the floor into a sitting position. Her back to the wall, she could see the entire room. She was now in the spare room. The image of Jane, propped against the wall, blood soaking into the carpet and dripping from the walls made her sick. Whatever was in her belly, exited her mouth on the floor next to her. She used her bound wrists to wipe the bile from her lips, and she spat the rest from her mouth.

Mariska needed to get out of her restraints, or she had no chance for escape. She thought back to the many stories her mom had told her at bedtime. How to escape zip-ties had been one of them. She glanced at her wrists; the locking mechanism was facing her. Her mom had always said that was the weakest part, right? What was the first step? Another sound from the living room brought out new urgency. The man was now talking to someone. His mumbled voice was the only one she heard so he must have been on the phone. But with whom? Probably whoever he reported to. Was he determining her fate?

Break the ties, she thought. *You've got to break the ties*. The remaining portion of the tie was sticking straight up toward her, and she brought it to her mouth. Biting down on the tie she pulled it tighter. With her back against the fall, she braced herself from her feet and pushed up against the wall. Using all the strength she had in her legs, she pushed herself up into standing and hopped twice away from the wall. Bringing her hands up over her head, she took a deep breath and balled her hands into fists. With an exhalation, she brought her fists down as hard and fast as she could, into her stomach. Flaring out her elbows at the same time, the ties snapped.

Now to free her legs. Looking around the room, she spotted the hiding place for the knife her mom had insisted she stash. Three short hops and she lowered herself to the floor and slid her hand under the dresser in search of the knife. Her fingers closed around the handle and with a quick flick of the wrist, she cut the ties away. There was no way she would be able to escape out the front door. The giant in the living room would be unstoppable, even with the small knife she wielded. Per, Los Angeles fire codes, the apartment had a second exit, but she'd never used it. For all she knew, it wasn't even a real door. Located in the back of the master bedroom's walk-in closet, she'd have to move fast if she had any chance of making out alive.

Another noise from the living room, this time angry words from her captor. He said, "I have to kill her. She's seen my face."

Definitely the foul breath, man she'd encountered at the diner. Whoever he was talking to must have wanted her alive, for some reason. Mariska was sure it wasn't for her own safety. Whoever wanted her alive, could have wanted to kill her himself…or worse. The things her mother had told her happened to kidnap victims had provided many sleepless nights growing up, but it'd proven to be a valuable lesson tonight.

Mariska tiptoed to the doorway, put her back to the wall, and clenched the knife in her hand. Listening for signs that the man was coming, she found herself holding her breath. Letting it out, she snuck a peek around the corner. The hallway was empty, but the man's shadow was visible at the end of the hallway. The shadow grew larger and then smaller as he paced inside the living room. She stole one more look into the hallway. It was still clear. Now or never.

Rolling around the corner of the doorway, she stepped into the hallway. Her body felt like it was vibrating. The adrenaline that coursed through her body, making her heart race and her breathing shallow and fast, pushed her forward despite the crippling fear she tried to suppress. Mariska's feet felt light on the ground, but her movements seemed clumsy and exaggerated. The fight or flight response wasn't there for precision movements; it was there to make you stronger, faster, and able to escape the clutches of death.

A quick glance over her shoulder, she hugged the wall and side-stepped into her room. The smell of Jane's death accosted her. The woman's bowels had spilled out the bottom of her dress and mixed with the blood the saturated the room. Mariska reached for the door to close it but hesitated. Would he notice the door was closed? Did the door make a creak when it moved? She couldn't remember. If she didn't close it, she couldn't lock it. One less barrier between her and death. She hurried across the room and entered the walk-in closet. It was jam-packed full of all the shit she'd accumulated over the years. Boxes with Christmas decorations stood between her and the exit.

One by one, Mariska pulled the heavy boxes away from the door at the back of the closet. She wiggled her way around the rest of the boxes and inspected the latch that kept the door locked. Rusty, and metal, it was going to make noise. She knew it. Somehow, she was going to need to put enough obstacles between herself and the man in the living room to give her time to escape. A plan formulated and she went back to the bedroom door. Mariska took the door in hand and slowly, and with much effort, closed the door without making a sound. She then locked it. Step one, complete. There wouldn't be much time, so she hurried back to the closet and closed that door. Stacking the heavy boxes against the door, she completed the second barrier, without making a sound.

Sweat poured down her face and back. The fear hadn't subsided and the pressure of time was making everything harder. Mariska closed her hand around the rusted, metal lever and tried to move it stealthily. It wouldn't budge. It wasn't going to go quietly. Tightening her grip, she pulled harder. It moved, but not much. The scratchy sound of the metal pieces against each other made her pulse quicken. Had it been as loud as it sounded inside the closet?

She braced herself sideways, with both feet on the wall and both hands on the lever. This time she used her body weight to help force the door to unlock. Gritting her teeth, she pulled with all her might. Her legs began to quiver with effort, and hands threatened to let go, as they were slick with sweat. *Please, please, please open*, she kept saying to herself. One final strain and the lever gave way. The screech of metal echoed through her eardrums like a trumpet blast.

Footfalls rushed down the hallway. It hadn't been her imagination; he'd heard the noise too. The bedroom door rattled as he tried to open it. There wasn't much time for her to escape. She pushed at the unlocked door, but it didn't move. It was rusty and stuck in place, just like the lock.

"Shit." Mariska kicked at the door. "Come, on. Open, you bitch." She took a step back and rammed it with all her might. The door gave way, sliding open with a scream of metal on metal.

Behind her, she heard the bedroom door crash open. The man had broken through and was now trying to push his way into the closet. The boxes wouldn't keep him out for long. Slam, slam, slam, the man kept trying to force his way inside.

Mariska looked over the side of the doorway; there wasn't a landing or stairway. A metal ladder bolted to the exterior of the building was her only way down. It would have to do. She turned around and stepped back over the side, bracing herself with both hands on the doorframe. One step down, and then the next, until she was able to grab the ladder with both hands. The man inside was making progress. She heard the pile of boxes fall.

Shimmying as fast as she could down the ladder, she made it to the bottom, but there was still at a ten-foot drop to the concrete-covered side yard, below. Mariska looked up as the man's head poked out from the doorway. *Shit*, he was close. His head disappeared as she hung from the bottom rung. He reappeared, holding a box over his head. She let go and fell to the ground below. The heavy cardboard box landed right next to her with a crash. He was working his way out onto the ladder, and she struggled to her feet. She scanned the ground around her; she'd forgotten to bring the knife with her, she was now completely unarmed. A new sense of urgency coursed through her body and she ran for the street, preferring the busy street to the deserted alleyway behind her.

Without looking over her shoulder, she raced down the side of the grocery store and out onto the street. Into traffic, she rushed onward. Tires screeched around her and drivers honked. It was dark, and the street lights did a poor job of illuminating her path. Across four lanes of traffic she ran and stuck to the shadows on the other side of the street. She squatted down behind a blue USPS mailbox and waited for a second. Peering around the side, she searched for her pursuer. He stood across the street, under a light post. Angry looking and fidgety he scanned the street and sidewalks on both sides with his hand shielding his eyes from the light above him. The longer he looked, the angrier he appeared. He took his phone from his pocket and made a call.

Mariska couldn't hear what he was saying, but by the way he punched the light post and kicked at the ground, she was sure he was getting the ass-reaming of a lifetime. A few more minutes passed as he searched the darkness for his prey. Then, he turned on his heels and marched back the way he came, toward her apartment. She fought back the rising fear and stood, backing into the shadows next to the tall brick building. The business was closed for the night, but she hadn't planned on going inside.

She patted her pants pockets. The bead and tooth were still there, along with her cell phone. Suffering from the physical pain of the assault, the emotional pain of finding Jane murdered in her apartment, she wasn't sure what to do. She could call Theresa, David, her parents, or the Detective to help her. She was tired, and her pace was slowing down. She wouldn't be able to keep going much longer, so she pulled her phone out and placed the call.

"Detective Wulf?" Mariska cried into the phone. "I need your help."

CHAPTER TWENTY-SEVEN

A cool breeze came through the open car window, drying the sweat from Mariska's brow. The city never slept, and now she wondered if she ever would again. Wulf had picked her up at a gas station; she'd been hiding between the garbage can and the last row of pumps. The worry on his face had pulled the tears from her eyes, and that's where her memory began to fade. He'd had a lot of questions, and she was pretty sure she answered all of them, but specifics didn't seem to matter right now. Jane was dead, and her heart was broken. It hadn't been easy, but she'd convinced Wulf to take her by her apartment to get her laptop and a change of clothes she kept in her car. He brought her there to retrieve the items from her car while he officially called everything into the department. Within a few minutes, the parking lot was swarming with cops, ambulances, and a CSI team.

"Where can I go now?" she asked.

"I'm going to have to take you down to the station and take a statement." His face betrayed this tough-guy demeanor. The look of pity on his face tore at her soul, and she bit back a new round of sobs for her beloved, Jane.

She nodded and rested her head back in the seat while he drove her to the precinct headquarters. A numbness washed over her, and everything seemed to happen as a blur. Somehow, she managed to answer his questions—not that she remembered what most of them were. Although, she'll never shake the sickening feeling of being asked if she'd killed her friend.

Detective Wulf looked up from his computer. "How about I get you home? I'd be happy to take you to your parents' house."

She shook her head. "Have my parents been informed about Jane?"

He nodded. "Yes…I'm sorry for your loss."

"Is my mom okay?" she asked, tears welling up in her eyes.

"How could she be?" Wulf reached across the desk and held her hand. "How could either of you be?"

She wiped a tear from her cheek. "I can't face them…I feel like this is all my fault." She shook her head. "Can you take me to a hotel?"

They got up from the desk and walked to his car in the parking lot. He unlocked the door and rushed over to open the door for her. She got in and closed the door. He got in the other side and sat in silence for a few moments before turning on the car.

"Are you sure you should be alone tonight?" He turned to face her, the concern in his eyes brought the tears back to hers.

She shook her head and closed her eyes. Tears running down her cheeks in a steady stream. He pulled away from the station, and she didn't open her eyes until car stopped and he turned off the engine.

They were now parked outside his home, a small Spanish-styled two-story, in West Hollywood. The neighborhood was quiet, almost too quiet, by Los Angeles standards. But the sound of a dog barking in the distance seemed to bring her back to the here and now from wherever her mind had taken her for safekeeping. Before long, she started hearing the sounds of sirens in the distance—traffic motoring down Santa Monica BLVD a couple of streets away.

Detective Wulf broke the silence between them. "I would be happy to take you to your mom and dad's…or your friend David?" He used his electronic controls and reclined his seat a touch. Crossing his arms over his chest, he waited for her to answer.

She shook her head. "I still need to apologize to him, before laying something like this on him."

"Apologize? You didn't mention anything about the two of you having a fight?" He straightened up in the chair and looked at her.

His expression was deadly serious, almost accusatory. Like she'd left something out when he originally questioned her.

"I didn't mention it, because it isn't anything for you to worry about. He got awarded a grant at work. And I flipped out on him."

"When?"

"Tonight…that's why I was home alone when I found, Jane. I'd left him at the restaurant and took an Uber home."

"Why did you flip out on him? Aren't you friends? Wouldn't you be happy for him?"

"Sheesh," Mariska said. "I'm a real, bitch. Aren't, I? I mean, he's my best friend, and I basically accuse him of stealing my grant. *My* grant. As if I somehow own the Museum's money."

"Wait a second. You're saying that the same grant that you were awarded was pulled and given to him?"

"Sort of. There's only one grant approved every year or two, and it was my year. But since the La Brea Woman's remains went missing, David pursued his own grant even though he should have known I was going to her back."

Wulf whistled high and long. "If he knew that you were getting her back then I'd say he's cold as ice."

"That's why I got so upset, but then I started thinking…if the money wasn't going to me, it needed to go somewhere." Mariska threw her hands up in the air. "Might as well go to him, right?"

"Yeah, but he didn't tell you about it?"

"No, he didn't. But that was because he didn't have a chance. I mean, it was practically a certainty that I was getting awarded money. Maybe, he'd given up on the idea of even getting it until it was taken from me. I…don't know."

Wulf sat back in his chair and looked out the window. Mariska turned and looked out of hers. There was no way she was going to go to her parents' house, or to David's. Too many emotions. Too much sadness.

"How about I take you to a nice hotel? I'll come back in the morning and drive you to your apartment so you can get your car? Sound good?"

She shook her head. "I don't think I'd feel safe in a hotel. Not tonight…not, alone."

He let out a sigh of resignation. "Okay, you can stay here in the spare bedroom if you'd like?"

She turned to him and smiled. "Aw, thank you. I didn't want to ask, but I really hoped you would offer it to me."

They got out of the car and in the front door. Once inside, Wulf's demeanor changed. No longer a hardened cop, but a gracious host.

"Can I get you something to eat or drink? Maybe a sandwich? You mentioned you never got to eat dinner."

"No, thank you. I'm really not that hungry."

He showed her through the foyer and into the kitchen, anyway. The room was large and open, with great appliances and finishing-touches Mariska hadn't expected. Wulf opened the fridge and took out two bottles of water, handing her one.

"Thanks," she said.

"Come, on." He motioned for her to follow him into the living room.

The room was comfortable but didn't look like he spent much time there. Surprisingly, clean for a bachelor, or at least the bachelors she'd spent time with. The large, plush, leather recliner she sat in, conformed to her body. Immediately, she felt herself relax into it. Her aches and pains began to ebb.

"Is there anything I can do for you, right now?"

She shook her head. "I think I have everything." Mariska squeezed the arm of the chair. "This will do me just fine."

"Oh," Wulf said. "I didn't mean for you to think you had to sleep out here in the living room. I have an extra bedroom with a decent mattress for you."

"It's no trouble. I don't mind sleeping out here."

He didn't say anything, but opened the bottle of water and took a few swigs. He put the bottle down on a coaster and let out a sigh. "You've been through so much this evening. I bet you're exhausted."

"Yeah, it's been a shitty night so far." She took a drink of the ice-cold water. It soothed her sore throat. Her voice was still a bit scratchy from yelling and being choked. "I guess there is something I can use if you have it?"

"Anything," he said.

"Any chance you have some aspirin? I've got a sore throat and a killer headache."

"Definitely." He stood and faced her. "Come with me. I have a bottle in the medicine cabinet in my bathroom."

He reached out his hand and offered support for her to stand. She took it. Grasping his head, she registered his warm touch. His hand melted around hers and it felt nice. Pulling hard, she stood easily. But whether it was the lack of dinner or mild dehydration, she felt woozy with the change in position. Mariska stumbled forward, but Wulf caught her before she lost her footing. Locked in an embrace, she pressed her face against his chest and held tight to his waist. Despite the late hour, he still smelled fresh and clean. He readjusted his stance and lifted her up and placed her feet back firmly onto the floor.

Mariska smiled and wiped a stray hair from her face. "Thanks. Not sure what happened, but at least I didn't hit the floor."

"Good thing. Are you sure you're all right?" He leaned down and looked her in the eyes.

Glancing away, she felt her face blush. She nodded, and he led her by the hand to the stairs that went up to the second floor. She grabbed her bag as they passed by and went with him willingly. Up the creaky wooden stairs and down the hallway, they passed a bedroom and then a bath. Into the master bedroom they went.

"Have a seat." Wulf walked her to the bed where she sat on its edge. Hands in her lap, knees touching each other, her posture was upright and uncomfortable. "I'll grab you the aspirin. Is extra strength, okay? I think that's all I have."

He disappeared into the bathroom; the light came on as he entered. She craned her neck to see inside, but couldn't make out much from that angle. "Yeah, extra strength is fine. I'll take two."

Wulf reemerged with the medication and his bottle of water.

"Here, you go."

She took the pills and stretched her neck from side to side. "Thank you."

"You're welcome." He looked behind him at the clock beside his bed. "It's really late. I think I better get some shuteye if I hope to be functional tomorrow. I haven't slept well this past week."

"Funny you should say that. I haven't either."

He went to the door. She followed him.

Mariska grabbed him around the elbow. "Can I ask you a something?"

"Of course." He turned and faced her. They stood in the doorway, and she could feel the warmth of his body despite the small distance between them. She took a tiny step back but bumped up against the doorframe.

She looked away for a second. "Will my parents be interrogated?"

"About Jane?"

Mariska nodded.

"Yes, tonight."

The pit in her stomach, deepened. She crossed her arms. "Okay."

"Your parents were Jane's emergency contact, so they were notified immediately, but they'll be questioned as soon as the detective assigned to the homicide can get there."

She shook her head. "Please tell me they won't be hauled down to the station. I don't think my mom could take it."

"The detective will most likely pay them a house call." He looked at his watch. "I'm sure they've already been questioned if you want to give them a call."

"I don't know what to say to them." She spotted a small trash can in the corner of the room. She felt like vomiting.

"I totally get it." He squeezed her arm. "I'll show you where you can sleep for tonight."

The last room on the right-hand side of the hallway was the spare room. Across the hallway was the guest bathroom. Wulf walked with her to the door but stopped short of going inside with her. He motioned to the bathroom. "Feel free to use the shower. I bet you'd like to clean up a bit. Also, there are some old clothes in the dresser in here. They probably won't fit you all that well, but you're welcome to anything in there."

Mariska turned to him. "I really appreciate you…for everything you've done for me."

She gave him a hug and a soft kiss on the cheek. It was his turn to blush. He smiled, nodded and walked back to his own room. Mariska watched him leave. He turned back and looked at her as he closed his bedroom door behind him. Turning back and doing the same to her door, she sat on the bed and contemplated going to sleep. She was exhausted, but somehow, not ready to close her eyes and drift away.

Kicking off her shoes, she slipped out of her dress and let it fall to the floor. It was covered in dried blood as was her legs and arms. She snatched the dress up from the floor, wadding it up and threw it into the trash can next to the bed. She shuddered and then fought back the tears that were bubbling just below the surface. Mariska hugged herself for a second, stuck in place, both physically and emotionally. She swallowed hard. Her painful throat wasn't getting any better, and when she looked in the mirror above the dresser, she saw the bruising and swelling from her chin to collarbones. That bastard could have killed her, but he hadn't. Why? Who was he? Who did he work for? The uncertainty of it all spurred her on and broke her spell of indecision.

Opening the dresser, she pulled out a large T-shirt and running shorts. At least it had a draw-string to keep them in place. In her panties and bra, she poked her head out of the bedroom and saw the coast was clear. Tip-toeing into the bathroom, she closed the door behind her and enjoyed a nice hot shower.

Feeling relaxed, refreshed, and ready to settle down for the night, she reentered the bedroom and locked the door behind her. The clothes were loose and flowy, but not warm, and the bedding looked soft and inviting. Pulling back the comforter and sheets, she slipped into bed, adjusting the pillows behind her so she could sit up. Sinking into the mattress and letting the soft, clean sheets caress her weary body, she contemplated flipping the light off and letting herself sleep. But there was so much she needed to know. Sleeping wouldn't bring her answers. Not, right now, anyway.

Twenty minutes of work and then sleep, she told herself. First things, first. She unzipped the bag and opened it. In the back inside pocket, she'd stashed the tooth and beads. Opening the pocket, she reached in and felt the objects in her hand. With a sense of relief that they were still there, she closed it back up for safekeeping. Then, sliding the laptop from the bag, she turned it on and waited a minute while it loaded. On the screen she had two choices, the first was a folder icon labeled LBW, for La Brea Woman. There was no doubt it contained some recovered data that had been scrubbed from the laptop. The other icon was a folder with a skull and cross-bones on it. She double clicked it.

The screen flashed bright white, and a storm of black pixels swirled into a vortex of white and black, slowly coming to stop, forming a list of names on the screen.

Ingrid Ashton

Katherine Wellington

Robert Stevenson

Peter Grassland

Mariska wasn't sure where to start. She knew Kathy was vying to become the face of the Page Museum, but what did she have to do with this mess. And, Mariska's father? How did he fit into all of this? And who the hell was Patrick Grassland?

She clicked on Kathy's name. The screen filled with twenty-three different folders each labeled with a date and the word, *Payment.* Mariska opened the first folder and inside was an image of an electronic deposit into Katherine Wellington's bank account. The amount was twenty-five thousand dollars. Twenty-five thousand dollars? She couldn't be making that much as the office assistant, let alone the off chance she'd been made the face of the Museum. The institution relied on donations to remain open and functioning. A closer look showed the deposit came from an anonymous source, labeled only by a number-letter code: *9q5dptqjn.* Each of the other folders had the same deposit amount from the same anonymous source letter-number combination.

Mariska wracked her brain. What could this mean? Was Kathy involved with the La Brea Woman's disappearance? If so, she could be involved in the attacks on her and the death of Jane. A surge of anger rushed through her. If she had something to do with this, Mariska would make her pay. Pay, dearly.

Mariska's hand trembled over the keypad as she prepared to open the file labeled with her father's name. Did she want to know how he fit into all of this? How could she not look? She owed it to the La Brea Woman, to Jane…and to herself.

Right as she was about to open the folder, her phone started ringing. She picked up the cell phone and saw it was an incoming call from her mom. A sick feeling in her stomach grew as she came to the realization that they must have been notified about Jane. She let the call go to voicemail. Seconds later, her phone began to ring again. This time, it was her dad. She ignored it and turned off the computer, putting it back into the bag.

A series of beeps, as texts started rolling in, no doubt from her mom and dad. The knot in her belly tightened, but she turned off her phone, anyway. *Not tonight. I can't*, she thought. Mariska turned off the lamp next to the bed and sank into the bedding. She hugged the pillow against her body, squeezing her eyes closed to keep the tears from falling. Another round of buzzing from her phone. She pulled it off the nightstand and looked—it was her mom.

"Mom?" Mariska's voice squeaked.

"Honey are you okay?" her mom asked, her breaths coming quick and loud through the receiver.

"No," she said. "Mom, she's dead. Jane's dead."

"I know." Her mom took a deep, audible breath. "Your father and I want you to come home."

"I'm safe. I'm with the detective." How could she tell her mom it was too hard to face her? That somehow not being homemade this less real? "I'll come by soon…I promise."

"I love you, baby."

"I love you too, mom." She made a kissing noise, and her mom returned it. "I have to go…please hug dad for me."

Her stomach revolted as she disconnected the call and she lunged for the trash can next to the bed. Life wasn't ever going to be the same.

CHAPTER TWENTY-EIGHT

Wulf had tried to fall asleep, but with Mariska a couple rooms away, he couldn't get his mind to turn off. It hadn't been more than a few days since he'd first started working on this investigation and it'd been an even shorter time since he'd taken her off the suspect list. And yet, he was drawn to her with more than his mind. He knew better than to let his feelings get the better of him. It wasn't professional, and he was better than that.

So why can't I sleep?

He got out of bed and started pacing his room. The floorboards squeaked every time he came within three feet of the bedroom door, and he'd turn around and head back in the opposite direction.

There was something about this case that wasn't adding up. He'd already met with a few of the key players, or at least he suspected them as such. But he hadn't made much headway. Everyone he'd met, with the exception of Mariska, was hiding something. For him the question had never been why was the La Brea Woman taken, but why did someone want to kill Mariska?

Squeak.

He stood in the doorway of his room, uncertain as to what to do next. Deep down inside he wanted to run into the guest room and scoop Mariska up in his arms. He wanted to ask her everything about her life, not as part of the investigation, but as a way to get to know her better. He shook his head.

Stop being stupid. This can't happen. This won't happen.

He walked down the hallway and stopped at her door. Her door was closed. Wulf put his ear to the door.

Stop being a stalker.

There wasn't a sound coming from her room. She must have been asleep. Which after all she'd been through, was a good thing.

Turn around and go back to bed.

Wulf rapped his knuckles on the door. He waited a second or two but didn't hear an acknowledgment of his request. He knocked again, this time a little louder.

"Come, in," Mariska said. Her voice was soft and had he not had his ear pressed to the door, he wouldn't have heard her.

He turned the knob, and pushed the door open, just enough to pop his head through the open space.

"Hey were you asleep?" *Of course, she was asleep. You're such a jerk.*

She sat up and wiped the hair from her eyes. *Were those tears in her eyes?* Even half asleep, this woman was stunning. And the best part being, she didn't even realize it. Mariska stretched her arms high above her head and yawned.

"Is everything, okay?" she asked, wiping a tear from her cheek. *She's been crying.*

"Absolutely." He paused for a moment. "Well, to be honest, I was having trouble sleeping." *Truth.* "There's something about this case that's messing with my subconscious." *Lie, you just wanted to see her again.* "Are you sure you're okay?"

She nodded and then tucked her legs up out of the way and offered for him to sit on the bed in front of her. *He wasn't the only one telling half-truths.* He took one tentative step and then hurried over to sit. He ran his fingers through his hair and let out a long sigh. Turning to her he said, "Things aren't adding up. I've got a weird feeling about this entire thing."

"What part?"

"Motive. I can't pinpoint one. Or, at least I haven't been able to find one solid enough to help me point fingers." Wulf tapped his finger on his chin. "I mean, sure the La Brea Woman is a valuable piece of history…and to you maybe even priceless. But on the black market? I haven't come up with much demand for her."

"Not much demand?" Mariska crinkled her nose. "How would you even determine that?"

"We have people that work within the dark web, cyber trading…that sort of thing. Most black-market stuff is done online these days. Not like twenty or thirty years ago when people met in dark alleys and abandoned warehouses." He snickered, but she didn't find it as amusing as he did. "Anyway, we didn't get any hits on our searches for her."

"None?"

"None. There wasn't anyone looking to purchase her or sell her." He shrugged. "It makes me think that whoever took her was planning on keeping her for themselves."

She didn't say anything for a few moments. He could tell she was processing everything he just told her. Hugging her knees a little tighter she cleared her throat and broke the silence in the room.

"I have something to show you." Mariska swung her legs off the bed and padded across the room. Opening the top drawer of the dresser, she pulled out a laptop. "I don't know what all this means yet, but it might be important."

After turning on the computer, she came to sit next to him on the bed. She smelled great, the soft scent of peach shampoo still breathed from her damp hair. The screen came to life, and the two sets of icons—LBW, and the secret files—came onto the desktop screen. One was marked LBW: La Brea Woman. And the other was marked as a secret set of files.

Mariska double-clicked on the file to open it. A list of names came up on the screen.

"What are these?" Wulf asked. "I see you dad's name and Ingrid's…who's Peter Grassland?"

"I'm not sure," Mariska said. "I need to look into all that. But when you click into each of the names listed, there are bank accounts associated with them."

"Bank accounts? Hmm, I thought I ran a search for bank accounts…at least for the members of the IRB, and your father. Sorry," he said, putting a hand on her shoulder. "I have to run background checks and search for things like this on anyone that could be a suspect."

She shook her head, "No, I get it. I say better to eliminate the innocent people so they can go back to living their lives."

"That's exactly how I feel about it."

"So, I'm assuming I came back clean as a whistle…or, you wouldn't be having me stay in your home?" Mariska said with a knowing look.

"You're wise beyond your years. I have cleared you from my suspect list." He turned and faced her with a very serious look. "For now."

They had a stare off for an uncomfortable moment. But then she smiled, realizing he was kidding around…or, at least mostly kidding. Mariska yawned again. "I'm really getting tired. Would you mind putting the computer back in the drawer for me?"

"Not at all." He got up and went over to the dresser. When he turned around, Mariska was already curled up under the thick comforter. Her slow, shallow breathing, telltale signs she was already asleep.

He turned to leave, clicking off the light as he went out into the hallway. But as he began to close the door behind him, a thought came to mind. *Those accounts could be an important clue.* Hurrying into his room, he grabbed a flash-drive.

Wulf peeked around the door and looked into the guest room. Mariska was still quietly sleeping, her face partially covered by the bedding. He tiptoed across the room and with as much care as he could manage, slid the drawer open, and pulled out the computer. He looked back a couple of times to make sure he wasn't being watched. Flipping open the laptop, he opened the files and moved them over to the flash drive one at a time until they had all been successfully copied.

After replacing the computer, he slunk back out of the room, only stopping for a moment to whisper, "Goodnight, Mariska." He closed the door behind him and went back to his room.

Without even trying, this woman had him by the heartstrings.

Whatever it took to keep her safe, he would do. But there was no way to be everywhere at once, and so he needed to solve this crime. He only hoped he'd be able to get to the bottom of it before it was too late—too late for Mariska and too late for them.

CHAPTER TWENTY-NINE

Mariska had thought about asking Wulf to come along with her today. She was going to meet Theresa for some lunch and conspiracy talk but still wasn't sure how much she should tell him. First things, first—she needed clean clothes that fit.

She parked her car at the mall and hurried inside. At some point, the police would let her back into her apartment, but Wulf had suggested it wouldn't be until sometime this evening. The department store was busy, but she knew where her usual brands were displayed. Mariska made a beeline to the back of the store and started rummaging through the table display of shirts. It was a nice light blue that would make her eyes pop, or at least that's what David had said in the past. Pants, she needed pants. As long as she could find the right shade of jeans, the shoes she was wearing would still work fine.

Around the large upright display, Mariska hurried. She grabbed a pair of jeans in her size and went to the changing rooms, but stopped short of the attendant. Slowly, she turned around. The store was filling up with shoppers, but that wasn't the problem. Something was off. She looked around the room some more, craning her neck to see over a display in the distance. She could have sworn someone was following her, she could feel it.

"Ma'am?" the attendant said behind her.

"Yes?"

"Are you ready to try those on?"

Mariska looked at the items in her hand and then looked back into the store. There wasn't anything out of the ordinary, but her senses were piqued. "I'm ready." She handed the clothes to the attendant who led her to the changing room.

The small booth was fully enclosed, the wall when from floor to ceiling, but there wasn't a lock on the door. Usually, that wouldn't bother her. The attendants knew their job well and kept track of which rooms were occupied and which ones weren't. But without a lock, she felt extra vulnerable. No time to be picky.

"Just try on the clothes and get out of here," Mariska said to herself.

She made quick work of the shirt. It fit okay. The jeans were perfect. She started to take the pants off when she heard the attendant come into the changing area. Mariska stopped and listened. The attendant shuffled through the room; her feet didn't seem to clear the floor. Mariska hadn't remembered that when she showed her to the changing room.

Mariska put her ear to the door and listened. A soft, whimpering sound. What the hell? She bent down, low and tried to look under the door. She got down on all fours and put her face against the carpeted floor. Two sets of feet, one female, and one male. The attendant's feet were touching the floor, only at the toes. She was being dragged. A flash of memory back to last night when Mariska was being choked made her suck in air.

The killer stopped. He must have heard her. The attendant hadn't told him what room she was in. He took another step and then suddenly threw the woman to the ground. Her head bouncing off the floor right in front of her changing booth. Mariska bit back a scream. The woman's eyes locked with hers. The attendant started to cry out, her face contorted in pain. The side of her face swollen and red, her eyes puffy with streaks of makeup down her cheeks. But before she could make a sound, a crushing hand came down and snatched her by the hair. With a quick jerk, the monster smashed her head into the floor. Mariska watched as the woman's consciousness drained from her eyes.

Mariska put a hand to her mouth to keep from gasping. She saw the woman take in a breath and then another. She was still alive. But how long would Mariska still be breathing? She crawled backward away from the door and stood. The frantic search for a way out or something to protect herself yielded nothing. She buttoned her jeans and put on her shoes as silently as possible. A quick inventory of possible weapons produced very little. She opened her purse. Car keys, a nail file, and hairspray. On the floor, there were some wire hangers and small metal pins in a pin cushion on the wall. She was going to die.

The sound of the first booth door being kicked in sounded. There was little she could do now. She turned in a full circle looking for something. Anything. That's when she saw it. A pair of flip-flops under the bench. A plan formed. She dove for the sandals and cushion of pins. One by one, with shaky hands, she pushed the pins through the top of the rubber soled flip flops. First one and then the other. Until they were two thinly spiked porcupines. She tucked her purse in the back of her waistband and then put the sandals on her hands like a pair of gloves.

Slam. Slam. Her door was next. She stood on the bench at the back of the booth and widened her stance. Perched like a predator ready to pounce. Her heart was racing, and her muscles shook. Without options, it was kill or be killed, time.

Slam.

The door to her booth slammed open at the very moment she threw herself toward the killer. With both hands up above and in front of her, she slammed them down on the side of his face and the other across his eyes, nose, and mouth. She felt the pins tear through his flesh, some of them pushing back into her hands as they hit the bones of his skull. He cried out in shock and pain. He stumbled backward as she used her shoulder to shove him. Take steps back, she tripped over the unconscious store clerk and fell to the ground. Without a second thought or a look back, Mariska bolted for the emergency exit, dropping the sandals as she went.

She hit the door with both hands as an alarm sounded. She kept going. At least, the attendant will get some immediate help when the security runs into the back room to find the source of the alarm. Around the side of the building, she kept going. She needed to make it to her car. If she could make it without anyone stopping her, she'd be fine. Pulling the purse out of her waistband, she increased her speed. Two more rows of cars to go and she would reach her destination. With a quick check behind her, she was relieved no one was following.

She fished her car keys out of the purse and clicked the unlock button and the car beeped, five vehicles away on the left. Slowing to a speed-walk space, she visually swept the parking lot. A smattering of people, parking, walking to and from the stores, and standing around talking with each other was all she saw. She jumped into the front seat and immediately locked the door and turned on the car. Her hands shook violently as she reached for the steering wheel. A couple of deep breaths. In, and out. In, and out. Making a fist and then opening her hands again multiple times, she felt the trembling ebb.

Mariska placed the car in drive and eased out of the parking space. Continuing to take slow, steady breaths, she successfully brought her heart rate back to a pedestrian pace. *Marie Calendar's* wasn't very far from where she was so all she needed to do was keep herself calm. It was now more important than ever to meet up with Theresa and try and get to the bottom of this before she wound up the next lifeless body on the floor.

Before she realized it, Mariska pulled up in front of the meetup spot, then had second thoughts. Was she putting herself and Theresa in danger by meeting? She'd been careful to make sure she hadn't been followed, but if she parked out front, they'd be easy to find. There would be more parking around the corner on Curson Avenue, across from the Museum. Half a block away, she parked and paid the meter. Checking behind her, she slung the computer bag over her shoulder and grabbed her purse. She was fifteen minutes late, but she was sure Theresa would wait for her. Glancing over her shoulder again, she shook her head. He hadn't followed her. There was no way. Not with the physical damage she caused him today. It would take him a few days to regroup. Wouldn't, it?

She looked once more, but this time three parked cars away she saw a man in a black leather jacket and sunglasses looking her way. He was smoking a cigarette and didn't look away. She turned to run but stopped herself. It's time to call a bluff. If he was going to kill her, he wouldn't be watching her on a busy street where there are hundreds of witnesses. Mariska marched toward the man.

"Hey, asshole." She stopped a few feet away from him. This wasn't the same man who'd attacked her, but he looked shady as shit. His dark sunglasses hiding his identity she wouldn't have been able to pick him out of a lineup. For all she knew, he was in Wulf's book of jackasses that are wanted for recent crimes committed in the area.

He turned and looked at her. Taking a long drag on his cigarette, he dropped it to the ground and smashed it under the toe of his shoe. "You need something, lady?"

"Stop following me, or I'm calling the police." She pulled out her cell phone. "I don't know who the hell sent you to hurt me, but you better back off."

"Look, you, crazy bitch," he said with his hands raise, palms out. "I don't know what you're talking about. I'm on my break minding my own business."

She looked at the car he was standing next to. A black limousine. Shit, now she's picking fights with innocent people. Or at least people that have nothing to do with trying to kill her.

"Oh," she said. "Just, stay away from me." If her adrenaline wasn't still pumping through her veins so hard, she would have been embarrassed. Instead, she hurried down the sidewalk toward the restaurant.

Mariska pulled the door open to Marie Calendar's and went inside. It took a few seconds for her eyes to adjust to the low light compared to the high-noon brightness of a sunny summer day in Los Angeles.

"Can I help you?" the hostess asked.

Mariska smiled, "Yes, I'm looking for someone. She is probably already here."

"Feel free to look around, if you'd like."

"Thank you." Mariska walked up the steps to the main level of the restaurant. She wove her way through the tables when she heard her name being called.

In the far back corner booth, Theresa waved her over. Mariska slid into the booth across from her.

"Are you, okay?" Theresa asked.

Mariska straightened her hair and looked at herself. Her clothes were rumpled, the tags still attached. The right shirtsleeve had an inch-long tear at the seam. She shook her head. "I don't even know where to begin."

Theresa reached across the table and rested a hand on Mariska's. "The beginning."

Mariska let out a sardonic chuckle. A waiter walked by, and Mariska reached out and took him by the arm. He looked surprised but remained pleasant.

"Can I help you?" he asked.

"Yes. I desperately need a drink." Mariska opened her purse to find her identification. "Here." She handed it to him.

He looked at it and handed it back. "What can I get you?"

"I'll take a shot of vodka with a lime…make it a double."

Theresa was about to get overloaded with dangerous information that could put her life at risk, and Mariska needed to self-medicate, to make it all okay.

CHAPTER THIRTY

Mariska slammed back the double shot of vodka as soon as it arrived. The waiter didn't even have a chance to leave when she handed him back the empty glass. "Thank you," she said.

"Anything else?" he asked.

Mariska looked over at Theresa who shook her head, no. "Maybe in a few minutes?"

"Of course." The waiter smiled and walked over to his other tables.

There was a moment of silence while Mariska pretended to look through the menu. Her mind still spun with the morning's events. Theresa dropped her menu on the table and cleared her throat. Mariska didn't look up, she knew what she wanted—all the details, but Mariska didn't want to talk yet.

"Come on," Theresa said. "Spill the beans."

"What?" Mariska played the fool and ran her fingers through her hair for a second, but then put her menu down and looked up.

"You come in here, late. Your makeup is smeared. Your hair is a mess, and those clothes…what happened to you?" Theresa sat back in the booth and crossed her arms. It was clear; she wasn't going to take no for an answer.

Mariska looked over her shoulder to double check for potential eves-droppers and then leaned in closer so she could speak in a low voice. "The past two days have been awful. I was attacked at my apartment, barely escaped." She omitted the part about Jane because it was too much emotion to deal with right now. "I ended up spending the night at Detective Wulf's house."

"Oh my goodness. That's awful." Theresa uncrossed her arms and put her hand on Mariska's. "Are you sure you're okay? I can take you to the hospital to get checked out."

"I never want to go to the hospital again, if I can help it." Mariska pulled her hand out from under Theresa's and sat back against the booth. "I'm fine. Just tired and kind of sore."

Theresa didn't say anything for a moment, but she seemed to be scrutinizing her rather intently. "So, anything else you want to tell me?" Mariska couldn't help, but notice Theresa looked almost amused.

"Why are you looking at me like that?"

"You mentioned that you spent the night at the detective's house." She glanced at Mariska's blouse. "Your clothes are a mess…did you just happen to leave his place?"

Her intimation dawned on Mariska. "Pull your mind out of the gutter. Nothing happened between us. Geez, what do you think I am? I'm a mess because…"

"Because why?"

"I left out the fact, that I was apparently followed to the store and attacked in the dressing room."

"Damn." Theresa slapped a hand on the table. "Are you serious?"

"As a heart attack."

"I don't know what to say other than I think we should go to the hospital to make sure you're okay." Theresa shoved the menu to the end of the table and gathered up her purse to go.

"I'm not going anywhere. We have too much to discuss. If I don't get to the bottom of this, I lose everything. My grant, my career, and probably my life and the lives of my loved ones hang on the need for me to find who stole the La Brea Woman. If I can find out who did it, I'll know who's behind the attacks."

Theresa let out a sigh. "All right, then. We better get down to business. I can't imagine you're bulletproof and things seem to be escalating."

"Very true." Mariska leaned on the table with her elbows. "Did you know that David was given the grant that was supposed to go to me?"

Theresa didn't look surprised. She opened her purse and took out a small piece of paper and turned it to face, Mariska. It was a list and at the top of it was the word *Grant.* "I saw something last night when I was snooping through Dr. Snyder's office. On his desktop date-planner, he had written David's Grant. I was going to ask you about it."

"Yeah, apparently, since La Brea Woman's remains are missing, they assumed I wouldn't be using the grant money," Mariska said.

"Makes sense to me. Although, it sucks big time."

"Yeah, it does. But to make matters worse, when David graciously told me about it at dinner, I blew up at him. I took it as he went behind my back and stole it from me."

Theresa went to say something, but Mariska interrupted. "I know, I know. He might as well have the money since I can't technically use it right now."

"But?"

"But it still hurts, and I'm a horrible person."

Theresa chuckled. "No, you're not. You were shocked…that's all."

"I guess, but I could have been a much better friend about it."

"David is an awesome guy. Just apologize to him, and I'm sure he will be more than understanding about the whole thing."

Mariska hoped she was right. "I have something I have to tell you about. It's important, but could get me in deeper trouble."

Theresa's eyes grew bigger as she leaned in closer. "Tell, me."

Mariska opened her purse and slid open the zipper pouch inside the back pocket. "I found these." She placed the mystery tooth and remaining blue bead on the napkin in front of her.

Theresa reached for them, but Mariska blocked her hand. "Can't I look at them?" Theresa asked.

Slowly, Mariska withdrew her hand and nodded. Theresa took the items and turned them over and over in her hands, examining them for every detail…much like Mariska had done when she first took a good look at them. Theresa was learning quickly as an intern what it meant to study rare and important objects. Do it with an intensity as if you're never going to have another chance at it if you wait. Mariska let her take a few minutes to study them. Theresa put them back onto the napkin and slid it back across the table.

"Where did you get them? What are they, exactly?"

Mariska went to answer the first question, but Theresa kept going. "Why did you say you could get into more trouble for having them?"

"Those are all very good questions. To start with, I have to have your implicit promise that no matter what. No matter who might ask, you have to deny any knowledge of them."

"Of course."

"I'm pretty sure these artifacts are part of why I'm being followed, threatened, and attacked. So, denial of their existence will help protect you as well."

"What artifacts?" Theresa said, her eyes big and feigning innocence.

"Perfect."

Mariska took her time and laid everything out of the table for Theresa. Full disclosure. She'd been completely honest with her about how she'd found the artifacts inside the skull of the La Brea Woman the night she'd been attacked at the Fundraising Gala. What she'd done by taking the objects from the museum was theft, but it was also the only link they have left to her whereabouts and clues to who was behind her disappearance.

"It's a lot to take in," Mariska said. "Are you okay with all this?"

Theresa nodded. "Yeah. I think I would have done the exact same thing. It also explains why you went to Ingrid's house and why we went to the library to find those photographs."

"That's the other thing. Did you hear about the librarian?"

Theresa looked away for a second. "Yeah, I can't believe she died. She didn't look like she was unhealthy."

"Unhealthy? She was murdered."

"She was? The news said they found her body but didn't know what happened to her. I assumed…hoped she had a heart attack or something."

"Detective Wulf told me that she'd been killed."

"Shit, things are escalating for sure. Whoever it is that wants the tooth and beads are desperate enough to kill," Theresa said. "By the way, I don't recognize the tooth. Any idea what animal it came from?"

"None. It's way too large to be human. It's even too large to be a Mountain Gorilla, which wouldn't have been in North America, anyway."

"Could, identifying the origin of the tooth be important to why the killer wants it back? Maybe some kind of huge discovery? Maybe the person is desperate for the historical credit?"

Mariska took a second to let that roll around inside her mind. "That could be a possibility. But that would also mean whoever it is would be a scientist…wouldn't it?"

"I can't imagine who else would want the credit for a big discovery? But there could be another reason they want the tooth and beads."

Mariska gave her a curious look. "Lay it on me. I've been wracking my brain, but seem to have lost all my critical thinking ability."

"The DNA from the tooth could be important."

"Why? It's clearly not human, so it didn't come from the La Brea Woman."

"Yeah, but if you can identify the DNA of the creature, you might be able to trace it to a location where that animal lived…"

Mariska sat straighter in the booth. "And by identifying the origin of the tooth, we could extrapolate what humans lived in the area and thus the rightful ownership of the La Brea Woman's remains."

"Exactly. But where would you have the testing done? There are a few institutions in the area that offer DNA testing, but Dr. Snyder would probably find out." Theresa tapped her chin in thought.

"The scientific community here in L.A. are a bunch of gossips.

And, let's face it, loose lips will sink ships. We need an independent lab somewhere far enough away to not tie back to the Page Museum…any ideas?"

Theresa didn't answer right away. She picked up her phone and started digging. Mariska was about to change the subject and admit temporary defeat, but Theresa said, "I got it."

"Tell, me."

"Copenhagen."

"Denmark?" Mariska cocked her head to the side like a questioning Dire Wolf.

"The GeoGenetics lab at the University of Copenhagen. It's where they did all that groundbreaking DNA testing for the Kennewick Man. They were able to accurately identify which tribe he belonged to and thus ended a decades-long feud between the native peoples staking claim and the research institution that found him." The excitement in Theresa's voice was contagious.

"That's right. I remember that case well. I also remember Dr. Snyder saying it was the biggest waste of scientific research in recent memory. My guess is he doesn't have any connections with the University there. Which, for us, makes it the perfect place. Nice job, Theresa."

"Not to change the subject, but is your computer in your bag?"

"Yeah." She opened the leather case and pulled out the laptop. "I was going to show you a few things I found on here too."

"I take it you were able to get some of the files back from the tech-guy you hired over the internet?" Theresa asked.

"I would have asked you, but you'd suggested using a tech-nerd from the internet."

Theresa rolled her eyes with faked annoyance. "Hey now, I'm pretty good around a computer." She laughed. "Show me what you found."

Mariska turned on the computer and then slipped into the other side of the booth to sit next to Theresa. "There's suspicious financial files on here. I have no idea why they are on this computer, but my guess is that it was used to access the bank accounts of some very influential people."

"Like, who?"

"Katherine Wellington, Kathy, someone with the last name Grassland, and even…my father."

Theresa turned to face her. "Your father?"

"Yeah, but I don't know why. When I looked into Kathy's file, it had large sums of money going into her accounts."

"Who was depositing it? I know, she's rich and related to Hollywood director guy, but I can't imagine what she'd be getting paid this much to do."

"That's one of the other strange things. The money is being deposited from a series of numbers and letters. I have no idea what it means." Mariska pulled up the file and showed it to Theresa.

"Huh," Theresa said. "Very interesting. I don't see anything directly deposited by Dr. Snyder, but yesterday I overheard an argument between them. They were in his office, and I couldn't hear much. In fact, had Kathy not exited the office in a hurry I probably wouldn't have even been aware it was happening."

"So, you couldn't hear anything specific? Did Kathy seem upset when she was leaving his office?"

"I wish I had. When Kathy opened to door to run out, I could see Dr. Snyder standing in front of his desk with his arms crossed. He was shaking his head, and his face was bright red. Like, he better take his blood pressure pills, red."

"Was Dr. Snyder yelling at her?"

"I wouldn't say he was yelling, but the intensity of his scowl could have cleaned the tar off the mammoth bones." Theresa continued to scroll through page after page of computer files under Kathy's name. Not finding anything else of interest, Theresa closed out the file, but then opened the file labeled Grassland. "I wonder who… Oh that's interesting."

"What?" Mariska craned her neck to get a better look at the screen.

"Mr. Grassland owns One-and-Done Catering."

"Who?"

"That's the catering company used by the museum for their events," Theresa said. "I saw their files in Dr. Snyder's filing cabinet. From what I found, the museum has been using this company for the past few years. Every Fundraising Gala, ground-breaking ceremony or even small institution-backed birthday party gets fed via One-and-Done Catering services."

"Well, then I guess it makes sense that they would have money being sent to them by the museum. Although, a catering van would be an easy way to discretely remove the La Brea Woman's remains." Mariska pointed to the screen. "But that strange series of numbers and letters seems to be depositing money into their account as well."

"Very strange." Theresa nodded. She scrolled through some more files, looking for something. "I don't see anything else to indicate who Mr. Grassland is?"

Mariska pulled out her phone and said, "Let's Google it." She put in Peter Grassland, One-and-Done Catering, and Los Angeles into her search-bar. "There we go…looks like he's…oh shit."

"What? What did you find?" Theresa asked.

Mariska turned the phone, so Theresa could see the screen. "No, way."

"Yep," Mariska said. "Looks like Mr. Grassland is the Tribal Leader of the local Chumash people. The very same group that's been protesting every event the museum holds."

"But why would Dr. Snyder use a catering company if they hate the museum?"

"That's a good question."

They both were at a loss for words. Neither said anything for a little while, letting the revelation sink in. What would the museum gain by using that company? Who was behind the large amounts of money being deposited into the accounts?

"I'm sorry to have to ask this," Theresa said, quietly. "Did you happen to look into your dad's file yet?"

Mariska shook her head. "Nah, not yet. I'm not sure I'm prepared to see what's in there right now."

"Let's save it for later." Theresa closed the laptop and slid it over in front of Mariska. "What do we do next?"

Mariska thought about it for a minute and then shrugged. "I think I'll need to pay Katherine Wellington a visit."

"What about Mr. Grassland? It seems to me that he would be the obvious choice."

"And, say what, exactly? Hey sir, you don't know me, but I think you attacked me and stole museum property?"

"I see your point."

"I feel like I would be more comfortable going to Mr. Grassland once I have more information. I would think that if he was going to steal the remains, he could have done it years ago? He's had access for years. Plus, I'd like to believe he wouldn't jeopardize the tribe's chances of legally obtaining the remains so they can do what's best in terms of their culture."

"I agree," Theresa said. "Let's start with Kathy."

As Mariska got up from the table, her mind went wild with possibilities. Kathy and Mariska had a mutual dislike for one another, so what was she going to say to her? Throwing caution to the wind, Mariska decided to wing it. What could go wrong? It's not like Kathy was going to kill her, right?

CHAPTER THIRTY-ONE

Kathy Wellington's home was more of a palatial mansion fit for a royal family of thirty than it was a residential dwelling for a single person. Tucked away in a private, gated neighborhood, the huge mature trees shielded it from view. Mariska had to park on the main street and climb over the bricked wall that kept out the general public and hordes of gawkers. No easy feat in couture pants and bedazzled flip-flops. Her guess was there were other celebrities who also inhabited this well-guarded neighborhood, and they didn't want to be seen on the Where-do-the-Celebrities-Live Tours. The guard at the gate told Mariska she couldn't enter the premises unless her name was on the list—and it wasn't.

No sooner had she landed on the soft, manicured lawn inside the walled-off neighborhood, when she heard the hum of the security gate opening. Either a resident or someone on the list was being let in by the guard. Mariska looked for a place to hide. There wasn't time to be picky. She chose the clump of jasmine bushes that were being used to block the unsightly look of the electrical boxes used to man the gate and guard house.

Mariska peered through the lush greenery that smelled like a high-priced body spray and watched a beautiful white Rolls Royce inch past the gate. The windows were tinted, obscuring the passenger, but her heart started to race when she realized the driver was none other than Thomas, Ingrid's chauffeur. Why was Ingrid here? Must have come to see Kathy, but why?

After the car rolled past and went far enough down the street to be out of the line of sight, Mariska popped up and stepped around the shrubbery. Brushing off the errant leaves and twigs, she hurried through the grassy area until she reached the sidewalk along the main road. Checking her phone for directions, she determined it would be a quick walk. Maybe five or six houses separated her from Kathy's property. The only thing was each of these homes were on a few acres of land. Large trees shaded the grounds. High towering Italian Cypress trees lined the road, preventing anyone from seeing past, into the yards of the rich and famous. Clearly, privacy was important to everyone here.

Looking up and down the street, there wasn't a soul in sight. She didn't hear lawnmowers, kids playing, or even the sound of a barking dog. A light breeze rustled the treetops, and the sounds of birds chirping was the only signs of life. Truly, serene, but a little creepy to be in a big city and hear none of the man-made sounds that usually accompanied living here. Her sandals scraped against the pavement as she walked, but she had the feeling no one knew she was there. A quick check of her phone revealed she was one property away from Ms. Wellington's house. Kathy had become a B-celebrity of sorts when she was disgraced and expelled from school for plagiarism. Her father being the A-lister movie director, publically backed away from his daughter. Rumor had it a reality show was in the works, but that Kathy refused to do it once she started working at the Page Museum. Now, as the potential face of the Page Museum, she would get paid to appear at museum events and fundraisers. Also she would have her image on billboards, posters, and the sides of buses. She would even star in the museum commercials and narrate many of the educational materials made at the museum. All in all, she would be making a ton of money without having to put out much effort and in her own way could rise back into celebrity status.

Mariska stopped at the driveway that lead to Kathy's mansion. She had her own gate. The black iron rods were in stark contrast to the white stucco wall that lined the front of her property. She peered through the gate, the well-manicured lawn, bright clusters of flowers surrounding huge old Oak Trees, and bricked driveway, truly made her property one to envy. Mariska couldn't help, but wonder if Kathy even took the time to enjoy what she has. The few times she'd interacted with the woman, she seemed too prissy and fame-affected to spend any time outdoors where there might be bugs or a slight breeze that could upend a perfectly quaffed hairdo. Not to mention the grudge she seemed to carry around.

So, how was she going to get inside? There wasn't anything to use as leverage to climb over the wall. She reached out and pulled on the gate. Locked up tight. To the right, there was a control box and camera. If she'd been an invited guest, she could have pushed the button, smiled, and identified herself. The butler or whoever would then buzz her inside the grounds. That wasn't going to work. She looked up and down the street, no other cars headed this way which meant no one was going through the gate anytime soon.

Maybe there was a place to climb over around the side of the property? With a sigh of resignation to possibly getting scraped up and, or arrested for trespassing, she marched around the corner and into the thick barrier of coniferous trees. Many of the branches hung low enough to catch her in the face as she tried to push past them and at least twice her short hair got snagged, pulling her up short. There it was, the perfect spot to climb over the wall. The tree grew close enough to the wall that she could climb up and step over onto the thick, stucco wall. So, she climbed. Before she knew it, she stepped over to the top of the wall, and lowered herself down the other side, before dropping the last few feet to the ground below.

Once on the other side, with no way back over, she started second-guessing her decision. She could be arrested...would someone shoot her for trespassing? Oh well. She needed answers before she was shot by someone else, anyway. Deciding it was best to keep as hidden as possible until she reached the front door, she kept close to the wall and snuck nearer to the house as trees, fountains, and a beautiful gazebo presented itself for her to hide behind. After zigzagging her way to the side of Kathy's house, she stopped and reassessed her position.

Mariska, her back against the wall, snuck a peek around the

corner. In the circle driveway next to the fountain, sat Ingrid's Rolls Royce. She couldn't see if Thomas was in the car or waiting inside for his boss. To be on the safe side, she decided to go around back and see if she could find out what was going on.

Rounding the back corner of the home, she spotted the huge back patio. The floor of the patio was at chest level as the backyard sloped toward a ravine in the distance. She hurried over to the stairs and took them two by two. Not wanting to be seen, she ducked low and rushed to the side of the house. Never having been to Kathy's house before, she had no idea what part of the house exited onto the back porch. For all she knew, the large, glass, multi-paned double set of French doors lead directly into the main living space where Kathy was currently entertaining Ingrid.

It was risky to look inside, but Mariska couldn't help herself. Staying low, on all fours, she peered through the glass doors. Inside was a large open room with bookshelves lining the walls and a beautiful wooden desk against the far side of the room. She scanned again for any signs of Ingrid and Kathy. That's when they entered the room. Kathy made a sweeping motion with her arm as she showed off her vast book collection. Ingrid smiled politely but said nothing. Mariska couldn't contain a smirk as she saw the older woman was less than impressed with Kathy's things. She wondered if Kathy had ever been shown Ingrid's vast repository of historical and priceless collections. Probably, not.

Muffled words were now exchanged, but Mariska could still make out their conversation. This was exactly what she'd hoped for. Answers.

"Lovely home you have here, Ms. Wellington," Ingrid said as she sat in the chair she'd been offered.

"I told you, please, call me Kathy."

Ingrid smiled but said nothing.

"So, what do I owe this unexpected visit?" Kathy said.

So, it hadn't been planned. Ingrid was definitely up to something, Mariska thought.

"Can't one member of the Review Board, visit another, without an agenda?"

Kathy smiled, "No, I don't think so…as lovely as it is to see you."

Ingrid crossed her legs and laced her fingers together as she held her knee. "I supposed you're right." She leaned in a bit closer, bending at the hips while her back remained straight, proper. "There's been some interesting developments at the museum, and I think we need to discuss them."

"Ah, yes. The unfortunate incident at the Fundraising Gala. Despite, everything that happened, I'm happy to see we still raised more money than we did last year."

"Yes, we did. Plenty of money still in the budget for your P.R. campaign," Ingrid said. *Kathy had been offered the position after all?* Mariska could see Ingrid's indirect jab, indicating Kathy's position at the museum depended upon public donations, was not lost on her. The younger woman straightened up and squared her shoulders.

"Again," Kathy said. "To what do I owe this unexpected visit?"

Just as Ingrid started to speak, Mariska's attention was pulled away, into the yard. Behind her, she watched as, who she presumed was a gardener walked past, pushing a wheelbarrow. She remained still, not even turning her head to look back into the library. Any movement could call attention to her. A few agonizing seconds ticked by until he disappeared behind the pool house.

Mariska looked back inside and saw the two women still in conversation, but this time they were standing. What had she missed?

Ingrid shook her head and gave Kathy a look that caused her to stop speaking mid-sentence. Mariska could feel the tension between them. Both women glaring at each other without a word being said between them. Mariska held her breath and waited for someone to break their silence.

"I'm telling you, she's on to you," Ingrid said. "It's not a threat. It's nothing other than a friendly warning…between colleagues."

Kathy's back straightened even further. "That sounds an awful lot like a threat to me."

"Oh dear." Ingrid gave her a condescending look. "I've upset you. My intentions were nothing, but honorable. I mean, if my position at the museum was at risk, I would welcome a warning."

"But I've done nothing wrong."

"It's not about right or wrong, dear. Sometimes, it's about public opinion. Sometimes, it's about nothing more than good timing…or, bad in your case." Ingrid went to turn, but Kathy stopped her.

"So, what exactly are you trying to say?"

Ingrid's face hardened. "Oh sweetie, do I really need to spell this out for you?" Ingrid smiled, a condescending look crossing her face. "You found out something you weren't supposed to know. I'm telling you that if you reveal it to anyone…even *her*, I'll ruin you. Your new career here at the museum will be shorter lived than even your own father expected it to be."

"But I had nothing…" Kathy started to say.

"Like I said, public opinion can be difficult to survive." Ingrid turned to leave. "I'll be in touch."

As Ingrid walked out of the room, Kathy put her hands to her face. She was clearly upset, but she followed behind her guest to see her out. Was Kathy behind the La Brea Woman's disappearance? Who was she not supposed to reveal anything to? Something deep inside Mariska told her it had to do with her. It was clear, Ingrid knew more than she'd ever let on. Mariska's resolve to find out more answers grew stronger with each passing question.

A banging noise in the distance caused Mariska to turn and look behind her. Way at the back of the property, she saw the landscaper, emptying the wheelbarrow. There was a small building, way in the back, that she didn't know what it was for. The worker, done with whatever landscaping job he was doing, opened the side door. To her horror, Mariska watched as two large Doberman Pinschers stepped through the open doorway.

"Oh no." Mariska crawled on her hands and knees to the side wall of the porch.

The dogs played with each other for a few seconds and then the worker commanded them to sit. They sat, and he give them each a treat from his pocket. They must have known him, and this was their usual ritual, but what was going to happen when they saw her? She was going to be their next treat. She needed to get out of there—fast.

She crawled across the porch until she reached the far side where she scrambled down the steps. When she rounded the side of the house, she heard their first bark. They'd seen her, and there wasn't much time. Running as fast as she could, she jumped one bush, and then plowed through a bed of peonies, not slowing to see how much time she had left before their teeth sank into her backside.

Thirty feet to go, she heard the dogs snarl and whine with the excitement of the kill. She pushed forward, trying to gain speed. Without looking, she could hear them gaining ground—quickly, too quickly. As she neared the wall, Mariska didn't see an easy way over it. But without time to slow down, she jumped as she got close. Her body slamming into the stucco façade and her hands gripping the top of the wall. Pulling with all her might, she started moving up, her elbows almost to the top, when one of the dogs bit ahold of her sandal. She tried to shake him loose, but he pulled hard, nearly yanking her grip loose.

The other dog lunged for her other foot, but she managed to swing it up and over the top of the wall. Mariska wiggled, pulled, and shook her leg, trying to get the dog to let go. He wasn't going to budge. With a glimmer of hope, she felt the sandal start to come loose. Fully prepared to leave them behind, she pulled hard again. This time, the shoe slid off, and her foot came free. Before the dog could drop it and bit ahold of her foot, she swung her leg up hard and fell over the side of the wall with a thud.

A few seconds passed, as she listened to the two dogs, bark, snarl, and whine on the other side. A man's voice soon entered the mix, calling to the dogs to come. Well, trained as they were, she heard them expel air from their nose as if they were trying to get her smell out of them and then left.

She waited while her heart rate normalized, and her breathing came back under control before she got up to leave. What had she witnessed? How did Kathy and Ingrid fit into the disappearance of the La Brea Woman? There seemed to be more questions than answers, but at least she now knew two more people she couldn't trust.

CHAPTER THIRTY-TWO

For Wulf, the smell of the morgue brought back bad memories. It'd been three years but suddenly felt like yesterday that he'd found himself standing in this very place, struggling to find the courage to identify his wife's body. That night had been one the city would not soon forget—a late-night attack in the Emergency Room at the hospital. His wife, Julia, had been the nurse in charge that night.

Wulf shook his head trying to clear away the memories that wanted to come flooding back. It didn't work. That night had been a full moon. The two had even joked about the crazies coming out in full-force at night, and to be extra careful. Wulf hadn't given it a second thought until he'd heard a report of an attack come over the police radio.

The memories caused his heart to break all over again, a sinking in his stomach instantly souring it. He tossed his coffee into the trash and walked over to the window of the waiting room and tried in vain to forget.

Julia lost her life that night, and there wasn't a day that went by that he didn't wish it'd been him, instead. Wulf turned away from the window and crossed his arms, slowly lowering himself into the chair nearest to him. No, something was different…he'd changed. This place. The memories. The resurgence of emotion. They opened his eyes to a truth he hadn't thought possible. A day…make that a few days, had actually passed without him thinking about that night. What had changed?

Mariska Stevenson. That's what had changed. She'd entered his heart and mind, even though he hadn't been ready for it to happen.

"Detective?" Dr. Hernandez, the coroner, said. "You can come back and have a look if you'd like."

Why else would I be here?

"Thanks," Wulf said as he stood from the uncomfortable folding chair in the waiting room. He followed the doctor back into the autopsy lab.

The smell immediately intensified. Strong chemical smells mixed with the odor of death.

Gore.

Dr. Hernandez pushed through the metal door into the autopsy room, Wulf following on his heels. Lying on the stainless-steel table was the body of the victim, Jane Bergstrom. Mariska's former housekeeper was covered with a white plastic sheet, but sitting next to the table were metal bowls containing her organs.

Wulf stepped around the table took in the site before him. The woman had met an untimely end, that was clear, but the Coroner had details to share.

"What do you have for me, Doc?"

"Cause of death, exsanguination. But the brutality of this attack has me stumped."

Wulf cocked his head to the side, looking at the woman, as the doctor slowly uncovered the body. "What do you mean? Stumped?"

"This woman had been beaten," he said, pointing to multiple bruises on her face, arms, and legs. "Both of her legs had been broken. You see here?" He pointed to marks in the middle of both lower legs.

"Are those…?" Wulf leaned in for a better look.

"Yeah, tread marks from the killer's shoes." The doctor shook his head. "Both her tibia and fibula were broken, mid-shaft. I've seen injuries like these in people who've been stomped or trampled to death. Either way, the sheer force it takes to cause a Tib-Fib fracture is incredible."

"So, the killer is strong."

"Yes, but I think it's more than that."

"What do you mean?" Wulf cocked his head to the side.

"When you look at her other injuries." Dr. Hernandez pointed at her abdomen. "She was repeatedly stabbed in the abdomen. But no single stab would have killed her."

Wulf turned to the doctor. *This woman had been tortured.* But why?

"That look on your face, Detective, is the same look I had. I couldn't figure out why someone would torture this woman." Dr. Hernandez walked around to the far side of the table, standing across from, Wulf. "Can you hand me the enterotome?"

"The what?"

"It's the thing that looks like a long pair of scissors with a hook on one end of the blade."

Wulf found the instrument on the table and handed it across to the doctor.

The doctor put the weird-shaped scissors into the long gash across Jane's neck and opened them, effectively widening the gash. He then dug his gloved-fingers into the opening and pulled out a flap of human-tissue.

"Is that her tongue?"

"Precisely," Dr. Hernandez said. "She was given a Columbian Neck-tie, which in the past had been referred to as an Italian Neck-tie."

"I remember when I first picked Mariska up after the attack and she was so hysterical. She told me the woman's neck had been slashed, but I had no idea it was this bad."

"Terrible way to die."

Wulf shook his head and pulled out his phone. "Fuck. I need to find out more about this act…is it ritualistic?"

"What'd you find out?" the doctor asked as he covered up the woman's body.

"Basically, it's used as a way to intimidate and control the victim's family or associates. Symbolic of teaching someone a lesson. But it's also as a way to show someone either snitched or wouldn't give up information." Wulf crossed his arms. "Clearly, this woman wasn't a snitch. My guess is she was roughed up and tortured to make her talk. Whoever did this, wanted…needed, information. And, either Jane Bergstrom didn't know the answer or wouldn't give it…either way, she didn't give anything up and suffered for it."

"Do you have any idea what the killer wanted to know? From what I'd been told, she was in the wrong place at the wrong time…didn't live in the apartment where she was found."

"That's correct," Wulf said. "I don't know for certain, but I have a pretty good idea."

How am I going to keep Mariska safe?

CHAPTER THIRTY-THREE

Mariska sat in her car for a couple minutes outside her family's home. The sun had begun to set, and the beautiful orange and reds glowed over the ocean in the distance. What was she going to say to her parents about Jane? They were doing to ask her questions. There was nothing she wanted more than for all of this to have been a bad dream, but it was real—too real. With a pit in her stomach that she couldn't wish away, she opened the car door and went to the front door.

Reaching for the doorbell, she suddenly realized, even this was going to be different. Jane was no longer there to answer the door or greet her with wide open arms and a smile that cured anything that ailed her. The pit in her belly deepened, and she swallowed hard against the lump in her throat.

The normally pleasant door-chime seemed hollow and scratched at her nerves. A few moments passed with no sign of life. Should she have called ahead? If she had, Mariska would have come up with a thousand and one reasons not to show. She checked the time on her phone. Her parents weren't the going out late type people and were generally a couple of homebodies. They should be here. An unexpected panic started rising inside. Had something happened to them, too? She hadn't heard from them since the night Jane was murdered. They'd called and messaged her, but she hadn't really spoken with them. They'd been silent, since.

She fished into her bag for the key when the door made a click. Oh, thank goodness someone was home—alive. The door swung open, and her mom stood there, a living, breathing, zombie of her normal self. Her eyes were sunken, her face pale. Normally, whenever she saw Mariska, her eyes lit up, full of life, but not this time.

"Mom?" Mariska took a step toward her, arms widening into the offer of an embrace.

Leah's expression didn't change, but she brought a crumpled tissue to her eyes and dabbed away the tears. It wasn't until Mariska wrapped her arms around her mom that she felt her tremble.

"Oh, Mariska…I can't…" Leah let out a sigh that ended in a series of sobs.

Mariska squeezed her tight, slowly rocking back and forth as her mom softened. Seconds later Leah melted into Mariska's arms, and she soon shared in the heartache. Back and forth, in the doorway, they rocked from side to side. Mariska kissed the top of her head and smoothed her hair down in the back, soothing her the only way she knew how—the same way her mom…and Jane had soothed her as a child.

They released each other and Mariska closed the door behind them. Leah held her hand and led her through the entryway and into the sitting room. On the sofa, Mariska sat next to her while they held hands in silence. Every few minutes Leah used a crumpled tissue to wipe the ever-present tears from her cheeks.

"Is Dad home?"

Leah nodded. "He should be down in a minute. We saw your car in the driveway for a few minutes before you rang the doorbell. We weren't sure you were going to come inside."

Mariska kissed her mom's hands. "To be honest, I wasn't sure I was going to either."

Their eyes locked and Mariska knew she felt her sadness despite the lack of outward emotion. Mariska had always battled hard to remain in control of her emotions and seldom had her family seen her lose control of them. Tears flowed down Leah's cheeks, her bloodshot eyes swollen, and her nose began to run.

Mariska spotted a box of tissues on the end table. "You're going to need a fresh tissue." She jumped up and hurried to grab the box.

"About time you decided to show up," her father's voice came from the doorway.

She turned and saw her father standing there, hands on his hips, shoulders back, strong. Had she not known him so well, she wouldn't have even suspected he was hurting emotionally. But even his eyes were a bit puffy and red, no doubt from the tears of grief he was feeling.

Mariska ran to her dad and threw her arms around him. She breathed in his smell and nearly lost control of her pent-up sadness. She squeezed him snug around the midsection, and his arms closed around her, but he didn't tighten his hold on her. A hardness in him wasn't melting away like it had with her mom. He was hurting, but he was mad…at her. She pulled away and looked up at him.

"I'm so sorry, Dad." She held one of his hands in hers. His arms remained limp, disinterested in her apology.

"Your mother was extremely worried about you." He pulled his hand free and stepped around her on his way to join Leah on the sofa.

"I'm—" Mariska started to apologize once again, but her father interrupted.

"Sorry? Yeah, you've said that already. But where were you when we needed you?"

Mariska went to answer but stopped when she saw her dad's hand come up. "Jane was murdered…in your apartment. Do you have any idea how scared we were? How upset?"

Mariska didn't answer, simply nodded.

"No, I don't think you do," Robert continued. "We got an unexpected knock at the door from the police telling us Jane was found dead in your apartment. When we inquired about you, they told us there'd been a struggle…" His voice caught in his throat, and it nearly tore her heart out. He cleared his throat and swallowed hard. His finger now pointed directly at Mariska. "You should have come home to us right away. We needed you, and I know you needed us. How dare you…"

Mariska knew he was right and she hated herself for her own selfish weakness.

Leah's hand came up and pulled her husband's hand back down on his lap. Mariska didn't know what to say or do. She'd never seen her father this upset with her. The disappointment and distrust in his eyes and the anger in his voice pierced her like a spear through the heart. She was losing control. Her hands shook, and her knees grew wobbly. If she didn't sit, she would fall. Looking for a place to land, she took two steps and fell into a chair. Unable to look at her parents she buried her head in her hands.

"I'm sorry," Mariska said. "I'm so, so, sorry." She shook her head and clenched fists full of her hair, tugging at it.

She heard her mom say, "Robert."

Without looking, Mariska knew they were on their way to comfort her. She felt like a horrible daughter. She didn't deserve their forgiveness, but she desperately wanted it. Within seconds, she felt her mom and dad's arms wrapped around her, their bodies covering her in a collective embrace. Their sobs shook her but didn't move her own suppressed emotions. Mariska uncovered her face and wiped the bangs from her sweaty face. Her parents knelt around her, Leah holding her hands, Robert's hands on her knees. Mariska fell into her father's arms and hugged him, then her mom. She kissed her mom's tear-dampened cheeks.

"I really am so sorry."

"We, know," Leah said as she looked at her husband. He nodded and gave a reassuring, but flat smile.

It was getting late, and after all the emotional turmoil, Mariska yawned. Her mom and dad stood and offered Mariska a hand. She took it and got up from the chair. The three of them walked into the kitchen together, and her mom started to make some hot chocolate. Something that always soothed her before bedtime as a kid. Robert went over and sat on the barstool in front of the kitchen island. Mariska joined him. They watched in silence as Leah heated the milk on the stove.

"We need to work hard to put this awful tragedy behind us, so we can heal as a family," Robert said. Leah turned and nodded her agreement, although the sadness in her eyes was clear. "Jane will never be forgotten. She was a part of this family and will always have a place in it. We've already started funeral arrangements, and her burial plot will be next to ours."

"That's wonderful," Mariska said, a round of fresh tears welling up in her eyes. "I don't think I can ever get the image of what I saw out of my mind." She shook her head and clamped her eyes shut. Sobs wracked her body before her dad put a soothing hand on her back, pulling her into a hug. After a few moments, she sat back up and wiped away the tears. "I think I will need to throw myself back into work. It'll be a much-needed distraction. So, once we find the La Brea Woman, I can be reinstated at the museum."

Leah dropped the spoon she'd been stirring the milk with and let out a soft cry when it hit the floor with a clang. Mariska jumped up and ran around the side of the island and picked it up for her.

"Are you, okay?" Mariska said. Her mom's worried expression aimed at Robert drew Mariska's attention back and forth between her parents.

Robert slapped the granite countertop and stood. "Enough."

Mariska flinched at her dad's outburst.

"Robert," Leah said.

Mariska looked from her mom and then back to her dad. She'd missed something. Her parents passed a silent message between them, and her mom turned back to the stove and turned off the burner.

"What's going on?" Mariska asked, but her mom turned and left the kitchen without uttering another word.

"Have a seat," Robert said, pulling out the barstool for her to sit in. "We need to talk."

Mariska took a seat and waited to hear what he had to say.

"Your mother and I have been talking. We love you more than anything in this world, but we cannot allow you to continue this utterly ridiculous pursuit."

"Utterly ridiculous?"

"The La Brea Woman."

"What about her?" Mariska went to stand up.

"Sit," he said and tapped a finger on the island countertop. She sat, and he continued. "We have decided that we can no longer support you in your pursuit of answers. We understand your need to learn about her…considering how little you know about your own past."

Mariska knew his words hurt him to say. Her parents hated to acknowledge they weren't her biological family, despite the obviousness of it. She never felt anything other than love and support from them and loved them as her parents, but it was clear it bothered them when confronted about it.

"Dad, I need to find her."

"Why? Why do you need to put your life at risk? Why do other people in your life need to get hurt…" his voice caught in his throat again as his emotions began to rise. "Give me a reason that makes this all worth it."

Mariska went to answer, but her words went missing. Lost to emotion and her rising self-doubt. "Because…I have to."

Robert let out a long, slow breath through his nose. "In that case, we have to do this. As long as you are pursuing this dangerous and unnecessary goal, we will no longer be able to support you. As much as it kills us to tell you this, we will cut off financial support as well as ask you not to return to our home."

"I can't come home?" Mariska felt like she'd been punched in the gut, feeling instantly nauseous. "You're disowning me?"

The pain in his eyes was obvious, but he continued. "We cannot support your need to get yourself killed, and I cannot risk your mother's life so you can find the remains of a woman who's already dead. Dead, Mariska. This person you're looking for is dead…for thousands of years. Your mother and I are here in the now. Aren't we enough for you? Haven't we given you everything you've ever wanted?"

"Of course. You've both been the best parents I could have ever had. But this had nothing to do with you. I need to do this for me."

She shook her head. "I don't expect you to understand."

Robert threw his hand up in the air. "Great. It's settled then. You can stay the night, tonight, but then you're going to need to leave. When you've finished following this foolhardy pursuit, you can come back." He turned to leave the kitchen, but stopped and looked back at her. "I only hope you will see the error in your ways before you get yourself hurt. Your mother and I can't sit around and watch you do this to yourself."

Mariska's shoulders drooped as her father walked away. She put her head in her hands and clamped her eyes shut. Her apartment was still roped off by the police and wouldn't be available until tomorrow. But there was no way she was going to stay here.

Fighting the urge to run upstairs and beg for her parents' forgiveness and for them to understand why she needed to find the La Brea Woman, she tiptoed over to the stairway and looked up. The entire upstairs landing was deserted. Nothing, but darkness looked back.

She turned and took in the room. Would she ever be back? It would depend on if she survived everything she planned on doing. Running back into the kitchen, she pulled her purse up from the barstool and headed out the front door. Sending a text requesting asylum wasn't what she'd wanted to do, but at this point, she didn't have another choice. What had been done, was done.

"Please forgive me," Mariska said out loud as she drove away from her parents' home. She watched it slowly disappear in the distance, and a new feeling settled deep into her gut. Mariska was now completely on her own. Despite knowing she had credit cards and a savings account to fall back on, she really needed a hug. She swallowed hard to stave off the coming tears. Inhaling a deep, calming breath, she let it out slow and steady. The one person she needed right now was Jane and that was forever an impossibility. *I love you, Jane.*

CHAPTER THIRTY-FOUR

Mariska sat in Chief Peter Grassland's living room. His house wasn't a mansion in the outskirts of town, like Kathy's or Ingrid's had been. However, it was grand in its own right. When she'd first arrived, she walked right up to the front door. There hadn't been a gate or security guard to greet her.

The five-thousand square foot, white, two-story Spanish-styled home sat in the middle of a six-acre patch of land that was sought-after by every developer in the area. Or, at least that's what Theresa had told her when she'd called to get directions to the estate. When Theresa had mentioned it was in the heart of Beverly Hills, Mariska couldn't have imagined it. From the main street, the turnoff to get there wasn't well-marked, and if you weren't familiar with the area, you'd never know it was even there.

The furnishings inside were an eclectic display to behold. The entryway was modern, the walls filled with abstract paintings, the niches equally spaced down the hallway housed glass and metallic sculptures—some were ornate, while others were simple, plain.

She sat uncomfortably on a nineteenth-century sofa with an ornate gold and red patterned fabric. The front of the sofa's arms and legs were dark wood that'd been carved to reveal the look of leaves. Mariska squirmed while she waited for Chief Grassland to arrive, his maid had rushed to get him from the second floor, but he still hadn't arrived.

Might as well look around. The thick brown hair from the buffalo skin on the back of the sofa was beginning to poke through her top.

It made an already uncomfortable experience, far worse. She stood and walked across the room to look at the pictures on the table against the wall. Chief Grassland and his family were quite photogenic. Contagious smiles and excitement was evident in all the pictures. But that's when she noticed another framed photo on the small end table, under a reading lamp. She knelt down to get a better look. It was an older picture, from the look of it, dating back thirty or forty years. Chief Grassland appeared much younger, and their clothes reeked of the late seventies.

Standing next to each other, the younger Grassland and male teenager…maybe early twenties. It was hard to tell. They weren't smiling, although they clearly had affection for one another, the chief with his arm around the younger man's shoulders. The similarity between the two men was evident, and she suspected they were father and son. She stood back up and looked back at the pictures on the table. None of the others contained a picture of the young man.

"Sorry to keep you waiting," Chief Grassland said, as he walked into the room.

Mariska twirled on her heel, hurried across the room, and offered her hand. He accepted the greeting. "It's great to meet you, Chief Grassland. My name is Dr. Mariska Stevenson."

"Please, call me Peter," he said with a huge smile. "Let's leave the Chief part to the members of my tribe, shall we?"

"As you wish." She was shown to the same sofa she'd rather not sit in and asked to have a seat. Reluctantly, she complied. "I'm really sorry to come here unannounced."

"Do not be sorry, my dear. I'm an old man. Any time a beautiful young woman wants to come and visit me, I will gladly accept it." He smiled and took a seat in an armchair adjacent to her.

Mariska smiled and folded her hands in her lap. "I'm not sure if you are aware of this or not, but I work at the Page Museum."

His eyes narrowed ever so slightly. "I knew you looked familiar, but couldn't quite place your face." He shrugged his shoulders. "One of the perks of getting old, I suppose. So, what do I owe this visit?"

"I have some bad news," Mariska said.

"Bad, news?"

"Yes." Mariska shifted in her seat. "The La Brea Woman's remains have been stolen."

She wasn't sure what she expected from this old man. A confession? Some kind of emotional outburst? Anger? He offered nothing. Peter Grassland, sat in silence for a few moments, just long enough to make her start to sweat.

He broke the awkward silence. "I'd heard rumors of such an incident. I'm disappointed that the Page Museum didn't come to me personally to inform me of such a terrible thing. As you may be aware, I have, on the behalf of my tribe, been requesting her remains to be return to us."

"I am aware of that fact." Mariska cleared her throat before pressing on. "I was awarded a grant by the museum to study her remains. I had hoped that through my efforts, I would be able to identify without a shadow of doubt, the rightful heirs to which the remains could be return too. The night I was to be officially awarded the grant, I was attacked in the basement, and the remains were stolen."

The man's eyes betrayed his disappointment and anger. His mouth tightened into a thin line, and Mariska worried what he was going to say next. He took a deep breath and let it out slowly through pursed lips. "Very upsetting. So, what is the nature of your visit? To provide this old man with devastating news? Seems a cruelty I hadn't expected from you."

"Oh, no." Mariska reached out. "I don't want to upset you. I just wanted to provide you with all the background information first. My goal is to find her remains. I want to continue with my research, so I can hopefully return her to her rightful people."

He straightened in the chair. "So, how can I be of assistance? Surely, you haven't come here looking for her? You don't suspect my people or me, do you?"

She was on shaky ground right now. Almost everyone was a suspect in her mind, at this point. But how could she say that without offending him? "I'm not here to accuse anyone of anything. I have some questions that I think might shed light on her whereabouts…or, at least possibly give me an idea of who might have wanted to take her."

"Since this is the first I'm hearing of this, I can't imagine I will be of much help. But I'll be happy to tell you what I know." Peter sat back into the chair and crossed his leg.

Mariska smiled. "That sounds perfect. If nothing else, I'd like to learn more about the La Brea Woman and the tar pits from your perspective. Knowledge is power, as people like to say."

"Would you like something to drink, before we get started?"

"No thank you, I hope not to take up too much of your time."

She made herself comfortable on the sofa before she continued. "I've seen some pictures at Ingrid Ashton's home dating back to when the La Brea Woman was found."

"Yes, that was a long time ago. Even before, this old man was born."

"There was a young Native American man in the pictures. Do you know who that could have been?" Mariska asked. "Was it a member of your tribe?"

"Yes. In fact, the man in the photograph was my father. I know it well, as our two families, the Grasslands and the Ashtons, go back a very, very long time."

"So, your father *was* present when they discovered her remains. Did he ever tell you stories of that day? And did any of his stories have any *interesting* or not-well known details you can share with me?" Mariska was fishing in the pond without any bait. She wasn't willing to reveal her own hand, but was hoping to persuade him to give up his.

He gave her a sideways glance before he continued. "Interesting or not-well known details. That's a curiously phrased question."

Shit, he's not as old and feeble-minded as he led on.

"My father was never the same after the La Brea Woman's discovery. He always said he knew deep in his bones that she belonged to us. Then, these white men scoop her out of the ground and put her on display. Like some kind of animal, unworthy of the honor she should have been provided through the time-honored rituals of our people. Then as soon as we begin our fight to have her returned to us, the museum removed her from display…only a small plaque remains stating one set of human remains have ever been found in the pits. It's like our history is being wiped clean."

Mariska's heart ached as she listened to him speak. His father's pain had been passed down and become his own.

"Did your father ever mention anything unusual about the body?"

"One that he always felt curious was how she was found with her arms wrapped around a small dog. It would have been unusual for someone to have domesticated a small canine during that time…or at least, that's what the history books say."

"You're right. Commonly accepted research indicated that canines weren't domesticated until later in the America's. However, to be honest, the timelines of the people of the world are constantly shifting. Changes are always being written in as further research is completed and new discoveries are made."

"My father only mentioned one other strange thing about the La Brea Woman discovery."

Mariska sat up straighter on the sofa. "Yes?"

"He mentioned that it ruined his friendship with Mr. Ashton. Apparently, they had been fast friends from childhood. That all changed when they found the remains."

"Other than the obvious, did he mention why?"

"Not anything specific. He said there were two discoveries made that day. When pressed about the second discovery, he would grow quiet and change the subject." Peter leaned in closer to Mariska. "You have to understand; in those days, we had respect and honor-lines…even within the family that could not be crossed. When my father said, no, he meant, no."

Damn, it. Did Peter Grassland's father know about the tooth and beads?

"Does the Chumash or any other local tribes have legends

surrounding creatures that may or may not actually exist?"

Peter looked at her like she'd lost her damn mind.

"I know, that's a really strange question," Mariska said with a laugh. "I've heard rumors about creatures with large teeth, specifically eye-teeth, that don't match anything else we've discovered up to this point. I'm just wondering if you've heard anything about these creatures…maybe in folklore or tradition."

"There is a legend amongst our people that is told to misbehaving children." Peter smiled and a snicker escaped his lips. "They are called the Night-howler. Many other names come to mind like Bigfoot and Yeti, but all referring to the same legend."

"Night-howler, huh?"

"Yes, the legend says that children that misbehave or don't do as they are told will be taken away from the tribe in the middle of the night. This mythical creature lives in the forested areas and howls at night…thus, the name. Anyway, it's a traditional story passed down from generation to generation. I can remember sitting up some nights waiting for the creature to come and take me away after I disobeyed my father." Peter laughed again as the memories were relived.

"It's too bad that there hasn't been any proof of these Night Howlers in the fossil record. I bet it would be easier to get the kids today to behave if we had found them."

"It's probably for the best." His voice changed from light-hearted to deadly serious.

"How, so?" Mariska wasn't smiling anymore.

"Legend has it that the bones of the Night Howler are sacred. Anyone possessing them without the proper authority is cursed."

"Cursed, how?"

"Not sure, exactly." Peter stood and stretched. "As far as I've ever heard, there's never been any bones in possession. My guess is they don't exist, so there was never a need to elaborate."

Mariska stood. She had a feeling with the mood in the room having shifted so drastically, her time here was up.

"Can I ask you a personal question, Peter?"

"Certainly."

"While I was waiting for you I took a look at the photos on your table."

"Ah, yes. Some of the best photos we as a family have taken."

"They certainly are." She paused for a moment. "I was wondering about that one." She pointed to the one under the reading lamp. "Who is that young man in the picture with you?"

His expression hardened, and he took a moment to answer. Clearing his throat, he said, "That was my son."

"Was?"

"He passed away a long time ago." Emotion began to rise up into Peter's voice. He cleared his throat again. "He was a troubled youth. Got into drugs. A similar story to so many other families that have suffered such a great loss."

"I'm so sorry for your loss." Mariska looked away so she wouldn't cry.

Peter shook his head, no doubt pushing the emotional memories back into safekeeping. "I'm surprised you didn't know about him?"

Mariska gave him a quizzical look. "Oh, yeah? Why's that?"

"No reason, I suppose. You'd mentioned you were friends with Ms. Ashton. I assumed she told you."

Definitely, not friends, Mariska thought. She couldn't imagine why Ingrid would have brought it up, other than Mariska having seen old photos of Peter's father. Maybe she would have to ask Ingrid about it the next time she saw her.

Mariska shook his hand and walked with him to the front door. In the driveway, Mariska saw the catering van parked in front of the house. That reminded her of another question she had. "Are you having something catered today? That's the same company we use at the Page Museum for our events."

"Yes, a birthday party for my grandchildren. Twin boys." He puffed his chest out a bit with pride. Surely, he had to know if she looked into it, she'd find out he owned the company. But she decided to let it drop…for now.

He stopped her before she left the house. "I would be very

careful if I were you."

"Why's that?"

"Whoever took the La Brea Woman's remains is still out there. And, if you have something in your possession that they still want or need, they won't stop until they get it. Remember, they've already hurt you once, they can do it again."

The image of Jane sprawled out on Mariska's bedroom floor, blood soaking into the carpet and dripping from the walls, made her shake her head. "It's too late for that."

They've already hurt me more than you can imagine.

CHAPTER THIRTY-FIVE

Mariska parked the car in the parking lot behind David's apartment. After leaving her parent's house, she'd called David and asked if she could crash at his place before she paid Peter Grassland a visit. She got out of the car and opened the trunk. Inside, she pulled out the computer bag. Slinging it over one shoulder and the purse over the other, she hustled across the parking lot. The darkness of night hadn't used to bother her as much as it did now. After being attacked and stalked this past week, she was a bit jumpy. A man throwing a full garbage bag into the dumpster made her jump. She pulled the straps of her bags closer to her, and she picked up the pace.

David's apartment was on the second floor of a new and enormous complex that stretched a full city block. She was almost to the staircase that lead to his place when something caught her attention. Someone was following her. Mariska stopped and turned to look behind her. The shadows were playing tricks on her, right? The lampposts retrofitted with LED lights cast some of the most glaring and hideous looking shadows she'd ever seen. A noise to the left turned her on her heel, and she ran the rest of the way to the staircase. Two by two, she dashed up the concrete steps and pounded on his door. With her back to the door, she searched the grounds below for any signs of danger while she waited for David to answer the door.

Nothing. No sign of anything other than the man who'd been throwing away the trash, walking back to his own place on the other side of the courtyard. The door opened behind her, and she stumbled backward as she'd been leaning against it.

"Oh, my gosh," David said. "Mariska, are you okay?"

She tossed her bags into his apartment and hurried inside. "Yeah, why? I'm good. How are you?"

David closed the door. He started to step toward her, arms out for a hug, but she reached past him and locked the door.

"Are you sure you're okay?" he asked.

She hugged him. The familiarity was nice. He was a solidly built man, which made her feel a little less on her own. "I'm better, now."

He tightened his arms around her. They stood in the entryway in an embrace for a few moments. Then, David kissed the top of her head, and she pulled away. She'd lingered a touch too long. Mariska smiled. "Thank you so much for letting me stay here tonight."

David waved her gratitude away as if he'd done nothing of importance. "You're more than welcome to stay. I have to ask you something though."

"Sure." She went and sat on his sofa. "But before you do, any chance you have some wine?"

He smiled. "You're in luck. I just picked up a box at the grocery store."

Box? They still made boxes of wine? "Great," she said. "Would it be a bother to have a glass?"

"No trouble at all." David disappeared into the kitchen.

She needed a couple minutes to clear her head. She owed him a huge apology, and she needed a minute to formulate the right words to say. He deserved more than an apology, he deserved the grant, and she intended on telling him so.

He returned with two glasses filled with a pinkish liquid. "I hope a Rosé will be suitable for you."

Not her favorite, but she smiled anyway. "Of course. Thank, you."

Mariska took the proffered drink and sipped it. It was too sweet for her taste, but she appreciated the attempt. "Oh, yum. That's surprisingly good."

"Really?" He took a sip, smacking his lips as he swallowed it down. "Not, bad, huh?"

She leaned back into the soft sofa and rubbed her hand across the leather surface. Was this new? He hadn't mentioned getting new furniture. Wow, she'd been a terrible friend, lately. He would have normally taken her with to pick it out, spent days mulling it over with her while they shared dinners discussing such a purchase.

"You like it?" He sat next to her and rubbed the cushioned back of the sofa.

"It's so comfortable. I love it." She yawned. "Man, I'm tired."

"Long day?" He leaned back. "So, what gives? Why the sudden need to see me? I think the last time we saw each other you accused me of stealing your grant."

He removed his dark-rimmed glasses and rubbed his eyes. But when he put them back on, he looked at her differently. It was clear he was still hurting from the other night. She'd cut him deep, and she was sorry for that. She sat up on the edge of the sofa cushion and leaned in, putting her hand on his knee.

"David, I want to apologize for my behavior at the restaurant. I think the news about your grant hit me unexpectedly hard and I lashed out."

"You sure did." He took another sip of wine.

She followed suit, taking down half the glass. "I'm sorry. I know you didn't do anything wrong. In fact, I'm happy for you."

"You are?" He arched his eyebrows in surprise.

"Of course I am. You're my best friend, and you're getting to do some amazing things in your career. You deserve this grant and many more. I know your future is bright. And, I will support you in any way I can…you know, once I'm reinstated at the museum."

"Mariska…do you think that will happen?" His question hit her stomach like a sucker punch. "I don't mean to be hurtful, but Dr. Snyder thinks you were involved with the theft of the La Brea Woman."

"That's absurd…you believe me, don't you?" Mariska pulled her hand away from him.

"Yeah, I believe you. But it doesn't really matter what I think."

"It matters to me," she said.

He looked at her for a moment in silence. "Okay, let's say you get reinstated. Would you want to be my assistant on this Dire Wolf project?"

She swallowed her pride and nodded. "Absolutely. I'd love to help you." It wasn't a total lie. She would love to help him get to the bottom of why this Dire Wolf was so much larger than the others found at the Page Museum, it'd be a fantastic achievement for him and an honor to be a part of it. It's too bad they both couldn't have received a grant.

David drained his wine, as did she. He said, "I'm surprised you're not staying with your parents. I always thought that was your home away from home."

"It used to be." She wouldn't…couldn't, go into all the gory details, but she'd offer him something. "You remember my family's housekeeper, Jane?"

"Yeah, that cool older lady? You two are super close, right?"

A sob came out of nowhere. She broke down, gut-wrenching heaves of sadness poured from her eyes and lungs. Was that what wailing sounded like? Before she took a second breath, he was next to her on the sofa, his arms wrapped around her. She didn't pull away. She didn't speak. He rocked her back and forth, her face pressed against his chest, her tears dampening his shirt. A few minutes passed in slow motion, locked in a pathetic embrace of emotion and regrets, Mariska hated herself at this very moment. She wasn't this weak and vulnerable, but she couldn't stop the tears.

"I'm sorry about your shirt," Mariska said as she sat up and brushed at the makeup smears she'd left behind.

"Don't be." The kindness in his eyes and the softness of his voice and touch made her fall back into his embrace. He hugged her tight and continued to rock her back and forth. His soothing words of comfort and the way his hands caressed her hair, made her hold on to him, not ever wanting to let go.

Some time passed without a word being spoken. Her emotions slowly stabilized, and she felt herself regain control. When she sat up, she felt a little dizzy. No doubt the blood was rushing away from her head after being forced there during her uncontrolled crying. She wiped away the residual tears and used the tissue David offered to wipe her nose.

"Pretty classy huh?" Mariska said with a sad, bitter laugh.

"I think you're amazing." He brushed away the bangs that'd matted to her forehead. "I'm here for you if and when you want to talk about it."

"Thank you." She looked away. David could gather that Jane had died, but was kind enough not to ask for clarification. Not right now, anyway. "Is there somewhere I can crash for the night? The sofa?"

He looked a bit surprised for a second. "Don't be silly. I have a bedroom."

She knew the apartment was a one bedroom. There was no way he could afford a two-bedroom on his salary. Not in Los Angeles where the apartment prices increased by the minute. Was she ready to share a bed with him? Friends could share a bed, right?

"You look scared," David said with a smile. "Don't worry; I'm not asking you to un-friend-zone me. It's just two adults sleeping in the same room."

"Oh, yeah. For, sure." Mariska followed him into his room.

Thankfully, he had a king-sized bed which would make sleeping possible without having to spoon. After freshening up in the bathroom, they got into bed together, and he turned off the bedside lamp.

"David?"

"Yeah?"

"Thank you…for everything." There was so much more she wanted to say but didn't trust herself at the moment.

He reached under the covers and grasped her hand in his and squeezed it. "Anything for you."

She rolled over and placed a hand on his chest, her face against his shoulder. They stayed in this position for a while. David's breaths grew long and slow as he drifted off to sleep. Mariska started to feel that familiar tug of sleep. The weightlessness soothing away the recent aches and pains and offering her a reprieve from the mental and emotional stress she'd been under.

A soft buzzing noise came from the front room. It was her cell phone. Was her dad calling to apologize and beg for her to come home? It stopped. She'd check it in the morning, but right now she wanted sleep. Seconds later, the buzzing returned. Whoever it was must have really wanted to talk to her. Mariska looked up into David's peacefully sleeping face. A flutter of emotion she hadn't expected or wanted surprised her. *Don't be stupid, Mariska,* she thought. *Don't make any unnecessary emotional attachments.* She sighed and slowly extracted herself from his bed, ever careful not to wake him.

Tiptoeing into the other room, Mariska fished the phone from her purse. It wasn't her dad, but an unknown number. Badger. A series of texts telling her that she's in danger started coming through. The last text said: *It's time to go. Copenhagen will give you the answers you seek.*

How the hell did Badger know about Copenhagen?

The wad of cash she withdrew from her trust fund earlier in the day could get her to Europe, but it wouldn't help her book a flight at this hour. She needed to do that online with a credit card. Had her dad frozen the cards or would he do that in the morning? They were her cards, but her father was a joint cardholder in case of emergencies. Mariska looked back toward the bedroom. David was still asleep. She needed to remain silent. If he found out she was going there, he would surely tell her father and ruin everything. She grabbed her laptop and took out one of the credit cards. A quick search for a flight to Copenhagen revealed a seat available on a five A.M flight. It wasn't first-class, but since it was last minute, the price seemed nearly as expensive. She checked the time, two in the morning. She didn't have much time to get there.

Mariska yawned. Oh, hell. She could sleep on the flight. With a wish upon a star, she typed in the credit card number and clicked submit. The computer system thought about what it was doing for a few minutes, but then the fifteen-hundred-dollar plane ticket price was accepted, and she messaged herself the boarding pass. Without much time to spare, she closed the computer and packed it away in her bag. Trying to remain silent, she debated on writing him a note before she left and decided it was necessary. She pulled out a small piece of paper from her bag and wrote him a message.

David,

Thank you for everything you've done for me. I didn't want to wake you before I left, so I am leaving you this message. No matter what happens to me, please know I've cherished our friendship. I will be in touch as soon as I am able.

With much love, Mariska.

She pulled open the door to leave and looked back into the apartment. The small apartment was dark, and she couldn't see past the soft green glow from the clock on the end table. If David had watched her go, he'd done so in silence and from the shadows. Mariska mouthed the word, *goodbye*, before pulling the door closed behind her.

Was she making a mistake not telling him? There wasn't time to dwell on her decisions. She needed to swing by Walmart and pick up some essentials and then make her flight. There was a few more hours before her dad would wake up and cancel her credit cards, and she needed to make the time count.

CHAPTER THIRTY-SIX

Mariska finished checking in with the airline and went to sit in a row of chairs near security. Folding her arms in front of her, she scanned the throngs of early morning passengers hurrying to their gates. People of all walks of life, age, and size mixed together into a loud, bustling crowd. It would have been easy for the killer to hide in plain sight. Was the man who wished her dead here? Did he know where she was going?

Mariska yawned. Damn, it was too early to be tired. She still had a long day ahead of her, but hopefully, she'd get some sleep on the plane.

"Is this seat taken?"

Mariska looked up and smiled. Detective Wulf had come through in a pinch. "Thank you so much."

She'd begged him to stop by her apartment and get her passport. There wouldn't be a way for her to even take this trip without it. And, since she didn't have full access to her apartment yet, he was the only one who could get it for her. Wulf went to hand her the passport, but when she reached for it, he pulled it back.

"Where are you going?" he asked.

Mariska hesitated. "I can't tell you."

"Can't, or won't?" He still hadn't given her the passport. "I believe I'd mentioned to you that you shouldn't leave the city? There's an active investigation going on."

She looked up at him with a sad, desperate look—large eyes, pouty lips.

"That's not going to work."

Mariska blinked a few times, allowing tears to well up, which caused her vision to swim.

"Damn, you're good." Wulf sighed. "I can't believe I'm not going to handcuff you right now and take you somewhere safe."

She arched an eyebrow.

"Don't give me that look. I need to know where you're going." They locked eyes. "I need to make sure you're going to be okay."

She wiped away her fake tears. "I'm going to Copenhagen. There's a university there that does DNA analysis. It's cutting-edge stuff."

"Why the hell do you need DNA analysis?" His skeptical look was mixed with surprise like he couldn't believe he'd missed something. "Unless you've got the remains stashed somewhere."

"No, nothing like that." She didn't like how he immediately accused her of withholding evidence…even though she hadn't told him everything. "I…happened upon a discovery, of sorts."

"So, what you're telling me is you found something that will point to the whereabouts of the La Brea Woman?"

"Well, not exactly. I think it might help me solve an even bigger mystery."

"Bigger? I think you need to explain further. And, since I'm not a brainiac scientist like yourself, you might need to start from the beginning."

Mariska pulled the tooth and bead from her pocket and covertly showed it to him. "It's a tooth. Non-human. Unknown origin…at this point. I'm hoping that if I can DNA test this and find out what animal it comes from, it could help point to the region that the La Brea Woman's people came from."

"Okay," Wulf said, rubbing his chin. "Why Copenhagen? Why can't you just go to a local university that processes DNA?"

"That's a great question." Mariska shifted positions, squared her shoulders as her excitement began to intensify. "Back in the mid nineteen-nineties, a nearly complete skeleton of a human male was found on the bank of the Columbian River. He's now known as the

Kennewick Man. Anyway, there was a legal battle that ensued where the Native Peoples of the area wanted him return to them for a culturally proper burial. But the men who found him argued that they had no way to prove who the rightful descendants were so the ownership would fall back on them since they discovered him."

"This sounds a lot like what's happened with the La Brea Woman. So, what happened?"

"They took a sample of DNA to Copenhagen and had the university test it. They are on the forefront of DNA analysis, and they have the most extensive peer-reviewed studies and DNA repository in the world." Mariska put a hand on Wulf's leg. "It's the only logical choice we have."

Wulf furrowed his brow, arching one eyebrow. "And, by doing this, you can find who her rightful descendants are, and possibly who stole her?"

She shrugged. "Unless you have any better ideas?"

"Where did you find the tooth? And why didn't you tell me about it before?"

"That's the thing. I found it inside the La Brea Woman's skull the night she went missing, and I was attacked."

"The tooth was just rattling around inside her skull, and no one else had seen it before now?" Wulf seemed skeptical, at best.

"Not, exactly. The tooth, along with nine hand-carved beads were found inside a pouch, inside her skull. The pouch was old, but not something that would have been around fifteen thousand years ago—more like early 1900's. So, someone within the last hundred years stashed it there, but why? I'd like to find out." She shook her head. "It may or may not have anything to do with her theft, but I need to find answers wherever I can at this point."

His eyebrows were pinched together in the middle, and he cocked his head to one side. "So, going back to what was in the pouch. There's beads as well?"

"Yes. Well, sort of. I mean, I have one left. The other eight were stolen from my apartment the first time it was broken into. Somehow they missed this one in the chaos they left behind." She pulled out the blue bead and showed it to him. "See, these markings? I think they represent star systems or constellations."

"Is that significant?"

"It might be later. If I narrow the location down to a specific area, and there happen to be multiple tribes in the region, this could narrow the search further." She shook her head. "I'm grasping at straws here. I'd like to get this solved before anyone else is hurt or killed."

They sat in silence for a moment.

"I mean, even if we can determine who her descendants are, it doesn't mean they took her or even still exist," Wulf said.

"That's absolutely true." Mariska put the tooth and bead back into the pouch and then into her front pocket. "But it would be a good place to start looking. And, if nothing else, once we find her, we will know who to return her to."

"In a weird way, it makes sense." He shook his head. "I can't believe I'm going to allow you to leave. I'm disavowing knowledge of these items, but make sure you bring them back with you."

"Allow me?" Mariska laughed. "I'm not under arrest, am I?" She offered her wrists for him to cuff.

He looked at her hands. "Be careful what you wish for."

They both smiled and stood, and then she threw her arms around him and hugged. It was meant as a thank you hug. Thank you for letting me do this. Thank you for helping me. Thank you for being so kind. But soon, the hug felt different. Mariska sensed an energy between them. She breathed in his scent—Earthy and warm. Her belly tingled. She could have stayed there forever—his warm, strong arms, securely wrapped around her. She opened her eyes and froze. In the distance, among the crowd, she caught a glimpse of David. But then the crowd swarmed around that spot, and his image disappeared. Had he been there? Looking to the left and then right, her heart began to race. Was her mind playing tricks on her? Could exhaustion and guilt make someone think they saw someone that wasn't there?

Wulf whispered in her ear, "I don't want you to go." His voice instantly releasing her from the spell she'd been pulled into.

She pulled away from him and looked up into his eyes. "I wish you could come with me, but I also know I need to do this on my own. You have to stay here and keep looking for Jane's killer."

He nodded, and she backed away toward security. Turning away, she hurried through the first checkpoint, but looked back and saw he was still watching her. He was such a good man, but so was David. It'd been so long since she'd felt anything even remotely romantic for anyone. She'd spent so much time focused on her work and schooling, she hadn't had time. But now in the midst of her world falling apart, there were two wonderful men who made her rethink her decision to remain single.

"Come on, Mariska," she said to herself. "Focus, and get this shit done."

She went all the way through security, fighting her desire to look back at Wulf…to see if he was still watching her. To see if David was really there? After retrieving her things from the conveyor belt, she hurried to the gate. Sitting down for a moment, she took out her phone and called Theresa.

"Hello?" Theresa sounded tired.

Mariska checked the time and cringed. It was a bit early to call but too late to hang up now. "Hey, there. So, sorry to call you this early, but I needed to tell you I'm sitting in the airport. I'm headed to Copenhagen."

Theresa's voice brightened. "Oh, cool. So, what can I do to help on this end?"

"I figured you could help me analyze whatever information I'm able to get."

"Sounds good to me. Who's your contact at the University?"

Mariska took a moment to think. Contact? Shit. "I…I didn't even think of that."

"You're going to need to have someone on the inside over there to get you in the door, let alone perform the testing. I bet they are back-logged for months, if not years with remains needing to have their DNA analyzed."

Mariska could hear Theresa typing while she talked. "I'm open to suggestions. I guess I didn't really think this through very well."

"Not to worry. I'll see what I can do while you're flying. I have a friend at the University of Copenhagen. He and I went to undergrad here in the States, but he pursued his doctorate over there, and I stayed here."

"You are awesome. Thank you. What is your friend's name?"

"Edgar. He went by Eddie when we were together. Really nice guy, but it's been a while since we've spoken. I can tell you this, he's brilliant, can keep a secret, and owes me a favor."

"Sounds…interesting. You'll have to tell me the whole story when I get back."

"Sure, thing," Theresa said. "Hey, Mariska?"

"Yeah?"

"Be careful."

"Thank you, my friend. I'm sure I'll be fine." Mariska looked behind her at the store opening up for the day. "I will call you when I land."

"Safe, flight." Theresa hung up the phone. No, doubt she was already getting things organized for Mariska. She was truly the best partner-in-crime anyone could ask for.

Mariska got up and went into the store. She grabbed two Los Angeles sweatshirts, one pair of shorts, headphones, phone charger and international outlet adaptor, some much-needed toiletries, and the latest copy of her favorite author, Carlie Lemont's book, *Murder at a Discount.* A hundred-dollar-bill covered the cost, and she went back to the gate. She sat, only to hear her flight called for boarding. Getting into line, she filed toward the front like cattle to slaughter.

She handed the airline attendant her boarding pass when the computer beeped, and the light turned red. "Is something wrong?" Mariska asked.

The attendant looked confused for a moment, taking the boarding pass with her to the computer. Butterflies formed in Mariska's tummy. The attendant took long enough for a few passengers behind her to start grumbling. She took a couple deep, cleansing breaths, and tried to relax. The woman returned with a smile on her face.

"Here you go, Doctor Stevenson." She handed Mariska a new boarding pass. "You've been upgraded to first class."

Mariska took the slip of paper with her new assigned seat and said, "Really?" Sure enough. Seat 2A. Window and first-class, just what Mariska liked. "Thank you."

She headed down the ramp toward the airplane, when her phone buzzed with an incoming text message. Mariska didn't recognize the number, but the message said: *Enjoy your flight. Badger.*

How did he manage that? And that's when it hit her. She had a contact number. This was the first time she'd been sent a text by him from a number other than *Unavailable.* Maybe, Badger knew something she didn't, and she'd need his help? Mentally preparing for the long flight ahead and the unknown situation that awaits her, she took an antihistamine to help her sleep on the plane. She had a feeling she was going to need every ounce of strength and rest she was going to get.

CHAPTER THIRTY-SEVEN

Mariska's legs felt stiff and weak as she hurried through the airport. It never ceased to amaze her how sitting in a luxury-seat on an airplane for an extended flight could take more out of her than running a half marathon. She only stopped long enough to get a Starbucks coffee and power-shop through the Marc Jacobs store on the way out—she still had plenty of room on the credit card. She needed clothes that would be appropriate for meeting with some very important people at the university. A new stylish backpack, three shopping bags filled with clothes, her carry-on, purse, and iced coffee in hand, she exited the airport. The flight she took from the Los Angeles airport had been delayed, and by the time she landed in Denmark, it was the next morning. No wonder she was exhausted.

The Copenhagen airport was a flurry of activity. Thousands of passengers rushing to the gates, standing in line at security, and even shopping at the shops that lined the long hallways of the terminals. Mariska was in a hurry but took a moment to appreciate the beauty of the airport itself. The Danish people clearly had an eye for art as the high glass walls, and multi-level styling reminded Mariska of a high-class American mall, rather than a busy transportation hub. Outside, the airport was equally as busy at this hour. People, taxis, buses, and carts overflowing with luggage swarmed in a chaotic mass of life and humanity. It wasn't an ideal place to make a phone call. Mariska looked for a deserted corner where she could put her things down and contact, Theresa.

"Dr. Stevenson?" a man's voice behind her said. She froze for a moment. Who else knew she was here? She hadn't expected to meet Theresa's contact, Edgar until she made it to the University. "Dr. Stevenson?"

Mariska turned and saw a tall, lanky man, with broad shoulders holding a sign with her name on it. The man's tailored suit was expensive, and his shoes looked like Italian leather. This cabbie knew how to dress, not to mention the taxi business must be good in Denmark. He was looking right at her with a questioning look on his face. Before she could respond, he turned to the side, looking further into the crowd of people leaving the airport. He said, "Dr. Stevenson?"

She hurried over to him. "I'm Dr. Stevenson. Did Theresa send you?"

He bowed his head ever so slightly and motioned toward a car parked at the curb a few feet away. She saw it was a very nice, black Mercedes with dark tinted windows. There wasn't a taxi sign on the window, but she wasn't in Los Angeles anymore. Did the city of Copenhagen require their taxis to mark their vehicles somehow? There wasn't time to research it. She took a second to look at the man once again. His eyes were averted as if he was unwilling to make direct eye contact. Sign of respect? He wasn't of classic European descent. His dark skin and beard made her think he could be from the Middle East somewhere. But if Theresa sent him, he must be legit.

He motioned for her to come with him. "Please, Dr. Stevenson, we must go." His accent was thick, but from where, she couldn't tell. Without further hesitation, she went against everything her mother had ever told her about survival in a strange city. Mariska could hear her mom's voice inside her head, telling her it's better to die at the scene than to be taken alive. She shrugged her shoulders and threw all of her bags into the backseat and got in—closing the door behind her. Sealing her fate one way or the other.

The man got into the front seat and started the car.

"Can you please take me directly to the Hilton? I have some important business at the University but need to check in to my room and get freshened up; it was a long flight." Mariska smiled as she spoke.

The man behind the wheel looked at her through the rearview mirror. His eyes were kind but mysterious. He didn't seem like the usual cab driver she'd become used to in Los Angeles. "Absolutely, Dr. Stevenson. I will take you to the Hilton right away."

As he pulled away from the curb, he raised the glass divider between the front and back seats. She sat back in the comfortable leather seat and took a long, cleansing breath. Mariska was finally getting somewhere on this investigation. All she needed to do was meet with the University, have the tooth DNA analyzed, and make it back to the United States in one piece. The La Brea Woman was within reach—she could feel it. She closed her eyes and thought back to the last time she'd seen her. The ancient woman, lying in a wood and glass storage container. It was made to exact specifications to preserve her remains. Preservation was the key to learning and understanding. The more intact DNA and trace evidence that could be recovered from her body the more they could learn about her and the time period in which she lived. What had the weather been like the day she died? Had she ever been a mother? How had she lived? The answer to these questions and the thousands of others that Mariska had thought about during the years of research she'd already done could be answered…if only, she had her remains to examine.

The car lurched and pulled her out of her thoughts. Traffic must have been heavy. Not surprising considering how close they were to the airport.

What was she going to wear? She put one of the bags in her lap and started mentally putting together an outfit when she realized, she hadn't reached Theresa yet. Would she be awake? Mariska pulled out her cell phone and connected the call. It rang a few times before going to voicemail.

You've reached, Theresa. I can't answer the phone right now. Please leave a message, and I'll get back to you as soon as I can.

"Hey, Theresa. Sorry to call you so late. I just wanted to let you know I made it safe and sound to Copenhagen, and the driver is taking me to the Hilton. Can you call me or message me regarding where and when I'm to meet up, Edgar at the University?"

Mariska hung up the phone and sighed. If Theresa was already asleep, how was she going to get everything she needs within the next couple of hours? She would try and call again, once she got to the hotel. "Stop stressing, Mariska," she reminded herself.

The tires squealed a bit as they turned the corner. She looked up and the driver's eyes locked with hers. A sinking feeling pushed deeper into her belly, and she felt for a seatbelt. There wasn't any. She looked for any signage or stickers in the windows to indicate which company this cab represented. Nothing on the side windows, so she turned and looked at the back window.

No stickers. No placards.

She put the address of the hotel into her phone to see how much farther it was to get there. The little blue pin indicating her destination blinked and then the route to get there highlighted in red. She was only a couple kilometers away now. At the next right, she should be able to see the tall building from the street.

Suddenly, without warning, the car tires screeched, and they made a left turn.

They were going the wrong way.

"Driver, we were supposed to turn right."

Without saying a word, the driver made another left turn, nearly sideswiping a car parked on the corner.

"Hey." Mariska knocked on the window divider. "You're going the wrong way."

The man said nothing but looked at her in the rearview mirror. His eyes no longer looked kind. Her heart began to race as the man's speed increased. The next corner sent her sidelong into the door. The bags sitting on the seat next to her softened the collision, but not by much.

"What the hell are you doing?" Mariska pulled herself back up into sitting and began banging hard onto the window with a clenched fist. "Stop the car. Let me out." She kept banging on the window.

Another hard turn and she slid into the door again, this time sending a searing hot pain into her hand. She scrambled back onto the seat and saw two of her knuckles had split on impact with door. Blood started to well up into the gash, but there wasn't time to worry about such superficial wounds. This madman was going to kill her. Throwing herself across the back seat, she slid to the other side of the car and pulled on the door handle.

It was locked. The door didn't budge no matter how hard she pulled on the handle or slammed her shoulder into the door. Before she'd come up with what to do next, the car screeched to a halt. She looked up, out of the back window and saw she was in front of the Hilton hotel. The car rocked, ever so slightly, as the driver got out of the front seat. She watched as he circled the car and opened the door for her. She recoiled deeper into the car. He looked in and offered his hand.

"Dr. Stevenson, you must hurry."

"Get away from me." She backed all the way up against the door of the backseat. No matter how far she went, it wouldn't seem far enough.

Who the hell was this guy?

"You must come with me. You must hurry."

There were people walking the streets, riding bicycles in all directions, but no one seemed to see this madman as he tried to grab her out of the backseat. "I'm not going anywhere with you."

He squatted low. "I'm sorry if I've scared you."

"Well, too late for apologies, asshole." Mariska grabbed her things and held onto them like a security blanket.

The driver looked around him and stood for a second. Leaning down again he said, "You have to come with me now. There is little time for this nonsense." He grabbed his cell phone.

It was ringing.

"Yes," he said. "She is here." The driver looked at her and shrugged before disconnecting the call and putting his phone back into his pocket. "We have been followed."

Followed?

She looked at her current position, crammed into the backseat of a stranger's car that doesn't unlock from the inside. Mariska was being stupid, and she knew it. The man offered his hand, and she accepted it. He pulled her across the seat, grabbing her belongings as he closed the car door behind her. He ushered her away from the car toward the front of the hotel where a large cement planter containing well-manicured and sculpted bushes and flowers, obscured the view from the street.

The driver pulled her by the elbow and a few more feet away from the street before he stopped and faced her. "You must be careful."

"What's going on? Why were you driving like a maniac if you weren't here to kill me?"

He shook his head, his eyes taking on a fatherly softness. "I'm not here to kill you, doctor. Much the opposite. Heed my warning. Be careful, we were followed."

"By who?"

He looked behind him, and she heard the sound of screeching tires. He turned back to her. "Go around and enter through the back. It will be safer. Less obvious." He nodded and looked away. "I leave you now."

With no real answers and a renewed feeling of paranoia, she wanted to pepper him with questions. But she knew she wasn't going to get any more answers. He took a few steps away from her and turned back, but kept his gaze averted. "You are here. You are safe. Badger has been repaid." He walked away, disappearing behind the large cement planter as he went to the street.

She waited a few seconds before she saw him pull away. His car sped down the street and out of sight. He had been sent by Badger, not Theresa? If she was going to survive long enough to see this adventure to the end, she was going to need to pull her shit together. Heeding the advice of the stranger, she grabbed her things and hurried around the side of the hotel and exited through the back—ever diligent to keep herself hidden along the way.

CHAPTER THIRTY-EIGHT

Blood-tinged water circled the drain. Steam from the hot water felt good on Mariska's face, despite fogging up the mirror and obscuring the view of her reflection. Her knuckles were missing a layer of skin from being thrown about in the back seat of the cab, but they didn't hurt too badly. Except for when she tried to move her fingers, or let her hand hang down by her side, or even wash out the cuts in the hot water. Then they hurt—bad enough to make her angry.

She turned off the water and wiped the moisture from the mirror and caught a glimpse of her reflection. Not too bad, considering she hadn't had much sleep in three days, and she kept getting assaulted. After brushing her hair, teeth, and applying enough makeup to hide her fatigue, she padded out of the bathroom and into the bedroom of the hotel suite. It wasn't much of a room by Los Angeles standards. The stark white walls and minimalist furnishings were more for functionality than they were for aesthetics. There was a small table and chair across from a small screen television. She would be able to set up her laptop and do some work later.

Sitting on the edge of the bed, she rummaged through her things making sure she had the right clothes to wear for today's meeting at the University. She selected a nice pair of pants, blouse, and sensible shoes. Not normally one to wear sneakers unless she was working in the field or exercising, she decided it made the most sense. She wasn't familiar with the University, or how long of a walk she'd need to do. The three-inch heels wouldn't feel that great after a few minutes of pounding the pavement not to mention how difficult it would be to don shoe covers if she was allowed inside the clean-lab where the DNA analysis took place. As soon as she'd finished getting dressed, her phone rang.

It was Theresa. "Hey there," Mariska said.

"I'm sorry it took me so long to get back to you."

"No, worries. Shouldn't you be sleeping? Not that I mind you helping me out." Mariska stood and tossed her dirty clothes into the corner next to her carry-on bag.

"Nah, I had to get up super early today anyway."

Mariska debated telling her about the cab ride but then figured, full disclosure was the best policy. "I took a cab to the hotel, and things got crazy."

There was a moment of silence, but then Theresa said, "Oh really? How, so?"

"This tall Middle Eastern man had a sign with my name on it, and he was calling out my name. Next thing I know, I'm in his cab, and he's driving like a maniac down the streets. I'm was tossed around the backseat like a bag of groceries when he screeched to a stop at the hotel."

"Sounds like he was trying to get you the best fare. You know how cabbies drive," Theresa's concerned voice didn't match her dismissive words. "You didn't die, right?"

"I would normally agree with you, but then he told me that I was in danger."

"Well, yeah. You were in danger of getting into an accident." Theresa's joke fell flat, and they both grew silent. "I'm sorry. I just wanted to lighten the mood. You're not in Los Angeles anymore. I figured you'd be safer away from the thug who's been stalking you around town."

"Yeah, I thought so too. But I'm starting to think the cab-driver was right. He suggested I use the back entrance of the hotel and so I did. I kept a low profile while I checked in, but I felt like I was being watched."

"Did you see anyone…suspicious looking?"

Mariska thought for a second. There had been a couple guys in business suits sitting in the lobby, but they never once looked in her direction. Come to think of it, no one really looked in her direction—except the front desk clerk. "I guess not, but it was Badger who sent the driver was sent to pick me up."

"Badger? How did he know you were in Copenhagen? You didn't tell anyone else you were going there, did you?"

"I told Detective Wulf, but other than him, no. And, get this, Badger upgraded my seats on the plane to first class. When I made reservations, there hadn't even been any first-class seats available. I have a feeling this guy has a lot more power than we ever thought. Or…" Mariska's voice trailed off.

"Or, what?"

"Or…a lot of people owe him favors."

"Favors? What do you mean?" Theresa asked.

Mariska remembered how the cab driver's expression was mysterious but kind. And then how when they were being chased, his eyes grew hard, and he'd driven like a professional…a guy who'd done that before—alluding pursuers. But when he mentioned Badger sending him, his expression had changed into a fatherly, concerned man. Almost like he was remembering a time when he'd been helped. Like he was paying it forward."

"Wow," Theresa said. "I wonder who the driver really was, then. I bet he wasn't really a cab-driver."

"All I know is, he said that he'd delivered me safely to the hotel and his debt to Badger had been repaid."

Another couple of beats while Theresa processed the information. "Well, I don't know quite what to say."

"There really isn't anything to say, I guess." Mariska sat back down on the edge of the bed. "I'm grateful Badger has been helping us. He really didn't have to. Although, it makes me wonder what I'm going to owe him in return?"

"That's a good question, but if you didn't ask him for the help, do you really owe him anything in return?"

"You think it's out of the kindness of his own heart?" Mariska asked with a sardonic laugh.

"Maybe. Or, he really respects you," Theresa said. "Anyway, I wouldn't worry too much about all that right now."

"Nothing I can do about it right now I guess."

"I do have some information you'll want to write down, or at least commit to memory."

Mariska quickly scanned the room but didn't find a pen or paper. "Lay it on me."

"As you know, the contact at the University was a friend of mine—his name is Edgar. He will be meeting you around lunchtime. I wasn't able to get a specific time because he will be between classes at that time."

"Okay, but what does he look like?" Who knows how many people would be named Edgar and that was all she knew about him.

"That's a tough one. I haven't seen him in years…so."

Mariska laughed. "Give me your best guess."

"He's a touch over six-foot tall, athletic build, nice smile."

"Oh, geez." Mariska sensed Theresa's unresolved feelings about this guy. "What color hair and is he brown, white, or green?"

Theresa laughed. "Last time I saw him he had electric blue hair…I bet that's changed. He was either Hispanic or Asian. Maybe a combination of the two? I'm not sure, I never asked. All I remember is his blue hair and blue eyes. Contacts, of course. You are to meet up in front of the University. There will be a statue out front, somewhere, and he'll be waiting. Just remember, there are multiple buildings which are associated with the institution. You want the main one. It'll be built of brown-stone and look really old. I'm told you'll know which building it is when you see it."

"Great, thank you." Mariska jotted down a few more notes. "When I meet up with him, is there anything you'd like me to tell him? It sounds to me like you two had a…thing."

"A thing?"

"You know." Mariska smiled. "A summertime romance."

Theresa coughed. "I just inhaled my coffee."

"Oh, sorry," Mariska lied. "If there's a message I can pass along, I'd be willing to do that for you."

Silence.

"Hello?" *Had Theresa hung up on her?*

Theresa cleared her throat. "Just tell him I send my regards."

"Your regards?" To each their own, she supposed. "Okay, will do."

"I'm sending you a driver to take you to the University. Don't worry about money, the fare has been prepaid."

"Prepaid?"

"Yeah, there's a cool app I downloaded. I can hire a driver anywhere in the world. It's easy and secure. The driver will arrive in twenty minutes. Driver's name is Andus, and he'll be driving a black Mercedes."

"Seems like everyone drives a black Mercedes in this city," Mariska mumbled under her breath.

"I didn't catch that, I think you were breaking up."

"Oh, nothing. I'll be ready. Thank you for all your help. I'll text you as soon as I meet with the University."

"I hope it all goes as planned."

"Me, too." Mariska disconnected the call and walked over to the window facing the street.

Below was a bustling city. The street was filled with cars, bicyclists, and people walking here and there. Looking further up the street, there were vendors lining the streets as well as shops filled with wears. Couples holding hands, kids frolicking, Mariska could imagine the sounds of laughter and life. No matter how far from home she found herself, people were still people. The same things that drove Californians drove the Danish. Love, happiness, hate, fear, hunger…sex. Humans were humans. She closed her eyes and pictured the La Brea Woman. What kept her going? Was it the constant struggle of survival? Did she have to fight off Saber-Toothed Tigers? Had she and the short-faced bear crossed paths? Or, had she had a child of her own? Was it the innate need to keep her child safe that kept her going?

She opened her eyes once again. The waterways across the street looked inviting. She saw people in the distance, rowing boats past the hotel, and it looked like fun. Her heart warmed at the idea of having fun. Playing, like she did as a child. She'd been too serious, for too long. The La Brea Woman becoming an obsession she'd been unable to shake, one she'd sacrificed for, one she'd nearly died for. Is it even worth it? A pit formed in her belly as she thought about giving up. No, she couldn't stop now. She was too close. She owed it to herself, Jane, and even to the La Brea Woman to find out answers. To bring her home and deliver her to those with a rightful claim.

Mariska patted the front of her pants. She'd forgotten to put the artifacts in the pocket. She checked the time; she had only a few minutes left. She hurried over to the dirty clothes and pulled out the tooth and bead. There hadn't been time, but she wanted to make sure they were in good condition. They both appeared undamaged, but for the first time, she noticed that they were still speckled with tar deposits. In the holes that had been burrowed through them to make into a necklace, they had bits of tar clinging to the sides. Also, along the sides of the tooth at the top by the root, tar had remained. Tar would continue to seep out of the objects over the course of years, the very mechanism that preserved the tooth and bead in the first place. But this tar had been there for a while, she'd just been too preoccupied to notice it before now.

She smiled. With the tar present, there was a significant possibility that DNA could be extracted. The very thing that entombed and killed so many creatures, the tar, would be the substance that preserved the root. And along with the root, any genetic information it contained. Once she got the objects back to the labs in the United States, she could carefully remove the tar and inspect for other clues. Possibly, find tiny evidence of insects, seeds, algae spores…anything that might give her an idea about the climate or habits of those living during that time period. With a renewed sense of purpose and excitement, Mariska put the objects in the woven pouch and back into her front pocket for safe keeping. On her way, out of the hotel room, she threw her purse into the backpack and put it on…nostalgic feelings of her college-years came flooding back. She couldn't help but smile as she shut the door behind her.

CHAPTER THIRTY-NINE

Mariska stepped out of the cab after paying for her fare. The car drove away leaving her in front of the University of Copenhagen. She was used to the universities in the United States. Often, they were sprawling campuses with large swaths of open land—park-like and pristine. The institution of higher learning before her now was nothing like she was used too, although not any less impressive. Smack dab in the middle of a huge metropolis, what made the building stand out from the others was its age and grandeur. The oldest University and one of the oldest buildings in the city, it was founded in the fifteenth century. Despite housing and being utilized for hundreds of years, it had stood the test of time—surviving two world wars.

The huge stone structure that stood before her was a testament to the impressive building standards that went into such a landmark. The University stood more than four floors tall and was topped in the center by a copper dome that had turned green with time and patina. As Mariska stood in front of the famed site of advanced genetic research and testing, she could feel the familiar tingle in her stomach. It was usually a sign she was in the presence of something significant and meaningful. In this case, possible answers to the many questions that have plagued her for years.

The metallic ring of a bicycle bell as it passed within a foot of her, brought Mariska back to the here and now. The large paved area in front of the university was filled with students on bicycles. Each of them with a backpack or messenger bag weighing them down. A sympathy pain in her low back ached as she remembered hauling around a bag filled with three in thick books, binders, and enough computer paper to make herself a tree.

Suddenly, Mariska was shoved from behind. Hard enough to cause her head to snap backward and for her legs to give way as she fell forward. Adrenaline-fueled veins limited the pain of impact, but her mind immediately went to the worst-case scenario. She'd been found. Whoever had followed her after the airport, was on her.

She rolled to her back, kicking up with both legs at once. Whoever it was suffered a direct blow to the chest and fell away from her. Rolling back onto all fours, she pushed herself up to stand. Fists clenched and raised in front of her she took a step toward the man on the ground. Her heart pounded, and she fought the urge to run away. A second more of hesitation, she kicked the man as hard as she could in the back. He cried out in pain, arching his back and putting his hands up to protect his face.

"Wait," the man said. "I'm sorry I knocked you over. I didn't see you."

Who was this guy?

Mariska took another step closer to get a better look at the man's face. Since she'd stopped kicking him, the man slowly lowered his hand to his side. She didn't recognize him. He wasn't the goon who'd attacked her back in Los Angeles. Shit, had she assaulted a student? Mariska offered the man a hand. He didn't take it at first, looking at her like she was a crazy person…and maybe he was right.

"I'm sorry I kicked you," she said. "Take my hand. I'll help you up."

"Oh, you're American," he said. Taking her hand in his, he pulled up and stood from the ground.

Mariska looked up at the young man and smiled. He was rather easy on the eyes. He looked a little bit Asian and a little bit African. But his eyes. His eyes were the lightest shade of brown she'd ever seen…with a hint of green. He stood a solid six foot four inches and had broad shoulders and deep chest.

"Yes, I'm from the United States. I don't recognize your accent?"

Mariska said.

"That's because I've lived in so many places." His smile was soft, and his teeth were surprisingly white and straight. Perfect, actually.

"Are you American?"

"Yes, but I have dual citizenship. I'm Canadian and American." He looked around a few of the students that had stopped and watched after the initial collision. "I think we're being observed."

Mariska looked toward the left and waved. Smiling and waving, until they all got the idea she was fine, and so was the other guy.

He offered his hand, "My name is Eddie."

The Edgar she was here to meet? What were the chances?

"Eddie? Do you happen to know, Theresa?" Mariska asked.

"Theresa?" A quizzical look crossed his face. "Do you mean Theresa Krieger?"

Mariska smiled, "The one and only."

Eddie's eyes lit up with sheer happiness. A smile and laugh followed. He clapped his hands together. "You must be Theresa's friend, Mariska?"

"That's, me."

"What are the chances?" he said. "I was hurrying here to meet but didn't see you. I'm sorry I ran you over."

"And, I'm sorry I kicked you…multiple times. I've had a rough couple of days."

"Not to worry. Theresa didn't tell me too much, just asked me to meet you here and introduce you to the department of genetic mapping's lead researcher." He shook his head with disbelief. "How is Theresa doing? Is she well? I've…really missed her."

This guy had it bad for her friend Theresa. The forced chipper tone to his voice and the rapid-fire questions told the tale. Had Theresa broken this man's heart? What had happened between them?

"She's doing very well. As I'm sure you know, she is an intern at the Page Museum in Los Angeles." Mariska wasn't going to go through her friend's entire history but wanted to give the poor guy some information.

"Aw, man. That's fantastic. She's such a great student. Beautiful…as she is smart." Eddie's voice trailed off a bit. "You know we used to call her a badger in class."

"Badger?" Mariska couldn't help but think about the man who had been helping her when she least expected it. "Why, Badger?"

"It was just a nickname…mostly, it was just me who called her that. She could do anything she set her mind to. Tenacious." He shook his head. "I swear there wasn't a problem too big for her to solve."

The look in his eyes and the way he seemed to glow, made Mariska wish she'd not pushed every man who ever tried to get close to her, away. Work wasn't everything. Right? Mariska could have delved into this guy's story over coffee and been perfectly happy, but she was on a time-crunch. She looked over her shoulder and scanned the sea of people rushing this way and that, making their way to classes or work. No sign of anyone watching them. Maybe she hadn't been followed here, but who really knows.

"Thank you so much for being willing to meet me here. I am desperate for help."

"Absolutely, Theresa is quite…convincing." He took a deep breath. "What exactly are you needing here that you can't get back in Los Angeles?"

"I need to have DNA testing done."

"On, yourself?" he asked.

"Not exactly. I've found some interesting and very old objects that may contain DNA, and I need the results fast." She looked behind him at a couple men in suits quickly approaching. "Friends of yours?"

Eddie turned and looked behind him. He shook his head, "Nah," he turned back to her. "It's finals week, and there are so many students presenting their doctoral thesis over the next couple days. You'll start to recognize them. Dressed up in suits, panic on their faces, and usually hurrying from one place to the other mumbling to themselves."

"Ah, yes. I remember those days." There wasn't time for a trip down memory lane. "Anyway, after the incredible work this university did pertaining to the Kennewick Man a few years back, you can hardly blame a gal for coming."

He nodded and shrugged in agreement.

"Would you be kind enough to take me to see the head of the genetics department?"

"Absolutely," he said. "Would you like a tour of the school on the way?"

Mariska smiled, "That'd be great. Thank you."

He offered his arm, and she gladly accepted the gesture. They hurried arm in arm, to the front entrance and inside. As soon as they entered, Mariska felt like she'd been teleported back in time. Sure, the university had been updated since the fifteenth century, but probably not in the past hundred or so years.

"Wow, this is a trip back in time," Mariska said.

"Yeah, you get used to it after a while. I hardly even notice anymore."

"It's hard to imagine the cutting edge technological advances in genetic testing and research happen in this place." Mariska kept walking but looked every which way, but the direction they were headed.

"The oldest, least updated areas are the entrance and the library. And, according to some of my classmates, the dorms aren't anything to envy." He flashed that award-winning smile.

It was clear to Mariska why Theresa liked this guy so much. He could snatch the knickers off a nun.

"What can you tell me about the university? Anything I need to be aware of?"

"It's one of the oldest universities in the country. Well, known for its genetic research. But you already know that. Otherwise, it's just like any other one I've been in." He shrugged. "I think there's around twenty-five thousand students here at any given time of the year, except for breaks, of course."

"This is a pretty grandiose building, but I'm surprised it can hold that many students."

"Well, there are actually four separate buildings associated with the university. They aren't connected to one another, or even on the same property. Spread over the city, taking over areas as expansion became necessary. This is the main building with general education classes and the library."

"Where is the genetics lab?" Mariska asked.

"That's behind this building and across the street. We could have walked around, but it's shorter to cut through and then exit out the back." He kept walking and pointing out different little historical pieces of art or plaques of famous people that attended the university. "Once you've been here a while, you get to know all the shortcuts. It's important if you have back-to-back classes in different parts of campus."

"I can imagine it would be," Mariska said. "So, you've mentioned the library a few times. Can you show it to me? I'm thinking that while the lab is running my genetics results, I can hang out in the library and do some research or maybe some pleasure reading."

"Of course, right this way." He dropped her arm, but then slid his arm around her back and led her through a set of huge wooden doors.

Mariska stepped into another world. The University of Copenhagen's library was something to behold. Beyond anything she'd ever seen in person. It was like she was on the set of a Harry Potter movie. From floor to ceiling, there were shelves for books. Two floors, each with twelve-foot ceilings. Row after endless row of books, ladders attached to the selves by rollers for easy access to top shelves.

"This is absolutely, unreal. It's…amazing."

"I knew you'd like it." Eddie smiled and looked around the expansive room. "I've spent so many long nights here, researching, studying, and trying to get over…someone." He didn't elaborate, but Mariska suspected he meant, Theresa.

"Wow, I don't think I'd ever want to leave this place. Is there a Special Editions section?"

"There is a repository of ancient texts and important books in the back of the library. But it's off limits to anyone that doesn't have the right level of clearance or privileges within the university."

"And, how would someone get that clearance?" Mariska asked.

"You'd need to be a tenured professor, or have written authorization to access the repository. There is a training protocol that goes along with it as well. You know, to ensure that people are wearing gloves when handling the books, and of course, no food or drink allowed."

Mariska laughed, "Well, duh."

They shared a moment of laughter, but then Eddie said, "You'd be surprised. I guess rules were made in response to stupid behaviors."

"You're probably right. Okay, take me to your leader."

Eddie pulled her along past the seemingly endless rows of books, out the back door, and then outside onto the street. Without a word, he started down the deserted street, lined by buildings of different colors and materials.

Where was everyone? She glanced behind her. No one. Mariska turned to Eddie, again. He was determined, focused on where they were going. She hesitated ever so slightly, and he must have felt her slow. He smiled.

"Everything, okay?" he asked.

"Yeah." She looked around. "I have a strange feeling about this place. Or, maybe it's just me."

"What do you mean?" He kept walking, and she followed.

"Where is everyone? The front entrance was swarming with people, but it's like a ghost town here."

He tightened his hold on her arm, "Nothing to worry about. Class is in session. There'll be a street full of people within the hour." He stopped and faced a tall, cement building. There wasn't a single window to be seen, and only one door. "We're here…the genetics lab."

"This is part of the university? You've got to be kidding me? Where are the windows? Where's the sign, for god's sake?"

"The genetics lab also contains some of the more…how, do I put this? Sensitive materials that bad people would want to get a hold of."

"Sensitive materials?"

"Plutonium. Or, that's what I've heard, anyway. The building has no windows, is securely fortified by thick concrete walls, and has only one way in, and two ways out."

"Wow, I had no idea."

"They don't advertise this sort of thing. The less the general public knows, the better. The building is a deterrent from theft as well as terrorist attacks. Sadly, this is the era we live in. Terrorism can happen anywhere and usually happens when you least expect it."

Eddie turned back to the front door and entered a series of numbers into the keypad next to the door. A hiss and the sound of the door unlocking sounded immediately after. Eddie pulled the door open and looked behind him, making sure they were still alone.

"How do you know all this? And, have access?" Mariska asked.

Eddie smiled. "I'm Dr. Tora's assistant. We should hurry, she'll be waiting for us." He motioned for her to come inside. "Are you coming?"

Mariska hesitated, but just for a moment. She stepped through the door and into the unknown. A second later, the door closed and sealed behind her.

Here we go, she thought.

CHAPTER FORTY

The closer Mariska got to Dr. Tora's office, the more nervous she became. But she hadn't come all this way to give up now. She absently touched her front pocket where she'd hidden the tooth and bead that needed to be analyzed.

Eddie stopped in front of a frosted glass door and turned to face, Mariska. "We're here."

"Is there anything I need to be prepared for?" Mariska asked. "Anything, really. Like, is Dr. Tora mean? Does she have a hideous mole on her face I wouldn't be able to stop staring at?"

"I've got a few freckles, but nothing hideous, I assure you," Dr. Tora said as she rounded the corner.

Shit. "I'm sorry, Dr. Tora. I'm just a bit nervous. This has been a very long and difficult journey for me…the past few days have been rough." Mariska extended her hand. "I'm Dr. Mariska Stevenson."

The two women shook hands.

"It's a pleasure to meet you," Mariska added.

"Pleasure is mine." Tora furrowed her brow and cocked her head ever-so-slightly to one side. "I've heard some very *interesting* things coming out of California."

Interesting. That's an understatement.

"Indeed." Mariska nodded. "I don't know all of what you've heard, but I doubt I'd be remiss to confirm most of what you've heard…unless you've heard anything negative about me."

Mariska offered an awkward laugh, and Dr. Tora simply smiled and arched her brow.

"Please," Dr. Tora said as she unlocked the door to her office. "After you."

Mariska, followed by Eddie, and then Dr. Tora filed into the office, and the door closed behind them.

"So, tell me, Dr. Stevenson…what can we help you with? I'm sure they have DNA analysis back in California? Am I right?" Dr. Tora said as she sat behind her desk and clasped her hands together. "Please, have a seat."

Mariska and Eddie sat in the chairs in front of the desk. She couldn't help, but notice the décor of the room. Floor to ceiling dark wooden bookshelves. Textbooks and other works of academia filled them. A few framed photos on the walls, desk, and bookshelves seemed to chronicle Dr. Tora's rise through the ranks at the University. Absent was one of her children or a spouse. No doubt, she was married to her work…much like Mariska had become over the years.

"You're absolutely correct, Dr. Tora." Mariska's words came out quick and to the point. "I need your help for a couple of reasons. One, I need the results quickly. Two, this is the premier genetics lab in the world. The work you did with the Kennewick Man, changed lives. And, I want the same result. I want the truth." She paused for a half second. "I *need* the truth."

"And, your reputation tells me you want it done with the utmost accuracy."

"That's absolutely correct. Oh, and without any fanfare." The last thing she needed was for Dr. Snyder to catch wind of this.

Dr. Tora gave her a quizzical look. "Fanfare?"

"I need to keep the results hush-hush, but just for the time being." Mariska shifted uncomfortably in the chair before leaning forward toward the desk. "There's controversy surrounding the missing La Brea Woman remains as well as to the rightful and legal ownership of the remains themselves. So, as you can see, I need to keep this between us…for the time being."

"Understood." Dr. Tora sat back in her chair. "Correct me if I'm wrong, but I heard rumors that you're in danger. There was an attack, of sorts. At the Gala?"

"Correct. It's been a rough couple of days. That's for sure." *Rumors sure get around quickly within the scientific community.*

"If remaining silent is what's best for the situation, I will do so." She nodded toward Mariska. "You have my word."

"Thank you, Doctor."

Mariska and Dr. Tora shook hands once again, solidifying their pact and bond over the greater good of science, knowledge, and understanding.

Mariska started to reach into her front pocket to retrieve the objects to be tested when Dr. Tora stopped her. "Please, if you are getting ready to show me something you want tested, let's wait and do this inside the lab. I like to examine things in a controlled setting."

"Absolutely," Mariska said, silently chastising herself for making such a rookie move. She had been so excited to get the process started, she'd been willing to dispense with protocols. "Lead, the way."

Eddie stood and offered his hand to Mariska who accepted it. The three scientists left through the back door to Dr. Tora's office and entered a stark hallway that lead to the genetics lab.

"Is this the back way?" Mariska turned to Eddie for the go ahead.

He nodded, "Yeah, we're getting VIP access this way. No signing in through the front desk. There won't be a record of you being here…"

"That's what you wanted, no?" Dr. Tora asked.

They couldn't have been more, right. "Yes, thank you so much."

At the end of the hallway, there was a set of double doors. Metallic, and locked. A keypad next to the doors blinked red as they approached. Dr. Tora flashed her ID badge over it with a beep. She then typed in a series of numbers followed by the sound of the doors unlocking in a clack of metal on metal.

Eddie pushed the doors open and held them while the two women entered first. Inside the lab, everything was white and the intense change in light, momentarily hurt Mariska's eyes. She held up her hand to shield her eyes.

"Takes a minute at first. The lights are really bright, white, and flat. Helps us to see things under microscopes. And, it helps identify if something becomes contaminated by foreign substances," Eddie said. "This lab is the greatest thing I've ever experienced." He beamed from ear to ear. He really loved the work he was doing here. Mariska felt a bit envious of the young man. She loved her job too, but it hung in the balance.

"Should we be in here without lab coats?" Mariska asked.

"Oh, this isn't the clean testing area of the lab. This is where students start working with the equipment, getting the hang of things. Hands-on, training. Once they start actually doing research and testing things, they will do it over there." He pointed to the far side of the lab. It was labeled CLEAN LAB, in more languages than Mariska could even identify.

"Follow me, please." Dr. Tora hurried on her way toward the clean-lab. She took a moment to look at Mariska's shoes. "Thank goodness you wore something sensible. I can't tell you how many times, women come in here wearing three-inch heels."

Mariska cringed on the inside; she would have too had it not been for the simple fact she hadn't brought a pair that went with her slacks. "Of course not. I know how to dress for work."

She gave Eddie a look to convey she was totally bullshitting his boss. He acknowledged it with a smile but said nothing. Dr. Tora brought them over to a changing room of sorts. It reminded Mariska of a decontamination chamber where someone would strip down and be scrubbed free of nuclear fallout. There were clean-suits hanging from each locker. The light-blue suits were covered in plastic indicating they'd been cleaned. Dr. Tora indicated to Mariska and Eddie she wanted to have them sit on the bench in front of the lockers. They complied without a word.

"Eddie, I know you already understand the importance of keeping the Clean Lab, clean." She turned to address Mariska. "But from what I know, you're used to digging around in the dirt and tar, less focused on preventing cross contamination. Is that correct?"

"That'd be correct, yes."

"Very well, I trust you're professional enough to receive my instructions, one time, and follow them precisely." Dr. Tora paused and waited for acknowledgment from Mariska.

Mariska nodded.

"Before entering the Clean-Lab, you will don one of the suits hanging up behind you. You will also wear a head covering, which is basically a hairnet on steroids. In the lockers, you will find the hairnet, shoe-booties, gloves, facemasks, and goggles. If you need help getting into any of the equipment, let myself or Eddie know. We will help you."

Marisa raised her hand.

Dr. Tora acknowledged her with arched eyebrows.

"Once we put the suits on, aren't the suits going to be contaminated by our DNA and anyone else that may have been in this room?"

"That's a great observation. And true. After donning the suits and equipment, we will go into the negative pressure entryway. The doors will close, and a heavy burst of hair will blow contaminated materials from the suit and collect them into a specially designed air filter in the floor of the room. It will be at this point, the door to the Clean Lab will automatically unlock and slide open allowing us to enter the lab."

Eddie turned to Mariska. "It's really cool. Reminds me of a science fiction movie the first time I went in."

"Great, let's get started." Mariska jumped up from the bench and opened the locker behind her.

Dr. Tora stepped over to her. "I like your enthusiasm. It'll be a pleasure to work with you."

Mariska watched as Dr. Tora pulled on a pair of dark blue latex gloves. She opened a plastic bag the size of a standard manila envelope. "Place your artifacts in here. Once the suit is on, we won't be able to access anything in our pockets until we leave the Clean Lab."

Mariska dug into her pocket and pulled out the old woven pouch. In this light, it was easy to see how worn it was. Dirty, from years of use and from being hidden inside a skull which continued to seep tar from its porous bones. She took a deep breath and placed the pouch into the clear plastic specimen bag. Her trepidation was not lost on Dr. Tora.

"Here, Dr. Stevenson." She handed the bag back to Mariska. "You can hold on to this until we are ready to examine the items.

"Thank you." Mariska took the bag and held it to her chest for a moment. It felt good to have the items back under her control.

The two women exchanged an unsaid acknowledgment of respect and appreciation for the other's lifetime of efforts and struggles in a male-dominated profession. Mariska took the bag and placed it on the bench while she put on the suit and other necessary equipment. The suits were extremely light but didn't breathe, at all. She became thankful of the steady air conditioning, no doubt, to help keep those in the suits comfortable.

Now, standing in the negative pressure room, Dr. Tora said, "Are we all ready?"

"Yes," Mariska and Eddie said in unison.

Dr. Tora pushed the red button on the wall. The door between them and the locker room closed with a hiss. Two seconds passed before a suction from the grated floor turned on. Then, without warning, a blast of wind hit her in the face, followed by one in the back and then from the ceiling. The entire process took a minute to complete. They turned to face the door leading to the clean room. A series of beeps and then the red indicator light on the right side of the door turned green. The door unlocked with a click and it slid open with a hiss of air.

Mariska followed Dr. Tora and Eddie over to the back corner of the Clean Lab. The bright white light, white walls, and floor stood in stark contrast to the metallic tables and bright flashing lights on the electronic equipment within the lab. A stainless steel, examination table, surrounded by some electronic equipment that Mariska couldn't identify sat open for their use. Mariska stood alone on one side with the other two facing her from the opposite side of the table.

"Okay, Dr. Stevenson. Show us what you have." Dr. Tora's tone grew even more serious than before.

Mariska placed the plastic bag on the examination table and removed the pouch, placing it on top of the plastic. With a nervous hand, she opened the pouch. This would be the first time she'd shown anyone else the items she'd taken from the museum. She poured the contents into her gloved hand and placed the pouch back down on the table.

"What do we have here?" Dr. Tora was immediately intrigued. Her enthusiasm made Mariska's heart happy. Someone else saw the significance of the find.

"I found eight beads and this tooth."

"What happened to the other seven?" Eddie asked.

"My apartment was broken into, and this is all I have left." Mariska put the tooth down and held the bead under a lighted magnifying glass for the other two to see it more clearly. "Do you see the series of tiny holes bored into the bead? I've identified it as a constellation. The other beads had already gone missing this point, so I wasn't able to investigate them further. But I suspect they all contained images of the night sky."

"What's the significance of that?" Dr. Tora asked. "I'm not an anthropologist so please forgive my ignorance."

"Understandable," Mariska said. "I feel that the more information we have regarding whoever made them might help identify who they belong to. For instance, in the United States, certain Native tribes were known their study of the night sky. One, the Chumash tribe in California. Another, the Hopi, in Arizona. Pawnee, in the Midwest. Just to name a few. I was unable to find any definitive link between this one constellation and a legend or story that would identify the Chumash tribe."

"Ah, I see. So, you're hoping that the tooth might yield some more answers." Dr. Tora reached for the tooth. She held it up to the magnifying glass. "The root is intact, I have a feeling we will be able to gather enough material to run a DNA test. I need your permission to drill a small pin-sized hole into the side of the tooth to extract the needed material for testing. We can use the hole that is already there as a starting point to minimize further damage."

"You've got it," Mariska said, knowing this was the only way to extract the DNA material. "I know you'll do it with the utmost care."

Dr. Tora nodded in agreement.

"Can I take a look?" Eddie asked, motioning at the tooth.

Mariska said, "Yeah, sure."

Dr. Tora handed him the tooth and reached for the pouch. Mariska walked around to the other side of the table and pointed at the small hole in the tooth and went all the way through. "See that?" Mariska said. "I think this was used as jewelry."

"Looks like it to me as well," Eddie said. "I can't imagine this is a human tooth? I mean unless it came from a giant."

"You're right. I have yet to identify what creature it came from. I'm hoping that the DNA test here will help me to classify it."

Eddie looked confused. "What will that help you find?"

"If I can get a positive identification on the tooth. Knowing where that creature came from would help me narrow down the tribes in that area. Maybe, just maybe, between that and the constellation information, I can narrow it down even further."

"Have you examined the inside this pouch?" Dr. Tora asked.

Mariska shook her head. "Actually, no. I haven't. Why?"

"Look at this." Dr. Tora inverted the woven fabric, turning it inside out. "There's a long red hair, interwoven into the threads of the pouch.

"A red hair?" Mariska moved over to get a closer look.

Sure enough, a long red hair had embedded itself into the pouch. Was it from the La Brea Woman? Surely not. Maybe it was from whoever owned the pouch and found the beads and tooth?

Dr. Tora reached for a tweezer and with a steady, trained hand, extracted the hair on the first attempt. She held it under the light of the magnifying glass. "We've got a rootball."

"Rootball?" Mariska asked.

"The hair can be DNA tested. The root system is intact," Eddie said. "We would still be able to do it without the root, but we would be limited. There are three types of DNA that can be gleaned from the root, but only one from the hair shaft."

"So, what are you telling me? Can you identify who the hair belongs to?"

"Not without a comparison sample…unless there was one already in a database somewhere to compare it to." Dr. Tora flipped on a few machines as she prepared the area for analysis. "Otherwise, we will run the DNA test and can tell you the person's heritage. We can also keep the information on file for future comparison."

Mariska's excitement continued to grow. This could be a game-changer for her. "Please run the DNA test on the hair. It might help me in the future. Might as well do it while we are here."

It suddenly dawned on Mariska. Could she have them run her own DNA? She knew virtually nothing about herself. She was found outside the museum in the dumpster as a newborn infant. Her heart rate increased as the possibilities grew.

"One more favor," Mariska said to Dr. Tora. "Can you run a sample of my own hair?"

"Why?"

"It's a really long story."

Dr. Tora eyed her for a moment. It was difficult to read her expression considering she was covered by a mask and goggles. "Against my better judgment." She motioned for Eddie to turn his back and they turned away from Mariska.

Mariska quickly pulled up on her cap and yanked out a few hairs. "Oh, would you look at that?"

The other two turned back around, and Mariska held up her hair, root-balls intact. "I found these hairs too."

"Place them on here." Dr. Tora laid a clear glass dish in front of her. "Eddie and I will run the tests on the tooth and hair samples. You might as well take the bead with you and wait outside."

"How, long do you think it'll take?"

"Long enough that you should find something to keep yourself busy for a while. The results won't be available for a few days, but the tests will be completed in a couple hours," Dr. Tora said. "The longest part is waiting for the computers to do their jobs."

Mariska hesitated. Eddie smiled with his eyes. "We'll take good care of the tooth. I promise."

Mariska took the bead, placed it back into the pouch and headed for the exit. "I'll be in the library. Will you come and find me when you're done with the experiment?"

Eddie nodded. "Of course."

"Thank you, both." Mariska turned to leave. A pit of anxiety formed in her gut as she walked away. She turned back once before going into the negative pressure room and saw the two scientists hard at work.

Let them do their jobs, Mariska. This is the only way to get the answers you want and need. She stepped into the negative pressure room and pushed the red button. A rush of air blew away all the tiny particles that had collected on her suit but did nothing to clear away her worry and uncertainty.

Now, which way was it to the library?

CHAPTER FORTY-ONE

The University of Copenhagen library was amazing. The sheer volume of books and knowledge that was contained in this one room was overwhelming. Mariska wasn't sure where to start looking or even what she was looking for, exactly. She started by meandering down row after row of the first floor of the library. Each book she pulled from the shelf was in a language she didn't speak. *Better keep looking.* A ladder situated at the end of a particularly interesting row that contained some very old books looked like a great place to climb.

She scaled the ladder, all the way to the top shelf. Pulling at random, she selected one rather thin and dilapidated book. Despite Mariska's inability to read French, she found that it dated back to the seventeenth century. Climbing back down to the ground, she held the book in her hands, closed her eyes, and imagined the man that had written it. He must have been someone of importance, or at least influential in whatever field he worked, to have his book saved and passed down for future generations.

These ancient volumes on various topics, in diverse languages, were the fossils of the written language. They were of great historical value and taught us so much about the process of science and what it meant to be human.

Mariska scanned the surrounding area to see if she was being watched, before putting the book to her nose and inhaling. It had the undeniable old-book smell—an intoxicating sweet, grassy, mustiness that made any true bibliophiles' toes curl.

Hugging the book close to her chest as if it somehow imparted its history and experiences to her through osmosis, she looked for a nice quiet place to sit. At the end of the long aisle, Mariska stopped and looked around. There was a comfy chair that was empty in the far back corner of the room. Perfect.

She settled down into the chair when her phone buzzed with an incoming text message. It was from David asking her to call him. Mariska's stomach sank with guilt. She'd left in the middle of the night, without so much as a goodbye. She was about to text him back but hesitated. What would she tell him? If he knew she was in Copenhagen, he'd freak out and tell her parents. His concern for her wellbeing would override his ability to see things from her point of view. He'd be thinking he was doing the right thing, but he'd ruin everything. No, she would call him tomorrow, from the airport on her way home. Better send him a text, though, or he will worry.

Hey David, I can't talk right now. All is well. I'm taking a spa day today. I'll call you tomorrow.

A spa day? *That does sound nice*, Mariska thought.

Her mind drifted to Detective Wulf. She wondered what he was up too, had he found out anything pertaining to Jane's murder? Had he made headway in the theft investigation? Had he come any closer to clearing her name so she could have her job back? Mariska selected his number from the contacts list and put the phone to her ear.

Detective Wulf answered on the second ring. "Mariska? Are you, okay?"

"I'm good. I made it to the University without any trouble." Omitting the frightening cab-ride to the hotel, she figured, a little white lie never hurt anyone, right?

"Great. I've been trying to get ahold of you pretty much all day. When are you coming home?"

"Tomorrow, evening," Mariska said. "But by the time I get back to Los Angeles, it'll be the next day. Jetlag is going to kick my ass, I have a feeling."

"I didn't get all that…breaking up…" Wulf said—the connection was bad. It amazed her that technology existed to look at and analyze DNA strands in bones of extinct creatures, but she couldn't get a clear phone call on the cell phone to save her life.

"I'll be leaving Copenhagen, tomorrow night." Mariska raised her voice and spoke a bit slower.

She heard sounds of static and no verbal response.

"Hello?" Mariska said, looking at her phone to make sure she was still connected. "Can you hear me?"

"…didn't get all…" *Static.* "I have to tell you something…important…" Static. "David…"

David? "What about, David?"

"You have…be…danger—" Wulf's words were cut off.

"Is David in trouble?" Mariska sat up straight in the chair. "Wulf? Hello? Is David in some kind of danger?" She looked at the phone again, it'd disconnected. She tried to call him back, but couldn't get the call to go through. "Dammit."

Was that why David had asked her to call him? It didn't matter to her now if he knew where she was. Her heart raced as thought about the possibilities. Was he, okay? Plugging in his number on the phone, she placed a call to him. No signal. "Shit."

Mariska stood and started wandering around the library in a desperate attempt to get a signal. Nothing. Maybe she needed to go outside? Still holding the old book in her hand, she shoved the phone in her pocket and hurried down the aisle to return the book to its proper place. She climbed to the top and slid the book into place. As she turned her head to start her decent, she froze. At this height, she could see the entire first floor of the library. How could this be?

The man that'd attacked her in her apartment was creeping down the row of books at the far end of the library. He was wearing a black leather jacket and dark blue jeans. His aviator sunglasses obscured part of his face, but she'd recognize that thick neck and mean-looking, dumbass face anywhere. He must have seen her enter the library, but didn't know exactly where she was. How the hell did anyone even know she was in Copenhagen, let alone at the University Library? The cabbie had warned her yesterday, that she'd been followed. Mariska scanned the room for an exit. Spotting one at the far end of the room, her stomach sank. She would have to pass by the goon to make it outside.

She watched as he ducked around the next aisle, headed in her direction. She descended the ladder on shaky legs. Instinctively, she touched her front pocket where she'd been keeping her artifacts and last remaining link to the La Brea Woman. Her hand came up empty. That's right; she'd left them to be analyzed in the lab. A new panic set her heart racing, and a deeper pit tore its way through her insides.

Fuck. She wasn't going to leave them behind, either. A plan formed. Sneak past the bad guy, make it to the lab, retrieve her belongings and head straight for the hotel. If she could barricade herself inside the room, she should be able to hold out until tomorrow evening, when her plane was scheduled to return home. *Simple, right?*

Running to the end of the aisle, she snuck a peek around the end. She didn't see him. This time, she crouched low, and looked around the end and waited until she saw the man sneak around his own aisle on his way toward her location. A minute passed in agonizing slowness. But sure enough, the man popped his head around the side. He looked left, then right, before heading down the next row of books. He was no more than fifty feet away from her and closing. Mariska looked up and down the aisles. The far end of each row, butted up against the wall, so there was only one way in and out of each one. The goon, once again, looked around the end of the row across the aisle, now four rows away. She was running out of time.

She hurried back down to the end of the row, against the wall. She knelt down to the floor. No way could she make herself inconspicuous enough for him to overlook her. That's when it dawned on her. It was all about timing. The bottom shelf had fewer books on it than the mid and upper shelves. Frantically, pulling out books and placing them on the shelf above and to the side of her she cleared away a section of books wide enough for her to fit in. Reaching through to the other side, she pulled books from that side as well, placing them out of the way.

Mariska climbed into the cleared space, fitting inside well enough that she wasn't sticking out on either side. All she had to do was wait until he passed her row, then sneak back out and wait at the end of the row. As soon as he moved another row down, she would have a minute to run to the exit before he reemerged. *It'll work—it had too.*

Fear escalated as she waited for her moment to move. The sound of her heart beat loudly in her ears, and she wasn't sure no one else could hear it. She held her breath a moment and shifted just enough to the left to see past a book on the shelf in front of her. Her body flinched when the goon stepped into view. Trying to make himself look less conspicuous, he would step around into the next row of books, look up and down the center aisle and then pretend to look at the shelf of books—but only for a moment. Then he began the process all over again. Systematically, making his way through the library. Almost nothing escaping his notice.

The man lowered his glasses on his nose as she looked up and down the center aisle once again, before moving to the next row—this time to the row she was directly across from. He paused, looking down her row, longer than the others. Had he seen her? Something must have looked off to him. Mariska felt dizzy, and she slowly let out the breath she hadn't remembered holding. She dug her nails into the sides of her thighs, but barely even felt it. Her breathing quickened as he stood looking down the aisle. What could she do? There was nowhere else to hide or run.

Like a cornered animal, she felt the fight or flight response taking over her logic centers of her conscious mind. Everything in her told her to run. Run for your life, Mariska. But wouldn't that mean certain, capture? *Hold still. Remain silent*, she thought. A moment before she rolled out from the shelf and ran down the aisle, screaming for help, the goon returned to his normal pattern. He looked up and down the center aisle and moved down to the next row. Sweet relief washed over her. There was still a chance of surviving this.

A minute later, he moved down another row, and she slid out from the bottom shelf. Sneaking down the row, she waiting until he moved one more row to the right. *Run like hell*, Mariska told herself. And, that's exactly what she did. Willing her legs to move she thundered down the middle of the library, heading straight for the street level exit. Without turned to look behind her she hit the exit door with a thunderous clap of metal on metal. The door swung open, and she barely slowed as she made a wide turn out into to the street.

Remembering the way to the concrete, windowless building that housed the lab, she ran full steam ahead. Her legs started to burn with sudden burden being placed on them. This was the right way, wasn't it? Mariska lost a half step of speed as she contemplated the possibility of going the wrong way. As she passed the large building on the left, the University Lab came into view. Located mid-block on the left, the tall, grey concrete building looked like a beacon of hope. She was almost there. A few more steps and she'd be at the front door.

Stumbling the last step, she caught herself on the door. Out of breath, she pulled on the door-handle. Instantly felt sick. It was locked. The keypad situated next to the door blinked red. She looked and felt around for anything that looked like a doorbell, but came up empty-handed. Looking up the street, she saw the goon emerge from the library exit in the distance. He took a moment before he spotted her and then started running in her direction. Frantically, she started tapping in series of numbers into the security pad.

Nothing.

Pounding her fists against the door with all her might, she started to shout at the top of her lungs. "Let me in." Mariska's voice cracked with emotion and pitch. She continued to pound her fists as she looked on in horror. The man was coming, fast. There was nowhere to go. She could run, but he would overtake her.

Back against the door, she prepared to fight. Fists balled up at her sides; she glanced around the ground looking for something heavy she could wield.

Nothing.

Her heart pounding feverishly in her chest, she wanted to cry.

She wanted to scream but knew she needed all her strength to fight the incoming threat. Mariska took a step away from the door, and put up her fists, widening her base of support, just like her mother had told her to do if she needed to fight.

Then, suddenly, without warning, she heard the door behind her unlock with a click. She turned as the door opened inward, and Eddie stepped out through the opening. Without a second of hesitation, Mariska threw herself through the opening, pushing Eddie down to the floor. Sprawled out on the floor, she used her legs to kick the door closed behind her. It shut with a life-saving slam, followed almost instantly by a pounding of fists. The enemy had been mere steps behind her.

"What the, hell?" Eddie said as he peeled himself off the tiled floor.

Mariska had already scrambled to her feet. There wasn't time for an explanation. She grabbed his hand and started pulling. "Take me back to the lab, or we're all dead."

"What?" He pulled himself up with Mariska's help.

"Take me, now. Dammit, Eddie just do what I'm telling you." Mariska started pulling him down the hallway as the furious sounds of pounding grew more intense.

There wouldn't be much time before someone either heard the commotion out front or had to leave the building. Once one of those two things happened, Mariska would be out of time…with nowhere to go.

CHAPTER FORTY-TWO

Mariska repeatedly pushed the red button on the locker room wall that led into the lab.

"You have to put on the containment-suit before you can go into the Clean Lab," Eddie said as he slid his legs into the light blue plastic jumper. "No one will unlock the negative pressure room until they see the suit…trust me."

Mariska blew out a huff of air in annoyance. "Fine." She reached for the nearest clean suit and started putting it on.

Once they were both fully gowned up with the jumper, goggles, head cap, mask, foot covers, and gloves, Eddie pushed the button. The door slid open, and they entered the negative-pressure room. Waiting for the rush of air in all directions made Mariska tap her foot with the impatience of a child waiting to open their Christmas gifts. A rush of air to the face followed by a flashing green light signaled her wait had come to an end. The door slid open behind her, and she and Eddie hurried over to the back table where Dr. Tora typed commands into the computer.

"Oh, good," Dr. Tora said as they arrived at the workstation. "I am almost done with the tests."

"Great," Mariska said. "I need my things and to get out of here."

Dr. Tora turned and looked at her with surprise. "What's going on?"

Eddie said, "There seems to be some people following her. I heard the man pounding on the front door, trying to get inside."

Dr. Tora looked from Eddie to Mariska, and then to the work

she was about to complete. "This will only take a minute. I'll hurry. In the meantime, Eddie go to the phone and call down to University security. Tell them that there is someone outside the Lab building causing a scene." Eddie went as he was told.

"Thank you," Mariska said. "I might need help finding a back way out of here."

Dr. Tora nodded. "We'll do what's necessary."

She turned back to the computer and started typing in more commands. Mariska looked over her shoulder and saw she was finalizing the steps needed to run the DNA comparisons.

"Have you extracted the DNA from all the samples?" Mariska asked.

"Yes, the DNA was present in both hair samples as well as the root system of the tooth." Dr. Tora continued to type into the computer. "The quick part is pretty much done. Now we will have to wait for the computer to compile all the data and then sort through millions of other DNA sequences to find a match…if one exists."

Mariska looked around the examination table for the tooth but didn't see it. "Where's the tooth? I want it back."

"Of course. I have it here." Dr. Tora reached into the drawer and pulled out the woven pouch.

Mariska took it and examined the contents. Sure enough, the tooth and bead were safely inside. She closed the pouch and unzipped her suit.

"What the hell are you doing? You can't expose the lab to outside contaminants."

Mariska froze in place. "I'm so sorry." *Dammit, I fucked up—again.* She shoved the pouch into the front pocket of her slacks and re-zipped her suit. "There's no telling if that guy got inside."

Eddie returned from his phone call. "Security said there wasn't anyone at the front door when they arrived. They are going to pull the security camera footage, but it'll take a while."

Dr. Tora and Mariska exchanged glances. "He wouldn't have just given up," Mariska said. "That tells me he's inside."

The door to the negative pressure room hissed open, and two people walked in and went over to the table next to theirs. The men were fully dressed in the appropriate attire, and Mariska couldn't make out anyone's face, but based on their general size she knew without a doubt neither man was her assailant.

Mariska shook Dr. Tora's hand. "Thank you so much for all your help. How long do you suspect it'll be before we have the data analysis back?"

"I suspect it won't be too long. There are a couple of samples that are currently being computed, but I've pushed for this to be moved up as a priority. I will contact you as soon as I have something," Dr. Tora said. "Please leave all of your contact information with Eddie."

"Definitely."

At the examination table next to them, the two scientists were looking at a bone under magnification and bright white light. Mariska couldn't hear what they were discussing, but from this distance, the bone looked human. She craned her neck to see past the man's shoulder. Sure enough, it was a human clavicle. It looked old, dirty…almost as if it had been stained by tar.

The shorter scientist had a German accent and said, "That's an astute observation." He pointed to the midshaft of the bone. "As you suspected, the bone has an old fracture with bone remodeling present."

"Meaning, the injury was sustained pre-morbidly? And, the person lived long enough to have bone regrowth?"

"Yes, you're absolutely right, Dr. Heuston."

"Please, call me, Caleb."

Mariska heard the doctor respond and his voice seemed familiar, but at the same time she chalked it up to being an American accent. It was surprising how much she felt drawn to anyone else hailing from the United States when overseas. Still, something about this guy started sending up red flags.

Mariska felt flushed, faint—suddenly claustrophobic inside the isolation suit. She staggered backward ever so slightly. Eddie placed a steadying hand on her elbow, preventing her from moving. She looked at Dr. Tora and Eddie and put her finger up to her mouth as if to say, "Shh."

"I need to get out of here, but I don't want to draw any attention," Mariska said.

"Are you feeling all right?" Eddie asked in hushed tones.

"I don't know how much time until the man who followed me here finds me. Better to make my getaway now."

Dr. Tora moved to the right, stepping between Mariska and Eddie. She came toward her and whispered, "There isn't another way out of here. You're going to have to go back through the negative pressure room."

Mariska nodded her understanding. She looked up at Eddie and said in a soft voice, "Will you come with me?"

"Of course." He gave her elbow a squeeze of reassurance. "I won't leave you alone again."

Dr. Tora's voice returned to normal volume. "Thank you, Eddie, for all your help. I will have the results sent to you as soon as they are available."

"Wonderful," Mariska said. "I really appreciate all your help, doctor."

Mariska turned to Eddie and nodded. Without a word, they made their way past David's table and to the airlock. Eddie pushed the button to leave, and for a split second, it seemed the door wasn't going to respond. But with a hiss, it opened, and Mariska and Eddie stepped inside. She held her breath until the door slid closed and locked behind them.

"Do you have any idea who the man is that's chasing you?"

Mariska shook her head. "If I knew, I'd have already found a way to make him stop…before he killed, Jane." Mariska turned and looked behind her, back into the lab. "She was as close to me as my own mother."

"Wow," Eddie said. "I'm so sorry."

A second gust of high-pressure air blasted them from the back. "Do me a favor?"

"Anything."

The last blast of air hit them from the front. "If I don't make it back to the United States I need you to contact Theresa, Theresa. Tell her the same man who attacked me in Los Angeles had followed me here to Copenhagen."

Another gust of wind and then the door slid open, and they stepped out into the locker room. "I promise," he said. "I'll make sure you make it back to the airport…I won't let anything happen to you."

She wanted to believe him as much as he believed himself, but she'd seen what this man was capable of doing. They stripped off the containment garments and threw them into a pile at the back of the locker room and hurried toward the exit when Eddie stopped her.

"I think we should use Dr. Tora's office. It'll bypass the front desk and take us directly into the hallway. Might save some time, and minimize how many people we encounter."

"I'll follow you," Mariska said.

They turned, veering to the right and through a doorway into a long hallway. Three quarters down the hallway they stopped at a door, and Eddie punched a code into the security pad. The door lock disengaged with a click and he pushed the door open. Once inside, Mariska closed the door behind them.

Mariska reached for the front door of the office when Eddie stopped her. "Maybe I should go first."

Good plan. Mariska took a step back and allowed Eddie to go through the door first. He stepped into the hallway and looked both ways before signaling for Mariska to follow. After entering the hallway, she jumped with a start as the door slammed shut behind her. They exchanged a surprised look, but then let out a held breath followed by a quiet and short-lived, anxious laugh.

"Do you know how to get out of here?" Eddie whispered. "Just in case we get separated?"

She nodded. They ran-walked, side by side, down the hallway. Mariska looked behind her as they rounded the first corner and slammed face first into a human wall. She looked up into the face of a monster. The thug who had attempted to kill her back in Los Angeles stared down at her. His hand reached for her as she stumbled backward away from him. His powerful hand closed around her wrist like a painful vice-grip.

Mariska cried out in pain. She pulled away, hard, but couldn't budge him. Eddie jumped into action. His fist collided with the attacker's jaw, throwing the man's head back. Mariska pulled again and managed to free her arm.

Eddie jumped on the man's back, squeezing the man around the neck with his arm. Mariska jumped into the fray, kicking the man between the legs with every ounce of strength she had. The man fell to his knees with a thud.

"Get out of here, Mariska." Eddie struggled to remain on top of the giant man. "I don't know how long I can hold him."

Mariska hesitated for only a second. She turned and ran for the exit, the sounds of the struggle behind her grew more intense with each step. She stopped at the exit at the far end of the hallway and looked back. Eddie and the killer were locked in a dance of death. She fought the urge to run back and help.

Eddie yelled, "Get out of here."

She closed her eyes and pushed back through the exit and stumbled out onto the street. Looking both ways, she wasn't entirely sure which direction to go. The sound of voices drew her attention down the street. She went toward the voices. Safety in numbers? She hoped so.

Rounding the corner, she found herself in the middle of a street market. Signs indicating no motor vehicles indicated the rules of the road. There were people everywhere. Lining the street were vendors, both inside the buildings and outside in front on the sidewalks. Groups of people meandered from one shop to the next. It was all here, conversations in Danish, haggling between customer and merchant, laughter, and life. Mariska pulled up a map on her phone and located the hotel. It was close, no more than a few kilometers from this shopping district. Orienting herself using the compass app on the phone, she set out in the direction of the hotel.

Mariska shoved the phone back into her pocket after memorizing the directions and looked behind her to see if she was being followed. At first, she didn't see anyone. Sweet-relief settled over her until her mind shifted from preservation to betrayal. What was going on with David, and why was he in Copenhagen? Why was he with the man who was trying to hurt her? She continued down the street but felt like she was being watched. She looked around and saw an old man sitting in a rocking chair next to a cart. He smiled, and she crossed the street to greet him.

"Do I know you?" Mariska asked.

He shook his head. "I saw you."

"You saw me?"

"You were at the library. There was a man following you."

A nervous energy tingled her belly. "You were there?"

He nodded and continued to rock in his old wooden chair. "That man is still following you."

Mariska turned and glanced down the street. Sure enough, the monster walked through the crowd, stopping by each shop looking inside before moving to the next one. What was she going to do? There was no way she was going to make it all the way back to the hotel without getting caught.

She looked at the man's sales cart and saw it was covered in scarves, hats, and other fashion accessories. An idea lit up her mind. She handed the man a hundred-dollar bill and plucked a long blonde wig, sun-hat, and sunglasses from the display. She smiled and arched her eyebrows.

The old man smiled back and motioned for her to hurry. Mariska donned the disguise and meandered down the street. She never really stopped at any one place but did her best to appear as a local shopper. At the end of the street, she quickly flagged down a cab driver and got inside.

Mariska gave the cabbie the name of the hotel. "Please, hurry." She sat back against the seat and tried to calm down.

I want to go home? A single tear trailed down her cheek before she wiped it away. *No, there isn't time for me to have a breakdown. I'm stronger than this.* She thought back to her conversation with Detective Wulf. What had he been trying to tell her? She pulled out her phone and called him. The call went straight to voicemail. She disconnected and tried the call again. Without a single ring, it went to voicemail.

"Hey, it's me. I'm not sure what you were trying to tell me, but the guy that attacked me in Los Angeles is here. He's here in Copenhagen, and he's definitely seen me." Mariska paused, unsure of what to say next. What was there left to say? "I'll try and call you again, later." The phone beeped rapidly, and she pulled it away from her ear and looked at the screen. The call had disconnected. There was no way to be sure the message had gone through.

She turned off the screen and put it back into her pocket. I'll call him later. *If there was a later…*

CHAPTER FORTY-THREE

Mariska slid the room key into the slot and heard the high-pitched beep of the door lock disengaging. She cranked down on the doorknob and pushed the door open. Once inside, she closed the door by leaning back against it and slid down the door to the floor. An overpowering exhaustion took her from the conscious world to one filled with horrendous images that played out in her mind's eye. Sleep was interrupted by a slam of a neighboring hotel room.

She pushed back the cobwebs and monsters and stood. Her legs hadn't stiffened up, and her butt wasn't sore from sitting on the hard floor, which told her she hadn't been out long. Yawning, she tore off the hat and wig, dropping them at the door. The narrow entryway opened up to the main bedroom and bathroom. That's where she stopped, dead in her tracks.

The room had been ransacked. The mattress was lying on the floor next to the bedframe, all the drawers were open with clothes flung around the room. Her suitcase lay on its side, open, and empty, the lining torn out and sitting on the floor next to it. She felt the room start to spin. Everywhere she went, they followed. Was there anywhere in this world left that they couldn't follow her, find her?

Pulling out her phone, Mariska placed a call to Theresa.

"Mariska," Theresa answered. "Is everything, okay?"

"No." She took what was left of her suitcase and put it on the mattress. "I don't seem to be able to catch a break. Not even, here."

"What happened? What do you need?"

Mariska started to laugh. She had no idea, why, but she couldn't stop. Sitting down on the floor, she started throwing clothes into the suitcase. "The goon."

"What about him?"

"He's here," Mariska said. "He's here and tried to kill me, again."

"Are you fucking kidding me? You're not safe there."

"You're telling me? I was attacked at the University. I barely made it back to the hotel, only to find my room has been trashed."

"Get out of there…now. I'll arrange for a ride to the airport."

"My flight isn't until tomorrow night. What am I supposed to do until then?"

"What could be safer than being at an airport? I know it'll suck, but you can spend the night in the terminal. There will be armed guards, day and night," Theresa said. "Now, get the most important things you need and get to the airport. It might take me a bit, but I will have a car waiting for you within the hour. I'll make sure you know which one is your car."

"Can you also call Detective Wulf and let him know what's been going on? I haven't been able to reach him."

"Yes, of course. Anything else?"

Mariska cringed as she thought back to Eddie and how the last time she saw him he was fighting for their lives. "Have you heard from, Eddie?"

There was a long pause. "No, I haven't." Another long moment of silence. "Is he…okay?"

Mariska cleared her throat. "I'm not sure, Theresa. The last time I saw him, he was…in a struggle. He saved my life."

"Struggle? I'll call the university. Unless there's something else you need right now, I think I should get going." The pain in her voice made Mariska rethink her decision not to come to his aide.

But what could I have done? Mariska said, "Thank you for all your help…I hope he's all right. He's a wonderful man."

Their call disconnected and Mariska suspected Theresa had hung up. She hurried around the room grabbing up her clothes and putting them in the suitcase. Every time she packed for a trip, she could hear her mom's voice in her head. Telling her to pack an extra pair of socks and underwear because you never knew when you'd get wet.

Emotions well up inside her as she closed her eyes and saw her parent's faces looking back at her. She missed them so much more than she ever thought she could. Opening the front pocket of her suitcase, Mariska pulled out a clear plastic Ziploc baggie. *You never know when you'll get wet.* Placing her cell phone, wallet, and passport into the baggie, she pushed all the air out and sealed it. Shoving the baggie into her purse, she slung it over her shoulder. After zipping the suitcase shut, she pulled it to the hotel room door, stopping long enough to turn and take in the mess she was leaving behind. Stooping down, she picked up the disguise and put it back on. "I think I'm going to need this," she said to herself.

I also need to get the hell out of here. Fast. While there was still time.

Mariska stopped at the hotel bar to wait for her ride that Theresa promised would be within the hour. "I'll have vodka and soda with a lime, please."

The bartender brought it a few minutes later. She tossed some money on the bar and took the drink to go. Keeping to the edges of the expansive lobby, she found a discreet place to sip her drink. Pushing the suitcase up against the wall, she sat on it and crossed her legs. The drink was delicious, with enough fizz and lime taste to make it go down easily. A bit watered down, but tasty. She could see outside through the huge glass doors at the front of the hotel. A dark limousine pulled up, and a driver got out and helped a family load up their bags and get inside the vehicle.

She pulled out her phone and found, Badger's phone number. She knew better than to call him. He wouldn't answer anyway, so she sent a message. *I need immediate evacuation from the Copenhagen International Airport. I'm headed to the airport within the hour. Any help you can provide will be greatly appreciated.* The message showed as successfully sent, but there wasn't an immediate reply. Not that she'd really expected one.

Putting the phone back into the plastic bag, she shoved the whole mess back into her purse. A flash of light drew her attention to the street out front. The sun glared off a limousine that had just arrived.

A man holding a white sign got out and stood facing the hotel. Could that be my driver?

Mariska pulled her bag behind her and exited the building. Sure enough, the sign read *Preservation.* Theresa knew exactly the right thing to show the limo had been for her. Otherwise, she wouldn't have known if it was a setup or not. She hurried over to the driver and said, "You're my ride."

He looked her up and down. "Candace?"

"No, Mariska Stevenson."

He smiled. "You don't look like the description I was given."

Mariska pulled off the wig and hat. "Perfect," he said. "Let me help you with your bag." The man opened the trunk and put the suitcase inside and then closed the lid. He hurried over to the back door and pulled it open for her. He was very eager to please.

"Thank, you." Mariska tossed her purse inside and got in.

The man closed the door behind her and hurried around to the front seat and got in, started the engine, and pulled away from the curb.

He looked back at her in the rearview mirror. "I have instructions to take you to the airport. Is that correct?"

"Yes." She looked behind her. No one appeared to be following them. "According to the map on my phone, there are two ways to the airport. Can you take the less traveled one, please?"

He immediately nodded. "Yes, the route that takes us down by the water is longer but less traveled."

Mariska took out the plastic bag and took out the wallet. "Here," she handed him some cash. "I really appreciate you accommodating me."

"I've been compensated; money isn't necessary. Would you like some music?"

"That'd be great, thanks." Mariska looked out the window as the man turned off the main roadway. An old Ricky Martin song came on the radio. Funny, she only spoke English, the song was in Spanish, and they were in Denmark, and yet she recognized the song. Music truly was an international language.

The driver stopped at a stop sign and made a right turn. "We should be there soon, ma'am. Feel free to sit back and relax. I'll give you some privacy." He rolled up the glass divider between them.

Mariska looked up at him and smiled. She fiddled with her purse for a couple minutes. She opened her wallet and flipped through the pictures of her parents. They were so happy, with big smiles, posed perfectly for each shot. The last picture was of Jane. Mariska's heart ached for the woman that helped raise her. Emotions threatened to break her, and she couldn't let that happen. Not now, she still had a job to do. Putting the wallet back in the purse, she zipped it closed. The phone and passport went into the plastic baggie and then into her front pocket, along with a wad of cash. The driver had been so nice, and she planned on giving him a generous tip once they arrived at the airport.

Something caught her attention out the side window. She turned just in time to register the grill of a truck as it ran through a stop sign. Without slowing down, the truck slammed into the side of the limo. Mariska saw as the front passenger door, imploded, sending the car careening across the street. She was pushed up against the door and then flung across the backseat to the opposite side. Her head hit the window with a thud. The sound of squealing tires and crunching metal filled the vehicle.

The car hopped over the curb and slammed into the short stone wall that lined the roadway above the Danish Straits. Mariska lifted her head from the backseat and looked around the inside of the car. A motion-sick feeling made her feel dizzy and nauseous as the car slowly moved back and forth—teetering on the edge of the drop off into the water. She tried to pull herself up from the footwell of the back seat and climb further back to help tip the car toward dry land. But the more she moved, the car tipped further toward the water.

A moment later, the feeling of free-fall was cut short by the impact of the car hitting the water and Mariska's head slamming against the glass divider. Her face seemed stuck to the glass, and her body felt like it was made of lead. She struggled to move her arms and legs, but they were too heavy to lift. Her vision began to fade, but when she saw a trickle of blood trailing across the glass, she knew it was her own. Coughs wracked her body as she tried to take a deep breath. The impact had pushed all the air from her lungs, and it seemed impossible to refill them. A sob, erupted from deep inside and the last thing she heard was the sound of her own painful moans. It was then that her world went black.

CHAPTER FORTY-FOUR

Piercing cold water rushed into the vehicle and tore Mariska away from her unconscious state. She coughed out the mouthful of salty water as she gasped for air. She was face down against the glass divider separating the front and back halves of the limo. Picking up her head, she tried to orient herself to where she was and how she got there. It all came flooding back, much like the water that was continuing to fill the vehicle.

The driver.

He wasn't moving. The water had almost completely filled the front seat, and his head bobbed around, face-down, as the turbulent water continued to deepen. Mariska started banging on the window.

"Wake up." She didn't know his name. "Hey, wake up." The glass was thick and shatter resistant, no matter how hard she pounded, there wasn't a single crack. "Please, wake up." Mariska watched in horror as the last bubble of hair floated to the top of the front seat, and out a crack in the side window.

There wasn't anything she could do for him now. She needed to get out of the car, or she'd suffer the same fate. With all her might, she pushed herself up away from the glass divider and scrambled to the door. Pulling as hard as she could, the door didn't open.

Locked inside a sinking car.

The water was now waist deep and rising fast. Pounding with her fists against the side windows, she felt the skin of her knuckles split. Each punch, each bang, she left a little more blood behind on the glass. She went for the door on the other side, but with no avail. The door wouldn't budge, and the window was solid.

Shit. What would mom tell me to do? Nothing came to her. Hadn't her mom told her stories? Hadn't her mom shown her how to survive?

There was not time to panic, but that's what she did. Screaming for help, begging someone to save her, and pleading with God to intervene, all with the same result.

Nothing happened. No one came to her aide.

The water continued to rise, now up to her neck. Mariska's head was pressed hard against the back window; she looked outside at the ledge far above her. It had grown dark outside, but she could still see the outline of two people standing on the edge, watching her. Watching her drown.

Were they the killers? Was that, David?

She screamed again and started pounding on the back window, begging for help. The two figures didn't move, they weren't on the phone calling for help, they did nothing, but wait for her to die.

The water was now inches from the top of the car, a mere bubble of air left to sustain her. But for how long? Mariska knew she only had minutes to live and her heart raced with the adrenaline coursing through her veins. She was going to drown, and there wasn't a fucking thing she could do about it.

Mariska puckered her lips and pressed them to the back window, breathing in the last little bit of air, and started to sink back down into the seat. Eyes wide open, they burned from the salty water, but that was nothing compared to the burning in her oxygen-starved lungs.

Suddenly a memory flashed into her conscious mind. Her mom in the back seat of their car and she was showing a young Mariska the best way to cut a seatbelt with a Swiss Army knife.

The headrest.

Mariska blinked and brought some clarity back to her vision. She reached for the backseat headrest and pulled up, hard. It didn't budge. Fiddling as quickly as she could with the release mechanism, she tried again. This time the headrest came free. With a renewed sense of hope, she brought the metal prongs to the side window. Pressing the prongs against the surface of the glass, she pulled back, before slamming the metal into the glass with every last ounce of strength she had left.

A cracked formed and spread across the glass like a spider web. One more hard strike was all it took. The window fell away leaving a large empty space for Mariska to swim through. Popping up to the surface, she sucked in air, but immediately coughed and gagged, causing her head to sink below the surface once again. Kicking with her legs, she resurfaced and wiped the water from her face.

She heard voices from up above. It was now too dark to see who was speaking, but she thought she recognized David's voice. "Go down to the water and find her."

"Sure, thing, boss," the other man said. "What do we do with her, Caleb?"

"Kill her, you idiot."

There was a pause. Why did the guy call him Caleb? Was it really not David? Her head sank underwater, and she gasped when she brought her head back up. Water seeped into her lungs, and she began to cough. Their conversation stopped, and she knew they heard her.

That asshole betrayed me. If I get out of this alive, he'll pay for what he's done.

Fearing that they might come and find her, she slowly started swimming back and away from the car, whose trunk and back bumper still stuck out through the surface. Mariska managed twenty or thirty feet away from the wreckage when she heard a whistling sound. She turned back and saw something plop into the water between her and the car, accompanied by the same whistling noise. Looking up at the street, the two figures stood, partially illuminated by a streetlamp above them. They were holding something in their hands. Another whistle and plop, this time a bit closer to her.

They were shooting at her. Or, at least in her general direction. They must not be able to see her, but figure if she's alive they will minimize their risk of her survival by shooting her. The shock of it all had started to wane. David had once been her best friend. They'd nearly been, lovers. Why did that guy call him Caleb?

Mariska turned and swam quietly away, putting as much distance between herself and the kill-zone. Allowing the water-current to help, she drifted downstream until the crash site disappeared around a bend. After a few more minutes of passive movement, she kicked her way into shore. Seconds later, she pulled herself up out of the water and collapsed onto the muddy bank.

Lying on her back and looking up into the night sky, she gave herself a minute to catch her breath and come up with a plan. Despite being in a large city, she was able to view the stars and moon with so much more clarity than she could from Los Angeles. Or, was it a new appreciation of things she'd once taken for granted?

She identified the Orion's belt and a cluster of stars she'd known as the Seven-sisters. She smiled and thought once again of her parents. Had it not been for her mom, she'd never have made it out of the car alive. She'd be at the bottom of the Danish Straits, dead and bloated—fish-food. She shivered. The trauma she'd endured, the pain of betrayal, watching a man die in front of her, and the cold water and chilly air was taking its toll.

Constellations. The artifacts.

Mariska sat up and pulled the soggy woven pouch from the front pocket of her slacks. After opening it, she poured the contents into her hand. As she suspected, the water had no real effect on the tooth or bead, but the pouch might not be salvageable. No, matter. She put them back into her pocket when she felt her other pocket vibrate.

The cell phone was still working.

Retrieving the plastic baggie, she took out the phone and read the incoming text message. It was from Badger, and it said: *New flight information. Tonight 11:05 pm. American Airlines. Unless you need to delay the flight, just say the word.*

Delay the flight? Better not to question, how. She typed a message in reply: *Please delay the flight. I will get there as soon as I can.*

She had an hour and a half to get there, check in and get to the gate. Under normal circumstances that wouldn't have been a problem, but she was lying wet and muddy on the banks of the Danish Straits. Would a cab even stop to pick her up?

"Only, one way to find out," Mariska said to herself as she pushed up from the ground and tried to wipe away as much of the muck as she could.

It was a steep climb up to street level, and Mariska had fallen to her knees more than once—further dirtying her clothes and wasting more time she didn't have. Once she managed to get to the top, she took a deep breath and brushed off her jeans which were still sopping wet.

The street was pretty desolate at this hour, but not completely dark. The dim street lamps that allowed for star gazing did less than a good job keeping the shadows at bay. Each alleyway, each darkened corner near a closed business, made Mariska nervous. There was no telling where death was going to jump out and try and take her.

A set of headlights came around the bed and was steadily making their way in her direction. Was it a cab? Or a nice citizen that wouldn't mind taking a filthy, wet, stranger to the airport? As the car approached, she saw the markings on the side indicating it was a car for hire. She stepped off the curb, a foot into the street, and waved both hands hoping they would stop.

It was her lucky day. The car slowed and pulled over to the curb a few feet past where she stood. Mariska started mussing with her hair trying to make herself look less homeless and less like a possible threat in hopes that Cabbie would let her in the car. As she approached the driver, he rolled down the window and said something to her in Danish.

She shook her head and smiled. "I'm sorry, I only speak English."

His eyes grew wide, "You're American?"

Mariska nodded.

He got out of the car and opened the back door, "Here, get inside, you're going to catch your death of cold." The man didn't have an accent like she expected.

"Are you an American?" Mariska asked.

The man was in his mid-sixties, heavy around the middle, and was wearing a golfer's hat. He was adorable, in a grandpa sort of way. "I sure am. I moved here when I retired. It's so much safer being a cab driver here in Copenhagen than my hometown of Chicago."

She needed a hug and was tempted to ask for one.

He motioned once again for her to get inside the car and so she did. He got into the front seat and turned around. "Where are you headed?"

"The airport. I need to get home tonight."

"Where's home? If you don't mind me asking?"

"Los Angeles. I know I won't get home until tomorrow, but I need to get out of here." She looked away.

He didn't say anything for a moment. He used the turn signal and pulled out onto the street, "I'm not one to judge, but is everything, okay? You look like an absolute mess."

Mariska shook her head. "I will be…once, I get back home." She fought back the tears and swallowed the lump in her throat.

"Is there anything I can do to help?"

"Not unless you have some clean clothes."

As he continued to drive, he reached down to the front seat passenger floor and pulled out a duffle bag. "I can't guarantee how clean any of it is, but I keep all the clothes that get left in the car, in this bag. You're more than welcome to take a look." He tossed the bag into the back seat next to her.

This man had to be her guardian angel.

She unzipped the bag and began rummaging through the clothes. There were bras, panties, even a random shoe, but not a lot that she felt comfortable utilizing.

"I don't think…" Mariska started to say. "Oh, wait." She pulled out a light pink sweater and a pair of soft flannel pajama bottoms.

"Oh, yeah," he said, shaking his head. "Those were left in here last weekend. A girl and her guy got into an argument on the way to the airport. They were throwing things at each other in the backseat. I suspect the clothes are relatively clean."

Mariska gave the items a once over. No stains. Nothing sticky or crusty. A quick sniff test told her they smelled stale, but no body odor.

"These'll do nicely. Thank you so much."

He smiled. "I knew they'd come in handy one of these days."

"If you wouldn't mind keeping your eyes up front, I'm going to change my clothes back here." Mariska started to pull her arms out of the sleeves.

"No problem." The driver moved the rearview mirror, so it was facing out the front window.

The flannel pajama pants had an inside pocket that the bead and tooth fit in, along with her passport and cash, but she'd have to carry her cell phone. Which was fine. She'd probably buy some things inside the airport anyway and that included a bag to keep everything in.

They pulled up to the airport, and the driver said, "Here you go. I hope you have a safe flight home. Say hello to America for me."

"I sure will." Mariska handed him twice the regular fare. "Thank you so much for everything."

"You're welcome."

Mariska got out of the car and hurried across two drop-off lanes and into the airport. She had thirty minutes to get to the gate, but when she looked up at the departure board, it said her flight was delayed an hour.

"Thank you, Badger," Mariska said.

Plenty of time to get her shit together and go home.

CHAPTER FORTY-FIVE

Mariska stepped off the plane in Los Angeles and felt the sweet relief of being back on familiar ground. Realizing she was single-handedly holding up the rest of the plane, she stepped aside and found a seat to sit on in the terminal. She needed to regroup both physically and emotionally.

Her shoes had not fully dried, and her toes felt disgusting in the damp socks. She pulled out her phone and turned it back on—waiting a few seconds hoping someone had sent her texts, voicemails, or anything else that showed someone that cared about her while she was gone.

Nothing.

A few more minutes passed before the technology gods smiled upon her. A series of beeps came through in rapid-fire succession as her phone was inundated with messages. She smiled as she saw the list of contacts that'd contacted her: Wulf, Theresa, and her mom. Then she saw David's name on the list. Her stomach sank. After the hair-raising ordeal she'd gone through, she decided she'd need a few hours before she responded to her mom and then figure out what to do about her betrayer.

Mariska sent a quick message to Wulf and Theresa letting them know she was safely back on American soil and asked Wulf if he would be able to come and pick her up. He responded within seconds, letting her know he was on his way to LAX to get her.

Good, now I just need to get through customs, she thought.

Phone and passport in hand, she marched toward customs with

an excitement she hadn't expected. Was it because she was finally home? Or, because Wulf would be waiting for her on the other side? It didn't matter at this point; she needed to get home and put on some clean socks. She wiggled her toes trying to scratch an itch that wasn't going away.

The lines had moved slowly, but she made it through and out the other side unscathed. There was always that momentary fear that the customs agent wasn't going to let her through, but after a thorough once over, he had smiled and welcomed her home.

Now, where was, Wulf?

She walked past security and into the main part of the airport where there were people all around, shopping, eating, laughing, and rushing toward their gates.

"Mariska," a man behind her said.

She turned and saw Wulf rushing toward her, his arms stretched out wide. She stepped toward him, and they embraced. His strength wrapped around her. Mariska pressed her face against his chest and breathed in his scent. A moment passed before she released him and took a step back.

"Thank you so much for picking me up."

"Absolutely. I was so worried about you from the moment you'd left."

She smiled, "I think once I've had a chance to shower and change my clothes we will have a lot to discuss."

"I brought someone with me," Wulf said. He waved someone over to join them.

Mariska looked in that direction and couldn't help, but laugh. Theresa came over, and they gave each other a hug.

"You came too?" Mariska asked…her smile disappearing slowly as she grew suspicious. "Did something bad happen while I was gone?" She looked from one to the other. "Are my parents, okay?"

Wulf put a hand on her shoulder. "Yes, your parents are just fine. I talked to your dad yesterday. He said they're still mourning Jane's death. Your mom is having a hard time with her death which is understandable. And, of course, they're worried about you. Other than that, everything is fine on their end."

"Oh, thank god. When I saw you both here, I was thinking it was to break some devastating news or something." Mariska turned to Theresa. "So, what are you both doing here?"

Theresa said, "We were investigating a few leads together when we got your text that you were back."

"Great timing." Mariska grew very serious and put a hand on Theresa's shoulder. "Have you heard from Eddie?"

Theresa shook her head. "No, but I contacted the university. They said he is okay, but was sent to the hospital with minor injuries. There's going to be a full investigation of course, but I'm relieved he doesn't seem to be too badly banged up."

"Oh, thank God." Mariska let out a sigh of relief. "He saved my life."

"He's a great guy." Theresa blushed and looked away.

Mariska stepped closer and whispered in her ear. "I know he still likes you…a lot."

Theresa nodded.

"And I have a feeling you like him."

Theresa nodded, again.

"When this is all over with, I'm taking you to Copenhagen for a quick vacation…my treat." Mariska gave Theresa a hug. "How's that sound?"

"Sounds, wonderful. I hope I'll be able to manage it with classes and the internship."

"From the sound of your nickname, I'd say you can handle just about anything you put your mind too."

Theresa's eyes grew wide. Mariska giggled, but when she looked at the confused look on Wulf's face, she busted out laughing.

"I'll have to ask about this when we have more time," he said. "Sounds interesting."

Mariska nodded and then yawned. "Any chance we can find me a shower and some clean clothes before we start getting down to business?"

"Of course," Theresa and Wulf said in unison. All three shared a quick laugh.

Wulf then said, "Theresa filled me in on what happened to you in Copenhagen. I'm glad you made it home in one piece."

"Neither of you know the half of it. I'll have to get you both up to speed on the car ride home."

The three of them walked out of the airport and into the parking garage together. Mariska got in the front passenger seat started telling them what had happened, including the car ending up in the Danish Straits. Wulf and Theresa both looked shocked and kept interrupting her story to ask if she was okay. Once she was done relaying everything back to them with as much detail as she could remember, she yawned again. It was like the more pent up information and stress she got out of her system by relaying what had happened, the more tired she felt.

She watched as Wulf put the car into reverse and started drifting off to sleep before they pulled out of the space. The jostling car ride back to her apartment woke her up a couple times, but she hadn't realized she arrived until Detective Wulf gently nudged her. "Mariska…we're here."

She opened her eyes and stretched her arms high into the air. "Great, you two are more than welcome to come up with me."

Wulf and Theresa agreed, and they went single file, up the metal staircase. At the top step, Mariska tipped over the potted plant and took out the key she'd stashed there for emergencies.

"The key won't work," Wulf said.

Mariska then noticed the door locks were different than she remembered. "Who changed the locks?"

"Your father," Theresa said.

"Yeah, he gave me the code." Wulf reached past Mariska. "See you just have to put in this six-digit code and the door will automatically unlock. Your dad left the emergency keys in your bedroom."

"I guess he doesn't hate me then. The last time I saw him, I wasn't sure he'd ever speak to me again."

Wulf put his hand on small of her back and urged her inside. "I can assure you, your family loves you and would never hate you."

Mariska went into her apartment and looked around. Everything had been freshly cleaned, and she could even smell a hint of lemon disinfectant in the air. No doubt, her mom hired a cleaning crew while she was gone to try and erase the atrocity that took place here a few days ago.

"You guys make yourselves at home, while I get cleaned up." Mariska pointed the way to the living room and continued on to her bedroom. When she reached the door, she paused, unsure of what to expect once she entered the room.

Would every trace of Jane's murder be gone?

She slowly pushed the door open and was immediately met with the smell of a fresh coat of paint. It was clear that the apartment had not been completely redone yet, but all the blood was gone or at least hidden. The walls had been painted over with the first layer of primer paint, and the carpet had all been ripped out. The bare floors were ugly but clean. *Thank you, Mom.* Rubbing her face and pinching her eyes closed to get rid of the bad memories, she closed the door and blindly made her way to the bathroom. Stripping down to her birthday suit, Mariska turned on the water and let the steam fill the room before getting in. *I left out the part about David. I should have told Wulf and Theresa. They needed to hear the whole truth. I'll do it right after the shower.*

Letting the water wash away her tension and worries, Mariska wasn't sure how long she'd been standing in the shower when a knock at the door drew her mind back to the here and now.

"Mariska?" Theresa said. "Is everything going okay?"

Mariska wiped the water from her face and turned off the shower. "Yes, all is well. I'll be out in a couple minutes."

She stepped out of the shower and shivered. It was far from cool in the bathroom, but she felt nervous like something was wrong. But she wasn't sure what was off. Walking into the bedroom, the cell phone on the bed drew her attention. Picking it up, she sent David a message letting him know she was home in case he wanted to stop over. It couldn't have been him in Copenhagen…could it? It was someone named Caleb…not David.

Minutes later, after she'd changed clothes, and dried her hair, he replied: *I would normally say yes, but I'm visiting my folks for a couple of days.*

Mariska thought about that for a moment. She shook her head. He's lying. David had a terrible relationship with his family. He wouldn't have just up and went for a visit. Totally out of his nature. She replied: *That's great. I'm glad you're getting to see your family. Let me know when you get back into town, and we'll get caught up.*

No reply. *What was he up to?*

Mariska joined her friends in the living room and sat.

Wulf was the first to speak. "Do you need anything before we go? We don't want to be in the way."

Theresa chimed in, fully agreeing with the detective.

"To be completely honest with you, I'm not loving the idea of staying here alone tonight."

Wulf and Theresa exchanged looks of concern.

"I'd totally stay, but I can't tonight," Theresa said. "I've got a butt-load of homework to do, and I have to be at the Museum early to give the opening tour to a bunch of grade-schoolers."

Theresa and Mariska turned to Wulf. He grew red under the collar, and Mariska wanted to laugh. For a detective, he sure didn't play his hand close to his vest.

"Don't worry about it," Mariska said. "I have stuff I can do to keep myself occupied."

Wulf cleared his throat. "No, I think you should come and stay with me tonight."

Mariska smiled and slapped her knees. "Perfect. I'll get my things."

"Before you get too excited, there's something we need to discuss with you first." Wulf turned to Theresa. "Would you like to start?"

Theresa shook her head.

"Come on, guys. Why are you acting like a couple of weirdoes? It's like you're going to give me a fatal diagnosis, or something."

"Not exactly," Theresa said. "It's possibly bad news…if it's true."

Mariska looked at Wulf for explanation.

"I've been doing some digging," Wulf said, clearing his throat. "It's about David Beaumont. We think he might be involved in the attacks…or, at the very least the La Brea Woman's disappearance." Wulf leaned forward and put his hand on Mariska's.

Mariska's expression fell. "I know."

"You know?" Wulf sounded surprised.

"I left something out when I was telling you what happened to me in Denmark." She looked away, feeling guilty. "The accident that nearly drowned me was caused by David. Or at least I think it was him. I was treading water trying to remain quiet…they couldn't see me very well in the dark. I heard David's voice, but the weird thing was the guy that was with him addressed him as Caleb."

"Caleb?" Theresa said as she got up and sat next to Mariska on the sofa. A look crossed her face that said she knew more than what she was letting on to.

"Do you know something more about this?" Mariska looked from Theresa to Wulf.

"I'm not sure." She took out her cell phone and began scrolling.

"As part of the investigation, I've had to run background checks, interview, and run bank records on everyone involved. That includes the two of you." Wulf shrugged. "It's how this works."

"Yeah, I get that," Mariska said. "And?"

"And, David has had a few things come back as concerning…at least to me."

"Like, what?"

"There's almost nothing in the public record under the name David Beaumont. Other than the obvious things, he's earned a Ph.D. from UCLA, works at the Page Museum, and rents an apartment in a sketchy side of town…there's nothing. It's like his life started when he entered the doctoral program at the University."

I'm going to have to send Badger a message, Mariska thought. *Maybe he can help?*

Theresa said, "I ran a few internet searches with as much information as I could get from work. I managed to sneak into his employee files and honestly, there wasn't a lot to go on. His social security number was valid, so was his driver's license…but there was no activity related to his social security number until he entered college at UCLA."

Wulf then said, "We were concerned he might not be who he said he was. And, now I'm sure of it. That bastard tried to kill you, and we need to stop him before he can get to you."

Mariska sat back into the soft sofa. "And, I appreciate that. But it's so hard for me to accept this entirely. I mean, he was my best friend…for years." The absurdity of it all threatened to make her laugh, but her heart ached.

"Do you promise not to do anything crazy?" Theresa asked. "David's dangerous, and you need to stay away from him until the police can track him down."

Mariska nodded and crossed her arms.

Theresa gave Wulf a look that made Mariska think that neither one of them believed her.

"Anyway, I have some things packed in the event that one of you two were going to let me stay at their place." She shrugged and looked at the detective. "Are you ready to go?"

The three of them got up and met back at the front door. Mariska was the last one onto the stairway landing. She backed out and closed the door, locking it behind her. She grabbed Wulf by the elbow. "Thanks again for taking me in for the night."

"Anytime," he said. "I'm glad I can help keep you safe."

She gave his arm a squeeze and started down the stairs. Now, she not only had to prove her own innocence but keep herself alive while her best friend tried to kill her.

CHAPTER FORTY-SIX

A sharp pain knifed through Mariska's left knee as she climbed the single step to Wulf's front door.

"Ouch," she said as she started to lose her balance, falling into Wulf.

"Are you all right?" Wulf said, steadying her with strong, sturdy arms.

Mariska rubbed her knee. "Yeah, I'm okay. I banged my knee up on the way to the airport last night. Plus, I'm exhausted…and needy."

"As soon as we dropped Theresa off at her place, you fell asleep. I actually felt bad about waking you up to come inside." Wulf smiled. "You were sleeping so peacefully."

It'd seemed like forever since Mariska could remember feeling safe enough actually to sleep, peacefully.

"Thanks again for letting me stay the night."

Wulf unlocked the door and placed a warm hand to the small of her back, welcoming her to go inside in front of him. His hand felt nice, goose bumps began to form across her arms, and all the little hairs stuck up on end. Really nice. As she took the step up once again, she noticed her knee didn't seem to hurt quite as bad this time.

Wulf locked the door behind them and led her by hand deeper into the house. "I'm sure you remember the way, but I know you're tired."

"Seems like forever since I was here." Mariska looked around the home. She hadn't noticed how well the place was decorated before now.

Up the stairs they went, Mariska wincing every few steps, but doing her best not to let it show. At what point did she spill her guts about everything that happened in Denmark? Or, did she play it cool and keep it all bottled up inside? The twinge in her stomach as she began to instinctively push everything deep inside, out of view from the rest of the world.

They walked into the guest room that Mariska used the last time she was there. The bed looked inviting, but she would need a long, hot shower before slipping between the sheets. Mariska suddenly realized she hadn't brought the duffle bag up from the car. It had everything she'd need for at least a couple days. She turned to ask Wulf if he wouldn't mind getting it from the car when he placed the bag on the bed next to her.

She went over and unzipped it. "Thank you for bringing this up for me. I'd completely forgotten about it."

"Yeah, I kind of figured. You looked like you were running on autopilot…at best." He smiled and crossed the room. He began closing the plantation shutters. The room dimmed with each closure. "Figured you'd like your privacy."

Mariska nodded. "Yes, thank you." She walked around the bed and gave him a hug.

She felt his body relax into the embrace. Soon, his arms were wrapped around her in a protective cover. She could have stayed like this forever. His scent weakened her knees and made her heart race. She breathed in deeply and felt her throat tighten with emotion.

No. Don't do this, Mariska. Stop while you still can.

Suddenly, Wulf's words sounded inside her mind: *Everyone's a suspect.*

Swallowing hard, Mariska let her arms fall to her sides and leaned back away from him. He let her go, and she turned away and went and sat on the edge of the bed.

"What's wrong?" Wulf asked.

"Nothing." Mariska tried to push her rising anger away. Wulf was just doing his job. There wasn't anything they could do about their relationship until the investigation was over. "I'm just tired. I think the jetlag is getting to me. Not to mention all the crazy shit that happened over there."

"Speaking of, what *did* happen over there?" He came around the side of the bed and sat next to her.

Fighting the urge to lean her head against his chest and tell him every last detail, she simply shrugged her shoulders and said, "It's a long story."

"Okay, give me the Cliffs Notes version."

Mariska turned and looked the man in the eyes. His bright, beautiful blues were framed in the most lush, dark eyelashes she'd ever seen on a man. Why did men always seem to have such amazing lashes? She blinked away her wandering thoughts and forced herself to focus.

"Basically, I was successful in getting the tooth to the Genetics Department at the university for DNA analysis. While I was there, we discovered a long red hair in the pouch where the tooth and beads had been stored inside the La Brea Woman's skull."

"Oh, really? Who do you suspect it belongs to?"

"No idea, but the director, Dr. Tora said there was a good root bulb so DNA shouldn't be too difficult to extract and analyze."

"That's great." Wulf cocked his head to the side when he saw Mariska wasn't smiling. "Right?"

"Yeah, it's good, but there wasn't a sample to compare it too. So basically, we'll learn the ethnic heritage of the person, but unless there is a sample on file, we won't find out the identity." She shrugged. "And, I gave them a sample of my own hair."

"To compare with the red hair?"

"Not, exactly. I mean, sure they will most likely cross-reference them, but I was more interested in finding out who *I* am?"

The understanding dawned on Wulf—Mariska saw it in his eyes. And from his silence, it was also clear he didn't quite know what to say.

She continued, "Since I was found in a dumpster as an infant, I haven't the foggiest idea of who I am. It would at least be nice to find out where I get my blue eyes and super dark hair from. Don't you think?"

He nodded. "I can't imagine what you're going through. I came from well-documented, German immigrants who came to America looking for a better life in the early nineteen-hundreds. They started in the Midwest and migrated to California in the sixties. Pretty straightforward as immigration goes. You know the Germans, very specific, always keeping track of everything."

They shared a laugh.

"I guess. I wouldn't know."

Mariska's honesty tasted bitterness in her mouth, and Wulf's sudden cessation of laughter made her feel bad she was being such a downer. A long awkward silence followed.

"Anyway, I'm hoping to have the DNA analysis sent to me within a day or two. Dr. Tora was going to make it priority number one, and she was more than competent to do the job."

Wulf patted her. "Fingers crossed that you get the answers you're looking for."

Mariska held up both hands and crossed her fingers. "I'd be nice to have some answers for a change. I seem to have way more questions than answers."

"I know the feeling. That's pretty much how it works being an investigator. I never know anything for a certainty at the beginning of each case."

"But it seems that every time I get an answer, something happens and I lose all the proof of it."

"What do you mean?"

"The bank accounts I told you about before I left for Copenhagen. I had all that information on the computer that is now missing. My hotel was ransacked before I could leave the country. Not that it would have survived the Danish Straits."

"Oh, God. I still can't believe you went through all that." After a moment, Wulf shrugged and said, "Do you want the good news?"

"There's good news?"

He hurried out of the room. A few moments later, reemerging

with a laptop of his own. "Before you left, I copied and transferred files from your laptop to mine."

"How and when did you do that?" Her voice raised, a bit more than she'd intended.

"Maybe one of these days over a nice dinner or wine, we can exchange stories." He winked, and she smiled with one eyebrow raised. "It's my job."

He's pretty sneaky, isn't he? She thought.

"Okay, show me what you got." Mariska feigned annoyance and bumped him in the ribs with her elbow and rolled her eyes. "All this buildup, I want it to take my breath away."

He turned his head slightly to the side, eyes locked with hers, and raised both eyebrows. *Was that naughtiness in his eyes?* At that moment, Mariska could see herself wrapped up in his arms, under the sheets. She swatted him on the arm.

"I'm talking about the computer," she said, feigning shock and embarrassment.

Wulf smiled, broad and genuine. The more she blushed, the happier he seemed. Was she making a connection with this guy? *Not now, Mariska.*

He turned his computer a bit to the side so they could both look at the computer screen. Wulf double-clicked on a folder on the desktop, and after it opened, she realized what it was. The same icons she'd seen on the laptop she'd gotten back from Badger. One was labeled *La Brea Woman*, and the other held the bank deposit files. He opened that folder, and she saw her father's name, along with Katherine Wellington, and Peter Grassland.

"Now," Wulf said. "Do you remember how there was a mystery-number that was depositing large sums of money into these accounts?"

"Yes?"

"I found out what that number is, or at least what it represents." Wulf clicked on the identification number: *9q5dptqjn.*

Once it was highlighted he copied it into the Google header and pasted it, followed by GEOHASH coordinates. The screen zoomed out to show a revolving globe of the Earth. As it turned and zoomed in on California, it became clear.

"Those are like GPS coordinates?"

"Sort, of," Wulf said. "I had Theresa explain it to me, but she said something about Geohash being a geocoding system invented by some guy name Gustavo. Anyway, it was placed into the public domain, and it's a bit more complicated than GPS coordinates that we are all familiar with."

Mariska felt her second wind, and she pulled the computer off his lap and onto hers. "So, basically it's a lesser known system by which people can locate anything on Earth? Theresa sure knows a lot of techy stuff."

"She really does," Wulf said and looked away for a second. "There's some inconsistencies with her background…nothing illegal, but there's something not quite right."

"I hope that once all this is over with, I'll have more time to get to know her. She's a good woman, and I can see myself being friends with her."

"She's an interesting gal, that's for sure. I'll keep digging into it."

She playfully swatted him in the arm again. "Let people keep their secrets if they aren't dangerous ones. Now, getting back to the geohash thing?"

"Yes it's some kind of grid patterning with a… how did Theresa put it? A hierarchical spatial data structure that subdivides space into buckets of grid shapes."

Mariska stared at him for a second. "Easy for you to say."

"Yeah, I have no idea what I said," he chuckled. "Just like college, I put stuff to memory that meant nothing to me. I just remember it for the test."

"Well, you passed." Mariska clicked on the state of California and watched as the map zoomed into the exact spot marked by the geohash coordinates. "Well, I'll be damned."

"What is it? Do you recognize it?"

"Ingrid Ashton's home." Mariska turned the computer to face him.

On the screen was an aerial view of the old woman's sprawling estate.

"I wonder what her connection is to all of this?" Wulf asked.

Mariska felt a new sense of anger welling up inside her. If this old bitch had anything to do with Jane's death, she'd better start praying Wulf got to her before she did.

CHAPTER FORTY-SEVEN

The cell phone felt hot against Mariska's ear as she listened to it ring. Again, she was sent to voicemail. She'd been trying to reach David for the past hour, without success. She needed to play it cool. David didn't know she was on to him yet so she would still have the element of surprise.

"Where are you?" Mariska said under her breath.

It'd been days since she'd spoken to him, and she couldn't remember the last time that'd happened. A heaviness in her chest threatened to force out pent-up emotions she wasn't ready to deal with. Jane's death continued to weigh heavy on her soul not to mention her best friend's betrayal. Normally, she'd be spending time with her parents, talking out their feelings, working toward a resolution or at least a long heart-felt hug where she would be free to break down. But things were still strained between them.

Normally, the next best thing would be to spend an evening spent with David. He ultimately knew what to say to either cheer her up or at least put her mind onto other things. But that'd never happen again.

Another failed attempt, ending with her being sent to his voicemail. She turned off the phone and laid her head down on the feather-pillow on the bed. She was tired but too worked up to nap.

Her phone buzzed with an incoming call. Fumbling with the phone to answer it as quickly as possible, she didn't even look to see who was calling.

"David?" Mariska said as she answered the phone.

A short silence followed. She took a second to look at the phone display. *Detective Wulf.*

"No, it's me," Wulf said. "Why the hell would you be expecting a call from him?"

"Well…I don't think he knows I'm on to him. It's keeping with my normal pattern to call him and try and hang out."

"Yeah, but he's a wanted man." Wulf's irritation was coming through the phone loud and clear.

Fine, she thought. *I'll try to do it your way.* There was still a part of her that hoped she was dead wrong about David. It'd be like losing a brother if he was indeed the monster everyone suspected.

"I'm glad you called." Mariska changed the subject. "It's nice to hear your voice."

Silence met her ear.

"Did you need something?" she asked.

"I'm calling to see how you're doing. I can't believe you insisted on going back to your apartment."

"Why?"

"I would have thought you'd feel a bit safer staying with someone." Wulf cleared his throat. "I'd be happy to take you to your parents' house."

"I'll be fine here. The door has a new lock on it, and I have a lot here to do." The apartment was still a mess, and she needed to coordinate some new flooring and painting work.

"Would you like some help?"

The immediate flutter in her chest surprised her. *Was he looking for reasons to spend time with me? Or, was he just doing his job?*

"Thanks, but I'll be all right." She sat up in bed. "I promise if anything happens out of the ordinary…you'll be the first person I call."

He didn't say anything at first. "Sounds good. I'll check on you later."

"Thank you."

Just before she could hang up, he said, "Oh, and if you hear from David…will you let me know? Please?"

"Definitely," she said—meaning it.

She and Wulf hung up the phone, and she was immediately met by another incoming call. This time, it was from a number she didn't recognize. *Could Badger be calling?*

"Hello?" Mariska said.

"Dr. Stevenson?" It was a female voice.

"Yes, this is her." Definitely not Badger. "Who is this?"

"Dr. Tora, from the University of Copenhagen."

"Oh my god. I wasn't expecting to hear from you so soon. Before you say anything else…how is Eddie?"

"Edgar is doing well. He's out of the hospital…strong kid, that one."

"Wonderful. I'm going to forever be in his debt for saving my life."

"So, I've heard," Dr. Tora said, a sense of pride entering her voice. "I'm lucky to have him as part of my research team. He's a remarkable young man."

"Did they catch the goon that attacked us?"

"Unfortunately, no. When the campus security showed up, Eddie was lying in a pool of his own blood, knocked out cold. But being a research institute that we are…I collected samples of blood myself to aid the investigation. We are currently processing the DNA from them as we speak." Dr. Tora took a deep breath and continued, "Hopefully, we'll get a match on Interpol."

"Fingers crossed." She took a deep breath. "So, did you call me because you have answers about the DNA analysis from the hairs and tooth?"

"Yes, and I think you'll be pretty interested in the results."

Mariska's heart began to race, and she felt butterflies wrestling around inside her belly. "Give me one second; I want to grab a piece of paper to jot down some notes."

She rushed from the bedroom and into the kitchen where she had a notepad and pen. Sitting down at the kitchen table, she steeled herself. "Okay, I'm ready."

"I will also be sending you all the results in extensive detail to your email. There's too much data to go over on the phone, but I will be sending you the results and the methodology used for their interpretation. Along with that will be spreadsheets containing the statistical analysis behind each interpreted result providing you with the exact percentage of error to certainty."

Flashbacks to statistical analysis and research methodology classes made her wish she'd paid a little more attention in class. Instead, she'd studied to pass these classes, rather than embrace the process.

"That's great, thank you," Mariska said. "Give me the general idea, and I'll download the email as soon as you send it."

"Let's start with the tooth."

"Perfect." Mariska tapped her foot with a nervous energy she couldn't contain.

"We were successful in drilling a pinpoint hole into the root of the unidentified tooth. Despite traces of asphalt that had seeped deep into the tooth, the DNA was viable and was quite simple to process."

"Great."

"We then put it into the database at the University, which also compares samples from nearly all private and public research and educational databases held worldwide. We came up with no definitive match." Dr. Tora's voice fell flat, a hint of disappointment staining her matter of fact demeanor.

"So, where does that leave us? Were you able to glean anything from the sample?"

"Of course. We didn't fail."

"Lay it on me, Doctor." Mariska sat poised with the pen. The word TOOTH the only thing she'd written on the page.

"The tooth is from a previously unidentified primate."

"Primate?" Mariska said. "Are you certain?"

"With an absolute certainty. But we weren't able to classify it further. Another analysis ran through the computer looked at prehistoric bone and tooth samples that DNA samples were extracted and processed within the last fifty years."

"And? Anything match?" Mariska asked.

"Gigantopithecus. Or, at least what they suspect to be him. The bones were found years ago and recently tested for DNA. Those results were in our database."

Mariska's heart raced with excitement. She couldn't even write the creature's full name down on the paper before her mind went wild with possibilities. Gigantopithecus had been thought of as a myth for centuries. Legends from native peoples living in China, India, and even Vietnam had told tales of this creature inhabiting the dense jungles and wooded areas of the regions. Unfortunately, acidic soils of heavily forested areas, rarely leave behind skeletal remains, let alone fossils. Then, recent discoveries in China changed all that. Bones from the legendary creature turned up, and DNA had been extracted. Sure enough, primate, extinct, but placed as recently as one hundred thousand years ago.

This tooth could change everything.

"So, Gigantopithecus was in the America's, possibly as recently as fifteen-thousand years ago?"

"Dr. Stevenson, as you know conclusions such as that would be premature. Years of research are warranted," Dr. Tora said. "Now, keep in mind, the DNA is closely related to Gigantopithecus, but is not an exact match."

Bigfoot.

It had been widely speculated for years that Gigantopithecus, was actually the famed Bigfoot, which had been relegated to the pseudoscientific cryptozoology community. Often, pushed aside by the mainstream scientific communities and educational institutions as folklore and legend.

"Of course," Mariska said. "Very interesting results. I can't wait to get my hands on the DNA analysis and start my own research."

A sudden nausea overtook her as she realized she wouldn't be able to conduct any research unless she was cleared of wrongdoing by the investigation. She'd be damned if she was going to miss out on an opportunity such as this.

"Thank you so much, Dr. Tora."

"I haven't even gotten to the most interesting part, yet."

The hair samples. Even more interesting than the tooth?

"Oh, yes. Please, continue."

"Again, all the sample information and mathematical processing will be included with the email I'll send you as soon as we hang up. The red-hair had a very nice root-bulb, and the DNA was easily extracted. We were able to determine the ethnic heritage which was a combination of Scottish, Irish, and German. The sample came from a female of undeterminable age…however, by the condition of the hair shaft and dry root-bulb, it'd been inside the pouch you found it in for decades."

"Okay." Mariska wrote the information on the notepad. "What's the interesting part? You said this was better than what you found from the tooth."

"It's a matter of how you look at it, I suppose." Dr. Tora paused for a moment. "We compared it to your DNA. There was a statistical match indicating a familial connection."

"What?" Mariska's stomach surged into her throat. "Say that again."

"We were able to determine that the red-hair belonged to your maternal grandmother."

A sharp intake of air, Mariska's hand went to her mouth. She tried to speak, but her throat was tight, painful. She cleared her throat. And then again.

"Dr. Stevenson. Are you, okay?"

Mariska nodded.

"Hello?" Dr. Tora said. "Are you still there?"

"Yes," Mariska's voice was barely more than a squeak. "Are you certain?"

"Absolutely."

This brought her one step closer to finding out who she was. Where she came from. How she ended up in the dumpster the night her parents found her.

"Dr. Stevenson?"

"Yes?"

"There's more. Are you sure you'd like to hear this from me? Over the phone? It'll all be in the report…you can take your time to—"

"No," Mariska said. "I need to hear it, now…please."

"We processed the DNA from the red hair, and we got a hit in the system."

"A hit?"

"Yes, we were able to identify who your grandmother is." Dr. Tora paused for a moment. "Are you ready for me to continue?"

"Yes, please." Mariska fought hard against the rising emotions. Panic. Fear. Joy. They all seemed to hurt and yet make her want to laugh and cry at the same time.

"The name was provided by the computer system, but for address, phone number, and any other private information, you'd need a court order."

"Understood." *Tell me the fucking name…Please.*

"Ingrid Ashton."

With her last composed breath, Mariska said, "Thank you so much."

She hung up the phone and slid out of the chair and onto the floor. *Ingrid Ashton was her grandmother? What were the odds? She couldn't have killed, Jane. Right?*

Mariska closed her eyes tight and wept.

CHAPTER FORTY-EIGHT

Mariska didn't remember the drive over to Ingrid's place, but she stood at the old woman's front door and tried to muster up the courage to ring the doorbell. She wiped the bangs from her sweaty brow and after a deep breath, pushed the button.

A few moments passed before, Thomas the butler, answered the door. He opened the door and took a double take.

"Dr. Stevenson, was Ms. Ashton expecting you?"

She shook her head, "No, but if you wouldn't mind letting her know I'm here, I'd be more than happy to wait inside." Mariska started to move forward, trying to pass the butler on her way inside the house.

He stood steadfast. "I've been given implicit orders from the lady of the house, absolutely, under no circumstances, is she to receive visitors today."

Mariska cocked her head to the side and crossed her arms. "Oh? And why's that?"

"I'm sorry, but that's none of your business," Thomas said with a tone of annoyance as he started to close the door.

Mariska turned and noticed around the far side of the circular driveway was a dark-colored SUV. *Who else was here?* She made her move, shoving the door open with her shoulder. Thomas stumbled backward, and Mariska helped steady him before he hit the floor.

"Oh, goodness," Mariska said. "Thomas, you must be more careful. Here, have a seat." She helped him over to the chair in the entryway. "You should be more careful."

Thomas rubbed a growing bump on his forehead where the door hit him on her way in. The twinge of guilt did little to slow her down. She hurried down the hallway, listening for the sound of voices. Muffled, yet angry sounds came from deeper in the house. Mariska followed like a hound dog on the heels of its prey.

She stopped at the back of the home and listened. The voices were a bit clearer from this distance and definitely coming from the right. She turned and followed the sounds. The sounds lead her to a set of large, wooden doors. The ornate carved wood was dark with age and Mariska suspected taken from a historical site, years before such things were considered illegal.

Mariska put her ear to the door and listened. Two distinct voices, no doubt, Ingrid was one of them. But who was the man? She reached for the doorknob and went to turn it when she was interrupted.

Thomas had found his backbone once again and charged down the hallway toward her.

"Ms. Stevenson, how dare you come in here uninvited? I must ask you to leave at once, or I'll be forced to call the authorities. I can't imagine you want *another* run-in with the law." His haughty tone set her hackles on edge.

"I'll only be a minute. I need to talk to Ingrid." Mariska turned back to the door, reaching for the knob. Her hand was pulled away, sending a jolt of pain up into her shoulder.

Thomas wasn't messing around. And he was stronger than he looked. Mariska pulled her arm free of his grip and was a half second from punching him in the face when the door was pulled open behind her.

Mariska swiveled around and saw Ingrid standing there, looking at her with shock and a bit of humor in her expression. The older woman's white hair was pulled up into a loose bun at the top of her head, and Mariska tried to imagine it transformed into a bright auburn.

"Thomas, what's going on here?"

Thomas took a step back and placed a tentative finger to the large goose egg on his forehead. "I tried to politely ask Dr. Stevenson to come back at another time. That I had specific orders from you that there were to be no visitors."

"I'm sorry," Mariska said. "It was…an accident." She shrugged her shoulders and reached for his hand, but he backed away. "I was merely trying to come inside to see you. I guess we got our signals crossed." She feigned a pouty face and turned and looked over Ingrid's shoulders into the large library behind her.

Where was the man she heard talking?

Ingrid followed Mariska's stare and then stepped into her line of sight. "What can I help you with, Mariska?"

Mariska focused on the older woman's face for a moment. Was the anger in her eyes? Had she interrupted something important? Who was in there with her? Where'd he go?

"I need to talk to you…and I can't wait for another time. So…" Mariska put her hands on her hips.

Ingrid offered Thomas a pitied look. "That'll be all, Thomas. Go fetch some ice for your forehead."

It was clear that Thomas wanted to say more, but simply turned and walked away, his hand pressed against the injury. Ingrid stepped aside. "Well, come on in."

Mariska stepped into the library, and Ingrid closed the door behind them.

"What's this all about?" Ingrid said. "Are you, okay?"

Mariska turned to face her grandmother. There was so much she wanted to say, but her emotions were preventing her from saying anything. She balled up her fists and held her arms straight at her sides to regain control.

"Oh, dear. You're pretty upset about something. Here, come and sit."

Ingrid pulled Mariska over to the sofa in the middle of the room, and they sat together. Ingrid held onto Mariska's hand and squeezed it with support. "What has you so upset?"

Mariska looked into her eyes and for the first time, saw herself staring back. The speckles of brown and flecks of light green in

Ingrid's blue irises matched her own.

"I know you're my grandmother."

Ingrid sat up straight and placed her hands together in her lap, looking away from Mariska for moment. "How did you find out?"

"I had my DNA tested and compared to a strand of red hair I found. We were a match indicating a maternal grandparent relationship between us."

"Where did this red hair come from?" Ingrid turned to her. "And how did you trace it to me?"

"You don't seem surprised by this revelation."

Ingrid didn't say anything, but put her head down and closed her eyes.

Mariska felt a deep seeded anger she hadn't expected. "How long have you known? Were you ever going to tell me?" She scooted away from Ingrid. "Answer me. Where's my biological mother and father? How…how did I end up in a dump—?"

Ingrid wrapped her arms around Mariska, stopping her from finishing her question. The two women held the embrace long enough for Mariska's heart rate to settle down and Ingrid to compose herself. Once, the older woman pulled away, Ingrid wiped tears from her eyes and cleared her throat.

"You must have so many questions…I do too." Ingrid shrugged her shoulders. The story starts so long ago, I'm not sure where to begin.

"How about you start at the part where I was left for dead in a dumpster outside the museum. I mean, how long did you keep this a secret?"

"I only found out a few days ago myself."

"Really?" Mariska said. "And, how was that?"

"When you came to see me after your accident on Mulholland drive. I couldn't help, but notice some things about you…the say you sit, some of your mannerisms."

Mariska looked at the way she held her hand in her lap, one leg crossed behind the other. Ingrid sat in an identical pose.

"Even Thomas mentioned how much you look like your

mother…my, daughter." Ingrid's voice was strained with emotion.

"The way we sit doesn't make us related. How did you determine this?" Facts, not emotion, was going to get Mariska the answers she wanted—the answers she needed.

"You're right," Ingrid continued. "After you took a drink of the water I offered you, I had Thomas take the glass away, and we had it swabbed for DNA. I gave a hair sample for comparison. The results were mailed to me just the other day. As you can imagine, I was stunned."

"Stunned? You were stunned? How, did you not know about me, before now?"

"It's a long story."

"I've got time."

Ingrid's shoulders relaxed as she accepted the inevitable.

"My daughter, Jennifer, your mother, was a troubled child. No matter what I did…no matter how many programs we put her in, she couldn't shake the drugs and alcohol. I even put her in one of those Malibu rehab programs. Fifty-thousand dollars a month…supposed to be a guaranteed cure. But she always relapsed."

Mariska found herself pulled into the story, but waiting for the punch line. How did this messed-up teen, with every opportunity in the world laid out before her, end up throwing her own child away?

"Anyway," Ingrid said. "I tried everything. Then one day she came to me, telling me she was pregnant. Well, you can imagine I was less concerned about her being an unwed mother and more for the safety of her unborn child…you."

"Who's my father?"

"Well, you see, that's interesting you asked because you've met his family."

"I have?" Mariska's mind went wild. Who the hell was her father?

"You see, Jennifer and Peter Grassland Junior grew up together from the time of their birth. Playing together in the dirt at excavation dig-sites, naughtily playing catch with fragile bones that'd been unearthed. They were inseparable."

"So, I have Chumash blood in me?" Mariska asked.

"That's correct."

So, it was in her DNA to obsess over the La Brea Woman? She wasn't crazy after all. She was linked to this ancestor from thousands of years ago.

"Go on. What happened after you found out Jennifer was pregnant?"

"I sat Jennifer and Peter down and had a talk with them. I asked them if they planned on keeping you. They were so in love, holding each other's hands on this very couch telling me that they'd do anything to keep the baby and be together." Ingrid shrugged her shoulders and rubbed her hands against her knees. "I let them know that their sobriety meant everything then. No matter what, they had to keep clean. Of course they readily agreed with everything I was saying to them. And, quite honestly, I believed them. The sincerity in their eyes spoke volumes about their love for each other…and, you."

Mariska felt butterflies in her stomach. The fluttering making her feel sick. She swiped away her bangs from her damp brow.

"Everything started off great. They both lived here in this house where I could keep an eye on them. I had a steady stream of counselors come in and teach them about their addiction. Tried to instill in them coping mechanisms for when times get hard…when the addiction seemed to be winning."

"Tried?" Mariska asked.

"Yes, I tried. The counselors tried. They tried." Ingrid tucked an errant hair back into the loose bun. "All-in-all, we managed to get eight full months of sobriety about of them. Then, one day, Peter disappeared. Jennifer was frantic. She cried for days, calling everyone they both knew. It was clear to me he'd run off to get high. Being the good man he was, he hadn't tried to get Jennifer to go with him. But the draw to remain together was too strong for her."

"She went to find him, didn't she?"

"That's what I think happened. I even think she went to find him and bring him back to the safety of this home…but once she got out there, temptation was too great."

"How did I end up in the dumpster?"

"I'm not entirely sure," Ingrid said. "I didn't even know you were their baby until just a few days ago. The night you were born there was a fundraising gala at the museum. As you've undoubtedly heard from your parents, your mother heard you crying inside the dumpster. She crawled into that nasty, rusted metal container before her husband could stop her. When she reemerged, she was holding you in her arms."

"Yeah, I heard the stories. She rescued me from certain death. She is the bravest woman I know." Mariska felt her stomach tighten. She missed her mom and dad more than she could even explain. Somehow, she would make this right again. She'd give them a reason to be proud of her.

"When they found my Jenny and Peter a month later, dead from an overdose of heroin, my baby…was no longer pregnant. I had no idea what had happened to you."

"So, she gave birth, discarded me and went off to get high?"

"As awful as that sounds, I truly believe she waited to have you before she shot up. She loved you, Mariska. So many nights we sat in front of the fireplace and talked about you. What we thought you'd look like, what we hoped your interests would be. How we both hoped and prayed you'd never become addicted to drugs like your parents." Ingrid's eyes filled with tears and poured over and down her cheeks.

Mariska leaned into her and gave her a long hug until she felt Ingrid's body soften into the embrace. Soon, both women were rocking each other to comfort their overwhelming emotions.

"So…would it be weird for you to have me call you Grandma?"

Both women burst into a much needed and cleansing laugh.

"I'd like that," Ingrid said.

"Do my parents know about this?"

Ingrid paused for a moment, her eyes searching Mariska's, no doubt wondering if full disclosure was the right thing to do.

"I informed your father about it as soon as I got the DNA test results back. I have a feeling he has yet to tell your mother. I told your father that I would never say anything to anyone unless I had his permission. He's your father and has the right to make that decision."

"I think you're right," Mariska said. "I'm not sure how to even bring it up to him. Did he seem upset?"

"Visibly taken aback, but not angry. He has a cool head on his shoulders. I assured him, I would be as absent in the family as he would like me to be."

"And what did he say?"

"He said he needed to think about it."

Mariska smiled. "Yeah, that sounds like him." *How could he keep this from me?*

"Anyway, I let him know, regardless of his decision, I was going to be depositing money into an account in his name. The money comes from my estate and has always been earmarked for my grandchild. I always felt that you were out there…somewhere. And, I was prepared to leave this money for you even in the event of my death. Having determined your lineage, I felt it was only right to give the money to your father. He was apprehensive at first, but I can be very convincing." Ingrid gave a wink.

"Yes, I'm sure you are." Then it dawned on Mariska. That's what the deposit was in her father's name from the mystery account. It was part of her inheritance. What were the other deposits for then? *It's not important…there would be more time to discuss such things later. Plus, that's all police business anyway—Wulf's problem to deal with.*

Mariska had some other pressing matters to discuss with her grandmother.

"So, Grandma, who was the man I heard in the library when I first got here? And where did he go?"

CHAPTER FORTY-NINE

Wulf expected Mariska to go to Ingrid's house that morning. With Theresa's assistance, he'd dug up some information regarding their genetic connection—namely she found her way into the University of Copenhagen database. Theresa sure knew her way around a computer and had proven invaluable to their investigation. If she ever decided to change careers, he'd definitely make the suggestion to enter law enforcement through their cyber investigations team.

What he hadn't expected was that within minutes of Mariska entering Ingrid's home, a man came running out the back. From Wulf's vantage point, he was unable to see who the man was, but when he saw the man driving away in a dark SUV, he decided to follow.

The man drove very well, fully stopping at all stop signs, never went over the speed limit, and used his blinker every time. It gave Wulf no legitimate reason to pull him over, and he knew in this situation he needed to play by the rules. He couldn't risk doing something to compromise the already precarious case.

Wulf placed a call to Theresa.

"Hello?"

"Hey, Theresa." Wulf stopped the car behind directly behind the SUV at the stop light. Traffic was picking up, and he wasn't sure he was going to have much time to get information about this guy.

"Wulf? What can I do for you?" Her voice sounded suspicious. "Was I supposed to meet you somewhere and forgot?

"No, but I have a huge favor to ask."

"Sure, what's up?"

"Are you by a computer?"

A slight pause. "Of course I am."

"Can you run a vehicle plate?" Wulf asked. The light changed color, and he'd been distracted and didn't see the vehicle pulling away from him. "Shit."

"Everything okay?"

"Yeah. Hold on a second." Wulf pulled into the next lane and pulled around the car that'd gotten between him and the SUV. He quickly jotted down the plate, just in case they became separated.

"Can't you ask someone at the station to run the numbers for you?"

Wulf smiled, "Yeah, but you're quicker. You seem to find things at a whole other level…not sure how you do that."

"It's a gift, I suppose."

"You're not part of some underground hacking ring, are you?" Wulf couldn't help but laugh out loud.

Theresa didn't immediately answer. "Are you accusing me of something, officer?"

"I'm just kidding. Anyway, can you run it for me, please? The number is 87CT5GH."

Wulf waited for a few seconds. He could hear Theresa typing away on the laptop. Wulf came to a stop at the next light and watched as the SUV went through the yellow. Not illegal, but it pissed him off. He craned his neck to watch as the vehicle pulled away. Soon, it was out of sight as car after car turned right at the intersection and obscured his view. By the time the light changed back to green, he'd lost his chance.

"What have you got for me, Theresa?"

"I show that the car is registered to a Caleb Heuston in Los Angeles County."

"Caleb? I came across that name during my investigation…does the DMV report show anything about the driver?

"Some traffic tickets. Nothing all that important."

"You said the plates are for a car?" Wulf sped up and tried to pull into the next lane, but got stopped at the next light. "Dammit."

"Everything okay?"

"Damn, traffic gets worse every year."

"Yeah," Theresa said. "To answer your question, the computer says it's a 2012 Honda Civic."

"Shit, I knew it."

"Knew what?" Theresa asked. "What's going on?"

"I followed Mariska to Ingrid's house. After what you dug up about them being related, I figured she'd end up going there, but when she got there, a man came running out of the house."

"Who do you think it was?"

"I'm not sure, I was hoping that by running the plates, it'd tell us."

Theresa let out a sigh. "I'm going out on a limb here, but I suppose the vehicle you were following wasn't a 2012 Honda Civic."

"Precisely."

"Do you think Mariska's in danger? Do we need to do something? I'm at home, but can meet you wherever, whenever."

What would be the point? They had nothing to go on right now. "Nah, nothing we can do right now. I'll be sure to call you if anything else turns up."

"Oh, wait, Wulf? Before you hang up…"

"Yeah?"

"So…don't ask me how, but while you were getting all mad, I did some digging."

Wulf huffed, "Me? Mad? Spill it now or I'll ask you how you how you found out about Mariska's DNA test…I've always been told that such medical information would be protected by the Health Insurance Portability and Accountability Act, not to mention the University of Copenhagen's firewall security systems."

"What's that supposed to mean?" Theresa said with a laugh.

"It means, you shouldn't have been able to access it. That information is secured with government security software."

"Whatever, you want the information or not?"

"Lay it on me."

"Seems that this Caleb Heuston and David Beaumont live in the same apartment complex. Although, Heuston's exact address isn't available." Theresa paused for a moment. "What are the odds of that?"

"It doesn't prove guilt, but it's definitely interesting. Good work as always, Theresa. I'm going to start searching the police database for information about this Heuston guy. If you don't mind, could you do that on your end as well? It seems we aren't using the same databases."

"Anything to help the great Los Angeles Police Department."

"I appreciate it." He hung up the phone.

He wanted to speed back to Ingrid's house and tell Mariska to be careful. To watch her with David. But he'd already told her his concerns, and she didn't want to listen. Didn't want to see her best friend as anything other than that—the person she'd come to rely on for emotional support.

No, he needed proof. Something irrefutable…not easily explained away.

He put in David's address into his GPS. *Might as well pay this asshole a visit.*

CHAPTER FIFTY

Ingrid led Mariska by the hand through a hidden back-passage way located behind a false-fireplace in the library. *Damn this old woman is paranoid*, Mariska thought. But she was also the coolest, badass, octogenarian she'd ever met. Although, Ingrid still hadn't answered the question about who her male visitor was today.

As they walked through the wall, Ingrid flipped on a light and illuminated the entire hidden passageway. They continued to follow the main path, but Mariska noticed that there was a diverging hallway. She slowed and looked down the alternate passage, but just for a moment. Ingrid gave her a little tug and a warm smile.

"All in due time, Mariska. There's so much for me to show you."

They continued hand in hand the last few feet until they came to a large metallic door with a keypad and turning-wheel. The kind they used for bank vaults in the movies. Ingrid tapped in a code and a door unlocked with a chirp.

"Want to turn the wheel?" Ingrid asked.

"Nah." Mariska couldn't suppress her childish grin. She stepped closer, between Ingrid and the wheel. "I guess I'd better get used to it."

She took a hold of the wheel in both hands. The cold metal felt good against her sweaty palms. Tightening her grip, she cranked hard to the left. The wheel gave way with force and then easily spun around, opening the last barrier to the vault. Ingrid grabbed the handle next to the wheel and pulled back, the thick, heavy door opened without as much as a creak or groan.

The room in front of them was completely black.

"After you." Ingrid motioned her granddaughter in front of her.

A moment's hesitation, but then Mariska took the leap of faith. Her grandmother wouldn't kill her after all these years, would she?

As soon as Mariska foot crossed the threshold, the bright, white lights illuminated the room, momentarily blinding her in the process.

"You remember this place, right?" Ingrid said as she entered the room.

Mariska's vision started to return, although she continued to squint. It was the same hidden room that was accessible from the sitting room she'd been in on her first visit.

"How could I forget?" Mariska turned and took in the room. Something was different this time. "Looks like things have been moved."

"Why yes. Very observant, dear." Ingrid walked over to the one of the covered cases against the wall. "I have something very important to show you."

Mariska turned her attention to her and crossed the distance between them, stopping in front of the case. She looked up at her grandmother and felt an immediate tickle of butterflies deep inside her gut.

Ingrid slowly pulled the canvas tarp away from the case and let it drop to the floor. Even before Ingrid flipped the case-lighting on, Mariska took a quick intake of breath.

La Brea Woman

Mariska brushed Ingrid out of the way and started looking for a way to open the case.

"You'll need a code."

Mariska continued feeling around the edges of the glass enclosure, looking for a way inside. Ingrid took a step back and laughed.

"You're as tenacious as me when I was your age."

Straightening back to full height, Mariska turned to face her. And with a wickedness in her voice, that she hadn't expected. "Have you had her this entire time?"

Ingrid took a step forward, palms up bearing her innocence. "No, it's not like that." But Mariska kept going.

"Did you try and have me killed? Did you bash me over the head yourself? Or did you hire someone to do it?" Mariska shook her head. She'd just gone from elation to agony in a matter of seconds.

"You don't understand. Please." Ingrid tried to reach for Mariska, but she pulled away from her touch. "Let me explain."

"Not until you answer one question of mine first."

"Anything." Ingrid's expression was sincere, honest.

Was she finally telling the truth?

"Did you have anything…and I mean, anything at all, to do with Jane's death?" Mariska took another threatening step toward Ingrid.

Without as much as a flinch, or even a step backward, Ingrid's jaw tightened into a clenched position. Lips flattened into a thin line, and she tilted her head up slightly, giving her an air of indignation.

"How dare you?" Ingrid spat her words in disgust. "Are you seriously accusing me…your own grandmother, of *killing* that poor sweet woman?"

"Yes or no?"

Mariska and Ingrid were at a standoff. Both sticking to their position of being right.

Ingrid broke first, "Of course I had nothing to do with her death." Ingrid's eyes never left Mariska's. "I am not a murderer, and I value life over things…no matter how important they may be to me." Ingrid glanced at the display case, but then looked away.

Mariska crossed her arms and then turned around to face the La Brea Woman. She believed what Ingrid said, and started feeling guilty for her harsh words and accusations. There were just so many pieces of the puzzle that hadn't come together yet, and she wasn't sure they were going to at this point.

"So." Mariska turned to face her grandmother. "How did you find the La Brea Woman? And how long have you had her in your possession?"

"Actually, the last question is the easiest. I obtained her officially yesterday. She'd been missing for a while, so I was concerned that she may have been tampered with…you know, replicated or parts of her replaced by foreign bones. That sort of thing happens far too often in the antiquities and paleontological realms. Authentication was a must."

That all made a lot of sense to Mariska. "Where did you have her tested?"

"The only place I can trust. Or, at least the only place I can trust to keep it hush-hush." Ingrid walked over closer to the display case and bent down, admiring the skeletal remains. The smile and wonder on her face reminded Mariska of herself. "The University of Copenhagen has an incredible state of the art genetics laboratory. Which is kind of interesting considering it's one of the oldest institutions of higher learning in that part of Europe."

"Wait. You're telling me you sent her all the way to Europe and got her back with no questions asked? How is that possible? I was practically strip searched on my way home."

"No, I sent just a couple bones that I sampled from the remains at random."

A memory flashed into Mariska's mind. There was a doctor in the lab with her that day working with another specialist. He had a human bone…which one was it? Oh, that's right, Mariska thought.

"Was it a clavicle?"

"That's right…but how'd you know?" It was time for Ingrid to have a shocked look on her face.

"What are the odds of that shit?" Mariska said as she began passing the floor.

"Dear, you're starting to worry me." Ingrid reached out and took Mariska's elbow in hand and pulled her around to face her. "What's going on? Why is the clavicle significant?"

"When I was in Copenhagen at the same genetics-testing lab you sent the bones, I saw a man with a human clavicle. The bones looked old…old like her." She pointed to the box. "Who did you send there to test the remains?"

"It's not important, who I sent. What's important is I have possession of the La Brea Woman. We can now study her…learn who she was."

Ingrid was saying all the right things. *Is she trying to distract me from the truth?*

"The point I'm making is I was attacked while I was there. The man you sent there might have been involved. I can't imagine it's just a coincidence you sent someone to the same place I was and they aren't related somehow. It seems plausible to me…you know, considering everything." Mariska couldn't keep herself from revealing her one closely held secret. This woman seemed to suck the truth out of her.

"Considering what? It's obvious you have something you want to tell me…or at least haven't told me." Ingrid's curiosity shown on her face, eyes hungry for more information.

"You first."

"All right," Ingrid said. "The man I sent to Copenhagen to have the bones authenticated was Dr. Caleb Heuston. He's actually the one that acquired them in first place."

"Acquired them? You mean assaulted me and stole her…is that what you mean?"

"Now, now. Don't be overly dramatic. I have no reason to believe Heuston assaulted you. Like I said, he sold them to me. That's all I need to know."

"That's pretty convenient. Isn't it? And in the meantime, someone has tried to kill me multiple times and then slaughtered Jane." Mariska stared at Ingrid for moment. Upset and struggling to gather the rest of her thoughts. "And how did he happen to ask you to buy them? Isn't that a risky proposition? Selling stolen property. To the woman whose family found her in the first place?" Mariska shrugged her shoulders and arched her eyebrows, not attempting to hide her irritation.

"I can see that you're upset. I can also understand why."

"Can you?"

"Yes, I can. I promise you I would have never put you in harm's way. Not on purpose." Ingrid put a hand on Mariska's shoulder. "I promise."

Mariska sighed. "I believe you."

"Good. That's a start, isn't it?" Ingrid smiled. "I will help you find who's responsible for hurting you. I didn't find my granddaughter after thirty years to simply lose her to some madman."

It felt good have as many people on her side as possible, but she still wanted answers. "I need to know why you have her remains and why you aren't returning them to the museum. They belong to the Page."

Ingrid's eyes hardened as Mariska's words sank in. "They belong to the person who found them. My father and grandfather…along with the Chief's father, have the rightful claim. Considering they have all since passed, they belong to us now. It's been no secret that the La Brea Woman's remains have been sought after by the local tribes as well as my family." Ingrid crossed her arms and took a deep breath. "Don't you see, she belongs here? With people who love her and will take care of her…find out her truth. I'm offering you the chance of a lifetime."

"What do you mean?"

"You can study her, the La Brea Woman. Here, in my laboratory. With all my equipment and available resources at your disposal."

It was a chance of a lifetime, but could she betray the Page Museum? "If I worked here, I wouldn't be able to return to the museum, once my name's been cleared."

Ingrid nodded. "You're right. Your time would be better spent here, doing what you've always wanted. No more begging for money. No more putting all your hopes and dreams into the hands of the Review Board."

Mariska wasn't sure what to say. This old woman was quite convincing. What was the right decision?

"You don't have to make your mind up right this minute," Ingrid said. "Let it all sink in. give yourself time to make the right decision."

Mariska thought about it for a few moments. *This could all be dealt with later. No decisions needed to be made right this second. The most important thing was her grandmother hadn't put out a hit on her. But if not Ingrid, then who?* She thought about Detective Wulf. His kindness and concern for her wellbeing. Could he actually protect her from someone they didn't know. Someone that hasn't yet shown themselves?

"Was Dr. Heuston the man who visited you today?"

"Heavens no. I haven't even met this Heuston character in person. It was more of a black-market exchange sort of thing." Ingrid's voice lowered to a whisper as if not saying it too loud made it okay, somehow. "Anyway," Ingrid went to continue, but stopped and looked into Mariska's eyes. "I promised I wouldn't reveal who was here today, but since we are coming clean with each other…it was David Beaumont."

"David? What was he doing here?"

"That's actually none of your business."

"Spill it." Mariska crossed her arms and squared her stance. "He attacked me in Denmark."

Ingrid arched her eyebrows in surprise. "He did? I thought he loved you?"

"Love is a strong word, but I never thought he wanted to do me harm." Mariska felt the pit in her stomach deepen. "Tell me. Why was he here?"

"He came asking for more money. He claimed it was for the Dire Wolf study." Ingrid shrugged his shoulders. "Personally, I felt the grant should have been more than enough to cover the research…no matter how great the find was."

"Wouldn't the proper procedure be to resubmit a proposal?"

"Absolutely," Ingrid said. "I assumed by his methods he was looking for some under-the-table handouts. Totally unacceptable. But to be fair, we didn't get that far in our discussion because you showed up. He didn't want you to see him here…something about you getting upset about him being awarded the grant."

"I can't believe this guy." Mariska put her hand on her hips with an exasperated sigh.

"Have you gone to the police about him? If he attacked you, it needs to be reported." She started moving toward the phone. "I'm not going to stand for someone hurting my only granddaughter."

Mariska placed a steadying hand on her as she tried to pass by.

"Detective Wulf is aware of the incident. The problem is no one's been able to locate the jerk."

"Oh, dear. And here he was in my home."

"As soon as we are done here, I'll call Wulf and let him know he's in the area."

Ingrid cocked her head to the side. "Is there something more you'd like to discuss?"

Mariska hesitated, then started to speak, but then stopped again. *What are you doing? Don't do it.*

She reached into her pocket and pulled out the bead and tooth she'd been carrying with her for days. Ingrid's eyes went wide with excitement.

"Where did you get these?" Ingrid reached for the objects, but Mariska pulled them away out of reach.

"Not so fast." Mariska waited a few seconds while Ingrid refocused on her, rather than the objects in her hand. "I take it you've seen these before?"

"What makes you say that?" Ingrid set her jaw in defiance.

"The cloth pouch I found them in had a red strand of your hair in it. So, my guess is you hadn't seen them since you were quite young." Mariska paused for a moment. "Am I right?"

A few tense moments passed while Ingrid's expression changed from defiance to feigned shock, and then settling on acceptance. "Okay, you're right."

"Tell me about them." Mariska held out the objects once again so Ingrid could have a good look, but not touch. Not yet.

"My father told me these bedtime stories almost every night, and they were almost always about the La Brea Woman. When my father dug up her remains, he noticed nine cubes of various colors and a large animal tooth among her bones. He hypothesized that they belonged to her and she must have worn them as a necklace. The beads and tooth have holes bore straight through them…something that hadn't been observed for this time period."

"That's what I was thinking too," Mariska said and then held up the bead. "I also noticed there were tiny indentations on them which after going to the Griffith Park Observatory, figured out they were constellations."

"Fascinating." Ingrid reached for the bead. "I hadn't been up this close since childhood. What do you think the significance of the constellations would be?"

Mariska handed the bead to her and watched as she held it close enough to see the intricate detail. "Their significance to the scientific community will need to be studied. For locating her origins, my guess is it would be a good way to narrow down a tribe or a group of tribes she may have belonged to. That way when DNA testing is done, it'll be more specific. Not all the local tribes are known for their knowledge of the night sky."

"Fascinating."

"What do you know about the tooth?" Mariska said.

Ingrid shook her head, a sad look formed on her face. "My father died before we started working on that part. And, when he died, the tooth and beads disappeared. I assumed he'd stashed them away somewhere."

"That he did."

"Where did you find them?"

"Inside the La Brea Woman's skull."

A sharp laugh escaped the old woman's lips. "I figured that codger would have hid them within the remains. At that time, the Museum had already taken her off display and kept in her the deepest bowels of the tombs. Trying, successfully, to keep her out of the public eye."

"I'm surprised you hadn't looked for them there. Considering how important they are to you." Mariska handed the bead to Ingrid for her to take a closer look at it.

Ingrid's face lit up as she took possession of the small, blue cube. "I've waited a long time to touch this." She shrugged and slightly shook her head. "I only wish we had the others."

"You don't have them?"

"Why would I have them? You're the one who took them from the body before it was stolen."

Mariska said, "I assumed that whoever stole her, was the same person that stole the other beads from my apartment."

"Oh, dear. No, I don't have them. I've got some private investigators working on the dark-web or some such thing. They are searching for them. I hope whoever has them wants to sell…at some point."

Mariska thought about the incident in her apartment. How her place had been ransacked. Her things violently strewn across the apartment. Broken. Shattered. "Maybe it was the beads and tooth then."

"What about them?" Ingrid focused on Mariska.

"I bet whoever stole them is behind attacking me…and ultimately, behind Jane's murder." She paused for a moment of thought. "But why?"

The two stood in silence for a few moments. Suddenly, Ingrid said, "You know, if the tooth is from an undiscovered animal and the beads point to the tribe that has ownership over the La Brea Woman…then they would be way more valuable on the black market than her remains."

"I had the tooth DNA tested, and it is from a previously unidentified animal…so, that makes sense. But why would the identity of the beads have such a high monetary value?"

Ingrid's face lit up at the mention of the DNA results. She'd no doubt be asking more questions about it. "The La Brea Woman is a well-documented find. She could pull a high price from someone who is willing to keep her secret and never want to resell her. In other words, someone like me. Now, to have the tooth and beads, that's a whole other matter. The tooth will fetch a high price from multiple groups trying to prove the existence of animals previously viewed as mythological or simply legends. And the beads, well, they will be worth a lot of money to anyone interested in legal possession of the La Brea Woman's remains. All-in-all, I would guess the lot could pull in ten million dollars or more to the right buyer."

"The prospect of having that kind of money could change a person." *Which included David.* Mariska needed to find out who was behind this before it was too late. As long as she had possession of the tooth and beads, everyone associated with her was in danger.

"As much as I'd like to stay and chat," Mariska said. "I have a feeling the person responsible for this is escalating. I'm going to leave these here with you." She gave the tooth and bead to Ingrid, who took them with a surprised look on her face.

"Really? You trust me with them?"

"Just keep them safe for me." Mariska turned to leave and stopped and looked back at her grandmother. "I have a feeling the danger is only going to escalate. If you're able to hide them away in this mansion…they're safer with you than me."

CHAPTER FIFTY-ONE

Day slowly darkened into night and Mariska hadn't even noticed until she looked up from her computer. Other than the glow from the computer screen, her bedroom seemed pitch black. Her apartment hadn't been returned to its normal state, she hadn't had time to redecorate and she hoped once she was able to get to it, her mom would be talking to her again.

She'd been researching this mysterious black-market buyer that had sold the La Brea Woman's remains to Ingrid. Who really was this man: *Caleb Heuston*? She needed to find out and there wasn't time to waste. After sending Badger multiple unreturned messages asking for help in her search, she decided to do the work herself.

One roadblock after the next met her as her frustration began to rise. Who was this guy? Was it even his real name? It would make sense that it was an alias, but Ingrid felt confident it was his given name. Or, at least that was what she'd said. All the usual Google searches came back with pretty much nothing. She then plugged the name into every social media platform she could think of, even signing up for a few of them, so she could have access.

Nothing of importance.

Mariska's cell phone rang.

"Hey Theresa. How are you?"

"I'm good. What are you up to?"

"Honestly, it'd be way better to tell you about my last twenty-four hours in person. It's been quite an eye-opening and emotional experience."

"Wow, let's get together tomorrow for coffee. I'd love to hear what's going on."

"Sounds, great," Mariska said. "So, what's going on with you?" She took a second to check the time. "It's almost midnight."

"Yeah, I'm sorry to call you so late."

"No worries. I'm up anyway. I haven't slept well from getting back from Copenhagen. How long is jetlag supposed to last?"

"I called because I was helping Detective Wulf out with some computer searches and one of the things we came up with was a guy named Caleb Heuston. Does that name mean anything to you?"

Mariska's heart pounded and her breaths quickened. "I was just looking up that name on my computer…did, you know that?" *Was her computer bugged?*

A short pause followed by a quick laugh. Theresa said, "No…not that I know of. Which computer are you using? Wasn't yours destroyed in Copenhagen?"

"I'm using my personal laptop. It doesn't have any of my research on it, but it still connects to the internet." Mariska lowered the screen but left it cracked open for a little light. "Tell me what you found…about this Caleb guy."

"Wulf followed a guy in a dark SUV and it was registered to Caleb Heuston. The strange thing is he lives in the same apartment complex as David. The address doesn't specify apartment number, so we aren't sure which building he lives in." A short pause followed this revelation. "Has David ever mentioned anyone by that name? Does he have friends in the building that you've met, but don't know their name?"

"You sound like a detective. Am I being interrogated?" Mariska asked.

"Sorry, it's been a long day. I'm running some behind the scene searches for Wulf…he asked, and you know how he is."

"Very convincing, huh?"

They both laughed.

"Can't say that I know of any of David's other friends. Honestly, I've never heard him even mention anyone at all by name. I kind of wondered if I was his only friend."

"It's pretty apparent that David's world revolved around you."

"If that were true, why'd he try to kill me?" Mariska ran her fingers through her hair. "It's still hard to accept. Has anyone at the museum seen him since I left for Copenhagen?"

"No one has. I've been asking around and literally everyone has been wondering if he quit."

"We know that's not the case," Mariska said. "Considering he had the Dire Wolf study locked down."

"Can't work on that much if you're wanted by the cops."

Couldn't argue with that logic. Where the hell was he? Mariska yawned. "Damn, I think my lack of sleep has finally caught up with me." She stretched her arms over her head while she tucked the phone between her chin and shoulder.

"I won't keep you," Theresa said. "I'll call Wulf and let him know you aren't familiar with the name either. Keep your eyes peeled. No telling who's involved in this mess."

"You're right, as always. I'm going to sleep. Thanks for checking in and I'll text you in the morning when I get up so we can meet for coffee."

"Great, sleep well."

Mariska disconnected the call and closed the lid of the computer, bathing her room in complete darkness. She was already in bed, so it was easy enough to put the computer on the floor and slide in between her comforter and sheets. The bed formed to her body and hugged her goodnight.

She closed her eyes for the briefest of moments when a loud thump at the far end of her apartment caused her eyes to snap open. Every sense was set on high. She held her breath and listened. At first, nothing, but a creaky floorboard between the kitchen and hallway sent her into full fight or flight. She grabbed for her cell phone and opened it. The screen opened to a missed call from Theresa and Wulf. She sent a message to Theresa: *Preservation.*

There wasn't time for more, as a creak just on the other side of her door declared the presence of the intruder. It was clear, she was the goal, and it wasn't a robbery. She sent a silent hope that Theresa would interpret the message to mean she needed help. Immediate help at her apartment rather than to meet at the Marie Calendars.

Her phone lit up with another incoming call. Saw it was Theresa and slid the phone under the pillow. Looking around the room for anything to defend herself with she saw a letter opener on the nightstand. The door to her room started to open, and she quickly threw the covers to the side, freeing her legs. Lying back onto the pillow she looked longingly at the sharp, dagger-like letter opener. Could she get it before the intruder entered the room? She looked back at the door; it was open.

She closed her eyes, as she saw the figure of a man enter her room. Her heart pounded as she pretended to sleep, scenarios flipping through her mind like a picture book of horrors.

The floor creaked under the weight of the man who was now approaching the bed. She balled up her fists and bit back the scream that threatened to erupt from deep inside. Mariska snuck a peek through slitted eyes. The room was nearly pitch black, but the silhouette of a man with broad shoulders approached carrying something indiscernible between outstretched arms. The primal, fight or flight, surged to the surface. She slid her legs straight off the side of the bed, lunging for the letter opener.

Just as she closed her fist, the weight of the intruder was upon her, pushing her into the nightstand. Mariska's lower body was pinned, while her upper body was shoved down onto the top of the nightstand, sending everything on it crashing to the floor. A guttural snarl reverberated from her throat, tears streamed down her cheeks, and she pushed back hard against her unknown enemy. She couldn't make him budge. Within seconds the man showed what he'd been carrying on his way over to her bed, a Garrote wire.

The ligature tightened around her neck, and she gasped for air. With both hands, Mariska grabbed for the wire, digging her nails into the soft flesh of her neck.

The wire was already too tight for her to breathe. Blood seeped out from the ever-deepening wound and ran down her neck, soaking into her shirt. Time was running out as her vision tunneled into points. Pins and needles buzzed in her eyes and cheeks and she was unable to take in a single breath. Her knees collapsed under her weight, and she slid to the floor. The sudden shift sent the man toppling onto her, loosening the ligature just enough for her to gasp a breath of air.

The rush of fresh air into her lungs caused an eruption of coughing. Phlegm mixed with tears drained out of her nose and into the back into her throat. She gagged. Her vision remained blurred by the tears, but by rolling on to her back, she could see her attacker right himself. She was close enough to see his face, but when she looked, his head was covered by a black ski-mask.

He scrambled to his feet and took a threatening step toward her. Mariska used both hands to push herself back and away from him, and then groped for anything on the floor she could use as a weapon.

One more step and he'd be upon her. Unwilling to let him out of her sight, she padded the floor around her, desperate for something to save herself. A piece of broken glass. Just as the fingers of her left hand closed around the shard, the man leaped toward her and stomped down hard. The glass sliced deep, into the palm of her hand. A pitiful whine leaked out from her soul, and the man struck her hard across the mouth with an open hand.

Blood dripped down her chin and onto the floor. The nauseating taste of blood filled her mouth forcing her to spit or choke.

"Pathetic bitch!" the man growled under his breath.

The voice was familiar. Who was he? Was it the Caleb man everyone has been searching for?

Next to the man's boot lay her only chance at survival—the letter opener. Fueled with rage and fear, Mariska dove for the weapon. Despite her pinned left hand, still stuck under the man's shoe, she reached for the handle of the shiv, securing it with her right. The move caught him off guard, and he shifted his weight when he tried to intercept. Her left hand came out from under his foot, allowing her to pull it safely away. He grabbed a fist full of her hair and yanked, hard. Her head snapped back, but she'd already achieved her goal. The man tightened a strong hand around her neck and hoisted her up to stand.

With all her might, she jabbed the blade through his thin T-shirt and into his stomach. The pointed metal slid right up to the handle with surprising ease. Blood gushed from the wound, covering her hand and wrist. The heat of the thick liquid caused her a momentary lapse in concentration. He started to pull away, and she tried to tighten her grip on the small, slippery handle. When she pulled back on the blade, it slipped from her fingers. Her only weapon was stuck inside her enemy.

The man hobbled another step back, stunned into inaction. Mariska rushed at him and once again grabbed for the opener. One hand on the weapon and the other against his chest, she pulled back with all her might. A sucking sound and a gush of blood caused her to step back, away from the gore.

The masked man growled and clenched his fists. With a renewed strength, he lunged forward, arms outstretched to grab her. She readjusted her grip and plunged the weapon into the man's neck. He collapsed to the ground. Mariska tried to run but tripped over his downed body. She fell atop him, coming face to face with the murderer for the first time.

Their eyes met. They weren't the eyes of a stranger. With a shaking hand, she snatched the top of the ski mask and yanked it from his head. A nauseating recognition washed over her as she watched her friend David gasp for air beneath her. His lips began to move, but the weapon had punctured his trachea, preventing his words from making sound. A steady gurgle of wasted breath spewed from the hole in his neck.

Tears filled his eyes and were matched by her own. His lips mouthed, "I'm sorry." And then his body began to shake. Blood ran from his nose and mouth and continued to bubble up from the slit in his throat.

Sobs wracked her body. She watched as the life drained from his eyes and the pain in his face relaxed out to a smooth, lifeless, expression. "Why? David, why?"

Sadness and anger of betrayal. The loss of her best friend and the acknowledgment their long-standing relationship had been based on lies, weakened her. She slid off him and collapsed to the floor next to his body.

The sound of sirens grew louder until coming to a stop outside her apartment. She closed her eyes and rolled to her side and cried, curled up into a ball. Mariska barely registered the sounds of her rescuers entering her room, guns drawn, orders flying.

She didn't care about any of it. She was tired, and she was done.

Someone rushed to her side and scooped her up into their arms. Mariska didn't bother to even look. It didn't matter. Not right now. She allowed herself to go limp and she was carried from the room and placed onto the couch in the living room.

"Mariska?" Detective Wulf said. "Are you hurt?"

She didn't answer.

"You're covered in blood." She could feel his hands all over her, looking, searching for the source of the blood. "Are you hurt? There's an ambulance on the way."

Mariska opened her eyes. She showed him her hand, the gash deep, but she could still move her fingers.

"Oh, no," Wulf said, undoing his tie and wrapping her hand up tight. "You're safe now." He hugged her against him, his warmth felt good to her cold, numb body.

"He's dead," she said.

"Yes."

"I killed him." She started crying once again. Her shoulders moving with each gut-wrenching heave. "I killed him."

"You didn't have a choice. He came here to kill you." He continued to hold her, her sobs slowing until they stopped.

"I know." She came up to sit, facing the detective. "How'd you know it was him?"

"Theresa." Wulf wiped the tears from her face with the thumb of his hand. His kindness threatening to send her into another sobbing fit.

"She must have gotten my text?" Mariska said. "I was hoping

she'd tell you I was in trouble."

"Yeah, she called me right away, but I was already on my way."

Mariska looked at him with confusion. "Really?"

"Yeah, Theresa, found a connection linking Caleb Heuston and David Beaumont. They were the same person."

Mariska shook her head, trying to make sense of it all.

"Let's talk about this later," Wulf said. "When the ambulance gets here, I expect you to get on it and go to the hospital for a full check."

Mariska went to protest but stopped when she saw the look in his eyes. Stern, but caring, Wulf wasn't going to take no for an answer.

"Okay, but will you do me a favor?"

"Anything." Wulf squeezed her good hand.

"Call my mom," she said, tears welling up once again. "I need my mom."

He hugged her as the paramedics entered the apartment to take her to Cedar Sinai Hospital. "I'll come for you as soon as I'm done here."

The paramedics asked her if she could stand and she walked with them, arm in arm, to the front door. She turned back to see Wulf watching her leave. She offered him a sad smile before exiting the apartment.

From this moment on, her life would never be the same.

CHAPTER FIFTY-TWO

Wulf waited outside Mariska's hospital room with Theresa and Mr. and Mrs. Stevenson. The doctors had told them she wasn't in any immediate danger, but they were attending to her wounds. The pit in his stomach threatened to turn the stale coffee he was consuming into a recreation of something straight out of the Exorcist movie. He put the cup down on the table next to him and went over and sat next to Theresa.

"Should it be taking this long?" Wulf said.

Theresa looked at him with a curious look. "You're worried, aren't you?"

He didn't respond but looked back at the closed hospital door. He closed his eyes for a moment and imagery from the night of his wife's murder flashed through his mind. The same sickening feeling settled deep inside him. He swallowed hard and cleared his throat.

This wasn't the time for a trip down memory lane.

"I didn't think she'd be in there for so long. All I knew about was a wound on her hand." Wulf sat back into the chair and crossed his arms.

"That's true. They need to clean out the wound and stitch her up. But she'd also been strangled. The ligature mark is going to leave a scar…or at least they said it was a possibility."

He shook his head. "That fucking bastard," Wulf whispered under his breath. A rage inside him squashed all the other feelings he'd just been feeling moments ago. "If I could get my hands on him…I'd fucking kill him."

"Mariska did that for you," Theresa said. "And, I'd suggest when you see her, you keep in mind what she just went through. Anger and rage aren't what she needs right now. Despite David being an asshole, he was still her best friend, and I'm sure she is hurting on the inside too."

But he tried to kill her. How could someone care about someone who tried to kill them?

"I'll keep that in mind." He took a deep breath and looked over at Mariska's parents. They were sitting on the far side of the waiting room, holding each other in a sad, but comforting embrace. He'd better go talk to them—try and offer some kind of reassurance. The look on her mother's face reminded him all too much of his late wife's mother that night. A mix of sadness and fear etched across her face, eyes filled with tears, and a crumpled tissue clenched in her hand, at the ready—in case bad news was delivered. He turned back to Theresa, "I'll be right back."

He got up and walked across the room; each step grew heavier as he approached. "Mr. and Mrs. Stevenson, may I have a seat?"

"Absolutely," Robert said. "Please, sit."

"Thank you." Wulf sat next to Leah Stevenson. "I wanted to tell you both what an amazing daughter you have. She survived so much over the past few days, but never gave up on her beliefs, goals, and her determination was beyond anything I could have imagined. You've raised a brave young woman."

Leah dabbed a tissue to her eyes, and Robert said, "Thank you." He then put his hand on his wife's leg as she leaned her head into his shoulder. "Her stubbornness can sometimes be confused with bravery, but we are sure proud of her. We hope her injuries aren't something that'll give her regrets in the future."

Wulf thought about his statement for a moment. Scars could last forever, fading with time, but possibly never going away. Would, Mariska look at the scars on her hand and neck in the future and see an accomplishment or a defeat?

The door to her hospital room swung open and a doctor came out, pulling off his mask as he exited the room. The smile on his face instantly changing the mood of the waiting room from worry to hopeful. Everyone stood and approached the surgeon in a half-circle.

"Mr. and Mrs. Stevenson?" the doctor asked.

"Yes?" They said in unison. Leah held onto her husband's arms with what looked like a death grip.

"Your daughter has been through some trauma as of late. We conducted a full body examination. Other than some bruises, in various stages of healing, she has no broken bones and no new head injuries. Having said that, she had a laceration on her hand that required stiches. Luckily, it wasn't deep enough to affect her tendons and ligaments. Mostly, it's just painful and will take some time to heal."

"Oh, that's a relief," Wulf said, looking from Theresa to Mariska's parents. He watched as their expression registered the relief of good news. "How about the garrote wound?"

"We examined the trachea for signs of damage, but other than some bruising, there wasn't damage to that structure. But she may have a scar on the left lateral side of her throat. The ligature dug into her skin on that side along with fingernail marks as she attempted to dig out the wire while being strangled. I've seen these marks before, but not on anyone that had survived. She's a lucky young woman." The surgeon turned to her parents and address them specifically. "Your daughter will make a full recovery."

Leah threw her arms around her husband and they rocked each other back and forth while Theresa turned to Wulf and smiled.

"I'm so happy she's going to be fine." Theresa hugged Wulf. "Good job, mister."

"Me? I got there too late to help her. Plus, you're the one who cracked the case. You still haven't explained how you figured out that Caleb Heuston and David Beaumont were the same person."

Theresa pulled him aside, away from Mariska's parents. "I know my way around the computer. And, once I set my mind to something, I don't give up until I've solved it."

"You're like a bulldog."

"My nickname in college was Badger…my friend Eddie used to call me that all the time." She grew quiet after mentioning his name.

Badger, huh? He might have to search into that a little more at another time. "How is Eddie doing?" Wulf asked.

"He's out of the hospital and we've talked on the phone every day since Mariska went to Copenhagen. I'm happy to say he's coming back to Los Angeles for a visit."

"Glad to hear he's doing okay. When is he coming? I bet Mariska would like to see him too."

"Next week." Theresa smiled. "I didn't realize how much I missed him."

Wulf nudged her with his elbow. "You really like this guy?"

"I'm not talking to you about this…not right now, anyway." Theresa's face flushed red.

The hospital door opened and drew their attention. They watched as Mariska's parents went in to see their daughter.

Theresa started walking toward the door and turned to address him, "Are you coming?"

The nervous feeling in his stomach deepened as he thought about the woman sitting in the hospital bed. He wanted to see her. He wanted to rush to her side and hug her and not let go, but that couldn't happen—not right now.

"I'll catch up with you later," Wulf said. "Please let Mariska know I said hi and hope she's feeling better soon."

Theresa cocked her head to the side and nodded. "See you later?"

"Sure." Wulf turned and walked away. He turned back as Theresa disappeared inside the hospital room, the door slowly closing behind her.

He had an investigation to finish so he could move on with his life—pursue the things he wanted to without official rules getting in the way.

CHAPTER FIFTY-THREE

It'd been five days since the attack and Mariska was finally able to sleep throughout the night. The sleeping pill had helped, but it was great to finally feel rested. She sat behind her desk and looked around the office.

Dr. Snyder had offered her the position of lead paleontologist back yesterday, but she'd declined the offer. The box sitting on the desk was filled to the brim with her personal things she hadn't gotten back the first time her office had been cleared out.

A sinking feeling filled her belly as she thought about all the great times she had in this office. The first time she'd discovered a new, previously unidentified fossil. The long nights putting together the perfect grant-proposal to study the La Brea Woman. Even, the time she and David shared a bottle of wine and a large pepperoni pizza when they'd found out Dr. Snyder was going to retire.

David. How could he have done this to her? The betrayal still stung like a fresh wound, but she hoped it'd fade in time. She got up from the desk and walked around to the wall across from her. Her diplomas had been framed and mounted onto the wall years ago, and she'd almost forgot to take them down.

She reached up and plucked each one off the wall and hugged them against her chest. Was this a final goodbye? After everything she'd been through, good and bad, could she really say goodbye to this place? But could she stay and move on like nothing had happened?

A knock at the door tore her away from her musing.

"Come in," Mariska said.

The door pushed open, and Dr. Snyder came inside. At first, he didn't make eye contact, but simply stepped around inside the office, looking at all the empty wall spaces and a clean desk. He shook his head.

"Have you thought about my offer?" he asked, turning his attention to her.

"I have."

"And?"

"I think I need a little more time."

Snyder nodded, "How much time are you talking?"

"I've already spoken with Human Resources. They said I could take up to six months paid leave…considering everything that's happened." Mariska hated sounding weak. But she had a plan, and this seemed the best way.

"I understand. HR informed me of your decision a few moments ago, and for that reason, I've decided to postpone my retirement. I can't very well leave this ship without a captain."

"Captain?" Mariska arched her eyebrows. "What are you saying?"

"I'm saying that until your return in six months, I'm going to remain as head curator and manager of this institution," he arched his back and puffed out his chest. "Once you've returned, I am handing over the responsibility to you."

"Me? Really?" Mariska blinked away her astonishment. "Just a few days ago you wanted me fired. Crucified and blackballed from this field."

"That was before I realized you were completely innocent." He shrugged. "It also doesn't hurt that the museum hasn't been this full—and had this much press—in decades. It seems your popularity might just reestablish this institution as *the* place to visit. I was even contacted this morning by a popular travel company that wanted to put the Page Museum on their list of *Must-See* places in Los Angeles."

So, this had nothing to do with her merit as a scientist and everything to do with money and popularity. Whatever, that was fine with her. Maybe, after a six-month hiatus, she'd be ready to return and take control of this place. Bring it back to life with the intention of its founders—to bring the latest and greatest scientific discoveries to the populous, and to inspire future generations of scientists.

"I'll let you think about it, but trust me, Dr. Stevenson, we'll be making you an offer you can't refuse."

Mariska nodded and gave a tentative smile.

"Now, it seems there's a few people who want to see you."

"Who?" Mariska asked.

"People. I don't know. They're waiting for you in the lobby. I'd suggest hurrying up we'll be opening soon, and I don't want a big spectacle."

"Of course." Mariska paused while Dr. Snyder opened the door for her to walk through first. She carried the box herself as she hadn't been offered any assistance.

Down the long hallway in silence she went until she reached the entrance to the main lobby. Dr. Snyder opened the door, and she stepped through to a round of applause. Standing in a group was Theresa and Eddie, her parents, Ingrid, Kathy, and in the far back stood, Detective Wulf. His mouth smiled, but his eyes seemed sad.

"I can't believe you all came out to see me off," Mariska said. "You're all too sweet. Thank you."

Theresa and Eddie stepped forward and gave her a hug. "We sure are going to miss you around here, but I know you'll be back," Theresa said.

"You're probably right. And, Eddie, I'm so happy to see you. How are you feeling?"

"Much better. Got banged up, but nothing too serious."

Mariska put the box down and gave him a big hug. "I wouldn't be alive right now if it hadn't been for you. Thank you."

"Nah, you're a tough woman. I bet you would have done a better job than I did." Eddie side hugged Theresa.

His gesture wasn't lost on Mariska who gave Theresa a wink. "Well, you two go and enjoy your time together. I hear classes will be starting back up again soon at the University."

Eddie nodded. "Yeah, but I'm contemplating transferring back to USC."

The glow on Theresa's face could not be hidden. They were back together and neither one seemed willing to put that on hold again. "Sounds wonderful to me. You both had better keep in touch with me."

Theresa hugged her again. "You couldn't get away from me. Even if you tried."

Mariska watched as they walked away hand-in-hand. Turning the detective, who'd moved up close as he had something he wanted to say.

"You kind of disappeared after the attack. How've you been?"

He blushed. "I've been okay. Busy…still working the investigation."

"David Beaumont. Guilty as charged."

"True," he said. "Although there's a lot more that goes into it. We still haven't found the La Brea Woman. I'm sorry." He looked away as if he'd failed her.

She smiled and reached out and grabbed his hand, giving it a squeeze. "I know, it'll be okay. Will I ever see you again?"

"I'd like that." He leaned in and wrapped his strong arms around her.

His body felt so good pressed up against her. She felt her heart race and her face grow hot. After a second she realized she could feel his heart pounding against her as well. She pulled away and held his hands in hers.

"Thank you for everything. I don't know how I would have made it through all this mess without you."

His eyes searched hers, and his intensity made her look away, the moment severed. "I'll let you know when the investigation has been completed."

"That'd be great." Their gaze met, eyes locked, searching for more. "I miss you." She looked away, turning to pick up the box.

"No, let me help you bring this to your car," he rushed past her to get the box.

"Why thank you."

Wulf hauled the heavy box off the floor and went for the door.

Mariska hurried over to her parents and gave them a hug. She'd seen them earlier that morning, but she would never take their presence for granted again. Standing next to them was Ingrid. They would all be eternally connected from now on, for the remainder of their lives. Mariska saw her mom and Ingrid exchange a look of profound respect and concern for not just her, but for each other. Her parents stepped aside, and she hugged Ingrid.

"Our agreement still stands?" Mariska asked in whispered tones. "If we determine who her rightful descendants are, we return her?"

Ingrid's eyes searched hers for a moment before she nodded—no doubt a difficult acknowledgment.

Ingrid whispered in her ear, "I'll see you on Monday…bright and early?"

Mariska whispered back, "I wouldn't miss it." She then stepped back and arched one eyebrow and said, "I've got six months."

Ingrid nodded and stepped closer to Mariska's parents. She watched as Ingrid and Leah began commiserating about something. She heard the words apartment and decorating and assumed the worst. No doubt, within the next few days her apartment would be refurbished and rehabbed into whatever they decided.

That's okay, Mariska thought. *I'm going to be too busy anyway.*

As she made her way to out the front door, she turned and looked back at the museum. Inside to the far wall was Zed, the largest and fully intact Columbian Mammoth ever unearthed at the La Brea Tar Pits. To the right stood a giant ground sloth and extinct short-faced bear. The thrill of working here wouldn't soon go away, and she was confident once she was finished doing what she needed to do, she'd be back.

Her internal dialogue was cut short when she saw Kathy watching her from behind the Saber-toothed Tiger display. Kathy was now the face of the museum, but for how long? If looks could kill, there's no doubt she'd have finished Mariska off. A chill ran through her body as she closed the door behind her. Shaking off the eerie feeling of new enemies, of the unknown, and potential dangers that still awaited, Mariska hurried to her car. As she approached the car, she became immediately aware that Wulf was nowhere to be seen. The box sat on her trunk, but as she searched the parking lot, there was no sign of Wulf's vehicle.

She used her remote to unlock the car and took the box off and opened the trunk. Mariska put the box into the trunk, and she noticed a piece of white paper folded and tucked into the top of the box. She pulled it out and opened it. Her belly immediately fluttered with a million butterflies as she read his note.

Mariska:

I wanted to wait for you, but couldn't. Not because I didn't have time, but because I didn't trust myself. There is so much I want to say, but none of it is appropriate at this time. I promise you that as soon as this investigation is completed, you'll hear from me again.

Wulf

Mariska folded the paper and put it in her pocket. She heard the sound of a car engine, and she looked. At the far end of the parking lot, Wulf's car pulled out into traffic, and he sped away.

She wanted to see him again. She wanted to rush to his home and wrap her arms around him and never let go, but Mariska still had secrets. He was still looking for the La Brea Woman. Would his investigation lead him to her and Ingrid or would they be able to keep that private?

Mariska slammed her trunk closed and got into the front seat of her car. She looked back at the museum.

She placed a call on her cell phone.

"Hello?"

"Thomas? Hi, it's Mariska."

"Oh, hello dear. Miss Ingrid isn't here right now. Can I tell her you called?"

"Absolutely," Mariska said. "I'm actually headed out to the estate. Ingrid wanted me to meet her there."

"Oh, great. See you soon." Thomas hung up the phone.

Mariska got behind the wheel and shut the door. Ingrid assured her that the La Brea Woman would be returned to her rightful people as soon as they were able to determine it. They would mysteriously find her remains off an anonymous tip and her remains would be made public. With their research completed, they would be able to point to her descendants and the museum would have no other option but to return her. It was simply awful what the museum had done to this woman and her legacy. *Times have changed*, she said to herself. People had evolved as a society, right? The public would want her returned…and that's what she was going to ensure. That was the plan, anyway. There was still a lot of work ahead of her but she looked forward to it.

Why wait until Monday to start? She put the car into drive and pulled away from the museum.

The La Brea Woman's secrets had waited long enough. It was time to tell her story.

THE END

ACKNOWLEDGEMENTS

There are so many people I need to thank for supporting me through the process of writing this book.

Ricardo: Thank you so much for putting up with me. I know that I was a pain in the butt to be around at times and this book took a lot of time to research and write. I wouldn't have finished it had it not been for your support and encouragement.

Leah: You have and always will be my sister-by-choice. The family you pick is often closer and more supportive than the one you're born with and I couldn't be happier to have you as part of my life.

My friends/family: I can't thank each and every one of you enough for supporting me and loving me. It feels good to have so many of you encouraging me through the hard times and helping me feel that this crazy idea of being an author is possible.

I hope this book will make each and every person who has been with me through this process proud. This project was a labor of love and I tried to incorporate the things I find important and interesting: history, science, and a good mystery.

ABOUT THE AUTHOR

Charles Lemoine is a Midwest transplant to the land of cactus, coyotes, and diamondback rattlesnakes. A traveler and collector of fine-things, he met his better half in the City of Angels. When he's not trying to save the world, one geriatric patient at a time, he spends his time drinking coffee, eating pizza, and playing with his three, adorable rescue-dogs. Having an interest in the arts, he also spends quite a bit of time writing and creating beautiful glass mosaics, the flashier the better. Mostly, he enjoys spending time with friends and family who share his sense of humor and are willing to laugh at the most inappropriate times.

97490694R00246

Made in the USA
San Bernardino, CA
23 November 2018